REJECTED FATE

ELEMENTAL WOLVES: SPIRIT ASCENDING

BOOK 1

by

Elena Forest

SYNOPSIS

I was the pack's shameful secret… until the day my twin was killed by a monstrous wolf and I was forced to take her place.

Born powerless and without a wolf, no one knows I exist. Which means slipping into my sister's world while I hunt for her killer should be easy enough… except when it comes to Hunter Weston—heir of our rival pack, my sister's chosen mate, and my number one suspect.

Broodingly mysterious and sexy as hell, Hunter is as unreadable as he is observant, and he knows there's something off about me. His rejection will be swift and severe if he discovers the truth. With danger right on my heels, and new powers awakening within me, there's a very real chance he might.

But the more I get to know him, the harder it is to stay away, which poses a problem. With war looming on the horizon between our packs, our mating is the only thing keeping it at bay. Unless my father, the Alpha, decides to retaliate before I can prove Hunter's innocence… or guilt.

If I don't find my sister's murderer soon, there will be more blood spilled, starting with my own.

REJECTED FATE

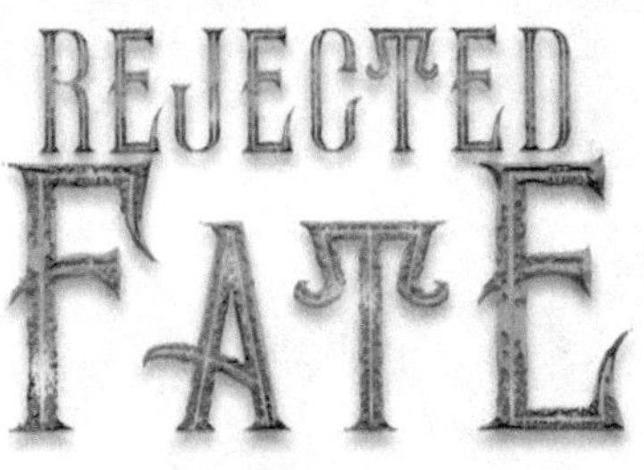

PACK HIERARCHY

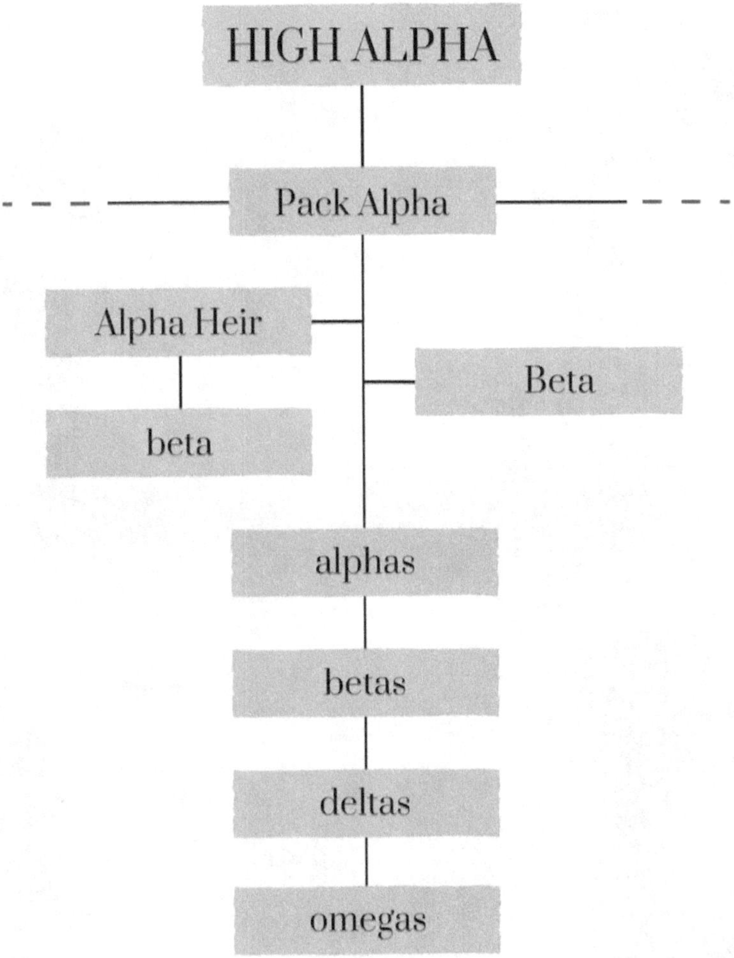
HIGH ALPHA
Pack Alpha
Alpha Heir
beta
Beta
alphas
betas
deltas
omegas

Madison

If there were one thing the Alpha of the Stormborn pack hated most, it was my disobedience.

Eluding the enforcer he had posted outside my cottage and sneaking through the forest in the middle of the night was the pinnacle of defiance. Especially since I'd been warned my entire life to stay out of sight, out of mind.

I doubted that meant waltzing right up to the Alpha's estate as if I lived there. Given that I was one of his daughters, it should have rightfully been my home.

Unfortunately, fate was a fickle mistress.

The anger that typically rose whenever I thought of my

father got the best of me, and I grimaced as I stepped a little too hard.

The ominous crunch of forest debris that littered the ground easily gave away my position.

Shit.

The breath caught in my lungs and my body froze while I waited to be found. I didn't want to think about what the punishment would be for my offense, but if I could pull this night off, the risk would be worth it.

Sadly, I wasn't that lucky. Powerful footfalls thundered through the trees, and the unmistakable, elemental scent of a Stormborn wolf—the petrichor of a fresh rainstorm and the sweet, yet sharp, aroma of damp earth—had fear shivering down my spine. My fight-or-flight response kicked in, but there was no time.

Born no better than a human, with no wolf or magic, I was a disgrace to my father's lineage and the outcast of the pack. I would never be able to outrun the wolf shifter heading directly toward me.

Think, Madison. What would Kenna do?

My identical twin sister, Makenna, or 'Kenna,' as most everyone called her, was crafty, cunning, and confident. If personality alone could dictate what we shifted into, she would undoubtedly be a fox.

Thinking like her gave me an idea. Though it was a long shot, I hurriedly pulled down my hair and combed my fingers through the light blonde tresses until it settled softly around my shoulders, flowing down my back.

Straightening my posture into something I hoped appeared confident, I continued walking toward the Alpha's lodging. My steps were nearly silent, but the steady thrum of my pulse wasn't as easy to hide.

Glowing blue eyes emerged in the darkness, and the low,

menacing growl of the enforcer made the fine hair on my nape stand on end. If I had a wolf inside of me, she would have growled right back and asserted her alpha dominance. Instead, I drew to a halt, threw a hand over my heart, and feigned a laugh to cover the spike of fear that released a burst of adrenaline into my bloodstream.

I hated that reaction, but as the lowest member of the pack without any of the benefits a wolf would have provided me, this guy could royally kick my ass.

Thinking quickly, I noted the unique pattern of sky-blue markings on his grey coat and the black shock of fur that created a "sock" on his back left paw. If there were one comparison to make between being exiled and being the pack princess, it was that my sister and I both knew the merry-go-round of enforcers stationed to watch us twenty-four seven. Except they guarded me like a prisoner while they protected Kenna like a precious gem.

"Damn, Reynolds. You scared the shit out of me," I scolded, pleased with the note of confidence that filled my voice.

The wolf yipped, but it wasn't a happy sound. Stormy magic enveloped him. Much like the charge that filled the air just before a wicked thunderstorm, unmistakable electricity tingled over my skin as he shifted. Tiny mountain ranges of goosebumps erupted along my arms, but I resisted the urge to rub my hands over them in an attempt to smooth them back down.

At the sight of the naked man standing before me, I averted my eyes quickly, trying not to wrinkle my nose in disgust. It wasn't that the enforcer was ugly, because he wasn't, but no one needed to see his flaccid bits bobbing in the wind.

"Madison," the gravelly voice of the newly shifted wolf

snapped. The cross-body bag I'd seen the enforcers wear to keep their clothing with them during shifts ruffled, and a zipper sounded. Blessedly, he stepped into a pair of sweatpants, saving his modesty and my eyes. Then he went right back to scolding me. "What the fuck are you doing out here?"

"Madison?" I scoffed, playing up the righteous, mildly offended tone my sister would use from being misnamed. I propped my sweaty palms on my hips. "Reynolds, you must be getting old."

The jab made his glower deepen, and he sauntered closer. I held my ground, seemingly unaffected by his presence. I was naturally wary of the enforcers. Over the years, I'd learned to have a healthy respect for the power they held. While I wasn't that scared little girl any longer, I tried to keep out of trouble and off their radar. Their priority was the pack's safety. Even from me and the weakness I apparently represented.

Shaking the bitter thought away, I raised my chin and stated boldly, "I'm clearly Makenna."

I hoped the power of suggestion worked, because I was clearly *not*.

My sister and I might be twins, but our upbringing made us as different as fire and water.

Reynolds' gaze dropped downward, sliding over my old clothing and slip-on tennis shoes. I didn't look bad, by any means, but I certainly wasn't wearing name brands like my sister would've been. My shorts and tank top were modest finds from the local thrift store, but I doubted the enforcer knew anything about fashion. Still, my heart beat faster and I swallowed, praying to the moon above that he was a few fries short of a Happy Meal and wouldn't notice the differences.

Raising a brow at his clear assessment of my body, I did my best to play the part. I waved him off, dismissing him and heading on my way as though I hadn't a care in the world. Kenna was always poised and self-assured, so I tried to be the same. Honestly, I'd always wondered who I'd be if fate had dealt me different cards.

What would it have been like to grow up alongside Kenna? To have her power and influence? To be loved and cherished by the same pack who ostracized me without ever questioning my father's orders?

"Makenna?" Reynolds repeated, sounding confused as he trailed after me while I tried to remember which path to take through the woods. It'd been so long since I'd made this trek, a handful of times over the years at most, but I couldn't let him see my indecision. If he figured out I was lying to him, it wouldn't bode well for me.

The enforcer's towering six-foot-five frame dwarfed my own. I was an entire foot shorter than him and vastly outmatched.

As Madison, the knowledge of just how much damage he could do to me if he caught me in a lie was intimidating, but Makenna had never been cowed by the enforcers.

Why would she? They'd never hurt a hair on her head. Me, on the other hand? I'd only tested the boundaries my father had set a few times, and I'd quickly learned to pick my battles carefully.

Tonight was one I'd gladly fight. While the risk was high, it was necessary, even if it meant I got caught and roughed up in the process.

Reynolds inhaled loudly behind me, and I wrinkled my nose at the idea of being so blatantly scented. Call it my human sensibilities, but there were certain things I would never understand without experiencing them myself, and the importance of scent to the wolves was one of them.

My senses were better than the average human's, but scents were just smells to me. Wolves, however, used them to identify individuals and packs, and up until our kind had been cursed, to find their fated mates.

His sniff just made me want to do a pit check to make sure my deodorant was working in the summer heat of early June.

But Makenna would never, so I trudged on, climbing over a fallen log and weaving between some trees, growing tired of how the enforcer matched my pace. He stayed only a foot behind me. Oppressive body heat warmed my back. I was on the verge of telling him off when he called me out.

"You don't smell like Makenna. What shit are you trying to pull, Madison?" The way he spat my name sounded dirty. Like he'd rather eat a lemon than wrap his tongue around the syllables.

I ducked under a branch, pulling it back so it wouldn't snag my hair, then promptly released it, enjoying the huff of annoyance from behind me where it'd hit Reynolds in the chest.

"I was just visiting her. Why do you think Madison's scent is on me?" I knew for a fact that our scents mixed whenever my sister and I were near each other. We were too alike, and though anyone who had spent significant time around us knew our signatures to be distinctly different, those less familiar may not pick up on the nuances.

In Reynold's case, I just needed to plant the seed of doubt, then water it until it grew and he left me alone. The sooner, the better, before he shifted back to a wolf and called for reinforcements, or worse, hailed the Alpha.

"If you are Makenna, and I'm not saying I believe your

story, you shouldn't be out here so late. You know your father doesn't approve of you visiting your sister."

No shit, Sherlock. Why did he think we had to sneak our visits? Even at twenty-one years of age, the Alpha controlled our lives. Any freedom he granted us was kept on a short leash.

"I was just saying 'goodbye.'" The imposing silhouette of the Alpha's house appeared through the trees, the white siding almost glowing under the midnight moon. Sighing, I turned to face the enforcer. "She's my twin," I retorted, as if that explained everything. To me, it did, but other people rarely understood the bond between siblings who had shared a womb.

"I don't know." Reynolds scrubbed a hand over his face, and I knew I'd gained a little ground.

I snagged a flower growing nearby, needing to fidget with something before I screwed up and did something decidedly 'Madison' that would give me away. "Surely you can let this slide?" Tucking the flower into my hair like I'd seen my sister do many times, I turned on the charm. "It can be our little secret."

Tilting my head, I tried to jut out my bottom lip in the pout Kenna was famous for. Would it look the same on me? Or did my face look scrunched up like a pug's? I hoped for the former.

"I'll be gone tomorrow, anyway. Daddy doesn't need to know." It nearly *killed* me to call him 'daddy.'

You're just acting, I reminded myself even as my stomach churned from the wrongness of it.

"Fine. Go, and I'll watch your return from here." Reynolds widened his feet and crossed his arms, looking like an immovable wall of human flesh among the trees.

"Thanks, Reyn." I smiled sweetly, using the nickname

I'd heard others call him before hightailing it out of the woods.

A breath wooshed from my lungs, and I counted my blessings that I hadn't been found by someone else. Someone like Juno or Crenshaw. I'd never have pulled that stunt off if it had been one of the more astute enforcers.

Goddess above, I half-cursed, half-prayed and looked at the waxing gibbous moon in the sky. *I never want to do that again.*

I hurried around the house, figuring Reynolds would assume I was using the front door, since it was closer to 'my' room. The shadows covered my advance, and I timed my steps to avoid the other enforcers lounging nearby. Smoke from their cigarettes wafted in the evening breeze, helping to disguise my scent, and their low chatter told me they were distracted.

I didn't know this group very well; the perimeter enforcers were different from the ones my father stationed to guard his private dwelling. Luckily, that would work in my favor. If they caught my scent, they'd most likely think it was my sister's, even if their deeper instincts told them something was off about it.

It took longer than I'd have liked to sneak along the front of the house—if you could even call it that, given the place was the size of a mansion—but I finally rounded to the far side and breathed a sigh of relief. I was close. Studying the landscape, I tried to remember the layout of my sister's home from the last time I'd been here. Though it'd been years, not much had changed.

Slipping beneath Makenna's balcony, I searched the ground until I found what I was looking for. Crouching down, I snatched up a small pebble from the landscaped beds surrounding the massive house, then hid in the formal garden just beyond. The stone was cool and smooth in my palm. I tossed it in the air a few times, testing its size and weight, then took aim and let it fly.

The ping on the glass door was flawless. Ducking back down again, I stayed out of sight while I watched the familiar flowery curtains that obscured my view inside. I waited for the telltale flutter that told me she was opening the door, but a minute passed, then two more. Still nothing.

Did I dare throw another? What if someone else heard the small clink from inside? Once wasn't suspect, but twice?

Normally I'd have admitted defeat, rather than chance getting caught by my father, but tonight was different.

Kenna was officially moving to live with her future mate's pack tomorrow, and I wasn't sure when I'd get to see her again. I hadn't come this far, risked this much, to fail now.

Not tonight of all nights. Besides, this was the day every year she snuck out to see me. It was tradition, fifteen years in the making.

My fingers dipped into my pocket to retrieve the note she'd sent asking me to meet her here tonight with a hastily drawn map to remind me of the best paths to use. It was definitely her handwriting, and I confirmed I was in the right place. Shoving it away, I stared up at her room.

Biting my lip, I made the decision. Sneaking back to the walkway, I scooped up a small handful of pebbles before bleeding back into the shadowed garden. Rolling them around in my palm, I selected one and let it sail. Warm, yellow light flicked on in one of the downstairs rooms. It'd been so long since I'd been inside the house I wasn't sure which room it was or who might be inside.

Barely breathing, I ducked out of sight once more and stayed as still as possible.

Dammit, this is a bad idea.

After a solid five minutes had passed and nothing happened, I dared a peek over the flowery bush I was hiding behind. Those same curtains sat unmoving.

My fist tightened around the stones, branding them into my palm, and I pursed my lips. This had been our plan, and I knew deep down she wouldn't blow me off. We never missed a chance to see each other, our visits all too short and sporadic as they were. Since we were separated as children at the age of six, she'd faithfully gone against our father's wishes and snuck out to see me.

So where is she?

Unwisely, I threw one last stone, convincing myself I'd leave if this one didn't get her attention. The outside floodlights flicked on, the pool of warm yellow light infiltrating my hiding spot. I cursed, backing deeper into the shadows of the garden.

A cell phone chimed in the distance, cutting off the happy chatter of the enforcers as they answered. Deep in the woods, wolves began to howl, their echoing cries blending into a haunting melody.

My heart dropped to my feet, and anxiety reared its ugly head. I knew who'd made that phone call, who'd alerted the perimeter wolves of a potential threat, and yet, I couldn't stop staring at those overly cheerful curtains.

My sister was one of the only people who meant anything to me.

Something was wrong. It had to be.

Before I could wrap my mind around that thought more fully, a large hand clamped over my mouth, and I was hauled backward into a hard body on a muffled scream.

TWO

Madison

I struggled in vain as my feet left the ground and my captor dragged me deeper into the shadowed garden.

Chiseled muscles were like stone against my back. With my arms pinned firmly against my body, I wiggled and wrenched myself from one side to the other, trying desperately to break the fucker's hold on me.

The thick arm banded around my middle tightened ruthlessly, squeezing more of the air from my lungs. I did my best to suck in a breath past the hand clamped over my mouth that nearly blocked all my airways.

It wasn't enough.

Dots coalesced at the edges of my vision, darkening what I could see: tall hedges sweeping toward the sky, blocking any view of the Alpha's house.

I closed my eyes against the onslaught of dizziness and panic that washed over me in all-consuming waves. Thankfully, pine and the sweet fragrance of a million flowers filtered in, helped ground me, and gave me clarity in the midst of the chaos.

Fight. Fight for your fucking life. If this ass reports you to the Alpha, it'll be nothing but unimaginable pain.

An unpleasant shiver crawled down my spine at the reminder of the few times my father doled out my punishment personally. It'd been a long while since I'd made him mad enough to visit my hovel deep in the forest, but I'd learned my lesson, even if I didn't always heed it.

You didn't piss off the Alpha.

And if you were going to chance it, you didn't get caught or there'd be hell to pay.

I had to get away.

Unfortunately, none of the moves I'd learned in my informal self-defense training would work well on a shifter with three times my strength. If I had my wolf, we would have been more evenly matched, but I'd have to work with what I had.

Opening my mouth, I bit down on the guy's fingers at the same time I mercilessly kicked my heels. One after the other targeted the only parts of the guy's body I could reach: his shins.

A pained curse flew from him, and my mouth tugged into a remorseless smile behind his palm. My plan, albeit scrappy and ill-formed, was working.

Taking him unaware, I pushed my face hard against his

hand only to reverse the motion, throwing my head back to connect with his chin.

"Shit! Mads, calm the fuck down," my abductor commanded, his tone a low warning. I froze at the informal use of my name.

That voice… I knew that voice.

The struggle bled out of me, and the extra adrenaline coursing through my body made me shaky.

A moment later, I was set down. The grip on me eased and I heaved a deep breath, finally able to breathe again as my feet met the thick bedding of the forest floor. His hands fell away, and I swiftly turned. The fire of my anger fortified me and kept me steady as a curse formed on my lips.

"Dammit, Jasper," I scolded quietly, pushing against his bare shoulder in retaliation. I decided I wouldn't feel bad for the teeth marks or bruises I'd given him during his stunt. His shifter healing would take care of those quickly enough. "You scared me half to death and nearly made me pass out."

Other than a fleeting wince of regret for forgetting to use more restraint with me, he didn't even have the decency to look sorry.

"Knowing your father, I think I just saved your life." He shoved a hand through his sandy blonde hair. Cut shorter on the sides, it lay in messy waves on top of his head, giving him a devil-may-care appearance that more than worked on him. "I'd ask what the hell you were thinking, but your sister already filled me in on your plans."

"You've seen her?" I asked, fully skirting around the disappointed note in his voice.

He didn't approve of my risk-taking, having witnessed or been ordered to participate in the aftermath more than once over the years. He may be one of my father's enforcers, but he was the only person I considered a friend. As loath as I was to admit it, I understood his concern. I'd never want to witness him bullied and beaten either.

But those same years that forged our friendship had hardened me. I wasn't the delicate young flower I'd once been. For better or worse, I could handle the outcome of my decisions.

"I was in her security detail today, and she told me about your plan to meet tonight. Little did she know of your father's plan to host guests this evening." He leveled a hard look toward the house he'd just dragged me away from before flicking his attention back to my own. The muscle in his jaw jumped when he clenched his teeth, and he was silent for a moment, allowing his words to sink in.

Shit. I understood the implications easily, and a shiver of ice raced down my spine. Had I been seen by someone from another pack, my punishment wouldn't have been just fists and fury. It would have been my *life*.

I was my father's greatest secret, the living, breathing reminder of his only weakness—the hole in his legacy: a shifter born powerless and without a wolf. It was unheard of. If the other packs found out, they'd view him as less. It would jeopardize the power he'd worked to obtain, not just as the Stormborn pack Alpha, but with the alliances he'd forged with other packs.

Wolves were extremely territorial. They needed little provocation to attack, and I was the chink in my father's well-fortified armor.

When my wolf and my powers didn't emerge like they should have when I'd turned six, our own pack had turned on him. Other wolves who were strong enough to be contenders attacked first, starting with the alphas, then followed by my father's Beta and a handful of deltas who thought they stood a chance of victory.

One strong wolf after another fought for the title of Stormborn Alpha, each one eventually falling in a bloody heap at his feet. He'd proven himself as the strongest, most lethal among us, but that was against wolves who were ranked below him.

The Alphas of our rival packs would make far stronger opponents.

The weight of what I'd risked settled like an oppressive blanket over my shoulders, and I swallowed hard, my voice a mere whisper when I said, "I didn't know."

"I know," Jasper comforted, just as quietly, the accusation bleeding away. "Your sister means a lot to you. Of course you'd want to see her." Moving closer, he lightly gripped my chin and raised my face up to his. "I just wish you wouldn't gamble with your life."

The bright moonlight enhanced the highlights and shadows that fell across his figure, and his stormy grey eyes shone with intensity, "Your life means just as much as hers, and you almost risked it all tonight," he scolded lightly.

I swallowed hard and my mouth went dry. No one had ever said that to me before. It barely had time to sink in before I realized something almost as startling.

Jasper was standing close. *Really* close. The naked planes of his chest suddenly seemed more intimate than they had moments ago. However, it was the genuine sincerity radiating from him that truly made me breathless.

That he worried about me was foreign, yet nice. Other than Kenna, no one cared what happened to me.

"The pack would disagree with you," I murmured, unsure why I was arguing his sweet, albeit chiding, sentiment. I certainly valued my own life, but being at the bottom of the pack tended to mess with a girl's head after years of hatred and disdain over something I had no control over.

More than once, I'd wondered why my father hadn't just killed me when it became clear I would never shift. Surely, it would've been the simpler option, though I was immensely grateful he hadn't.

I used to think it was because twins were rare among shifters, so uncommon they were seen as a blessing from the Moon Goddess. While my father had always been aloof and cold, withholding any love and affection, he'd been proud and boastful of his twins. But being viewed as a blessing only made my downfall more painful, my inability to shift more shameful to the pack.

He could have killed me when I turned out to be 'defective' and rid himself of the problem I presented, but when he didn't, I convinced myself the reason was because, in his own way, he still wanted me.

It took years for me to realize it was because he *couldn't*.

Discovering such crushed the childish hope I'd once harbored that his mercy meant he cared, if only a little.

Bound by the Moon Goddess, he was forced to follow shifter law. He wasn't allowed to kill me for simply existing; he needed a valid reason. It would take a grievous crime against the pack, like outing myself, for him to justify killing me off. Yet, while he would love to be rid of me, he cared far more about holding his position of power, and that meant keeping my anomaly a secret.

So, I'd been exiled instead and heavily guarded. Meanwhile, my father spun an egregious tale about how I'd died, intent on keeping my failings concealed from the other packs.

Jasper shook his head slowly, looking sad. "The pack is

wrong. You're so much more than they see." His succinct surety caught me off-guard, and I sucked in a shocked breath.

His attention flicked to where my lips slightly parted, and I swore his eyes darkened.

He isn't going to kiss me, is he?

I had limited experience with people, let alone men. Other than the enforcers, I rarely saw anyone until Kenna had convinced our father to allow me to attend one of the human community colleges just outside pack territory. Even then, I had a bodyguard and rarely got to socialize outside the classroom.

Do I want him to kiss me?

I couldn't deny I'd thought about it, but something always held me back. Honestly, it'd been a non-issue until now. We'd never been intimately close like this before.

I was confused and unsure, but this definitely wasn't the time to contemplate it. The perimeter wolves could be drawing near, and we were still too close to the main house for comfort.

A light breeze whispered across my exposed skin, rustling the leaves and further breaking the moment.

I stepped back, pulling out of his grasp. Smoothing my hands down my rumpled clothing simply to cover my nerves, I blushed.

"Thank you, Jasper. For everything. I think I should get home." Hitching a thumb over my shoulder, I motioned vaguely toward where I lived, silently praying I could get back unnoticed.

I wanted to give him a message for Kenna, so this night —and the risk I'd taken—wouldn't have been for nothing. It would be better than failing completely, but the thought cut off abruptly when my friend smirked.

"Suit yourself, but you'll miss all the fun your sister has planned for you." Jasper crossed his arms. Raising an eyebrow, he challenged me as my own drew downward.

"Huh?" I had no idea what he was talking about.

"Come on. We need to get moving before we're caught and both of us get in trouble." Reaching for my wrist, he wrapped his fingers around it and tugged me into the forest, leading me down a trail he was obviously familiar with.

"What's happening?" I whispered, keeping pace just behind him.

"Once I learned what Makenna had planned, I knew if you two wanted to rendezvous tonight, we'd need a plan B. Your father's having closed door meetings tonight with some representatives from other packs; Kenna told him she was going out with friends, so she'd be out of his way."

Jasper picked up the pace, and I jogged to keep up. He kept his head on a swivel, scanning the shadows between the trees while listening for any signs of danger. I did the same, actively searching for unseen threats.

"Wait. So we're meeting up after all?" I couldn't contain my excitement, letting it roll over the slight frustration I had that he didn't tell me sooner.

Peering over his shoulder, he gave me a mischievous grin. "She's waiting for you outside pack territory. It's the only place that's safe for the two of you to be together."

The sound of more howls, this time closer than they'd been before, had our conversation drawing to a close. Jasper's grip shifted from my wrist to hold my hand, squeezing in silent reassurance that we'd make it. I hurried after him, trying to move as soundlessly as he seemed to.

Not long after, the trees broke apart to reveal a clearing where a dark sedan was parked. Digging the keys from the pocket of his low-slung jeans, he hit a button and the car unlocked with a click.

I hurried to the passenger door, but Jasper cleared his throat. Glancing up, I noted his sheepish expression. Lifting the remote, he hit another button and the trunk popped open.

"Oh, you have got to be kidding me." I eyed it suspiciously. "I have to ride in there?"

"Sorry, Mads," Jasper's apology was genuine. Reaching into the car, he grabbed a t-shirt and slid it on, tugging it down over the hard planes of his abdomen. "I don't like it either, but I need to keep you out of sight when we pass the perimeter. It's the only way."

I sighed, realizing he wasn't wrong, and moved to the back, scenting the heavy fragrance of the cedar planks I'd be sharing a space with.

"I've been doing construction on the side." Joining me at the back of the car, he nodded toward the interior. "The enforcers posted at the border won't think anything of the cedar smell, and it will help disguise your scent," he assured me.

He really had thought of everything.

As much as I despised being trapped in small spaces, it was no more of a risk than the rest of my night had been. It'd be worth it to see Kenna.

"In for a penny, in for a pound," I murmured. Taking Jasper's proffered hand, I crawled inside.

Once I was settled, Jasper grabbed the hood of the trunk, peering down at me with indecision on his face.

"Do it," I encouraged, ready to get this over with. The sooner we got out of here, the better. My anxiety spiked when another howl rose into the night barely a mile away. A distance a wolf could easily cover in mere minutes.

Jasper's features hardened and he nodded. "Stay quiet. It's not a long drive." Hesitating a moment longer, he added, "No matter what happens tonight, I vow to keep you safe, Madison."

I held on to that promise as he lowered the hood and cast me into the confined, inky darkness.

THREE

Madison

The walls felt like they were closing in on me with every passing minute. My heart raced, my pulse fluttering wildly in my neck despite the deep breaths I used to calm myself down.

By the time Jasper finally opened the trunk, I was on the verge of a panic attack. I crawled from the back, greedily sucking in fresh air. Cramped, enclosed spaces were not my thing, but the discomfort was erased when I heard the high-pitched squeal that pierced the night.

"Mads!" Kenna launched herself at me, and I laughed as she wrapped her arms around me in a bear hug. Barely stable on my feet, I hugged her back with a vengeance.

"Kenna," I replied happily. Out of the corner of my eye, I saw Jasper watching us from a few feet away and mouthed 'thank you.'

He nodded and took up a stance I'd seen him enact a thousand times before. Feet shoulder width apart, arms crossed, chin up, eyes scanning the distance. He went into full guardian mode, taking his promise to keep me safe seriously.

This far from the pack's land, threats should be minimal. Shifters tended to stick to their pack's territory, but I appreciated the effort all the same.

"Oh my God, I'm so glad you made it!" Kenna practically bounced on her heels with excited energy. It was contagious, and I found the stress of the evening melting away in her presence.

It was always like this. Like a piece of myself had finally come home. Like my heart was once again complete. We had a calming effect on each other we couldn't explain but chalked it up to a twin thing.

"I'm so sorry I wasn't home. I was worried you'd get caught." She bit her lip, her blue eyes so similar to mine swimming with concern. "I never would have sent that note and asked you to meet me if I knew Daddy was having people over. I swear. I should have checked. I'm so sor—"

I cut her off with another hug, this one quick, yet comforting. "I know. You'd never knowingly put me in danger. I chose to take the risk. It almost backfired, but we're here and we're safe." I didn't want to dwell on what could have happened. The night would be too short, and I wanted to spend it talking about her life and soaking up the time we had together.

Goddess knew how long it would have to last me until I got to see her again.

Kenna linked her arm through mine and half-led, half-dragged me through the parking lot that led to… a warehouse? Taking in my surroundings for the first time, I noticed the slew of cars that filled the dark lot and the two-story brick building we were heading toward.

"Where are we?" I asked, cutting into Kenna's apologetic retelling of the evening.

Her smile was positively wicked. "The Tipsy Crow."

"The night club?" Our packlands were located near Packwood, Washington, between Mt. Rainier and Gifford Pinchot National Forest. The Tipsy Crow was the closest club in the area, situated at the edge of the Yakima Valley, just outside the mountains. I'd heard my classmates talk about this place but never expected I'd ever see it myself. Excitement shot through me.

"Where else?" Kenna readjusted her oversized purse onto her shoulder and practically jogged in her heels toward the steel door with red, chipping paint that was the sole fixture at the back of the building. Guarding it was a massive bouncer Kenna handled with ease.

Music surrounded us when the door was wrenched open, and my sister squealed her delight once more as we entered with Jasper trailing behind shortly after.

Colored lights washed over the writhing bodies dancing in the center of the room, adding to the mystery and sex in the air. Thanks to the cloying scent of too much perfume mixed with the stench of sweat, my sensitive nose practically burned.

"You'll get used to it," Kenna hollered over the low roar of a million conversations and the rhythmic song blaring from the speakers, clearly seeing the way my nose wrinkled. "Come on."

Her hand clasped around mine, and I held on for dear

life as she pulled me along the path she fearlessly forged through the crowd. Finally stopping when she reached the bar, she squeezed her way between two college guys who bristled before they turned and spotted her.

Kenna smiled sweetly and tugged my hand a little harder than necessary, bringing me up to her side. The moment they saw her, their irritation fled, and their interest only grew when they noticed she had a twin.

"Hello, boys," my sister cooed and promptly began flirting before flagging down the bartender.

Despite being identical, it was hard not to notice the differences between Kenna and myself. Her hair lay in perfectly styled waves, and she wore a low cut top and a skirt that stopped mid-thigh. Expensive heels decorated her feet while I still wore my slip-on tennis shoes with my tank and frayed shorts. Our styles were completely different; hers was a product of her upbringing while I wore whatever I could get my hands on that didn't have holes in it. Kenna owned Louis Vuitton and Gucci, brands I'd only ever have a chance of wearing if someone carelessly threw them out and they ended up in the local Sift and Thrift.

I knew my sister would have graciously handed her clothing down to me if our father would've allowed it, but he hated me enough he refused even that courtesy. She'd wanted to sneak them to me herself, or have Jasper deliver them, but I told her it wasn't worth the risk.

We both knew it would be me who bore the brunt of his anger if we were caught. Pretty things weren't worth the cost of his wrath.

Kenna effortlessly chatted with the two guys while we waited for our drinks, and I tried to smile and nod at the appropriate moments. I felt out of my depth with the nuances of flirtation at which my sister was so skilled.

It made sense that those talents came naturally to her. She'd been groomed to lead the pack alongside her future mate. Her natural grace had been refined by her posh upbringing while my edges were left rough and jagged.

Though, if I were honest with myself, that was one thing I didn't envy.

My sister and I might not have much in common, thanks to our vastly different lives, but my exile meant no one cared about what I became, and there was a certain freedom in being mostly ignored.

Kenna, on the other hand, was always surrounded by people. There'd never been a day she wasn't being molded into a tool our father planned to use for political purposes. Even her mating had been arranged to serve the pack's best interests.

Just like me, she had no say over her own life. She may have had a more gilded prison than I did, but she was a prisoner nonetheless.

I recognized the same eagerness to escape I'd become so familiar with.

Perhaps we both needed this one night of freedom.

Maybe that was why I was quick to grab the flaming shot glass the bartender set on the worn, wooden counter before me. I needed to get out of my head and enjoy tonight.

Pointedly ignoring the men she'd been flirting with, Kenna turned to me and held up her drink with a melancholic smile.

"We might not be able to celebrate with a party and presents like we should've, but at least we have each other," Kenna voiced over the music. "Happy birthday, Mads. Make a wish."

Closing her eyes tightly, she blew out the flame and downed the bright pink alcohol, our favorite color.

"Happy twenty-first, Kenna." Following her lead, I squeezed my eyes closed.

I wanted to wish for more time with her. For another day, another week, another month, or even a year.

But it'd be a waste of a wish, a dream that would never see the light of day. Instead, I wished for the only thing I knew could come true.

One last amazing night together before we were ripped apart for the second time in our lives.

·)))) ● ((((·

"The guy behind you is so freaking cute," Kenna slurred, her eyes glazed and happy as she swayed to the music with her hands in the air.

"Aren't you already spoken for? You have to leave some guys for the rest of us mere mortals," I teased, enjoying the light, happy buzz that had pushed away my worries.

"We are literally identical," Kenna pointed out, easily understanding what I said through the noise of the club thanks to her enhanced hearing. "We even move identically." It was hard not to notice the similarities as we danced to the fast beat of the song. "Except for our outfit, the way we styled our hair tonight, and the slight difference in our scent, no one would be able to tell us apart."

"Maybe," I said, remembering how I'd duped Reynolds earlier. But it was a close call. He'd been moments away from calling my bluff.

"I think that puts us on an equal playing field." Kenna

nodded like she was agreeing with herself, her long blonde hair swaying behind her.

I just playfully shook my head. I didn't have the heart to tell her that as much as we wished differently, we'd never be equals. Instead, I hung on to my buzz like a stage five clinger, refusing to let reality deflate the fun little bubble I was living in.

Just for tonight.

"But, really. Don't you like Hunter?" I asked, truly curious about their relationship. She never talked about the guy she was about to mate with, and I knew nothing other than the idle chatter I'd heard from the few female enforcers who occasionally ended up on my guard detail.

Apparently, he was gorgeous, the strongest alpha the packs had ever seen. Next in line to lead the Ember Wolves, he'd have been my father's worst nightmare if his mating to Kenna hadn't been arranged and a tentative alliance formed between our packs.

Kenna hummed noncommittally, but her gaze left mine in a clear sign of avoidance.

I guess I couldn't blame her for not being thrilled about her arranged mating, but I was endlessly curious.

It was almost unheard of for the wolf packs to arrange a mating between heirs. The packs mostly kept to themselves, valuing their 'pure' elemental bloodlines over integration. They'd become very elitist in their thinking, so the mating between Kenna and Hunter was new territory for everyone.

I was sure my father, however, was tickled pink that the arrangement he'd set up years ago was finally coming to fruition. It was a power play for him to be tied in such a permanent way to the Ember Alpha, who also happened to be the High Alpha—the Alpha who ruled over all the other

Alphas and their packs. As much as my father hated the Ember Wolves, he knew they were more valuable as an ally than an enemy.

If he couldn't beat them, why not join them?

It helped that being the High Alpha's right hand would increase my father's standing and perceived power, and for whatever reason, the High Alpha agreed to the arrangement. There had to be something advantageous in it for him too—like territory, more warriors, or additional resources—but I wasn't privy enough to pack politics to understand the inner workings of the deal.

Selfishly, all it meant for me was that I was losing a sister. In another life, she'd have been mated off to a strong alpha contender within the Stormborn pack, and we would've been able to continue seeing each other during stolen visits. Instead, she'd been promised to the Ember heir shortly after her awakening, and she now was leaving, only to return for the occasional holiday, meeting, or pack function.

"Does that little hum mean you *don't* like him?" I pressed, suddenly worried about my sister's happiness. What if the guy was a complete tool? Or something even worse? I might not have much—okay, fine, *any*—experience with guys romantically, but I'd been around enough egotistical, pissed off enforcers to know the darker side some of the males of our kind possessed.

"I like him just fine," she answered. Her haze of alcoholic bliss diminished and her movements slowed as she continued to look away.

"You say that as though you're discussing the weather or tomorrow's breakfast menu," I quipped.

It struck me, then, just how little I really knew about my sister. Other than the basics and the fact that we were twins, we were almost strangers. Her life was so far removed from my own, I was constantly playing a game of catch-up. I didn't really know how she felt about any of this.

I tipped my head and studied her. "You can tell me the truth." I straightened the golden pendant on her necklace, hoping she'd take me up on the offer.

Kenna ran her hands through her hair to untangle the strands, then flicked it back with a toss I'd never perfect. "What's there to say, Mads? You think you're the only one Daddy controls?"

"Of course not," I shot back defensively. It was our last night, and I didn't want to fight. "I know you're just as trapped as I am. Your cage just comes with better pillows." I tried to joke to ease the sudden tension, but a small, half-hearted smile was my only reward.

"I have no choice who I mate with. I mean, *moon and stars*, Mads. I've been promised to mate with the next heir of the Ember pack since I was six." She laughed mirthlessly. "And Daddy made sure I couldn't do anything to mess up his plans. Hunter and I were bound six months ago by a moon witch he keeps on retainer."

The news that Kenna already shared a bond with Hunter was one thing, but surprisingly, it wasn't the most shocking part. I shook my head. "Wait. I thought the coven of moon witches were responsible for our curse over a century ago. Why the hell would our father trust one?" It made no sense. They'd cursed our entire kind. The spell they'd woven took away the greatest gift a wolf could receive from the Moon Goddess—a true mate.

"I don't know," Kenna shrugged. "She appeared about a year ago with information she wanted to trade for money, and they've been partners in crime ever since. Apparently, the curse is unbreakable, but a moon witch can bless two wolves and form a spell that simulates a fated mate bond. It's supposed to be way stronger than a chosen mate bond."

Kenna appeared dejected, and our movements continued to slow until we were two lone statues in the middle of a writhing sea of bodies. "Daddy offered the witch enough money, and she performed the spell. We've already gone through the first step—the initial bonding—and there's nothing I can do about it now." A pinched, forlorn expression worked across my sister's face. "Once Hunter completes the second step and bites me during the mating ceremony, it'll be completely irreversible."

Kenna blinked in rapid succession, pushing away heartbroken tears before they had a chance to fall down her cheeks.

"You care for someone else, don't you?" The truth was easy to see now that I was looking for it.

Kenna sniffed, took my hand, and pulled me from the crowd back to the bar where she hailed the bartender for another drink.

"You can't say a word to anyone," she ordered, her fingers tapping a staccato rhythm on the bartop.

Doesn't she trust me? I'd never, and I told her as much. Besides, who would I tell?

Some of the tension eased from her shoulders. "I know," she admitted. "You're one of the only people I can trust." She bit her lip and tucked her hair behind her ear. "He's actually meeting me here tonight."

Her blue-eyed gaze studied me, looking for condescension or judgment.

Worry immediately wormed its way into my chest.

"I want you to be happy. But are you sure you know what you're doing? The risk you're taking?"

Kenna released an exhausted sigh. "All I know is my life

is signed, sealed, and delivered in another twenty-four hours. You, of all people, know what it feels like to have no control, no say, in your own life."

I shouldn't condone it. I knew how hard it was to let yourself have a taste of something only to deny yourself in the end. It was how I felt every time I saw Kenna or went to school, only to return home to the same sheltered cottage alone, save for the rotation of enforcers.

A part of me was already grieving the time I'd be giving up with her if I had to leave already, but I wouldn't be selfish. Our one night of freedom wasn't just about our shared birthday or our goodbye. If Kenna needed this before giving herself over to our father's demands, I wouldn't begrudge her. Even though I thought it was a bad idea.

Just as I was about to tell her so, the air in the club shifted viscerally. A wave of power pulsed through the room, the tingle of it skating along my skin like a warm caress.

My sister cursed as I looked toward the door and saw two male wolf shifters stride through the entrance. Nose tilted up, the taller of the two drew a deep inhale, scenting the air, and I knew we were royally screwed.

Madison

The two shifters scanned the room, and I didn't wait to get a better look at them before I grabbed Kenna's arm and dragged her toward the ground. We weren't particularly tall to begin with, only five foot four, but I wanted to make sure we were out of sight.

To others, we probably just looked like two drunk girls searching for a lost earring, but I was already trying to see through the forest of legs toward the exits I'd noted when we'd arrived.

A girl in my position didn't have the privilege of a night out without making sure she knew her escape routes.

"Dammit. I thought he'd be tied up in meetings all

night," Kenna whispered with wide, wild eyes. "We can't let Hunter see us."

"Hunter?" I repeated in disbelief. Kenna's *mate*, Hunter? Our pack's greatest rival?

This couldn't be happening.

"And his beta, Tristan. They're in town to meet with Daddy and to escort me to the Ember pack in the morning. They must have wrapped things up early and come looking for me. I don't know how they tracked me down. Goddess, Mads! If they find out about you…" Kenna trailed off, but the weight of what she said settled over me like a scratchy, uncomfortable blanket. Suddenly, my skin felt too tight and my heart raced. The implications were too tragic to contemplate.

Moon Goddess above, this night just won't give me a break.

I held my hand up to my lips to silence her from saying anything more on the off chance they could pick up our whispered conversation from across the room, though it was unlikely due to the distance and the pounding beat of the music. Grabbing her hand tightly, I pulled her toward an exit.

Jasper, having already detected the newcomers, silently stalked toward us from where he'd been standing sentry and shielded us with his body as best he could.

"You guys need to split up," he said quietly as soon as he was within earshot. "It's your best chance at getting out of here without being seen together."

Kenna shot me a look and released a pent-up sigh. "He's right. You keep going. I'll find another way out and meet back up with you."

"There's a door at the front of the building you can use." Jasper motioned the direction to Kenna with a jerk of his head.

"You're going with her," I told him. "No arguments."

"Mads," he protested, but I held up my hand. We were out of time.

"Do it," I ordered, unused to giving such sharp commands. "Besides, it will look suspect if Kenna's without her bodyguard. All that matters is that I'm out of sight. If they catch her, there's nothing to be suspicious about. But me?"

Kenna nodded. "Come on, Jasp." She pulled on Jasper's shirt and started moving. "We'll meet you in the lot."

My friend looked anxious and unsure, then his expression changed to one of resolve.

"Head toward the car. Take cover in the woods, and I'll find you when the coast is clear," Jasper promised. He squeezed my arm reassuringly before the two of them bled into the crowd.

I blew out a nervous breath and pushed my way through the throngs of people, moving toward the exit.

My hand met the smooth metal handle of the side door at the same moment a large hand wrapped around my forearm like a shackle. Just like that, my escape plan disintegrated.

"Makenna." The deep voice shivered down my spine, and despite the fact it wasn't my given name, it somehow awakened parts of me that had long laid dormant.

The fine blonde hair on the back of my neck pricked upward at the alpha authority infused into that one uttered word. I could scarcely breathe while my mind scrambled for a way out of the inevitable: facing my greatest threat, even if he did think I was my sister.

"You shouldn't be here," the warning rumbled out of the man standing directly behind me.

Goddess, but those four little words had become the anthem of my evening.

For the second time tonight, I channeled Kenna. Spinning into his hold, I was ready to face him, but no matter how hard I tried, I couldn't force myself to look up. Fear that he'd see the lie in my eyes as clearly as rain during a summer storm kept my focus at chest level.

Though, if I were being honest, it was a *really* nice chest.

"What are you doing here, Hunter?" I accused after gathering my wits, taking a wild stab at his name from the possessive way he held onto me.

It wasn't a difficult guess. His beta, Tristan, would've had to have some major cajones to handle my sister this way. Kenna was an alpha herself, after all. And the future Luna of his pack. He'd never grab her so brashly. But Hunter? That was a different story entirely.

"I came to collect you," he answered, and my ire rose from the way he made it sound like such a chore.

Was this what Kenna had to look forward to? A life of being dictated to and babysat? No freedom? No say in her own life?

No wonder she doesn't want to mate with this guy.

"I don't need collecting," I said, tugging my wrist back toward my body in an attempt to break free of him, but all it served to do was draw us closer together.

"It's not safe to be out tonight," Hunter reprimanded. I felt his attention burning a hole into the top of my head, almost as if he was daring me to meet his penetrative gaze.

I scoffed. "Is it ever safe to be out?" The challenge slipped from my lips before I realized it may have been more of a 'Madison' thing to say.

I needed to be careful before I gave myself away. Then

again, this whole charade would be for naught if Tristan caught Kenna before she made it out of here. I flicked my attention past Hunter's imposing frame, scanning the crowd, hoping against hope my twin made it to an exit and had left the building. This was far too close a call for comfort.

Even without looking at him, I felt Hunter scrutinizing my profile. Was he looking for what made me different tonight? Did he know something was amiss?

Finally, he answered what I'd meant to be a rhetorical question. "We're always safe inside our packs' territories. It's when we leave we need to worry. You shouldn't have taken the chance."

His tone sounded scolding, as if he couldn't understand why I'd risked leaving the safety of our boundaries. Deep down, his rebuke was most likely concern in disguise. It may have come from a place of caring, but it struck me then. Didn't he realize there were just as many monsters within our guarded lands as there were beyond? Nowhere was truly safe.

At least, it hadn't been for me.

Hunter's experiences were most likely different. As the future Alpha of the Ember Wolves, his pack probably worshiped him, and rightly so. With only a small glimpse of him, I'd noted his strength and commanding presence.

It seemed the world couldn't touch Hunter Weston.

Daring to glance at him, my eyes cut their way up his defined chest. I drank in the sight of the hard planes clearly evident beneath his fitted black t-shirt and the tattoos inked down his arms, the same ones that peeked above his neckline. The sharp line of his square jaw was dusted with light stubble, and his shoulders were broad, his arms thickly muscled. He was like a chiseled Adonis, except his hair was dark brown. Styled shorter on the sides, longer on top, it swept effortlessly away from his forehead. Coupled with his thick, expressive brows, he possessed a dangerous edge I had to admit I liked. But it was his most striking feature that marked him as a predator and ensnared my full attention—a set of amber eyes which seemed to cut right through me.

Even within the shadows, the color was a rich gold interspersed with red that almost seemed to shift and flicker.

Ember wolf.

Any trace of doubt I'd had about who stood before me fled. Only an Alpha or an heir's elemental power would show in such an outward display.

As if summoned, a wave of his power crashed over me. The heat of it licked along my skin, warming me and warning me simultaneously. Where his hand gripped my forearm almost burned.

The effect was magnetizing, and something in me responded, daring me to draw inexplicably closer to him.

Some of the ire seemed to fall away as he studied me with an intensity I wasn't used to. "You need to come with me. I'm taking you home."

I shook my head. "I don't have a home." As soon as the words left my mouth, how true they were hit me with new clarity.

The Stormborn pack wasn't home anymore, what with my sister leaving tomorrow. Maybe it never had been. Somehow, I knew the same sentiment was also true for Kenna.

Our pack may have been her home all this time, but now she was being forced to leave, to join with the Ember pack. To mate against her will with Mr. Smoldering McHottie.

I mean… There were worse fates. But still. My indignation for both our futures intertwined until I tugged out of Hunter's grasp.

It was clear he hadn't been expecting that, and after a brief moment of puzzled confusion, his face darkened to something downright chilling.

"You're free to go, Hunter. I release you of whatever obligation brought you here, but I came out for a night of fun and dancing. I intend to do just that." I shocked myself with how brazen and bold I had become in the span of a heartbeat.

Brushing past him, I made sure not to make bodily contact, still worried he would pick up on the fact I wasn't my sister.

Kenna's signature had mingled with my own, thanks to the dancing we'd done earlier, and the cacophony of scents in the club helped muddle it even further, but if he got me outside, my ruse would be walking the thin tightrope between truth and lie.

The way my pulse fluttered in my neck and the butterflies jumbled in my stomach were additional reasons I needed to put some space between Hunter and me.

That man was far too handsome, and far too observant, for his—or maybe, my—own good.

Weaving between bodies, I pressed deeper into the club toward the dance floor. At first, it was difficult to maneuver, and I'd had to shoulder my way past people, but soon, they parted naturally, allowing me to pass.

I almost reveled in the newfound command I seemed to exude, until I felt that same lick of body heat pressing against my spine.

I frowned and cast a scathing look behind me at the towering man following far too closely, parting the crowds like the Red Sea. Everyone around us had unconsciously noted the predator stalking toward them and moved out of his way to dance off to the sides, giving him, and me by association, a wide berth.

Damn him. It was a handy superpower, and one I wish I possessed.

"You must be hard of hearing. I said you can go." I threw the retort over my shoulder and suppressed the grin fighting to bloom at the irritated line forming between his brows.

"You said you wanted to dance. So let's dance, Princess."

Princess. I almost snorted inelegantly. No one would ever call me that.

If only he knew how very far from the truth he is.

I stopped in the middle of the dance floor and turned to face him. "I'm not going to dance with you." I crossed my arms, belatedly aware of how the gesture pushed my breasts together, up and outward, forcing them against the neckline of my top.

While I wasn't flat-chested by any means, I also wasn't overly blessed. I was a decent B cup, but the way I was standing definitely made the girls appear bigger.

Hunter noticed, his molten stare scalding me as it dropped down my body. He stepped closer, and I sucked in a breath.

Way to poke the bear... or grumpy wolf in this case.

"If you want to dance, Little Wolf, go right ahead. But make no mistake. I'll be right here the whole time." Hunter crossed his own arms, the fabric of his black t-shirt pulling taut from the breadth of his arms and shoulders.

Damn. He looked delicious. Shadows played across the cut lines of his physique with every pass of the bright, colorful strobe lights. Red. Blue. Green. Yellow. They chased each other across his body, highlighting the hard press of his kissable lips, the array of intricate tattoos swirling down his corded forearms, the confident way he tilted his chin up just slightly, bolstering his authority over everyone around him.

And I wasn't the only one who noticed.

Women all around us were glancing coquettishly in his direction. For some reason, it set my teeth on edge.

Stop that. He's Kenna's mate, I cautioned myself, but the shocking fact remained. There was no denying it.

I was attracted to Hunter. Got perverse pleasure out of challenging him. But he was Kenna's, so I shut down my rising interest and locked it away in a place deep inside my heart where it would never see the light of day.

It wouldn't matter that she didn't want him; when they sealed their mating with bite marks and magic—the 'blessing' of the moon witch would finish binding them for life. This wasn't a path I could explore.

You'd think I'd be used to being denied the things I wanted in life, but this one stung. I didn't think I'd ever been as drawn to someone as I'd been to Hunter, but being born no better than a human meant I'd never take a mate.

That reality had never felt as stark as it did now, standing in the middle of this club surrounded by happy, drunk people. I felt keenly out of place, torn between two worlds, not truly fitting in either.

As we stood there, staring at each other, both of us locked in an elaborate game of chicken, I made a decision.

The people in this club? *These* were my people. Humans. Mundanes. I was more like them than I was the pack I'd been born into, and I wanted to be as happy and free as they were. Just for tonight.

Smirking, I relaxed my stance and shrugged.

"Suit yourself. If you want to watch me dance, enjoy the show."

I barely got to enjoy the deepening slash of his brows before I turned my back on him and began moving to the beat. With every sway of my hips, every swish of my hair as I moved to the rhythm, I relaxed, letting the stress of the evening melt away.

Things were looking up. Tristan hadn't found Kenna. I spotted the dark guardian, with his black hair and deep brown eyes, stationed off to the side of the dance floor, leaning against the wall, alert and ready if his friend called upon him. That meant I just needed to keep my distance from the brooding alpha behind me and everything would be okay.

I'd give myself time to enjoy the music and shimmy my way across the dance floor toward the exit on the other side. Hopefully Hunter would realize I was serious and he'd leave me to my devices. Once he was gone, I'd head for the woods and wait for Jasper to come for me.

No matter how long it took to execute my plan, I knew Jasper would be there. He'd been a loyal friend, proving himself time and time again over the years. Instead of simply guarding me, he kept me company when assigned to my security detail, and he was lenient anytime he was ordered by my father to dish out punishment. He'd encouraged my schooling, celebrated my wins, and comforted me during my lows. He indulged my fantasies about a normal life, one where things were different and I wasn't a dirty little secret. Slowly, he'd become one of the only people I could count on.

I felt bad knowing he and Kenna were probably

worried about me, but I knew they wouldn't come back inside and potentially make the situation worse.

They'd trust me to handle it, and I was.

I closed my eyes and lost myself to the song, dancing and jumping, swaying and throwing my hands in the air.

The crowd eventually eased and grew closer once more, forming a loose circle around me. A pair of hands landed on my hips and pulled me out of my trance. My lashes lifted and I spotted a good-looking college-age guy swaying before me.

This was a man I could allow myself to be with. He was tall and cute, with blonde shaggy hair and a dimple in his left cheek that formed when he gave me a lazy grin. The music was too loud for us to converse, so we just moved together, his hold on my waist growing more bold when I didn't shove him away.

A low, menacing growl sounded from just behind me, making me want to lower my head and wrench my neck to the side in submission.

My easy mood disappeared in an instant, and I gritted my teeth against the urge to submit. In another lifetime, I would have been an alpha, but the smidgeon of wolf genes I did possess wasn't enough to go toe to toe in a dominance battle with an heir.

Luckily, the oppressive wave of alpha power eased enough before I gave myself away and bared my throat to him.

"I think you're lost," Hunter addressed my dance partner, the tenor deep and forbidding.

His arm slipped around my waist tugging me into his body and away from the blonde. Every inch of me was pressed intimately against him, my back molded to his front. I felt positively cocooned by him, wrapped in his embrace. Hunter's hand splayed possessively over my stomach in an outward display of ownership.

I fought against the dark thrill shooting through me.

Holding up his hands, the blonde retreated. "I didn't know she was taken, man. S-sorry."

If I could have been a fly on the wall, I knew Hunter would have looked downright frightening towering over me. I could just picture his eyes smoldering with anger, his shoulders bulked with the presence of his wolf just beneath the surface.

In his wolf's eyes, someone had just pissed on his property, and now Hunter was retaliating in kind, marking *me* as *his* for anyone who dared to look.

Apparently, this man had a breaking point, and I'd prodded him enough to push him to the brink.

Slowly, purposefully, he turned me in his arms.

His eyes were deeper and darker, the color more russet than amber. The glint within was intimidating.

I swallowed, my mouth going dry again, my inhale jagged. An apology sat ready on my lips even as my mind scrambled to find another way out of this situation. Obviously, I'd miscalculated Hunter's resolve to see me home. The way Kenna had talked about their relationship, I'd doubted his interest, his dedication. Maybe he didn't see her—and now me, by proxy—as an obligation the way she did him.

He was a mystery, one I wanted to figure out.

But before I could say anything, before I could come up with a way to extract myself and get back to Kenna and Jasper, Hunter stiffened. His head cocked to the side and he seemed to listen to something beyond the obtrusive beat of the newest song blaring from the speakers.

Faster than he should have moved if he wanted to keep

his supernatural status a secret, Tristan was by Hunter's side.

The hold around my waist tightened a fraction as the two communicated silently. I strained to see past them, to listen for whatever it was that had them on high alert.

Focusing, I flexed the few heightened senses I did have and took in my surroundings. Nothing in the club seemed out of the ordinary. But then I heard it. The distant battle cry of a wolf. The howl was baleful, and I shivered from the daunting sound of it.

"Stay here," Hunter ordered, releasing me as fast as he'd claimed me.

I stumbled, righting myself before I fell on my ass.

"I'll come back for you when it's safe," he promised.

"Are you sure it's a good idea to leave her here?" Tristan questioned, something only Hunter's beta, Luna, or an Alpha higher in the pecking order could get away with given his position as a powerful heir.

The muscle in Hunter's jaw jumped, and he scrubbed a hand over his chin, contemplating. "Too dangerous to bring her with us. You stay back with her."

"Like fuck," Tristan cursed, then turned into my space, shutting me out by giving me his shoulder and back, though he knew I could hear him regardless. "I know you can handle yourself, but we don't know the full extent of the threat. You could be walking into a trap," Tristan threw a glare at me over his shoulder like I was the enemy.

Guess tensions on both sides of our pack treaty were high, our trust in each other brittle, given our tentative alliance.

Truthfully, I didn't blame them for their suspicions. It was a little too convenient that they'd chased me down outside pack territory into 'no man's land' where shifter laws became grey at best. But my father would never do anything to jeopardize the treaty he'd painstakingly put in place.

He'd be the loser in a battle between our packs, and though I hated to credit him with anything positive, he was too smart not to know that.

If there were any redeeming quality about the man, it was his concern for his pack and protecting them with his life. That they also provided him with his position of power and fed his ego was, let's just say, a convenient perk.

Either way, I knew what I needed to do. This was my chance to get back to Kenna and Jasper, and if there were truly a threat outside these walls, I needed to be with them and return to the safety of the Stormborn pack.

"Go," I pressed. "I'll stay safe."

Hunter pushed past Tristan and grabbed my chin. Not strong enough to hurt, but firm enough to let me know he was serious. He lifted my face until I was staring into the fiery depths of his hardened gaze.

"No," he replied sharply with a single shake of his head, seeing through me far too easily. That alpha command pressed down on me. "You'll stay *here* and stay safe."

I nodded, the jerky motion all I could manage under the influence of his demand. The higher a wolf was in the pack hierarchy, the less potent an alpha's command, but I was at the bottom of that proverbial totem pole.

Luckily, I wasn't a member of his pack. The magic of his request made me want to obey, but ultimately, my actions were my choice.

More howls sounded in the distance. He needed to go… and so did I.

"I need to hear you say it," he urged. He wasn't going to leave unless I promised.

I swallowed, and forced myself to comply. "I'll stay." The lie slid as smooth as honey from my lips.

I don't know if I was convincing enough. Hunter's gaze moved between my eyes, searching. For the truth in my words, or perhaps deeper, looking for the truth in the carefully constructed lie I'd been weaving since we met.

It didn't feel good to lie to him, I realized. But I would. I would do almost anything to stay safe. To keep my sister safe. And I wasn't a monster. I didn't want to see my father or the pack harmed, either, because of repercussions that led directly back to me.

Whatever he saw, it must have been enough.

Hunter released me and backed up. He studied me for a few long beats as he moved away, then turned and hurried for the door with Tristan in tow.

I didn't move, barely breathed, until I knew for sure he was gone.

The moment he stepped into the deepening night and the door swung shut after him, the presence I'd been happily drowning in since he'd arrived dissipated. I drew a deep lungful of air to clear my head and shake off the lingering effects of his power and then I was moving in the opposite direction.

I maneuvered toward the back door, the battered red one that led directly into the parking lot. Slipping through, I broke the promise I had just made and headed for the tree-line to the sound of another perilous howl piercing the night.

Madison

The warm air felt almost stifling as I raced through the parking lot, the new wave of adrenaline crashing through me fueled by my growing panic and fear.

Weaving my way through the cars, I tried to remember where we'd parked, looking for any sign of Jasper and Kenna along the way. They had to be here somewhere, but with the threat of wolves pressing down on us, I didn't dare call out for them.

Even if the wolves where from the Stormborn pack, catching my sister and I together wouldn't bode well, so I stayed quiet and moved swiftly.

I blew out a tension-filled breath when I spotted Jasper's car. Skidding to a halt, I peered through the windows, my relief deflating as I took in the empty seats.

They aren't here.

Frustrated, I ran my hand through my blonde hair and glanced around, trying to figure out where the hell they'd be. Remembering Jasper's instructions about keeping to the woods, I backed away and headed for the treeline. It was only then I noticed the slashed tires.

Deep gouges had been ripped into the rubber, the rims resting on the asphalt.

The cuts weren't the clean workings of a knife but jagged, angry tears made by force.

Someone—or some*thing*—didn't want us to leave.

The Stormborn Wolves would know Jasper's car and would never do this, which meant we were in serious danger.

My fingers went ice cold as my heart jumped into my throat. I turned and ran.

Only one thought pounded through my mind in time with my pulse.

Kenna. Kenna. Kenna.

Hunter was right. It wasn't safe outside packlands, and coming out tonight had been too big a risk to take.

How many packs out there would jump at the opportunity to use my sister as leverage against my father? How many enemies had he made in his years as Alpha of the Stormborn pack?

The numbers could be endless.

Peace among our elemental packs was tentative at best. I'd heard rumors that more often than not, the various packs were at each other's throats. And with my sister's looming mate bond sealing the treaty between the Stormborn and Ember wolf packs, it was entirely possible another Alpha was trying to sabotage the pending alliance. Or worse, forcing my father into uniting with them instead, using Kenna as a pawn in an elaborate political game.

Guilt swamped me. We wouldn't be out tonight if it wasn't for my desperate desire to say goodbye to Kenna.

Extending my senses, I caught a whiff of Kenna's scent on the breeze and picked my way through the forest.

I tried to stay as quiet as possible, but moving quickly soon outweighed my desire for stealth. Keeping totally silent was costing me too much time. All that mattered was finding Kenna and getting somewhere safe, so I pushed myself harder, pumped my legs faster, and hurried deeper into the forest.

The cover of trees grew thicker, their leaves and bark darkened to no more than shadowed silhouettes. Against the shine of the moon in the velvety night, the tall giants towered above me, but instead of the peace the forest usually brought, tonight it felt imposing.

Following the faint trail of Kenna's sweet floral and thunderstorm scent, I veered to the left, hoping my instincts wouldn't fail me. My heart lightened a fraction when her signature strengthened, the tendrils of it coalescing into something more tangible, but the next howl smothered that spark of hope into ash.

The haunting song of more wolves in the distance joined the first, some close while others were farther out. I recognized it for the ploy it was. Whoever was out here wanted to disguise their intent. Spread out and dispersed as they were, the enemy could be leading me, and anyone else out here, like Hunter and Tristan, on a wild, confusing chase.

I shook off the paralyzing reality of the danger we were in and kept going.

"Kenna, where the hell are you?" I whispered harshly, uncaring of the brambles that caught and tore at my skin or the visible path I was rending through the undergrowth. The scratches were nothing compared to the sting of fear, and finding my sister quickly was more important than remaining unseen.

Overhead, the clouds seemed to gather, and a hint of electricity hung in the air to tickle my nose.

Out of nowhere, a dark blur launched at me, knocking me off my feet and sending me careening toward the ground. A cry rose up my throat, but it was gone before it ever truly formed as the harsh impact knocked the wind from my lungs.

Gasping and spluttering, I sucked in air to replace what I'd lost while I scrambled to sit up amid the grass and leaves. My bearings returned to me just in time to see an onyx wolf with beautiful sky-blue markings disappear, shifting to reveal my sister's human form.

"Kenna!" The anger and pain from being tackled like a running back about to make a touchdown fled with my relief.

Kenna's hand smacked over my lips, and she held a finger to her own, signaling the need to remain quiet. I nodded, sat up, and moved into a crouch at her side. Ignoring her naked state—a phenomenon typical among the wolf shifters but always uncomfortable for me—I listened for whatever it was she heard stalking us in the woods.

An eerie silence settled over the forest, the critters that were usually out were taking cover and hunkering down. The leaves barely dared to rustle overhead, and I felt darkness creep in like inky mire. An ominous feeling slithered down my spine, and I knew Kenna felt it, as well, if her rapid breathing was any indication.

Gazing at me with wide, scared eyes, she slipped her hand into mine and squeezed.

Shooting from between the trees, a dark wispy form appeared. It flew above our heads, circling and weaving between the thick tree trunks.

I gripped Kenna's hand tighter and sent her a look I hoped conveyed 'What the fuck is that?'

I'd never seen anything like it; whatever it was, was clearly a threat.

"Mads," my sister hissed, snapping herself out of her fear and gripping my shoulders so I was looking right at her. "You need to run."

"Not without you," I whispered resolutely as another dark wisp appeared.

Then another and another.

Kenna gasped. "I don't recognize this magic."

"What element is this?" I pressed, hoping she'd be able to discern which of the wolf packs we were up against.

Upon birth, each wolf was blessed with an elemental power pertaining to Fire, Water, Earth, Air, Storms, Energy, Light, the Moon, or the Celestials.

Isolated as my life was, I was only familiar with the Storm magic I'd seen within the Stormborn pack, and there was no way this was our doing.

"I-I don't know." Kenna shook her head, eyes tracking the strange shadows as they flitted around us. "We need to move. I'm going to shift and you're going to climb on my back. Hold on tight." Her order turned more guttural as she started to shift.

"I'll just slow you down," I pleaded, wanting her to

leave me behind. I'd be dead weight, keeping her from sprinting at her full potential.

I could be the bait, lure the shadowed things away from her while she made a bee-line for home.

"Your best chance to get out of here is without me."

Kenna's low growl brokered no argument, and she roughly nudged me with her nose when her shift was complete.

She wasn't going to leave me behind.

The unformed shadows stalked closer, their movements predatory as they circled us like dinner.

Gritting my teeth, I swung my leg over and dug my fingers into her soft fur. Lowering my body until I was flush with her spine, I braced myself, my thighs tense against her flanks as she took off into the forest.

I wanted to gasp, to squeal, to scream, but I pressed my lips together and swallowed any sound as I dared a glance backward.

Sure enough, the wisps dove after us like a hoard of obsidian ghosts.

Kenna put on a burst of speed when they caught up, practically nipping at her heels. She swerved left, then diverted right, but they simply wove in and out of the trees, following after like the tail on a kite. Whichever way my sister moved, they mirrored.

The snarl that burst from Kenna vibrated through my chilled body. Adrenaline pumping, I tried to think.

What the fuck were these things, and why were they hunting us?

Then a thought struck. *Hunting? Or* herding?

"They're not chasing us," I gasped, my throat dry from the onslaught of warm air rushing against me from how fast we moved. My stomach rolled, my fingers locking painfully in Kenna's dark fur. "They're driving us somewhere."

Testing that theory, Kenna turned sharply, angling us directly toward our territory with new fervor, but it was no use. The shadows surrounded us, cutting her off. The first time, she pivoted and ran a different direction to escape their reach, but each time she turned toward home, they intercepted us.

"Go through them," I urged. If we didn't, we had zero chance of making it back.

Taking the risk, Kenna barreled straight through the dark essence.

Pain erupted in my head as a loud, untamed howl filled my mind. A dark chill engulfed me until even my bones were cold, then promptly heated until I felt like I was boiling alive.

Fairing no better, Kenna whimpered and whined until we broke free on the other side.

The fiery sensation burning along my skin slowly subsided, and the splitting headache eased with every foot-fall we placed between ourselves and the dark magic.

Then, out of the billowing, smokey shadows, the faces of vile, angry wolves began to form. Teeth bared, muzzles snarled, they floated like demented clouds, catching up and easily keeping pace at our sides.

Too easily.

They snarled and nipped at us as we ran, somehow corporal enough to be able to draw blood from both my sister and I. Their razor-sharp teeth left long scratches along my legs and Kenna's sides, and my sister sprinted harder, pushing herself past her limits with me on her back.

I almost went flying when she stumbled and missed a step, then squealed as she bucked and readjusted me until I was steadily seated once more. The shock of almost falling sobered me and chased away the effects of the pain.

The weight of our situation was as heavy upon me as I was against my sister's back, and the realization she was tiring quickly from carrying me squeezed my heart in a vice.

She's never going to make it.

She didn't even stand a chance of getting home, of evading this threat, with me clinging to her.

Kenna whined the moment she felt my grip ease, my fingers untangling from her fur. Her wild gaze flew over her shoulder, locking with mine.

"Run!" I yelled. "Run with everything you have."

Then, I pushed off her back and freefell for one glorious moment before I smashed into the ground, pain exploding throughout my body.

Madison

The pain was an all-consuming ache. My bones ground together, and my muscles pulled in unnatural ways. I finally came to rest against the debris-ridden ground with a pained groan.

Sticks and stones cut into my skin, leaving more bleeding gashes on my arms and legs. Leaves clung to me and tangled in my hair.

Still, despite the pain, I forced my eyes to open, rolled onto my stomach, and pushed myself up, crawling to my knees to make sure Kenna had kept going without me.

But what I saw froze my blood.

The creepy shadow wolves didn't stop. They followed

after her with more vigor, moving faster than they had before as they disappeared into the trees. It was almost like they wanted me gone and out of the way so they could get to her.

Dammit!

I pushed myself upright and broke into a hobbled run, uncaring of the agony my muscles screamed at me.

Fuck. That.

I had hoped the shadows would deviate once they saw an easy target... me on the forest floor. But they hadn't come after me when I bailed off of Kenna. They hadn't stopped or given me a second thought at all.

This is all about her... She's the one they want.

I followed the broken trail Kenna's wolf left through the undergrowth. Scrambling over fallen logs and brushing branches out of my path until a sharp, wounded cry sent panic tearing through me.

I stumbled as dread pooled in the pit of my stomach.

My legs ached, my calves burned, but I didn't stop moving.

Trepidation crawled up my spine like icy fingers when I crashed into a clearing and drew to a sudden stop.

My sister's beautiful black wolf stood in the center. Blood marred her pretty coat, the sky-blue markings saturated with crimson. It ran down in streaks from all the places she was injured, slicking her fur to her body.

Concern shot through me, but I had zero time to focus on her wounds.

Hackles raised and canines bared, she growled menacingly as the strange shadow wolves bled back into the forest.

Something deep in the shadows watched us.

My breath left me completely when a huge male wolf appeared. Eyes as red as the fires of hell, he stalked forward with bared, razor-sharp teeth. Smoke swirled off the beast, its coat nothing more than those same unformed tendrils of thick, onyx wisps. I watched with panicked awe as the last dark smoky cloud dove into his body, becoming part of him as he recalled whatever strange magic he held.

This wolf seemed to bleed from the shadows themselves as if he were born from the darkness. A heavy scent of sulfur hung in the air, and the stench of rotten eggs made me want to gag.

Realizing just how screwed we were, Kenna tilted her head back and released a long, loud cry for help. Her howl rose into the night—a call for her pack.

Return howls echoed in the far-off distance. Reinforcements were already on their way, but they'd never make it in time.

I had no skills with which to take on a wolf, especially one using such dark powers, but if I was going to die, I'd die fighting at my sister's side.

I bent down and scooped up the first tree branch of substantial size I could find. Narrowed to a splintered point on one end, I wielded it like a spear as the shadow beast snarled.

Fierce and precise, it lunged at Kenna. The two wolves locked in battle, their growls resonating into the air and tangling together until I didn't know one from the other.

But where her attacker moved skillfully, Kenna's offense was rough and her defense inexperienced, her training not nearly as refined.

Rushing forward, I took aim and threw the spear with every ounce of adrenaline-fueled strength I had. My scream was raw and angry. Fire felt like it licked up my throat and my heart nearly beat out of my chest. It pounded as though it was about to explode, my pulse racing wildly.

I watched the branch soar through the air and sail into the body of the beastly wolf. I had no idea if I'd be able to injure it, but when it slammed into the writhing smoke cloaking its fur, it sank deep.

A loud, angry, wounded snarl echoed off the trees, and Kenna used the slight advantage to bite into the wolf's leg.

Retaliating, he snapped his lethal jaws, the two of them entangled in a wicked dance of claws, teeth, and blood.

In the blink of an eye, the shadow wolf locked his open maw around Kenna's throat.

His red eyes then locked on mine with dark, deadly intent.

My gaze widened, and I rushed forward with a raw scream. "No!"

Everything happened in slow motion after that. His jaw clenched, tightening as he ripped into Kenna's neck. Blood sprayed across me as my aching body collided with my sister's attacker.

He barely budged, but he dropped Kenna's limp body before slamming his snout into my stomach, sending me careening backward.

I fell into a crumpled heap on the ground, sucking in air, then wrapping an arm around my tender rib cage.

"K-Kenna!" The cry stuttered out of me as my shocked gaze fell to her heaving body lying in a pool of ever-widening blood.

I didn't get the chance to move before the dark wolf prowled forward and stood over me. Tears tracked down my cheeks and the air rattled in my lungs as I shook from fear.

I was staring death in the face, a Grim Reaper in the

shape of a wolf that looked as though he walked straight out of the fiery pits of Hell. If hellhounds were real, I'd have guessed that was exactly where he'd come from, but I knew better.

This monster wasn't some myth or fabled tale. He was flesh and blood, a lethal combination of strength and power in the form of a nightmare.

Instead of ending me, however, the beast craned his neck and bit down on the branch sticking out of his side. Ripping it out in one fluid motion, he dropped it beside me with an irate expression narrowing his animalistic features. Blood poured from the wound but it sizzled away almost instantly, evaporating into curls of smoke before it ever hit the ground.

As he lowered his head and growled a menacing warning, his jowls lifted and rippled, baring his blood-stained teeth.

I was sure I was a goner, but the ending bite never came.

The crashing sound of something thundering through the forest at a fast clip had the dark wolf's ears pricking, and then, with one last deep, low snarl, he stepped past me and bled back into the forest as though he'd never been there, having torn my life to shreds and leaving me in the bloody aftermath.

A hysterical breath burst from my lungs, and I nearly hyperventilated as I crawled toward Kenna. Her blood soaked into the dark denim of my shorts and slicked my hands as I moved to her side.

Her wolf tried to whine, a breathy, airy, half-formed sound that broke my heart.

With shaking fingers, I pressed my hands against the wound in her neck, but it was too large to cover all of it.

My pulse pounded in my ears, and I lost sight of my surroundings. All I could see was dark fur and blood. So much blood. It covered everything—the ground, my clothes, my skin. The metallic smell of it threatened to make me puke. Desperately trying to think through my panic for something to fix this, I ripped off my tank and begged for it to be enough as I pressed it against her torn throat.

A blue spark of magic shimmered over her body, shooting along her fur like tiny lightning bolts as her shift ended and her wolf gave way to her human form.

"No! Why? Why did you shift?" A fresh wave of panic flooded me until I could barely breathe. Wolves healed faster than their human counterparts. "You need to shift back, Kenna. Please. Please shift back!" It was her only chance.

Choking on blood, she tried to talk, but I shook my head, my tears blurring my vision.

"Don't. It's okay. Help is on its way."

Just as the promise left my lips, a wolf covered in the typical sky-blue Stormborn markings burst out of the brush in a blaze of fury.

Jasper.

A mixture of grey, tan, and blue fur stood on end along his hackles, his teeth bared. On high alert, he scanned the clearing for any threats before some of the tension left his taut shoulders. But the moment his gaze landed on me and Kenna, he shifted back to his human form. Face pale, he rushed to our side.

"Mads," he pleaded. His timbre was tinged with a deep, rough quality from the wolf who stayed just beneath his skin.

"Where were you?" I accused, my voice wavering and hoarse from the emotion threatening to clog my throat.

"I was leading the wolves away from Kenna. They were drawing close and I… I…" He ran a dirty hand through his blonde hair and shook his head. "I was trying to protect you," he finally said softly, dropping to his knees beside me.

His hand was a comforting weight on my back, reminding me I was no longer alone.

"We have to help her," I sobbed. "Please, Jasper. Please help me."

Something hardened in Jasper's eyes a moment before he turned away and hid the expression from me. "She's not going to make it, Mads."

I shook my head, swiping a hand under my nose as I continued to cry, accidentally smearing blood across my face. The sharp tang of copper hung heavily in my nose.

Sniffling, my tears fell unchecked, leaving wet streams down my cheeks.

I refused to believe him. I wouldn't—couldn't—give up on her.

This wasn't happening.

Not her. Not my sister. My twin.

Kenna's blood soaked through the cotton and welled up between my fingers. Her breathing grew even more shallow, barely lifting her chest. Weakly raising her hand, she rested it overtop of mine, turning her head until we were looking at each other.

Jasper stood, then paced frantically along the treeline somewhere behind me, but he became nothing but background noise as I held onto Kenna and tried to slow her bleeding.

"Shift," I begged again, needing her to try and save

herself. "Shift back. It'll help you heal faster. You have to, Kenna. Please."

Instead of listening to me, her eyes dropped closed, her lashes fluttering against her cheek.

"Love… You…." Even with the last of her strength, her rasping words were a barely formed gurgle. They were so quiet, they were hard to make out under the shuddering, sobbing breaths racking my body.

"Don't do this to me. Don't leave me, Kenna. Please. Please don't go." I chanted nonsensically. Somewhere in the back of my mind, I knew she had no choice, but talking to her, begging her, believing she could change this cruel fate kept the spark of hope alive in my chest, and somehow, that was vital to my own survival.

Slowly, like the ebbing of the tide, the remaining life left her until her breathing stopped altogether.

The connection we shared dulled and dimmed to nothing but a glowing, fading ember.

No! No. This couldn't be happening. Sharp, visceral agony pierced me like an arrow. I felt like I was having an out-of-body experience, like my consciousness was trying to disconnect from the rest of me. I was both in my body and beyond it, a strange tingle working its way through my limbs as I grasped onto what was left of our connection.

I couldn't lose that too.

Bowing over her broken body, I wept, the sorrow so thick I was sure I would die right alongside her from heartbreak.

I ignored Jasper. I ignored the physical pain. I ignored the sudden heat radiating in my chest as I mourned for my sister.

Something inside of me pulled.

Then, without warning, Kenna's body began to glow a

vibrant teal. Lifting my head, my eyes widened and I gasped, hiccuping on the sharp inhale.

Rising from within her was the beautiful spirit of her wolf.

I fell back on my ass, scrambling backward to give it more room as it emerged to stand over her motionless body, peaceful in death.

It cocked its head, studying me curiously, waiting for something I didn't understand.

The warmth in the center of my heart reached new levels, the heat nearly scalding, and I pawed at the spot where the sensation seemed to emanate from. The very same place I'd always felt the indescribable bond of sisterhood.

"Help her," I begged her wolf, unable to contemplate what life would be without my other half.

But instead of rejoining with my sister or doing something magical that would save her life, her wolf bounded straight toward me… and dove into my chest.

SEVEN

Madison

The wolf's spirit, sealing with my own, awoke something in me that had always been absent, and everything changed.

A new sense of magic settled inside of me, a powerful thrum below my skin that felt overwhelming and strange. All my senses honed and sharpened far beyond what my limited power had been capable of. Smell and taste worked almost synonymously, the forest taking on new life. I could taste the dew forming on the leaves and smell the moss covering the trees as keenly as I could hear the crashing sound of wolves less than a mile out heading our way.

My vision sharpened as well. Suddenly, the world was

cast into high definition. The difference was staggering, but I could barely process what had happened. My mind was blown, my senses in overdrive. But none of it mattered to me.

My heart was completely and utterly shattered.

My sister…

I couldn't move my gaze away from Kenna.

Tears continued to stream down my face as I crawled back to her side, pressed my hands onto her chest, and pumped in even rhythms, trying in vain to bring her back. More blood spilled from the tear in her neck, and I stopped immediately. She'd already lost too much.

What do I do? I don't know what to do!

I had to act. This couldn't be it. It couldn't be the end. Kenna was counting on me. I was all she had right now, and I couldn't let her down.

I didn't know how to use whatever magic now seemed to reside within me, but I called on it the way I'd been instructed by the numerous tutors my father had enlisted after my failed awakening. It hadn't worked then, but I tried every damn trick they'd taught me now, hoping something —*anything*—would respond and help me. Magic tingled under my skin. I channeled it, pushed it toward Kenna, and prayed it had healing properties, though I knew that wasn't a Stormborn affinity.

All the while, I begged her wolf to go back, to use whatever magic she had to fix my sister. To heal her.

But no matter my efforts, Kenna's chest remained still.

"She's gone, Mads," Jasper whispered and lightly grabbed my arm to stop me.

I growled, literally growled, jerking out of his grasp to keep trying.

"Mads," he pressed again, this time more exasperated.

"She's not breathing. She was too gravely injured for even her wolf to heal. The very wolf I just witnessed you pull into yourself."

I wasn't ready to deal with how I'd just seen the spirit of my sister's wolf, let alone how it now resided inside of me. As far as I knew, that had never happened before. Wolves died with their human counterparts, two halves of the same soul.

So what the hell had just happened?

"Y-you saw that?" I didn't sound like myself.

I wanted to laugh. Not in mirth, but desperation. Because I didn't feel like myself either.

I was pretty sure shock was setting in.

Jasper gently took my hands.

He moved me until I sat back on my heels, then cupped my face, forcing my gaze off of Kenna and onto himself.

"That was incredible," he said in awe.

His hands slid down my neck, then glided over my shoulders and down my arms, barely making contact as he checked me over.

Covered in blood as I was, it was hard to tell if any of it was my own. Some of it was, but the majority belonged to my sister, the person he *should* be concerned with, who lay motionless only a foot away.

"Incredible?" I scoffed dryly.

Ignoring the sound of my disgust, he asked, "How do you feel?"

"How am I supposed to feel, Jasper?" I rasped. "My sister is… is…" I couldn't even bring myself to say it.

"Fuck." He pulled away and drove his hands into his hair, tugging hard at the blonde strands, staining them with the blood covering his palms. "You know what I meant. I saw the whole thing. It shouldn't be possible. I-I can't believe it."

I clutched at my chest, wishing with all my heart I could rip her wolf out and give it back.

"Oh, Kenna," I sniffed. "I'm sorry...."

It should have been me lying in her place.

Nothing was ever going to be the same again.

The sound of low growls broke through the treeline just before my father's enforcers did. Surrounding us, they circled the clearing and reinforced it, ensuring it was safe for their Alpha—Thaddeus Hale, my father—to enter.

Having shifted in the woods, he stepped from the trees fully dressed. His gaze quickly traveled over the gruesome scene before settling on me with excruciating censure.

"What have you done?" he growled, stalking forward and wrapping a hand around my throat.

I squeaked, scrambling to pry his fingers away as he lifted me straight off the ground like something out of a Star Wars movie.

Jasper jumped to his feet.

"Alpha," he dared to speak, to interject on my behalf. "This wasn't Mads—er, Madison's—fault." He'd quickly corrected himself, but I was sure my father caught the overly friendly nickname.

"Did you or did you not lure your sister out of the house tonight and coerce her into leaving pack lands for your own *selfish agenda?*" My father screamed the last two words, his face reddening.

I wouldn't tell him it was Kenna's idea to leave our territory, so I stayed silent while his grip choked me.

Dots formed along the edges of my vision, and my lungs screamed for oxygen.

Releasing a yell of anger, claws descended from the

Alpha's fingertips, and he raked them against my abdomen, leaving jagged gashes in my flesh.

I cried out, the sound hoarse and strangled, until he dropped me, leaving me in a wounded heap at his feet.

The wolf inside of me alternated between low growls and whimpers. Having her in my head was surreal. This whole night was surreal. This couldn't be happening. Not any of it.

Blood seeped from my injuries to further stain my skin. I clutched my stomach, the natural salt on my skin stinging the wounds.

They weren't life threatening, but they'd take me weeks to heal from. Weeks of pain and penance.

Or maybe I'd heal faster now there was a wolf inside of me. I didn't know. And it didn't matter. The injury was nothing compared to suffering through a shattered heart.

My father's disapproval hung in the air, but as hurt as I was, even though he could end me with such little effort, I wouldn't cower before him.

I'd just survived the worst thing that could possibly have happened. Nothing could touch me anymore. Not pain. Not death.

No one dared to lend me a hand, lest it be seen as a betrayal. If my father wanted me down in the dirt, injured and bleeding, then that's where I belonged in their eyes.

So I did it myself. With a gasp of pain, I stood, forcing my legs to hold me upright as my stomach screamed at me to stop moving.

While I struggled to my feet, Jasper hurriedly explained what happened from his point of view, though he kept the part about helping us sneak out to himself lest my father kill him for the offense. When he was done, my father nodded to a group of his enforcers, sending them scattering into the woods to search for the threat.

They wouldn't find anything. The task the enemy set out to accomplish had been done. If the shadowed beast didn't want to be found, there wouldn't be a trace of him except the damage left in his wake.

With a sharp jerk of his head, my father signaled one of his enforcers to bring Jasper a bag of clothing, and my friend dressed quickly. He pulled on loose sweats and a t-shirt to cover his nudity while I was left standing in ruined shorts and a bra.

My father brushed past me with a sneer, nearly making me stumble. Going to Kenna's side, he stooped over her body and checked her pulse for himself, assuring she was truly dead.

I couldn't watch. Turning away, I suppressed another groan of pain. Twisting at the abdomen was a bad idea. Tears swam in my eyes and my emotions threatened to choke me as much as my father's grip had. The strain of holding back a sob made my throat ache worse than the bruises forming on the column of my neck.

When my father whirled back around, he was pure Alpha, his face drawn with furious rage.

Not as young as he used to be, wrinkles pinched the corners of his ice-blue eyes and his blonde hair had grey streaks at his temples, but no one, man or wolf, would mistake him for anything less than being in his prime.

Power pressed down on me in unrelenting waves as he forced his Alpha command over me. Now that I had a wolf, it was easier to fight back, but I was still no match against my father's power. It brought me back to my knees, and all I could do was brace myself against the onslaught. My neck slowly wrenched sideways to expose the column of my throat even as the wolf inside me vibrated with angry energy at the involuntary submission.

I clenched one hand into a fist, the other digging into my side as I kept an arm wrapped around the gashes in my stomach. My nails bit sharply into my skin while I fought to remain somewhat upright.

The wolf urged me to push back against his authority, but I reined her in. This wasn't the time or the place. My father had lost a daughter in the same way I'd lost a sister. Deep down, buried in that cold heart of his, he had to care. Losing Kenna *had* to mean more to him than losing all his hopes and dreams for the future of his pack.

"Do you have any idea what you've done?" he scolded scathingly.

"I never meant for any of this to happen," I pleaded hoarsely.

A fresh bout of tears leaked from my eyes. His anger, though somewhat misplaced, was warranted.

I hadn't killed Kenna personally, but I was partially responsible. Some of the blame was mine to bear. If I hadn't jumped off her back, maybe, just maybe, we could have fought off the shadowy beast together and she'd still be alive. My guilt was caustic. Bailing off of her was supposed to give her the advantage, but all I'd done was left her alone to fend for herself. What I'd thought was the right thing to do turned out to be my biggest mistake, and somehow, I'd have to live with that.

I blinked against my tears. If we just hadn't gone out tonight, if we had obeyed orders, none of this would have happened in the first place. Kenna would still be safe at home instead of lifeless on the forest floor.

"Tell me everything. Spare no detail, Madison," he demanded, forcing me to recall every grim memory. The pain in my stomach was incomparable to the pain in my heart as I lived the night over again. I squeezed my eyes shut, but the nightmares refused to be blocked out, playing against the dark tapestry of my eyelids until I couldn't take it anymore.

I told him everything, though I left Jasper's name out of my story. I also kept the part about Kenna's wolf now residing inside of me to myself. That secret felt too personal to share, especially since I was still coming to terms with it.

By the time I was done, I had no tears left to cry. They ran down my cheeks, cooling rapidly in the early morning air. I barely felt the chill as numbness stole through me.

"It was a wolf? You're positive?" My father pressed, finally relenting the command he'd foisted upon me. I relaxed marginally, slowly unclenching my fingers and noting the deep, crescent shaped grooves left in my palm.

"Yes," I answered weakly. "There's no doubt in my mind it was a wolf. But I've never seen anything like him, and I don't know which pack he's from."

A muscle in my father's jaw jumped, and he turned to a woman I hadn't noticed before. The remaining wolves parted as a witch strode into the center of the clearing to join us.

Long, dark robes trailed along the ground, decorated with intricate designs made of silver thread that shimmered in the moonlight like it was woven from tiny diamonds. The pattern took the shape of stars, moons, and planets.

Moon witch.

This must be the lady Kenna had spoken about, the one my father kept on retainer.

The very one who had bound Kenna and Hunter together, solidifying their mate bond.

What was she doing here? Surely my father couldn't pay to keep her on staff around the clock.

Having her stand before me was disconcerting, and I subtly shifted to protect my sister's body with my own.

"She speaks the truth," the witch said, and I finally clued into the hint of magic in the air. She'd been working a truth spell in the background this whole time.

"Of course I am," I growled, Kenna's wolf adding to my anger. The audacity of that witch bitch astounded me. "Why would I lie about it?"

She gazed down at me, and what she believed to be true was so clear, it shocked me.

Did she seriously think I wanted my sister *dead*? That I had orchestrated the attack? Because I was pretty sure that was exactly the condemnation I saw written across her stupidly pretty features.

With dark hair, pale eyes and skin, and painted red lips, she looked like a queen among the shadowed, midnight landscape.

"Enough," my father barked, then stalked toward me. "Something's different."

Could he feel Kenna's wolf inside of me?

If I were smarter, or fuck, if I could feel again, I was sure I would have backed away from him. I stayed where I was, however, and didn't flinch when he pulled me to my feet. I swallowed my cry of pain as he grabbed my chin roughly and craned my head back until it was uncomfortable, all to stare searchingly into my blue eyes.

For a long, slow beat, he studied me, and then his power flowed freely. The call of the Alpha.

"Shift," he demanded.

I prepared myself, expecting to feel the pressure of my first shift under my skin, but it never came.

The wolf responded in a different way. No matter how I tried to warn her to stay back, to stay hidden, she emerged from my chest to make her presence known.

I whimpered, worried she was about to leave for good this time.

Without her, I'd feel bereft. She was a part of Kenna, and already a part of me.

It was crazy. I was sure something like this had never happened before.

It has to be because we're twins. It doesn't make sense otherwise.

Before we'd been separated as children, Kenna had shared everything with me from toys to clothes, and now we shared *her*.

The beautiful obsidian she-wolf stood regally beside me and faced my father with a coolness I admired. Just like me, she wasn't trembling in my father's presence, though her fortitude came from sheer strength while mine was born from the numbness that stole through me.

Chuffing in shock, the Alpha blinked in disbelief at her glowing, ethereal presence. "This is impossible."

The pack around us broke into harsh yips or whispers, depending on their form. It created a low din, and I shifted on my feet from the attention, feeling like a spectacle.

My father tried to force my wolf forward and away from me. It could have been because of the pack transition she was already going through, her bond with Hunter making her less susceptible to my father's orders, or the fact that she wasn't corporeal, her body translucent with a brilliant teal aura, but she refused to listen, sticking to my side like glue.

I reached out and ran my fingers through her fur, elated I could actually touch her, though I suspected others couldn't.

"Aether," the moon witch murmured, her melodic, sing-song voice carrying the notes across the pack.

Aether? What does that mean?

"Aether, the tenth element," she answered as if she could read my mind. "You're a Spirit wolf, my dear."

Tenth element? Spirit wolf? My mind spun. What was she talking about?

My father paled. "Th-that's…" he stuttered. It wasn't often he was lost for words.

So I finished for him. "Impossible?" I wanted to know more, but I couldn't pass up the opportunity to goad him. It wasn't smart, but it was damn satisfying to see his glower return.

Fuck him. If he would've let Kenna and I see each other like a normal family, even in secret, the need to sneak out would have been non-existent. Some of the blame was lifted from my burden and transferred onto his broad shoulders.

"There hasn't been a Spirit wolf in many millennia, which is why many don't know of its existence," the witch explained. "Aether is the lost element, and a powerful one." She looked at me with new respect, then turned to the Alpha. "Madison is going to be quite powerful."

Me? Powerful? Now I wanted to scoff. Was she sure she was talking about the right person?

"You will bring me any information you can find, Endora," the Alpha commanded more than requested.

Endora pursed her lips. "Not much is known about this element, but I will do my best to find out what I can. For a price, of course."

My father waved her off. "You should be acquainted with the way I do business by now. Bring me what you have, and we'll see what it's worth."

The witch smirked. "Then, I suppose I should find something worthy of your time. And your coin. Hmm Thaddeus?" she chimed, "You'll want to keep this a secret. If the other witches find out, you won't have one dead daughter, but two."

Watching the exchange was like watching an intricate chess match. You knew the moment one of them called 'checkmate,' and Endora was the queen, just as I'd suspected.

Her thinly veiled threat to betray what I was to the other witches in her coven wasn't lost on me or my father, though it did surprise me that he seemed to care about my wellbeing. *That's a first.*

Narrowing his eyes, my father all but growled. "You will be richly compensated for your silence, Endora, but this is now pack business." He jerked his head angrily toward a particularly strong beam of moonlight. He hated to lose.

Inclining her head with a pleased smile, she shared one last weighted look with me, then moved toward the patch of moonlight. As soon as it filtered over her, she drew upon her magic and disappeared, teleporting away.

I filed her name away. Consorting with witches was at the bottom of my to-do list, but if she had answers about what I was, I may need her. My father would never freely give me information unless it benefited him, and I didn't have many resources available to me. But right now, I couldn't handle anything else.

Spirit wolf, I repeated, rolling it around. It felt right, even if I didn't understand it.

Biting my lip, I hesitantly asked Kenna's wolf to rejoin me, hoping she'd jump into my chest as easily as she had the first time. Thankfully, she read my request, understood my desire, and obeyed easily. It shocked me that the link between us was as flawless as if I'd been born with her as my own wolf.

She filled the deep void I'd lived with my entire life. Kenna's last gift to me.

Bone-deep sadness settled in.

"I want Makenna removed discreetly. Take her to the cliffs and have her body burned before word spreads about what has transpired." The Alpha issued his orders, extending his power to make each wolf who'd witnessed the tragedy swear an oath of silence.

"Burned? Like an Ember wolf?" I gaped. She wasn't mated yet. She was still one of us. She deserved a Storm-born burial, to be laid to rest among her people on *our* lands.

My father growled. "Do not speak of their pack to me again," he threatened. "For all we know, they could have been responsible. A desperate ploy to end our upcoming alliance."

I hated that I couldn't disagree with him. A vision of Hunter earlier in the evening flashed into my mind. He may have been an ass at times, but he'd cared about me—about Kenna. It wasn't possible, was it?

The smoky wisps and beastly wolf who'd smelled of sulfur made me question everything.

I hated to admit it could've been Hunter, or even Tristan, but I couldn't vouch for their whereabouts. They were supposed to be in the forest, that's all I knew. And what about Kenna's boyfriend? I had no idea who he was or what pack he belonged to. The list of suspects who could've been involved in her murder were numerous and over-whelming.

The enforcers surrounded Kenna, lifted her body, and began carrying her away.

No!

I ran after her, the pain in my stomach making my head swim.

Snapping his fingers, my father summoned Jasper to contain me. A familiar body encased me, caging me in. The pain worsened, deepening as the band of his arms pressed across the injuries.

"Shhh," Jasper tried to soothe. His breath was warm against my ear. The rest of me was chilled. "This will be easier if you stop struggling."

"Why? Why are you doing this?" I pleaded as the wolves disappeared with my sister. It was irrational. She was gone, but I still fought and struggled to break free.

I was never going to see her again.

My father sneered down at me. "Collect yourself." Peering over my head, he motioned to Jasper. "Take her to the estate for now and get her out of my sight."

"I'm sorry, Mads," he murmured to soften his betrayal, then obeyed orders and carried me kicking and screaming back to the safety of our pack.

Madison

Even from far away, Hunter was imposing. Tall, broad, and strong, he stood out among the Stormborn's best enforcers.

"Get your hands off of her." His familiar, deep voice cut across the long stretch of yard as Jasper hauled me toward the front door of my father's house.

It stunned me that I could hear him given the distance, but my newly enhanced shifter hearing picked him up just fine.

Turning to the enforcers keeping him contained, he growled. "I'm a guest of the Stormborn Alpha."

"Not right now, you're not," Jasper called back derisively. "My Alpha has placed the entire pack under lock-down. Only those authorized are allowed in and out of his estate."

"I can assure you his orders don't apply to his daughter's bonded mate—the son of the *High Alpha*," Hunter growled, throwing around the weight of his position. "And I warned you to let her go, *wolf*." Ripping free of the enforcers who tried to detain him, Hunter shifted, hurrying toward us like a dark, avenging angel, leaving Tristan to fend off my father's enforcers before running after his alpha.

Between the pain and grief clouding my mind, I barely made out the outline of Hunter's large, imposing wolf against the surrounding darkness still cloaking the world in shadows. His fur was black with red markings that glowed like dying embers. He was about the same size of the beast who'd killed Kenna, but his markings gave me pause. The shadowed beast hadn't had markings, had he? And Hunter certainly didn't smell like the rotten scent of sulfur.

In fact, he smelled… *good*. Really good.

Jasper quickened his pace to avoid the angry wolf who snarled one last warning. The jostling hurt, and I gritted my teeth against the wounds that pulled with every step. His shirt, which he'd ripped off and forced over my head once we were out of my father's sight, was already stained with blood from the weeping gashes on my stomach.

"I'm following my Alpha's orders," Jasper barked at the approaching wolf, and his hold on me tightened.

I couldn't tell if it was edged with a misplaced sense of possession or if he just hated being issued commands from an alpha not of his pack.

Either way, I was pissed as hell. My anger was an easier

emotion to deal with than the overwhelming grief, and I'd latched onto it, using it as a balm, if only for a little while.

"Do what he says and let me go," I warned, but it came out weaker than I'd hoped. Truth was, after the night I'd had, and then fighting with Jasper all the way back to pack territory, I was spent.

"You know I can't do that," Jasper told me. Then softer, "Even if I want to."

I renewed my struggles, uselessly trying to free myself from the cage of his arms. I didn't want to feel bad for the position he was in, the position he was *always* in, suspended between friend and enemy. I couldn't. I didn't have room for those emotions beside the roiling storm of my own.

"You can't be with me and against me at the same time. It doesn't work like that," I scolded past clenched teeth.

Damn, my stomach hurt.

The wolf inside of me responded, pushing some of her power through me. It was strange to feel its effects, both a part of me, and yet, foreign, but it helped.

"I'm on your side, even when it doesn't seem like it," Jasper promised just as Hunter reached us with long, purposeful strides.

With a menacing growl, a wave of Hunter's alpha authority weighed against us, while his magic sparked with his shift. Jasper set me on my feet and released me, letting out a snarl of his own. I nearly crumpled to the ground, but Tristan skidded to a stop and caught me, steadying me and letting me lean on him for support.

Standing at his full human height again, Hunter domineeringly lifted his chin. "Touch her like that again, enforcer, and you won't live long enough to regret it," Hunter threatened, his power strong enough to transcend pack bonds and force Jasper to his knees with his throat exposed. He could easily end him here and now, though doing so would start a pack war. He left him on the ground, turning to me instead.

No one had ever stuck up for me like that.

I gazed up at the sexy, stark naked, powerful heir with new appreciation.

It wasn't for you, I reminded my shattered heart, tamping down any misplaced feelings before they could grow. I dropped my gaze from his, studying the intricate tattoo designs inked across his chest

I wasn't under any illusion. Hunter still thought I was Kenna. He thought he was protecting what was rightfully his, but I couldn't bring myself to tell him the truth. Not when I could barely admit it to myself.

Kenna was gone.

My heart hurt.

Tristan procured a pair of sweats from the cross-body bag he wore and tossed them to Hunter, who caught them with ease and stepped into them swiftly. Then, a strong set of arms scooped me up to cradle me against a hard, inviting chest.

Taking Hunter's help was a bad idea, but I was done being strong. I soaked up the alpha's strength instead, letting him sweep me into my father's house and up the stairs all while I swallowed back a hiss of pain.

I didn't think. Didn't worry. I simply breathed him in, his signature all smoldering campfires, smooth musk, bourbon, and leather. Though the stolen comfort was a temporary balm, nothing more than a Band-Aid against my pain, I leaned into him and took what I could get as yet another means of survival. But the lingering thought that his chivalry and kindness would be gone as soon as I told him what had transpired tonight, and who I truly was, niggled at my conscience.

His solace shouldn't be mine. It wasn't truly meant for me, and he deserved to know. But I just… couldn't.

"You're covered in blood," Hunter all but growled, anger flashing in his amber eyes, turning them to a flickering russet. He strode purposefully down a long hallway, and it didn't escape my notice that he knew exactly where to go when I barely recognized the layout.

"A lot of it," Tristan added darkly from where he trailed behind us. Gone was the man who seemed to think I was his enemy. His anger appeared to be redirected from me to whomever had hurt his future Luna. "I'm sorry I doubted you."

"If you had obeyed my orders, you never would have been in those woods to begin with," Hunter murmured, but there wasn't as much vitriol behind his censure.

"I couldn't stay," I growled in pure frustration, but he wouldn't understand until I told him the truth.

And then he won't care.

I pressed a hand against the wounds on my stomach. The shirt stuck to them uncomfortably.

Hunter stopped, and Tristan hurried to open a door. Kenna's signature flooded me as I was carried into her bedroom and set gingerly on her bed.

Tears swam in my eyes, obscuring what I could see. It'd been so long since I'd been here, but so much of it was oddly familiar. White furniture sat against the soft pink walls, the tops adorned with trinkets and things Kenna loved. A beautiful carved jewelry box, a wolf figurine, a hairbrush that looked as if it were out of a fairy tale.

It was the room of a beloved pack princess, so vastly

different from the dank cottage I was relegated to living in at the edge of the woods.

Hunter lightly grabbed my chin and brought my attention back to him.

"What happened?" he demanded gently, handling me with more care than I expected him to show. Gone was the hardass from the club who went head to head with me, but in his place was someone far more dangerous. A silent fury burned in his gaze, one that promised to tear down my enemies until they paid for what they'd done.

"We hunted the enemy through the woods, but every lead we followed led to a dead end," Tristen explained, driving one hand through his hair while the other gripped the strap of this cross body bag.

"They were leading us in fucking circles while they attacked you." This close to Hunter, I saw the way the muscle jumped in his jaw and the tension that pulled through his bare, tattooed shoulders.

He hated that I'd been hurt.

It only made me feel worse for lying to him.

Then again, as images of my horrendous night filtered through my mind, visions of the smoky, black wolf haunted me, and I was reminded that I may be alone with my biggest enemy right this very second.

Suddenly, hiding the truth didn't feel so wrong. If Hunter's pack was behind our attack in any way, I didn't want to let them know they'd succeeded. That was up to my father to decide. Entangling myself in pack business any more than I already had would be a terrible idea.

I'd never felt more like a chess piece in my life. Was this what my sister encountered every day—strategized moves in a political game neither of us had asked for?

"I don't want to talk about it," I told them honestly and

pulled away from Hunter. "I need to shower." It was the truth as much as it was an excuse to get away from them both. Locking myself in the ensuite and being alone was exactly what I needed.

"Out," Hunter ordered Tristan, and without a word, his beta slipped from the room. The door clicked closed, leaving Hunter and me alone.

Gently, the alpha pulled me to my feet, and then he was in my personal space, leaving barely any room between us. A low growl rumbled from his inked chest, and his fingers brushed away my hair to get a better look at my neck. I had little doubt about what he'd spotted that elicited such a dark reaction. My throat still ached from where my father had nearly choked me. The bruising probably already marred my skin like a macabre testament to the worst night of my life.

I turned my face away, staring at some inane spot on the wall. "I'm okay."

I'd never told a bigger lie, but Hunter didn't press.

Silently, he helped me to the bathroom. Now that the adrenaline was wearing off, the pain seeped in with a vengeance.

"You don't have to do this," I murmured as he flicked on the light.

Warm tones filled the room in mauves and pinks with golden accents. Makeup littered the countertops along with a lighted mirror. A perfume that enhanced a shifter's scent sat beside the faucet as did a variety of face creams and nail polish. My sister's whole life lay there waiting for her to walk back through the door.

I was a poor substitute.

In one swift movement, Hunter carefully lifted me onto the counter with ease, setting my ass on the cool marble.

Gripping my chin lightly, he moved my head this way and that, his gaze darkening with anger now that he had a better view of the deepening bruises decorating my throat. And that low, nearly indiscernible growl vibrated his chest again.

Gingerly, he lifted my borrowed shirt, pulling the stained fabric away from my skin. The dried blood fusing the shirt to my body tugged painfully at the raw gouges across my midriff. I hissed at the sting of the fabric being torn from my flesh and watched as fresh blood began to trickle from the wounds.

He swore as he surveyed the damage and helped pull my top off entirely. Tossing the ruined fabric into the trash, his hand pressed against my shoulder, skin on skin, as he made me lean back a little to get a better look at my injuries.

I braced my palms behind me on the counter to keep myself from reclining too far. Heat worked into my face when Hunter leaned down, folding his large frame above me. His face was so damn close to my breasts as he bent to inspect my abdomen. I wore a bra still, but with all the bare skin between us, suddenly the vast bathroom felt smaller.

He cocked his head this way and that, gaze searching while he scoured my body, looking for a graver injury to account for the amount of blood I wore. It covered almost every inch of me, the dry, tacky texture of it making my skin feel too tight. Rough fingertips skimmed lightly over my body, only stopping when he had assured himself I wasn't bleeding more profusely.

Hunter didn't seem to miss much. He had to be wondering where the copious amount of blood came from. Blood that smelled like mine… like Kenna's.

Her blood covered any differences in our scent, but once I showered…

He'll be able to tell I'm not her.

Instead of questioning me or drilling me for more information, he ran his fingers along the edges of the gashes in my stomach, inspecting them before rifling through the cabinets. He pulled out some medical supplies and set to cleaning out the claw marks.

I let him work in silence, only hissing when the alcohol stung. Bending at the waist, he blew lightly over the wounds to soothe them.

When he was done, he shook his head. "Forget the shower. You need to shift."

"No," I said too quickly, shaking my head. Scooting to the edge of the counter, I pushed against his firm chest, trying to get him to move so I could hop down. Truthfully, I didn't know if I *could* shift.

Or how to….

"Shift," he ordered, this time suffusing the command with that alpha shit he did.

"You can't just order me around," I bit out, but the wolf inside of me responded. I felt her just below my skin, her presence tingling with the power and magic that was so new to me. It was disconcerting and incredible at the same time.

But then, the faintest teal glow began to appear, and I panicked. She wasn't going to help me shift. She was going to walk out of my body just like before. I shoved her back, and the light disappeared just as quickly.

Hunter hadn't seemed to notice. He was too busy invading my space, bracing his hands on the outside of my thighs as he leaned into me. The man was immovable, and my effort to escape had only brought us closer.

Those amber eyes held me captive as his body heat

licked along all my bare skin.

Injured or not, I'd never felt more exposed in my life. It wasn't the shameful, embarrassing kind I'd experienced earlier when I'd been half-naked before an army of my father's enforcers. This was different. Almost intimate.

A blush stained my cheeks, and I prayed Hunter didn't witness his effect on me.

"If you shift, this will heal faster." Hunter lifted one thumb and skimmed it along the waistband of my jean shorts. "As your bonded mate, I can control your wolf, lend her some of my strength, and channel our combined power into healing to speed up the process."

It was more complicated than that. He was asking me to let him in, to give him access to a wolf and a power I barely had control over through the tentative mate bond I suddenly noticed thrumming between us—a bond that must have transferred when Kenna's wolf dove into my chest.

"No," I repeated.

Placing his hand on my waist, he squeezed just enough that my skin pulled, and I winced at the sharp bite of pain from the gashes only inches away from where he touched me.

"You're an ass," I growled, jerking out of his touch, then whimpering from the movement.

Hunter chuckled darkly. "Look who suddenly decided to get mouthy."

I froze, realizing I was acting like myself and not my obedient sister. I was treading in dangerous waters, unsure what to do or how to play this role when I was raw and hurting.

Luckily, Hunter wasn't done. "If I'm an ass, then you're a masochist. Everytime you move, you'll hurt. I could take it away." He tilted his head and studied me intently for a beat. "But you don't trust me, Little Wolf, isn't that right?" There was a hint of bitterness, a hint of challenge behind that taunt.

I was flying blind, unsure of his and Kenna's past or how I should respond.

"I can handle the pain."

"Suit yourself." Hunter pushed off the counter and stalked to the door. His grip on the wood was merciless as he sent a dark glower over his shoulder.

His face was all harsh angles, his glare molten and intense. His features tensed, the muscles in his jaw bunching with the clench of his teeth. It was clear he wasn't happy I'd been injured and, perhaps, even more so that I wouldn't allow him to help. That I didn't trust him.

"Just because you can handle the pain, Kenna, doesn't mean you deserve to. If you decide to trust me, your father set us up in the east wing, so you know where to find me."

He left me gaping as he left not just the bathroom, but the bedroom entirely, the door snicking shut in his wake.

Hunter Weston was a mystery. Everything about him was more than I expected. More 'alpha.' More intense. More, dare I say, caring.

But he was also wrong. The use of my sister's name sent me into a tailspin, the pain far greater than the sum of all my injuries.

I deserved to feel every ounce of that agony. I needed it. It helped remind me I was alive and served to fuel my anger over what had happened. It solidified my resolve.

Whoever had killed Kenna wouldn't get away with it. I was going to find her killer and make them pay. And then, I'd find a way to make my father pay for his sins as well.

Even if it cost me my own life in the process.

Madison

Aloud rap on the door jolted me out of a troubled sleep. Sitting up sharply in bed, I gasped, then groaned from the ache of my healing muscles as it all came flooding back to me.

The club. The fight. My sister.

"Who is it?" I croaked out, rubbing the exhaustion from my eyes.

It took me a moment to remember I was in Kenna's room. That my father's enforcers had locked me in and refused to let me leave. Exhausted, I'd finally given up the fight and cried myself to sleep.

My eyes felt puffy as I slipped from the floral covers and took in my surroundings in the light of day.

If there were any doubt my sister loved the color pink, her room would have squashed it. It made me smile.

The pink, flowery bedspread matched the curtains covering the sliding door that led to the terrace. The same curtains I'd stared at from the grounds below, hidden in the formal garden when I'd come to see her last night.

Being on the other side of those window coverings was surreal, but watching the maid—an omega—who sauntered into my room with a tray full of breakfast was even more so.

I debated making a run for the open door, but I'd never make it before the enforcers were on me. It's why I hadn't shimmied down the trellis outside Kenna's balcony. Enforcers were posted below, making sure I didn't leave against my father's wishes.

The smell of biscuits, butter, and jam drew me back into the present to the sound of my stomach rumbling. Bacon, sausage, and eggs filled a second plate and the scent had the morose wolf inside of me perking up. The strong scent of coffee wafted toward me next, making my mouth water.

I'd always been one of those people who needed coffee before I could properly function in the morning, and this morning I was pretty sure I'd need two cups just to get through the start of the day.

Apparently, the wolf felt the same way about bacon.

"Good morning, Miss." The maid practically curtsied as she set the tray down on a small round table near the bed. "Excuse the chef. Only a small breakfast was ordered to your room this morning."

This is small? I couldn't help but gape.

"Your father is waiting to meet with you," she continued.

And *there* was the catch. Any appetite that had emerged disappeared at the mention of my father.

Fear spiked, making my pulse flutter faster. After last night, he now had all the evidence he needed to kill me without recourse, but if he wanted me dead, he would have done it already. Right?

My stomach churned at the thought of seeing him, but I didn't let my apprehension show.

Tugging at the delicate nightgown I'd stolen from my sister's half-packed suitcase, I felt like an imposter as the maid scurried around, picking out clothing and setting it out on the bed.

"He expects you to be downstairs in half an hour."

I swallowed, forcing myself to appear calmer than I felt.

"Uh, thank you," I replied, rubbing a hand awkwardly across my healing stomach.

The gashes were raw, but they'd finally stopped bleeding thanks to Kenna's wolf. Apparently, she was able to lend me some of her magic, speeding up the marginal healing abilities I'd already possessed thanks to my genetics. Most of the small scrapes and cuts were now light pink lines, but the bigger injuries were still healing, including the bruising that collared my throat. My body still hurt, but the pain was tolerable, and I wouldn't complain. I was alive. At least, for now.

I'd never forget the way my father's claws had slashed into me. His fury was burned into my memory, and I wondered if that same rage awaited me downstairs.

The maid smiled kindly, noticing the way I traced my injuries. "Just know the whole staff is happy you survived the... *ordeal*... last night," she said, downplaying the attack and gruesome murder I'd witnessed. That I'd survived.

But in a way, I was almost grateful. I'd cried a million tears last night, and I didn't want to start again. In order to make it through this day, I needed to bury my emotions before I faced my father and whatever punishment he deemed necessary.

Processing what the woman said, my brows drew together. "They are?" The pack had always been happy to ignore me, so hearing they may actually care was confusing. It didn't feel right.

"Of course we are," she tsked. "Now eat up. Times a' fleeting." She left just as quickly as she'd swept in.

Sitting back on the bed, I pulled the table closer and picked at my food.

In the new light of day, I felt steadier. The sharp, stabbing pain of loss was just as visceral, but I focused beyond it until it became an ache in my chest I could breathe past. There were things to be done, and I focused on those.

My father wanted Kenna discarded discreetly, but I wouldn't let her life trickle away without some kind of funeral. I needed to find a way to commemorate and celebrate her life. She deserved more than the harsh ending and a botched goodbye.

Kenna was beloved by the pack. I was sure others would agree with me, even if we kept her death quiet until my father found out who killed her.

By now he would be in the middle of preparing for war with whichever pack had attacked us last night. I had no doubt he was plotting and scheming with his Beta, Griffon Ford, and top enforcers this morning. Luckily, that meant he shouldn't be focused on me for long.

As soon as Kenna was set to rest properly, I needed to

hatch a plan of my own and disappear. My sister had been my only tether to pack life, and if I could find a way to slip past the enforcers and run, I'd take it.

Hurrying through what little I could eat, I brushed past the dress the maid had picked: some overly cheerful thing with a short skirt and a low bodice that was far too bright given the circumstances.

I went into the closet to find something more appropriate and nearly choked at the sheer size.

The closet was as big as my entire cottage. Walls of clothing surrounded me with an entire wall of shoes lining the shelves at the back.

Overwhelmed with choices, I found a pair of dark wash jeans and a black shirt covered in lace. The sleeves extended past my elbows in a three-quarter style, though the neckline dipped into a *V* that was lower than I liked, but it was the best I could do. Kenna didn't own a lot of black clothing.

I cursed the pair of black heels I threw on when I couldn't find tennis shoes or comfortable flats. Since my own shoes were covered with blood and thus unwearable, I had to make do with the options I had.

Unused to walking in heels—let alone three-inch heels —I wobbled my way to the door, cursing the pain in my stomach that flared as I tried to keep myself upright. I practically fell into the hard wood, gripping the handle to steady myself only to find the door still locked.

I traded one prison for another.

"Hey," I banged on the solid wood begrudgingly. "Let me out. My father is expecting me, and you know he'll blame you if I'm even a second late."

I suppressed the small grin tugging at my lips when I heard Reynolds, the enforcer I'd duped last night, grumbling on the other side. A key rattled in the lock, and the door opened.

"Madison," Reynolds growled in lieu of a greeting, less than amused.

"Good to see you again," I snarked right back, confirming his suspicion that it was me he'd dealt with last night and not my sister.

Gripping my arm, he tugged me from the room. "Let's go."

Escorted by enforcers flanking me on either side, I staggered my way down the hall. By the time I reached the first floor, I was steadier on the heels, looking less like a baby deer finding its legs and more like a semi-functional human.

Led to a set of ornate doors that set my pulse racing, I paused, needing a minute to gather myself before they were wrenched open. This room, I remembered. The dining room, the one spot in the house I had the fondest memories of. The place we'd gathered as a family once upon a time to share our meals. The place my father spent hours teaching Kenna and I how to play chess, his favorite game. A game of strategy and skill, and as my father used to say, where you needed a better plan of action than your opponent in order to win. Even back then, he'd been calculated and cunning. Though my childhood couldn't be described as loving, it was all I knew. I used to look forward to coming here, to spending time together, but now I dreaded having to enter.

I blew out a breath, steeling myself to face my father, when Reynolds dug into his pocket and pulled out a small bottle. Before I knew what was happening, a puff of perfume assaulted me. I blew a raspberry, waving my hand through the air to stop the onslaught as he spritzed again and again.

What the fuck? I eyed Reynolds like he'd lost his mind, but I didn't get a reaction. Not so much as a sheepish shrug.

I was about to tell him that I'd showered and smelled fine when I caught the first notes of a familiar scent.

My brows furrowed, and I opened my mouth to ask him what the fuck he thought he was doing. But the enforcers decided I was out of time and pulled the doors open, presenting me to the room I was unprepared to face.

Seated at the head of a long table was my father, his guests occupying the other seats, enjoying a lavish breakfast spread.

Not what I expected….

I glanced around, trying to recognize who was in the room with us. None of them were familiar, but the scents that lingered and clashed together were a mixture of fire, water, mist, warm summer days, and damp earth. A small zap of electricity tingled my nose, and I realized I was surrounded by representatives from the various elemental packs.

Fire, the Ember Wolves. Water, the Calder Wolves. Earth, the Eden Wolves. Air, the Gale Wolves. Moon, the Lunar Wolves. Light, the Gilded Wolves. Storm, the Stormborn Wolves. Energy, the Conduit Wolves. Celestial, the Zodiac Wolves.

Someone from each respective pack was here.

But it was the tall, dark, and handsome man who stood sharply at my arrival who drew my full attention.

Hunter's focus bore into me from across the room. Breathlessly, I stared back, my body warming under his gaze as much as it had warmed under his grazing touches last night. Tension scorched between us, a push and pull that sucked the oxygen from the room.

"Ah," my father cooed, holding out his hand and summoning me.

Griffon, my father's Beta, was just inside the room, and he pressed a hand against my spine and shoved me forward, breaking my connection with Hunter, who growled a warning.

I stumbled, luckily catching my balance after a few steps and righting myself in time to see all eyes in the room centered squarely on me.

Hunter looked poised to slice Griffon to ribbons. I shook my head subtly.

He was a guest in my father's territory, alliance or not. I didn't need him going all dark knight. Besides, as soon as he learned just who I was, he wouldn't care to defend me any longer.

"As promised. Here's my daughter." My father smiled, and unease pricked at me. The glint in his eyes was anything but pleasant. "Come join us, Kenna," he enunciated.

I nearly stumbled again. *Kenna?*

My blood turned to ice at the sound of my sister's name and the narrow-eyed look of glee on my father's face.

Head spinning, I looked around the room at the expectant faces. Hunter had his palms flat against the table, studying me intently. Everyone became a blur as Griffon leaned in.

"Behave," the Beta warned roughly.

I wanted to growl right back at him, but the sound stuck in my throat. Gripping my elbow tightly, he escorted me to my father's side.

Once I was deposited beside the Alpha, I whispered harshly, trying to keep my voice down so only he could hear, "What are you doing?"

"Having breakfast, of course." The feral look on his face dared me to defy him.

Turning to address the room at large, his voice grew deep, his bellow echoing off the muraled twelve-foot ceilings—the images depicting Stormborn Wolves in all their glory, surrounded by lightning, howling in the midst of terrifying storms, leaving little doubt to any who gazed upon them exactly who was in charge here. "There are vicious rumors meant to undermine my reign as Alpha of the Stormborn Wolves. They say we were attacked last night and my beloved daughter Kenna was killed. You are all here to bear witness to the fact that she is alive and well, poised to seal our alliance with the Ember Wolves." He motioned toward Hunter, whose gaze hadn't strayed. He answered my father with a sharp nod of agreement as the room erupted in applause. "Let it be known that no scheme, no planned attack, is great enough to touch us. You are to take this news back to your Alphas and assure them our power and our allies are stronger than ever. Any who dare to cross us will meet a swift and violent end."

My head spun, my lungs struggling to expand, when my father made his decree. The manic energy he held suddenly made sense, as did the maid's reaction this morning.

She thought I was Kenna.

He meant for me to take my sister's place.

Pliantly, I let him remove me from the room, leaving the pack ambassadors murmuring in our wake. The harsh grip he had on my arm was sure to leave more bruises, a brand to remind me of this morning and the insanity brewing inside of him.

"You can't be serious," I said breathily as soon as we were clear of the room.

It was a death wish to challenge the Alpha in such a

way, but I didn't care. He was certifiable if he thought I was going to do this.

Pulling me to a quieter part of the estate where we were alone and shoving me into an alcove, my father released me only to close his hand around my throat, cutting off my airway. My already-bruised skin screamed. I gripped his wrist, trying to keep him from strangling me.

"Deadly," he growled. "Your life is worth nothing to me. Kenna's, on the other hand, is worth everything. If you dare defy me in this, I will see that you're killed painfully. And don't believe I won't. I rue the day you were born and would take great pleasure in ending your miserable life."

"You need me," I spluttered and gasped until he eased his hold, allowing me to suck in a precious gulp of oxygen.

"You will take your sister's life as your own. You will befriend her friends, you will parade yourself as my rightful heir, and you will uphold her mating. You are to seal our alliance with the Ember Wolves while you search for evidence that they are the ones behind the attack on your sister," he quietly raged.

He must be mad. He was talking about taking down Hunter's dad, Rhett Weston, the Alpha of the Ember Wolves. But it was so much more than that. In the hierarchy of our world, High Alpha Weston was at the very top. He was practically royalty.

That's when it dawned on me.

"You want his position," I uttered in shock.

Of course he did. My father would never be satisfied until he was *the* most powerful. Was this his ploy all along? Form an alliance with the Ember pack only to get close enough to undermine their Alpha and seize the position of High Alpha for himself?

"And now they've given me the perfect opportunity to

end their reign. When the other packs hear of their treachery, they'll have no choice but to join me and rise up with a force the Ember Wolves will never be able to match," he raved, already on a power trip.

Doubt crept in. "What if they weren't behind it?"

While the beastly wolf's red eyes and smokey tendrils were damning, there were many other packs who'd benefit from seeing my father's alliance with the Embers end. And what of Kenna's boyfriend? I was the only one who knew he existed, let alone could've been in the woods last night too.

"It has to be them," he snarled, too blinded by hatred for his rivals to see any other possibility. "Why else was the Ember heir in the woods last night?" he questioned, but he never expected an answer. "They wanted to end our alliance by forfeiting your sister's life. Do this. Get me the evidence I need to condemn the High Alpha, and I will release you. Once you've given me what I need, you will be free to live among the humans, far away from the reach of the packs."

He was offering me my freedom? It was all I'd ever wanted.

Until now.

My thoughts were a swirl of disbelief, but I didn't need more time to contemplate. Luckily, we had a common goal. We both wanted to see whomever was responsible for Kenna's death pay for what they'd done.

As much as I hated the idea of stepping into Kenna's shoes, literally this time, I didn't see another way.

Being Makenna would give me the access I needed to find out who killed my sister with the power, money, and strength of the Stormborn behind me.

As Madison, I'd have nothing but a vendetta and a death wish.

So, I agreed, even though I knew it was wrong, not to mention risky as hell.

"I'll do as you ask, but I'm not doing it for you. I'm doing it for Kenna."

"I don't care who you're doing it for," my father spat, "as long as it's done."

My skin crawled. I was siding with the devil.

My only solace was that my father didn't realize I only wanted the truth. I wouldn't conjure up evidence where it didn't exist. I wouldn't condemn his enemy if the High Alpha weren't to blame. The person responsible would be brought to justice. That was all that mattered to me. And I'd play his game to achieve it.

The spirit of Kenna's wolf—my wolf—rose to the surface, excited about my decision.

Turned out she wanted revenge just as much as I did.

"I knew you'd see my side of things." My father straightened and dusted off his clothing. Retrieving a small perfume bottle from his suit pocket, he pressed it into my hand. "I had Endora make this for you. It will mask the differences between your scent and Kenna's. Apply once every morning, and they'll never know the difference." I stared at it in disbelief, recognizing it as the perfume the enforcers had spritzed me with earlier. "And take this." He passed me a sleek device next, the same kind of cell Kenna liked to use. "When you find something of value to me, use it to call Jasper and arrange a meeting. He will securely and personally transfer the information back to me." With cold efficiency, he waited for me to apply the perfume and then pulled me from our hiding place and led me to the front door.

Omegas, treated no better than servants, traipsed up and down the stairs lugging suitcases and boxes from Kenna's room above.

"You're leaving now. Jasper will be your personal enforcer." My father waved a hand toward the man standing in the shadows, watching me with an unreadable expression.

I looked away from him. "I'd rather take Reynolds." And that was saying something.

My father gripped my face painfully and narrowed his eyes, his lips contorting into a cruel grin. "I don't think so. Jasper seems to have a vested interest in you and your welfare. He'll do what needs to be done to keep you on task as he knows what awaits you should you fail me yet again."

I glowered at my father, who looked overly pleased that he'd irked me.

"He'll be reporting back to me about your progress. Get me the evidence I need. Don't disappoint me, *Kenna*." He stressed the last word, putting every ounce of warning and deadly intent into it before striding off.

Jasper crossed to me and stood rigidly. "Your things are almost done being packed and loaded into the vehicles. Why don't I escort you to your room so you can double check you have everything you need?"

He held out his hand, imploring me to take it.

"Let's talk somewhere private," he murmured, just for my ears.

An apology swam in his eyes. For last night. For today. For the role he was going to play in my future. But I didn't want to hear it. I didn't have anything to say.

It had never been more clear to me that I couldn't trust him. Not fully. He was a lapdog for my father—an enforcer—and now, my spy, sent to keep me in line. It had been easy to blur the stark lines separating our lives when I was sequestered away from the pack, desperate for a friend to ease the loneliness, but I realized now how naive I'd been.

Whenever he found himself in a precarious situation, Jasper's loyalty would always side with my father. His Alpha.

And what other choice was there?

In my head, I knew he was just doing what he needed to do to survive within the pack, but in my heart, I was angry. I wanted to fault him. To blame him for his betrayals. The truth of our situation chafed, but my heart was already raw and bleeding, so I leaned into my anger.

I turned away, but he grabbed my arm tightly, tugging me back to face him.

"You don't have to do this. There's got to be another way."

I shook my head and pulled free of him. "There isn't."

"Please, Mads," he pressed.

"Kenna," Hunter's deep voice cut through me. Nervous butterflies fluttered to life low in my belly and my heart skipped a beat.

He'd stalked up so silently I hadn't heard his approach. *Shit.*

Had he heard our conversation? Did he pick up on Jasper's use of my given name?

I whirled to face him, and watched Hunter stride down the hallway, watching me like a hawk watches its prey.

And there was no doubt given the harsh, questioning slash of his brow that he'd heard absolutely everything.

Hunter

I stalked toward Kenna, pissed to see how close Jasper was standing to her after I'd warned him just last night to keep his hands to himself.

Spilling blood in another Alpha's territory was highly frowned upon, especially one as volatile as Thaddeus. But I didn't care if I started a war as long as it meant he removed his hands from the woman meant to be mine.

"You don't have to do this. There's got to be another way," Jasper whispered harshly to Kenna. Voice quiet, the enforcer tried to keep their conversation private, but my senses were honed far beyond that of an average wolf, and I heard him easily.

My jaw clenched tightly. Was he trying to convince her she didn't need to leave with me and join my pack?

His Alpha would view that as treason. For some reason, it didn't thrill me either.

I quickened my pace as Kenna shook her head. "There isn't," she replied, and yanked herself free of his grip.

Goddess help him if he left a mark on her pretty skin. She was still healing from the attack last night, and I didn't want to see her hurt any further.

Baring his teeth in a wicked growl, my wolf happily agreed with my desire for violence.

"Please, Mads," Jasper pressed.

Mads? My brow furrowed, gaze narrowing in on the pair. *Is that some kind of pet name?*

"Kenna," I called out, making my presence known. I scowled at Jasper, hoping he'd feel the full effect of my disapproval.

"Hunter," Kenna stammered. "I-I can explain." I was unsure what to make of them, but jealousy instantly sparked at the idea that there was more going on.

Unfortunately, Kenna wasn't as discreet as she thought, and I knew she'd been romantically involved with someone else recently.

Truthfully, it hadn't bothered me as much as it probably should have at the time. Our mating, a political match rather than a true mating, had been arranged for ages. Hell, it hadn't even bothered me when we'd been bound by the damn moon witch six months ago.

So, why then, did the thought of another daring to lay his hands on what was mine suddenly make me want to kill something?

The forceful possession that rose inside of me was new and unexpected. Last night, something between us had shifted. The mate bond that had been nearly dormant stirred deep in my chest for the first time, demanding I seal our magicked bond with a primal mate bite. My gums ached as my wolf rose to the surface, wanting to partial shift and reveal our sharp canines, but I held him back.

Eyes narrowed, I flicked my attention between the pair, wondering what Kenna needed to explain.

"I see more than you think I do, Little Wolf," I told her, and her face paled.

Was that an admission of guilt?

My fists clenched, my nails shifting to claws. Combating the strong desire to put Jasper on his ass for daring to move in on what was mine, I physically forced my claws to retract before I started a fight.

"You're dismissed," I barked at Jasper. His jaw jumped, and for a brief moment, he stared directly at me until the authority I held as alpha forced him to fix his attention beyond my shoulder.

With a sharp nod, he took a small decorative bottle Kenna handed him and strode off to finish orchestrating the preparations for her move to my pack.

My little mate shifted on her feet, tucking her phone into her back pocket before smoothing her hands down the sides of her jeans, over her hips.

Did I make her nervous? That would be new….

Before last night, she'd always been dismissive. Dutiful, even, but never nervous. But at the club, she'd been feisty and brazen. The woman had become an unexpected enigma, and I didn't know what to make of her anymore.

"I know we've had a pretty understanding arrangement so far, Kenna," I stated, "but you'll be living with my pack permanently now. Indiscretion will no longer be tolerated."

What the fuck was I saying? I'd never put rules on our mating before. And I'd never planned to.

But my wolf reveled in every word.

No one else would touch her again but *me*.

Kenna blinked, then blinked again, as though she hadn't expected the decree either. She blew out a breath and then practically smiled. "You're jealous."

I smirked. "I have no reason to be, now that we understand each other."

Kenna rolled her eyes. "Hunter, it's not like that. Jasper was just looking out for me." She stepped forward, that bold woman emerging once more. "But if you're going to put restrictions on our mating, then I expect it to go both ways," she said with a tilt of her chin, her pert little nose rising into the air as she stared at me.

Oh, but her fire called to me. No one else would get away with challenging me like this, but for some reason, I welcomed it from her.

Where had this girl been my whole life? While my interactions with her had been limited in recent years, both of us keeping our distance from each other, she'd always seemed so prim, proper, and reserved. A puppet for her father.

But this woman? She was strong and independent.

I didn't understand the change.

Kenna held her ground as I leaned into her, invading her space, enjoying the way her breath hitched as I gripped her chin.

"Making demands already?" I purred.

"No different than you." Her blue gaze flashed with the power of her element, a bolt of lightning across a stormy sky.

I thought I caught a hint of the same possessiveness in her eyes.

"You want me all to yourself?" I pressed, enjoying her little huff of annoyance.

"I'm only asking for fairness."

"Mmmhmm," I hummed but released her. "You can lie to me if you wish. But I see right through you."

There was that wide-eyed reaction again, but it disappeared almost instantly.

I narrowed my gaze, searching her face. There was something she didn't want me to see, something she didn't want me to know.

"I don't know what you're talking about." Kenna brushed past me and swept out the door, effectively ending our conversation as she ran from me.

I trailed her, enjoying the sight of her swinging hips and the rounded curves of her ass far too much.

Oh, yes. This girl had secrets.

For the first time in longer than I cared to admit, I was looking forward to having her around, if for no other reason than to uncover whatever it was she was hiding from me.

Kenna presented a challenge, and I wasn't known for backing down.

·)·)·)·)·●·(·(·(·(·

I tossed a bottle of pain reliever at Kenna as she squirmed for the millionth time in the passenger seat of my car. For some reason, she continued to turn down the pills I offered, preferring to suffer in silence during our drive, but my wolf grew more antsy with every wince and gasp she tried to conceal.

"If you would have let me heal you last night…" I trailed off, trying not to appear smug as she glowered at me.

An animalistic growl echoed through my mind, my wolf warning me to stop being such a dick.

"The injuries are healing just fine," she snipped back, but it didn't stop her from finally opening the bottle and popping two pills, chasing them with a chug from her water bottle. After seven hours in the car, she was hurting. Badly.

I didn't want to see her in pain, so I was glad she accepted the small peace offering and took the medicine. I didn't agree with her, but I understood why she didn't accept my help last night. Despite our long engagement, the two of us weren't that close. However, I'd never get why she refused to shift and allow her wolf to speed up her healing. If she'd slept as a wolf, the gashes on her stomach would have been almost healed and the bruising on her neck would have been nonexistent this morning.

Studying her in my periphery, I watched her fiddle with her purse, pulling out a small round compact. Prying it open, she used the small mirror and makeup inside to dab at the bruises, covering them until they were barely even faint shadows.

I suppressed the growl that threatened to rattle out of my throat, hating that she'd been hurt, that some asshole dared to choke her.

That you weren't there to keep her safe…

Every protective instinct I possessed rose, calling for blood in retribution. I gritted my teeth and swallowed down my anger. There was nothing I could do about it right now, and I needed to keep my cool. But I certainly wouldn't let the attack against my mate drop. I'd find out exactly what happened and make whomever was responsible for her injuries pay.

Satisfied with her handiwork, she put everything away and gathered her golden-blonde hair together, fastening it into a ponytail. I didn't think I'd ever seen her wear her hair up before.

The long column of her throat was exposed this way, and her scent, which had already permeated the small, enclosed space over the last several hours, wafted toward me in a stronger wave.

Her rainy, floral signature was undeniable, but there was something different. The underlying notes were somehow stronger, more tangible. I wasn't a poet, but I couldn't stop thinking about how the aroma reminded me of summer thunderstorms and jasmine blooming under a midnight sky. It was fucking intoxicating.

My cock twitched in my jeans, and I gritted my teeth to suppress a groan.

So far, the car ride with Kenna had been quiet and tense. I was overly aware of every little movement, every breath, every heartbeat, and her scent was driving me insane.

My fingers tightened around the steering wheel as my wolf sent vivid images of claiming Kenna through my mind.

Intense need flooded my system with every lungful of air; it still wasn't enough.

I wanted to drag her from her seat and place her on my lap just so I could bury my face in the crook of her neck and breathe her in.

The speedometer crept up with the pressure I placed on the pedal, my car racing down the highway. I needed to get out and clear my head before I did something stupid. Like acting on the impulsive wish to claim that pretty little mouth that was currently pursed as she flipped through the radio, unable to settle on any one song.

Blessedly, she sat back into her seat and distracted me with a question.

"Is there anything I need to know about your pack before I arrive?" she asked, smoothing her hands down the dark denim of her jeans again. A nervous tick. A new one. Her heart beat a little faster as she waited for my answer.

Curious…

"You've been to my pack's territory before, Kenna," I tried to ease. "Nothing's changed, except you'll be living there permanently while you wait for our mating ceremony and take your place as my future Luna."

"Right," she murmured. "So, I should just sit around and wait for you."

"That's not what I said."

"Not in so many words," she sassed, carefully crossing her legs and arms as she angled herself toward me in the car. "I assume I'll have new responsibilities? Something to keep me occupied while I wait for our mating to become official? Surely there must be some prep for becoming Luna of the pack."

Becoming a true member of my pack had never been part of Kenna's agenda before. She'd always seemed all too content to stay on the sidelines and reap the benefits of her position without truly engaging. Hearing her desire to become Luna, to work together to rule my pack one day, surprised me.

"There aren't any direct responsibilities to pass off to you, since I'm not yet Alpha. We also haven't had a Luna in years," I replied, my tone low. "Not since my mother passed. The pack will have to adjust, as will the distribution of duties."

Some of the vigor left her, and she reached for me, placing her lithe fingers on my forearm and stroking lightly. "I'm sorry. I wasn't thinking."

I'd never known Kenna to apologize. Just one more of the notable changes in her I'd witnessed.

"One of the few things we have in common." Kenna squeezed my arm, then her touch fell away.

Neither of us were strangers to loss, and it seemed she knew I didn't need her pity.

We fell back into silence as I took the exit, and a short time later, I steered the car onto the long lane that led into my territory.

The closer we got to home, the more Kenna tensed, gazing out the window while tapping a staccato rhythm along the tops of her thighs.

"Why are you nervous?" I noted, and flicked my eyes off the road for a moment to assess her more closely.

She met my gaze with an honest one of her own. "I'm joining a new pack. Stands to reason I'd be a little nervous about uprooting my entire life and starting over somewhere new."

I studied her in my periphery.

"You've started over before. I always got the impression you preferred being away at school or at the Summit over being at home."

Kenna bit her lip, worrying it between her teeth. "I guess this just feels different."

"Well, don't worry. The pack's already accepted you. They know your place in my life and what the alliance means to my father. They won't fuck with you." She didn't look convinced. "The full moon is in four days. I've arranged a pack run with a gathering afterwards to officially welcome you to the Ember Wolves. I know how much you like parties… and dancing, apparently."

A shit ton had happened last night, but even amidst the danger, I couldn't get the image of Kenna swaying on the dance floor of that club out of my mind. The insane surge of possessiveness and jealousy I'd felt when another man put his hands on her. I'd almost ripped him to shreds for daring to touch what was mine, a completely foreign reaction I'd never had when it came to my mate.

Until now.

All I could think about was the swing of her hips, the curves that taunted me under the flashing, colorful lights, and that sassy mouth I wanted to put to good use.

Fuck. I definitely needed fresh air. And a cold shower.

Instead, I cleared my throat and carried on. "It was supposed to be a surprise, but maybe that will help you feel a little better."

"That's… great." Kenna's faked enthusiasm didn't pass my observation.

She seemed far away, lost in her thoughts.

"Mmm," I hummed, narrowing my eyes in an effort to figure this girl out.

She just wasn't herself. Something was… different.

I tapped my thumb against the leather of the steering wheel, feeling the need to pry deeper. "I thought you'd be happier."

"I am! I just wasn't expecting it. You did that for *me*?" She glanced sideways, trying to catch my eye as I drove us up to the gate, as though she realized her first response wasn't what I'd expected and wanted to try again.

"Thought it might make your transition easier. Contrary to your opinion of me, I'm not a heartless bastard," I quipped, slowing the car and rolling down the windows as the enforcers approached. The perimeter of our territory was heavily guarded, with wolves spread out every few yards. I felt their curious stares as my mate smirked.

"No. Not heartless," she snarked. "Just a bastard."

One of the enforcers I considered a friend choked on a laugh before clearing his throat.

"Don't think I've ever heard someone speak that way to the heir-apparent," Kip said, barely containing his amusement.

"One of the perks of being me, I suppose." Kenna grinned cheekily.

Goddess, but her sass was a turn-on, even when I was on the receiving end of her sharp wit.

"What's this?" she questioned when another guard shoved a device through the window.

She recoiled, leaning heavily against my shoulder.

My brows drew down, a crease forming between them. "It's all right." I allowed myself to touch her, to massage her shoulder. The attack on her last night must have rattled her more than she'd let on. Made sense she was on edge.

"It's just the retinal scan, Miss," the enforcer, Marshall, informed her. "Same thing we use every time you come to visit."

"Oh," Kenna sat upright, and stared at it like it was going to bite her in the nose. "Of course."

I studied her while I tilted my chin and let Kip scan my eye, the validating little jingle singing out when it confirmed my identity.

"My father likes his technology." I shrugged while waiting for Kenna to lean forward and let Marshall do the same.

Swallowing hard, she lifted her face and let him scan her eye.

An error tone rang through the car.

"That's odd." Marshall tried again with the same result. "These things rarely malfunction."

"Technology never likes me." Kenna laughed nervously.

But I was in agreement with the enforcer. Something wasn't right.

Dark realization dawned. I'd felt it all along. As intrigued as I was by the new and, dare I say, improved Kenna, the changes in her didn't add up.

I wasn't one to ignore warning signs and red flags.

Gritting my teeth, I fisted the wheel.

No matter how long Kenna and I had been engaged, or how close we were to finalizing our mating, she was a Stormborn wolf first, and her loyalty would always be with her pack.

The Stormborn Alpha was up to something, and Kenna, or whoever the hell this was, had to be working with him. The magic to change appearances wasn't easy to get a hold of, but it wasn't impossible either. And everyone knew that Thaddeus had a moon witch in his back pocket.

Fuck me. How had I not seen this earlier?

Her conversation with Jasper flashed back through my mind, echoing as I replayed it quickly.

He'd said 'you don't have to do this.' If they weren't talking about her moving in with me, what exactly was 'this' and what did it have to do with my pack?

"I'm vouching for her," I spoke up, issuing the order to bypass the security checkpoint.

"Are you sur—" I leveled a harsh glare at Marshall for the mishap of questioning me. "Yes, sir." He nodded resolutely and moved away.

"Kip," I barked, and my friend bent to peer through the window.

"Have the omegas come to the gate to retrieve Kenna's things. The Stormborn Wolves no longer have an invitation to cross into our territory."

"On it," he agreed without question, already doing my bidding by the time I hit the gas, lurching the vehicle forward.

Kenna squealed and gripped the edges of her seat before falling silent. Tension pulled her muscles taut while her heartbeat galloped loudly in her chest.

I veered off the road and into a grassy clearing when we were far enough away from the perimeter where no one would overhear us. This distance from the heart of our pack offered complete privacy, and without her entourage following closely behind, we were well and truly alone.

I stalked from the car and rounded to her side.

"Hunter," she gasped when I yanked her door open, unbuckled her seatbelt, and pulled her from the seat.

Slamming her door shut, I backed her onto the car, ignoring the way her scent pulled at me and fueled my lust.

It all had to be part of her elaborate ruse. I'd never been this attracted to Kenna's signature before. Why now? It was just another warning sign.

The bond between us thrummed from how close I was standing.

Boxing her in, I braced my hands on either side of her and pressed in menacingly.

"Get off me," she all but growled, the warning clear in her rough tone. She shoved at my chest, but I didn't budge.

Her struggle only brought us closer together, and her cheeks heated from our nearness, her pulse fluttering wildly in her neck.

Giving in to temptation just once, I skimmed my nose up her throat, drinking in her scent.

Fuck, she smelled incredible.

My wolf panted, ready to rut, to claim.

I growled in her ear, every muscle in my body growing tense as I fought off the effect.

Pulling back just enough to allow her to breathe, I glared at her.

My voice was laced with gritty warning as I rumbled a question brimming with dark accusation. "Who the fuck are you?"

Hunter glared at me with wicked contempt, the fires of hate blazing in his amber gaze.

One that promised retribution for deceiving him.

I hadn't even made it one day, and already Hunter knew.

"I'm your mate, you asshole." I shoved against his chest again, uncaring that all my wolf wanted to do was draw closer to him. She had a completely different goal, one that included being beneath him.

Stop that, I scolded, but she wasn't the least bit contrite.

Thirsty bitch. Not that I could blame her.

Hunter looked positively gorgeous in his anger. His muscles rippled with the presence of his wolf, and his eyes danced with barely contained flames. The tattoos that crawled up his neck jumped when he swallowed, and his jaw feathered with the grit of his teeth.

This close, his smokey signature teased my senses until I was heady with it. The heat between us increased as his power threatened to emerge. It washed over me, making sweat bead on my skin. The red in his otherwise black and grey tattoos glowed molten, and his already broad frame bulked with his impending shift.

This close to danger, I should flee for my life, but I stood transfixed, witnessing his power and fury, all directed at me.

But beneath it, behind his hate, was something else, something… hungry.

"Don't toy with me, Little Wolf," he warned. His timbre was deep from the nearness of the beast within, but the husky notes were for an entirely different reason. "It won't end well for you."

I scoffed. "That threat is getting old," I muttered.

His wolf growled, but Hunter silenced it quickly. "Who's been threatening you?"

"Besides you?" Shoving against his chest again only brought him impossibly closer. "I'm the Alpha's daughter. I'm used to threats."

I artfully crafted my answer to avoid giving him the full truth.

I *was* the Alpha's daughter, just not the one he believed me to be.

Bending me backward until I was practically lying against his car, his chest brushed mine, sending pleasant jolts through my body that settled low in my belly.

"You're lying."

Partly, yes, but I couldn't admit it. The weight of what I needed to do settled on my shoulders with a vengeance. My father would kill me if I failed, and if Hunter found out, he'd have every reason to do the same.

I was an imposter, sent to betray our alliance. To find proof that his own father was behind the attack that had killed Kenna. Or worse, to conjure evidence of his involvement for my father to use as leverage against the Ember pack.

Wolves killed for far lesser crimes.

Witnessing the pure anger roll off Hunter, it wasn't hard to imagine him capable of wicked things. But had he killed Kenna? Was I in the clutches of a murderer?

The sharp yip in my mind disagreed.

Kenna's wolf—*my* wolf—didn't believe it. She trusted him, even when I couldn't.

"I'm warning you," Hunter growled, the rumble in his chest vibrating through me. "Do not test me. Tell me who you are and the Stormborn Alpha's plans, or face my wrath."

His fingers dug into the metal of the car, making it groan and leaving dents in the frame. Shadows shifted over his face as his image blurred in and out with distinctly more wolven features. A flash of fang, eyes burning as they searched for the truth.

"More threats," I spat.

"It's not a threat, it's a promise." Hunter all but growled the warning. When I was silent for longer than he deemed acceptable, he cupped one side of my neck. Thumb shoved under my chin, he forcefully tilted my head back until his gaze was boring into mine. "Maybe you need a little more convincing."

Heat built everywhere he touched me until it was nearly scalding. Fire licked beneath his skin, threatening to burn.

I swallowed but lifted my chin further and spoke with as much authority as I could muster. "I've already told you. You just don't believe me. I am the Stormborn Alpha's daughter, and his plans are for us to mate and unite our packs."

Another half-truth, another carefully worded answer.

Hunter chuckled darkly, the sound cold and disinterested. "I won't mate with someone I don't trust, *Kenna*," he emphasized the name sarcastically. "I won't put my pack at risk for a pretty face."

He thinks I'm pretty?

That probably wasn't the part of his threat I should lock onto, but no one had called me that before. My stupid heart pitter-pattered.

I sucked in a breath, keenly aware of how Hunter's body pressed into mine. Every hard inch was plastered against my soft curves, and I squirmed. Hunter's wolf rumbled in his chest, half-warning, half-purr. I gripped his shirt in my fists, unsure whether I wanted to pull him even closer or shove him away.

Why did Kenna's mate have to be sex on a stick? He was going to be hard to resist. I needed to keep my distance from Mr. Smoldering McHottie, if not for my sanity, then for my mission.

A wave of alpha power pressed in on me. Was he trying to force me to submit? To tell him the truth?

He really was a bastard.

I expected to sweat under his authority like I had at the club, to have to fight off his effect on me. Instead, my wolf rose from within, lending me her strength and refusing to bend to his will. She wanted to be seen as his equal, as his future Luna. Despite how much she wanted to mate with his wolf, even she had lines she refused to cross. I was grateful, and I held my ground.

His eyes darkened as we stood in a stare-off. Chests heaving, we breathed in the strong essence of each other's scents, neither of us willing to yield.

"Hunter," the sharp bark of a man infiltrated the moment and broke the suffocating tension. "I didn't bring your mate here so you could fuck her the moment you got her on pack territory."

I stiffened, and Hunter tensed more than he'd already been. Slowly, he peeled himself away from me and backed up, letting me straighten from where I'd been leaning against his car. Cool mountain air rushed between us, chilling my heated skin. When I turned, I spotted the High Alpha striding toward us from the motorcade parked just up the road. I didn't spare him a smile for the crude way he'd spoken about me, and I crossed my arms instead.

"Dad," Hunter bit out in a tense greeting.

Though his father was decades older, I could clearly see the resemblance in their dark hair, sharp noses, and defined jawlines.

"You pissed off the Stormborn Alpha by denying his pack entrance onto our territory as our guests. Care to explain?" His father glowered.

Hunter shrugged, unaffected by his dad's ire. "I had reason to suspect they were planning to make a move against us."

"I'd like to see them try." The High Alpha's glower turned into a vicious grin. "Their heads would've rolled before they'd so much as yipped. It would have been entertaining to see, even more pleasurable to send them back to the Stormborn Alpha as a present and a warning never to test me."

Chills chased down my arms from the sheer violence. This was a man easily capable of killing without an ounce of remorse. Just being in his presence made my stomach churn.

As much as I didn't want to care about him, I needed to warn Jasper that we needed to be extremely careful. A mad sort of danger rolled off the High Alpha, and I got the impression he wasn't a man you wanted to mess with.

We were treading in dangerous waters. My life had never felt more precarious than it did standing in the High Alpha's presence. Unconsciously, I reached up and touched the front of my neck.

I very much wanted my head to stay attached to the rest of me.

I gulped.

No matter which way I turned, I was surrounded by enemies. It was a stark reminder that the only person I could trust was myself.

"Kenna." The High Alpha turned to me, and I dipped my head respectfully. "I hope you will prove your loyalty to the Ember pack and your High Alpha by relaying a message to your father for me." He prowled closer, as if he needed to tower over me so I felt the full effect of his threat. "If he dares cross me, I will burn out his heart and take over his pack as my own."

"I am sure he knows just how powerful you are. He wants this alliance too much to jeopardize it." My voice stayed steady while the lie spun from my lips.

"Mmm," he hummed, and I felt his attention on me. Alpha power radiated from him, and it was stronger than anything I'd ever experienced. He was like the sun. I could only take glimpses of him, but I was unable to look at him directly without grave repercussions.

I couldn't quite put my finger on it, but there was something… off… about the High Alpha. Perhaps it was because I was standing so close, but there was an unhinged edge to the man that made me want to squirm uncomfortably beneath his scrutiny.

My wolf heeded his power, treading carefully so as not to challenge him.

"My omegas are bringing your things to your room as we speak and the pack is eagerly awaiting the arrival of their future Luna. Shall we?" He held out his arm and I glanced at Hunter, who stood stark straight, staring at me like this was a challenge. Like he wanted to see just how far I'd go in the charade he accused me of playing.

And damn him, but I wanted to prove myself. To show him I wasn't afraid. That I wasn't cowed by him or his father. I almost reached out to take the High Alpha's arm, but something inside me rebelled.

I took Hunter's hand instead, surprising him when I linked our fingers together. Light calluses were rough against my skin, and his hand was still warm from the blazing heat he'd held against me earlier.

"Thank you for the offer, High Alpha,"—I dipped my head in a quick show of respect—"but I'd like to show a united front to the pack by arriving with Hunter. If I'm to be their future Luna, they need to see us as a ruling pair."

The High Alpha hooked his arms behind his back and narrowed his eyes. He didn't like being told 'no,' much like his son.

Thankfully, we were interrupted by his second-in-command.

"Sir," his Beta called from the road, holding a cell

phone. "The Stormborn Alpha is demanding to speak with you."

"Just as expected. Looks like I'll get to deliver that threat myself." The High Alpha appeared almost gleeful about the prospect. "Hunter," he snapped, "take Kenna to the pack house and get her settled. Then meet me in my office in an hour."

Hunter's jaw clenched, but he agreed. "Yes, sir," he said coldly, diplomatically, and when his father turned and left us behind, he shook off my hand and gripped my elbow instead, leading me to the car.

Opening the door, he waited for me to get in before slamming it shut with more force than necessary. I used that brief moment of solitude to catch my breath.

Holy hell. I am never going to survive this.

The rest of the ride was short and tense, but I was grateful for the silence. I needed the time to collect myself and come up with a plan.

I needed to find a way to speak with Jasper in private, and I needed to find out everything I could about Kenna's life without raising red flags. Her belongings may hold some clues, though nowhere near enough to describe the relationships and connections she'd made. Still, maybe there was something in those boxes that would help.

Staring out the window at the passing scenery, I ignored Hunter to the best of my ability.

Through the trees, shapes started forming in the distance, becoming more solid the sparser the forest grew until we broke into a wide clearing that housed a small town, the heart of the pack.

Roads branched out in every direction, and around the clearing sat rows of different shops. I spotted a grocery store, a hair salon, and a number of clothing stores among the buildings. A cafe and a few restaurants were interspersed here and there, and a community center sat in the center of it all, a place for all pack members to congregate.

Hunter drove us past all of it, steered the car up a long drive that led to a huge, sprawling lodge surrounded by trees, and pulled to a stop at the top of the loop.

The house looked like a luxury cabin, except ten times the size. It appeared more like an elegantly rustic hotel than a home. It sprawled well beyond the size of my father's estate, and had enough space to hold most of our entire pack. I gaped, realizing this was my new home. It was a far cry from the small hovel I'd lived in.

I wondered how many pack members lived here. Being surrounded by people all the time was going to take some getting used to. While I was acclimated to living with constant enforcers watching over me, they'd always given me my space, guarding me from the forest, or at least from outside my home.

But this? This was like living in a college dorm or hotel. I was bound to run into people no matter where I went.

Living Kenna's life suddenly felt stifling. I'd have to find a place where I could be alone, where I could let down my guard and just be Madison.

For now, I shoved that thought down hard, locking it away as Hunter got out and rounded the car to my side. The last thing I needed was him seeing the truth written across my face.

If there were any hope Hunter had let our earlier argument go, it was squashed by the sheer condemnation he leveled at me through the window as he bent and pulled open my door.

The air was cooler this high up in the mountains, and it

cleared my head and cooled my heated cheeks when I stepped from the car.

But I only had a moment to enjoy it, because Hunter brought a heat all his own when he shut the door and leaned close.

"Don't for a minute think we're done here." His voice was deep and low as his hand pressed against my stomach to hold me against the car. The light scruff on his jaw abraded my skin when he leaned in, his lips brushing over my ear.

I closed my eyes and my breath hitched as pleasant little zings shot through my body. To anyone watching us, we looked cozy and intimate, like we were sharing a sweet private moment when instead, he was making me a deadly promise.

"You're hiding something, and I'm going to find out what it is."

TWELVE

Madison

Dread pooled in my stomach as Hunter's grim vow settled over me.

I wasn't stupid. He saw the differences between me and my sister. No matter how hard I tried to disguise my identity, I'd never act just like her. I wasn't privy to her past conversations, relationships, thoughts, or actions. Exiled as I'd been, I only knew a fragment of the full life she lived. Considering we saw each other once or twice a year, if we were lucky, what I knew about my sister could fit in the palm of my hand. As much as I knew her, I didn't know her well enough to pull this off without casting doubt.

Hunter was too observant for my lies. Distrust had been

bred into him, a trait all alphas seemed to possess. And I couldn't fault him for his suspicion. He wasn't wrong about me. I was an imposter, a liar, a deceiver, but what he didn't know was that I wouldn't jeopardize his pack if they were innocent.

Unfortunately the jury was still out, which meant I had to commit to the role I was forced into until I could prove his innocence… or his guilt.

How my father thought I could pull this off, I had no idea.

Talk about being thrown to the wolves…

This was his most asinine plan to date. And yet, I found myself wanting to succeed. I wouldn't sleep peacefully again until I knew who'd killed my sister.

That need for vengeance burned brightly while I greeted the members of Hunter's pack who'd waited for our arrival, wondering the entire time if one of them were responsible for the attack.

The wolves that were gathered looked at me with varying levels of interest. Some were truly curious about me. A few seemed excited by the prospect of having a new Luna soon, while others barely hid their contempt. It was hard to know if it stemmed from my being part of the Stormborn pack, if it was something personal to do with Kenna herself, or if it was simply because I was taking the most eligible bachelor in their pack off the market. The latter was an easy guess when it came to some of the scathing glances the women in the pack gave me.

Some welcoming committee.

I did my best to keep my interactions with everyone vague, feeling completely out of my element. If I survived this day with my secret intact, it would be a miracle.

Hunter's gaze burned into me the entire time, studying

every move I made, assessing me in the light of his new suspicions. I half-expected him to drag me away from his pack and demand answers, but then I realized this was a test. He wanted to see me squirm, to pinpoint the things about me that were different.

I felt like an ant trapped under a magnifying glass with a beam of sunlight ready to incinerate me if I made the wrong move.

Thankfully, someone called his name from the edge of the lodge, stealing his attention so I could breathe deeply again. Until I turned and saw a stunning woman walking toward us, beaming a bright, happy smile that only made her pretty face more radiant.

I stiffened, unsure of who she was or her significance to Hunter.

She waved, and Hunter actually smiled.

"Tristan," he barked at his beta, issuing more orders. "See Kenna up to her room."

"You're not going to walk me in?" I asked, unsure why I was pressing the issue. Hadn't I just wanted space from the imposing alpha? Why was I challenging him?

"You've been here before, right Kenna?" he challenged back. "I'm sure you could find your own way, but since I don't trust you, Tristan will be watching you while I'm busy."

Busy. With her.

Green jealousy rose with a force I wasn't accustomed to. I wanted to ask who she was, but there was no surer way of outing myself. Kenna would have known the pretty brunette. She would have known most of the pack by now.

I tipped my chin up, affecting what I hoped was a confident stance. "I don't need a babysitter. I can handle myself." I was bluffing. Just the idea of going inside and having to find my way around was intimidating as fuck. With my luck, I'd end up walking into a closet instead of whatever room Kenna usually stayed in when she was here to visit.

"You're right," Hunter stalked closer, leaning over me with an angry slash of his brows. "You don't need a babysitter. You need a warden."

"So, I'm your prisoner now?" I spat back, anger making my body rigid. My fists clenched, nails biting into my palms. The wolf below my skin rumbled her dislike. Above all else, she valued her freedom.

"You're whatever I say you are. Mate, Luna, prisoner, outcast… dead. You'd do well to remember your fate now rests in my hands."

His threat was like poison seeping into my veins. The realization that I was just as free here as I was in my previous pack made my heart sink. I'd simply traded prisons—from my old life to Kenna's to being at the mercy of the Ember Wolves. Hunter didn't trust me, and until I could prove myself to him, he never would.

But how would I do that when he was right to be wary of me?

Guilt ate at the edges of my conscience.

Instead of a snappy retort, instead of coming right back and pushing his buttons, I simply nodded, the energy to fight with him bleeding away. Seeming happy he'd put me in my place, he turned and strode away. I watched his back rippling as he unbuttoned his shirt and pulled it off, exposing his broad shoulders and golden skin to the world. His back was covered in tattoos, the intricate images cascading down to his tapered waist. I gritted my teeth when the girl, whoever she was, launched herself into his arms and hugged him tightly.

So much for his speech on indiscretion not being tolerated. That decree only went one way.

Sexist pig.

Still, I couldn't stop the angry beat of my heart or the way my eyes narrowed as he quickly stripped and shifted in a burst of smoky magic, leaving his clothing in a pile by the edge of the lodge. Nudity was normal, but I couldn't stop the flare of jealousy swirling through my gut, how everyone, including the ogling females behind me, had gotten an incredible view of his tight ass.

The sound of my wolf's possessive growl reverberated through my mind, nearly breaking past my lips.

Hunter was supposed to be mine. That he was content to disrespect me in front of his pack on the day we made our debut as the future rulers stung like a slap on the face. I had no right to his loyalty or his faithfulness, and it was insane to feel like I'd been wronged, but something deep in my chest tugged at watching his gorgeous wolf lope toward the woods.

In the light of day, and without the haze of pain and shock still clouding my mind, I took in the sight of Hunter's wolf. He was huge, standing nearly as tall as I did in human form. His fur was as dark as night, but depending on how the light hit it, I saw a glimmer of deep reds and maroons that revealed his element of Fire. Crimson markings curled over his back and legs, further marking him as a member of the Ember Wolves. Each movement was graceful, each powerful flex of muscle showing off his strength. There was no questioning that he was the heir-apparent, the future Alpha of the Embers. Hell, he had the potential to be the next High Alpha of our kind. His power charged the air, making me shiver. Pausing at the edge of the trees, he peered across the distance, pinning me with a look I couldn't decipher.

I took the opportunity to study him, trying to connect any similarities between him and the wolf who'd attacked us. Other than his size and black coloring, there was nothing distinguishable, and just like the first time I'd seen him, his markings gave me pause. No matter how many times I replayed the details of last night, I didn't remember the beastly wolf having any apparent markings amid his roiling, smoky fur. Strange. Didn't all shifters have markings? Had the smoky wisps simply hid them from sight? And was the dark, cloud-like matter a physical manifestation of power used to conceal, or was it simply how the shadowed beast appeared in shifted form?

My wolf pressed in, taking advantage of my doubt about Hunter's guilt. In her mind, he was innocent, and she wanted me to believe that as much as she did.

The mate bond pulsed like a physical rope connecting us, and my wolf whined, wanting to shift and go to him. She wanted to dig her paws into the dirt and fly along at his side. Muscles straining to hold her back, I swallowed and begged her to retreat, reminding her things were different than they'd been with Kenna.

We weren't normal, and if she emerged now, everyone would know.

It was a sure-fire way to get ourselves killed.

She huffed her frustration, but the tension below my skin eased until I was sure she'd acquiesced.

Hunter focused his attention over my shoulder for a long moment, staring at his beta, Tristan. Then he was gone, the shadows of the forest swallowing him as he disappeared into the trees.

Unfortunately, the brunette shifted a moment later,

shrugging out of her loose dress to join Hunter, trailing after him.

Okay, so it was possible he wasn't a psychopathic murderer, but that didn't mean he was absolved of *all* guilt. Cheating, for instance.

I gritted my teeth, trying to let that be the only outward sign of the emotions rioting through me.

"Let's go," Tristan motioned, grabbing my attention and drawing it back to the thinning crowd.

The lingering females smirked at me with cruel intent, happy, and perhaps hopeful, Hunter had practically cast me aside and shown the divide in our relationship so publicly. To them, it meant they had a chance. I had no right to Hunter, but my wolf surged to the surface and pushed a wave of pure power outward to warn them off him. They still sneered but there was less fire behind it, and they turned away quickly. Sauntering away in their own little groups, they left me to my own devices. It was impressive, and I gave her mental high fives while promising myself I'd find a quiet place to let her out soon. We needed to practice, figure out what we could do together… and what our limitations were.

With a sigh, I followed Tristan to the massive front door. Off to the side, I eyed another technological contraption. Pressing his thumb to the pad, it scanned Tristan's fingerprint and the door unlocked.

Dammit. I was hoping once I was inside pack borders, I wouldn't have to worry about physically proving my identity, but this place was determined to make my life more complicated.

Skirting inside on Tristan's heels, I counted my blessings that he didn't insist on making me scan anything. Then I counted them again once inside, grateful I didn't have to navigate this maze of a lodge alone. Getting lost was a real possibility.

The inside of Hunter's home was just as impressive as the exterior. Rustic hewn log walls gave the entire place a warm, cozy, cabin-like feel, even with the cathedral ceilings, floor-to-ceiling windows, and huge stone fireplaces set on each side of what I guessed was the living room. The entryway which opened into the living room just beyond had two beautiful curving staircases leading to a landing above that sported a rustic log railing with metal ballasts. The mix of wood and iron was so different from where I'd grown up, I found myself instantly falling in love with the vibe. Landscapes of the forest were framed and hung around the space, bringing the outdoors in as much as the sparkling glass windows did. Chandeliers made of antlers hung from the ceilings, and despite that it was June, large fires raged in the hearths.

Tristan caught me staring at them, and shrugged with a crooked tilt of his lips. "Ember Wolves—we like fire."

I chuckled wryly, thankful a number of windows were open to let in the breeze, keeping the temperature comfortable despite the dancing flames. "I can see that."

"I'm sure you're the same. You like rainy weather or storms or some shit, right?"

I took a minute to think about it. I'd distanced myself so far from the persona of a Stormborn that I'd honestly never considered what I may actually have in common with my birth pack.

"I do like the rain," I admitted as he led me toward an elevator off to the side of the entryway.

It dinged open, and I followed him inside after a flurry of omegas who'd been moving my things swept out.

Stepping inside, I memorized which button Tristan hit

to take me to my room, noting I was on the second floor. I followed him about halfway down, counting the doorways until he stopped outside of one. With a swift knock, he opened it and stepped back, waiting for me to enter first.

Knowing Hunter, I'd expected an actual prison cell complete with immovable silver bars, a shifter's weakness, but the room was beautiful. A queen-sized bed sat against one wall with a small fireplace directly across from it. A TV sat above the hearth on a rustic mantle and bookshelves lined either side. While the selection was sparse, I had no doubt I would fill those shelves if I could find a bookstore in town. Two doors were inset into the wall, and I guessed one led to a closet and the other to a bathroom.

The comforter on the plush bed was a soft pink, and the window had a bench seat lined with pillows that called my name.

It was nice. Nicer than anything I'd been given before. But my wolf growled a warning that made me tense and pay attention. Inhaling, I caught only the musty scent of dust and the strong chemical odor of cleaners. Peering around, I spotted a few cardboard boxes had been dropped in the corner, a far cry from the sheer number that had been packed from Kenna's room.

I whirled around and crossed my arms, raising a brow at Tristan who studied me darkly. Gone was the camaraderie from downstairs. Had it all been an act? A test?

"What kind of joke are you pulling?" I scolded.

Tristan cocked his head, crossing his own arms. His tall frame blocked the only way out of the room, unless I wanted to take my chances with the windows.

"Strange that you didn't realize this was the wrong room until you were inside of it, is it not?" He appraised me coldly. "Hunter said something was off with you, and I think he's right."

"You're testing me." I didn't put it past Hunter to order his beta to put me through my paces. I just kicked myself that I didn't see it coming sooner.

Lesson one: trust no one.

"And you fucking failed."

"Did it ever occur to you that maybe I considered your almighty heir had arranged for me to stay in a different room? How am *I* to know where you want me to sleep? Every other time I've been here, I was a visitor. Now I'm here to stay." I saw the flicker of uncertainty cross his face before it disappeared, but all I needed was that small seed of doubt. "Honestly, Tristan. I don't care where I sleep, so long as I have a place to myself. It's been a long day. This room will do just fine. Have the omegas bring my things," I ordered like I had the authority to make such a call.

Confusion clouded Tristan's unwavering stare, and I guessed it was because this room wasn't nearly as fancy or as big as others. Kenna would have demanded their best, but I was out of fucks to give and energy to care. He studied me for a beat longer, trying to find my angle, but ultimately his loyalty was with his alpha, not the woman who would be his Luna someday.

He shook his head. "Not happening."

Surging forward, he pulled me from the room and rested his hand in the center of my back, pushing me along the hallway, guiding me back to the elevator and up to the third floor. When the doors dinged open, a small hallway greeted us with a set of double doors and another finger-print scanning device Tristan made short work of.

Just my luck.

Pushing inside, Hunter's scent enveloped me. It was

everywhere. It filled the modern living room I was shoved through and covered the scent of food in the huge, open concept kitchen, growing stronger the closer Tristan marched me toward the two doors that sat side by side at the back of the space.

Opening one of them, he guided me inside, and I tried not to gasp at the sheer size of the bedroom. The downstairs room had been nice, but this room? This one was gorgeous.

The same logs made up all four walls, but soft white curtains hung from the windows lining the far wall, swept off to the sides and secured to allow the afternoon sunlight in. A huge king-sized bed sat against one wall, the posts reaching far above to create a canopy. White gauzy material was tied at each post, giving the bed a romantic look. More throw pillows than anyone needed were strewn at the top of the mattress, and I wanted to dive into them and take a much needed nap. A door opened to a large closet stacked high with Kenna's boxes. Another door led to an ensuite that I was itching to check out. But it was the third door that had my curiosity peaked and inquisitiveness pulling at my brows.

"That door connects you to Hunter's room," Tristan said smugly. "This is his apartment. Convenient, since he wants to keep an eye on you."

The wolf inside of me was practically running in excited circles at our proximity, but my excitement over the room dimmed. Adjoining rooms.

This entire suite screamed Alpha's quarters.

"Is this the late Luna's room?" I questioned on a breath.

Tristan glanced around as though memories were playing through his mind. Surprisingly, he was forthcoming. "The High Alpha used to live here, but when his wife passed, he moved out of the lodge and built a house more suited for a ruler of his position. This apartment was bequeathed to Hunter when he came of age. These are his private quarters. No one but a select few are keyed to enter. So again, it'll be the best place for him to—"

"Keep an eye on me. Yeah, I get it," I quipped. But I knew better.

Hunter hadn't made this decision last minute. It would take time to prepare a room to look this nice. There was barely a hint of dust lingering anywhere. It smelled fresh and clean. Ready for a new occupant.

He'd wanted me here before he'd had any suspicion about me. And now our proximity simply worked in his favor. My heart was being pulled in a game of tug of war, flattered that he'd been committed enough to have gone to such trouble, allowing me into the only place he had solitude from the pressures of leading his pack, yet annoyed he wanted to use it to keep me under his thumb.

Dismissing Tristan, I waited until he'd retreated and left the apartment before I closed the bedroom door and shut myself in. Resting my back against it, I dug my palms into my eyes and released a pent-up sigh. This was getting wildly complicated.

"What have you gotten yourself into..." I muttered to myself.

Crossing to the window, I stared off into the forest. The trees had always been soothing, and I needed comfort now more than ever, but knowing Hunter was out there with some girl only stirred the discontent churning in my stomach.

That he planned to keep a close eye on me was only going to complicate things between us and make snooping around for information harder to accomplish.

It'd only been one day, and I was already overwhelmed.

Balling my fist, I banged it lightly against the glass pane. I was caught in a cage of my own making, and all I could do was keep fighting. Fighting to stay alive. Fighting to find my sister's killer. Fighting the draw I felt toward Hunter, a man who understandably hated me, who could never be mine, regardless.

Lost in my thoughts, I didn't initially pick up on the feeling of being watched until it crept along my skin like ghostly fingers, raising the fine hair on the back of my neck like the hackles of my angry, agitated wolf.

Scanning the treeline, my heart picked up pace, the thrum of it thundering like a wicked storm. There at the edge of the forest was a smoky, wispy form, a dark, foreboding shadow watching me.

In a blink, it shifted into the darkness of the woods and disappeared.

Wrapping my arms around myself, I tried to chase away the bloody memories and the familiar chill that stole through me while I convinced myself my eyes were playing tricks. That I hadn't just seen a vestige of the beast who had murdered my sister.

Because if I had, there was only one reason he was here.

For me.

THIRTEEN

Madison

Early morning light brightened my window, and I padded across the room to peer out at the twilight woods below, scanning the treeline for any sign of unusual shadows or dark, beastly wolves. I didn't move away until the sun fully crept over the horizon and chased the shadows away, pushing them back into the trees.

Three full days had passed since I arrived at the Embers' territory, and I'd spent every one of them hyper-vigilant, half-expecting the "Shadow Beast," as I'd aptly named him, to find me around any corner.

It was silly to be so anxious when I wasn't even sure of

the evidence I'd thought I'd seen, but something deep within me refused to let my guard down.

If that beast were truly here, it meant one of two things, he was either a member of the Ember Wolves, or he was stalking me to finish what he'd started the other night. Or maybe both.

My hand skimmed over the newly healed wounds on my stomach as my mind churned over the facts. I was a loose end, the only other witness to his crime. For some reason, he'd left me alive that night when it would have been so easy for him to end me. It was a decision I planned on making him regret when I hunted him down and made him pay for what he'd done to Kenna. To me. To my life.

Forcing myself away from the window, I headed to the bathroom and washed my face before dabbing the water off my skin with a soft towel. Everything here was of the highest quality. Back home, my towels, like my clothes, had been threadbare, but now the best of everything had been provided for me. I felt a little guilty for enjoying it when I knew the ultimate price had been paid for me to have this rags-to-riches existence, however brief.

Catching sight of my reflection, I stared in the mirror. My hair hung in soft waves thanks to upgraded hair products, and my complexion was flawless, despite the stress I'd been under, also compliments of the high quality creams and facial scrubs I'd found among my toiletries. But all of it served to make me see someone else when I looked back at myself. I felt like a stranger.

I felt like Kenna.

Fear was a heavy weight. It'd be too easy to lose myself in this life that was never meant for me.

This is temporary, Madison.

The gentle yip from my wolf told me she didn't agree.

Insisting I was just as deserving, but that wasn't the narrative that'd been beaten into me, and the years of abuse weren't easy to shake.

Needing to find my sense of self-worth and cheer myself up from the anxiety that continuously had me on edge, I took my time with my makeup. I didn't have much practice with this stuff, and going slow kept me from poking an eye out.

That I was also procrastinating in an effort to avoid my *warden* was simply an added bonus.

The sound of Hunter on the other side of the adjoining door was maddening.

Keeping mostly to my room since my arrival at the lodge, I'd spent the majority of that time listening to his movements throughout the apartment, timing my daily trips to the kitchen around his schedule. I only snuck out to find sustenance when he left, doing my best to circumvent another run-in. Not an easy feat when you lived together, but I wasn't ready to face him again.

Unpacking had occupied me and kept me sane during my seclusion, but my wolf was growing antsy from being cooped up. Hell, so was I. The added pressure of performance anxiety didn't help matters either. My time to figure out whether I could shift was dwindling with the pack gathering and subsequent run *tonight*, and I felt her desperation just as sharply. The forest called to her even in the midst of danger, and she begged me to let her out.

I'd been on the brink of agreeing so many times in the past few days, but given the High Alpha's penchant for technology, I couldn't be sure I wasn't being surveilled within the apartment somehow. I'd searched every room for any signs of hidden cameras or microphones, and though I found nothing, my trust level was at a zero.

With the possibility of the Shadow Beast, the forest didn't feel much safer. Besides, even if I wanted to leave my room and go explore, I wasn't sure I'd be allowed to wander about Hunter's pack freely, given his suspicions about me. Their safety came first, and though I hated to admit Hunter wasn't a complete dickwad, his protection of his pack was admirable. I respected his dedication to his people.

That said, his threat about me being his prisoner was still ripe in the back of my mind. So far, I'd decided to keep to myself, but I wondered what I'd find if I tried the front door of the apartment, or the elevator, or the door that led outside. Would I be locked in? Was I free to leave?

I decided I needed to try.

Being in Hunter's apartment was stifling, regardless of the expanse.

His scent was everywhere, drowning me in pheromones that made me heady and low-key needy. My body was keenly aware everytime he was nearby, the bond between us seeming to flare brighter when we were closer to each other. The pull between us was magnetic, and the force drawing us together was becoming harder to resist.

Yeah, some fresh air was exactly what I needed, and I'd stay close to the lodge just to be safe.

Waiting until the door to the apartment opened and closed again, I breathed a sigh of relief and quickly opened my bedroom door to beeline it to the fridge. My stomach was rumbling angrily, begging for food.

I blamed my hunger for distracting me enough not to realize the strength of the bond hadn't faded. I wasn't proud of the squeak I released, or the small jump I gave, when I spotted my *mate*. My pulse thundered even as my eyes greedily drank in the sight of him. The traitors. Then again, I couldn't fault myself for knowing what I liked.

Hunter was sex and sin and every wicked thing in between.

"You've been avoiding me," he stated, crossing his arms and staring me down from where he leaned casually against the counter in a pair of jeans tailored to fit just right and a button down, rolled at the sleeves.

No shit, Sherlock. "You haven't exactly made me feel welcome," I snarked, gathering my composure and marching my ass to the fridge, overly aware of the silken short shorts and matching camisole I'd slipped on after my shower last night and worn to bed. They left little to the imagination, and my cheeks colored from being so exposed.

Planning to be alone, I hadn't seen a need to change into something less revealing, and while these pajamas weren't my usual oversized t-shirt and yoga pants, this was apparently all the servants had packed for night clothing—unless the lingerie sets I'd found wrapped in soft tissue paper with the tags still on counted.

"You haven't exactly earned my trust," Hunter bit back.

"And *you* haven't earned *mine*." I yanked the fridge open with a little too much force, making the condiments rattle on the shelves. A blast of cool air made me shiver in my state of undress. My boobs were free ranging, enjoying their time outside the confines of a bra, and my nipples hardened against the silk.

Out of the corner of my eyes, I saw Hunter's gaze rake down my top to focus on those hard little points. He swallowed and then his jaw clenched.

Jerking his gaze back to my profile, he replied coolly, "I don't need to earn your trust. I'm not the one with secrets."

"We all have secrets, Hunter," I retorted, searching the shelves for something to eat.

Where had all the food gone? I could have sworn there

were eggs in here last time I'd checked. Granted, I'd need to go grocery shopping if I planned on hiding out much longer. Though Hunter calling me out for avoiding him made me want to do the exact opposite. What was it about this guy that made me feel so defiant? I wanted to challenge him, to go toe to toe. It was almost… fun.

Pushing off the counter, he reached me in two strides and stood behind me while I stared into the empty fridge without really seeing it.

"Some of us have more secrets than others," he said, and that low, deep tone did funny things to my stomach. His heat along my spine and the chilled air from the fridge created a tantalizing mixture. My wolf urged me to lean into him when he braced one hand on the edge of the appliance, his other forearm resting on top of the open door, framing me within his arms. "Ready to share what you're hiding from me?" His words were so close to my ear, I nearly jumped again.

Goddess, this man was unsettling, always keeping me on edge.

"I'm not hiding anything," I bluffed.

"It's cute that you don't think I'll figure you out," he said confidently. "I *will* find what you're keeping from me. And when I do, you'll wish you had told me yourself," Hunter growled with a tinge of warning. "The time for leniency is now."

A whine pierced my skull, and it was clear which side my wolf took. She wanted me to open up to Hunter, but didn't she understand what was at stake?

It's our life, I reminded her. *Hunter could end us in an instant.*

The mate bond clouded her judgment, because she was positive he'd never do that.

I wanted to believe he wouldn't… but I meant what I said. I didn't fully trust him.

My mouth opened and closed as I fought with my wolf, but ultimately, I sealed my lips shut and whirled to face him.

"I'm on your side, Hunter." It was all I could give him. I'd given it a lot of thought and I was ninety percent certain he wasn't my sister's killer. If he were, he'd know he'd delivered a death blow to Kenna, and he'd never keep up this charade with me, which meant he was in the dark and most likely innocent.

I didn't care about the pack feud. In my eyes, we were only enemies if he threatened me or protected whomever it was who'd attacked Kenna and me, be it a member of his pack, or worse, his father.

Maybe I was naive, but I didn't believe he'd do that. Behind that grumpy-growly thing he had going on, Hunter seemed like a decent guy, a just leader. He was going to make a great Alpha. He protected fiercely, cared deeply, and took his duty and responsibility seriously.

After watching my father mismanage our pack for years, it was hard not to notice the good qualities in Hunter.

But just because I could acknowledge them, didn't mean I had to trust him.

Weighing what I'd said, Hunter finally responded, "For your sake, I hope that's true. But until I make a decision about you, we need to keep up appearances. I won't have my pack sensing a weakness in their leadership."

Right. Because running off with some pretty brunette the other day really helped sell our solid, loving relationship. I rolled my eyes, scoffing at the ridiculous double standard, stopping shy of a full-on, unladylike snort.

Straightening, Hunter ran a hand down his shirt to smooth out the wrinkles. "The pack run is tonight, and the gathering to celebrate you joining the Ember Wolves is immediately after. I expect you to be there. Your attendance is mandatory."

Hunter's order left no room for argument, not that he'd get one from me. This was the opportunity I needed to study his pack, to see them in their shifted forms and find out if any of them matched the Shadow Beast's description. Dangerous? Yes, but absolutely necessary to speed this process along. The problem, however, was that I didn't know how to shift… or if I even could.

How am I going to make it through a pack run as a human?

Still, it didn't stop me from saying, "I'll be there."

"Good." Hunter nodded authoritatively and strode toward the door. Stopping before he walked through it, he threw a cocky little smirk back at me. "Oh, and if you're hungry, you can eat at the cafeteria and mingle with the pack. I assume you remember how to get there?"

It was a taunt, a test, and I wasn't about to fail.

"Don't you worry about me." I tipped my chin, faking a confidence I didn't feel.

"If only," Hunter grumbled under his breath on the way out.

At the click of the door, I relaxed and shoved a hand through my hair, combing at the long strands.

Blowing out a slow breath, I spun and shoved the fridge closed, catching my reflection in the polished stainless steel.

I braced my hands on either side of my mirrored image. "You just can't stop bluffing, can you?" I chastised myself for the heap of trouble I was continuously digging for myself.

The pack run. *This is going to be a shit show.*

FOURTEEN

Madison

Worry ate at the edges of my mind every time I glanced at the clock and counted down the hours until the pack run. Pacing to the window, I stared down at the forest. It beckoned me like a Siren's song, and my wolf stirred restlessly. Hunter had goaded me to leave his apartment an hour ago, and now that I knew I wasn't a prisoner, I'd been working up the courage to take him up on the challenge and walk out the door.

Leaving felt dangerous. It meant run-ins with his pack and having to play the role of Kenna to perfection. Was I ready for that? So far, I'd been able to hide out, but I couldn't stay in here forever. And honestly, I didn't want to.

My wolf scratched at my mind encouragingly. Truth was, we were both going a little stir crazy, and if we didn't get out of these four walls soon, we were going to go mad.

Daring to take a chance, I left Hunter's apartment and took the elevator to the ground floor. The lodge was surprisingly quiet, but I snuck out the side door to evade any enforcers my mate may have tasked to follow me. I drew an invigorating breath of fresh air as I hurried to the edge of the woods, wanting to get out of sight as quickly as possible. The last thing I needed was a tail when I wanted to try and let my wolf out.

But as soon as I hit the treeline, I paused.

The shadows had me swallowing hard, and my anxiety about the potential danger rose sharply. I couldn't get the image of the Shadow Beast out of my mind.

The dark tendrils.

The blood.

Dammit. My breath caught as panic tried to swamp me. It took long moments before I was able to will away my fear and dread, sucking in steady lungfuls of air to ground myself.

You're okay. You need to do this.

I took one step into the trees, then another. Slowly, I forged on, staying to the patches of sunlight that broke through the canopy of leaves above.

See? You've got this, Madison. You're doing great.

The deeper I went into the forest, the harder my heart pounded. Every little sound sent fear skittering down my spine until I scolded myself that I was being paranoid and more than a little ridiculous. The Shadow Beast wouldn't attack in broad daylight. Probably. Hopefully.

My wolf yipped, letting me know she was also on high alert. I felt her magic ripple outward, and she soon sent a wave of calm through me, telling me we were safe. Closing my eyes, I used all of my newly heightened senses to double check that we were truly alone. Only when I was satisfied did I finally relax.

Exhaling slowly, I rolled my neck and shook the tension from my shoulders.

"Alright, girl. Let's see what we can do," I murmured.

Biting my lip, I stood awkwardly in the forest, trying to figure out what I was supposed to do. So far, my wolf had only appeared when others had demanded I shift, so I focused on that place in my chest where I could feel her. She was eager to respond, and I urged her forward, calling her forth until her presence was a vibrating buzz under my skin. This time when I felt the unrelenting press, I didn't hold her back. Before I knew it, she emerged effortlessly, walking right out of me and into her own glowing, ethereal existence.

The beautiful obsidian wolf stood before me, cocking her head and staring up at me with her sky-blue eyes like we'd done this a hundred times before. Her fur was so dark it gleamed like an oil slick, shimmering with hues of purple and blue. Swirling, tribal-esque markings patterned her legs, curling up her sides in a gorgeous display of azure color. Surrounding her was the same teal, glowing aura she'd had since she somehow became mine.

Propping my hands on my hips, I watched her with a smile on my face as she stretched her legs and then took off. She sprinted around the small clearing, weaving in and out of trees and prancing about, happy to finally be free.

I had a feeling she could have spent all day frolicking through the forest, but she felt my urgency as keenly as if it were her own, and after a few minutes, she came to a stop before me, peering up at me expectantly.

"We need to keep this short. Anyone could wander by and the longer we were out here, the greater the chance we'll be caught," I told her, ready to get to work.

Unable to help myself, I reached out and scratched behind her ears giggling when she leaned into my hand.

"Okay. Let's try to shift this time." Recalling her was as simple as asking her to come back, and she leapt into my body just as easily as she'd appeared.

Practicing easily ate up the hour I'd allotted, but no matter how hard I tried to force myself into a wolven form, it never happened. Each time, my wolf bounded out of me just like she had the first time. And each time, I grew a little more worried about the impending pack run.

Dropping to my knees in the leaves and forest debris that littered the ground, I reached for my wolf, who came to sit in front of me. My fingers dug into her soft fur, and I pet her neck.

"You are incredible," I told her, truly meaning it. "Having a wolf is a dream."

At least, it was if I didn't think about the way I'd gotten her. I tamped down the sadness that clogged my throat. This wasn't the time to lose myself to grief.

I sat back on my heels and ran a hand through my hair. "But it doesn't seem like we're going to master this shifting thing today, and if that's the case, what are we going to do about tonight?"

It was clear to me that I wasn't a typical shifter. At this rate, I didn't know if I even *could* shift. I knew nothing about being a Spirit wolf, and the Aether element was a complete mystery to me. I didn't understand the new magic that lived in my veins, and my lack of knowledge was putting me at a great disadvantage.

With a sigh, I stood and recalled my wolf. She licked my

fingers in silent support before bounding back into me and settling into place inside my chest. Tipping my face skyward, I sent a prayer to the Moon Goddess, asking her for help.

If I was going to survive the night with my secrets intact, I needed answers.

And I was almost out of time to find them.

·)·)·)·)·●·(·(·(·(·

I wanted to keep practicing, but soon my stomach was making its own demands. Ones that had me braving another potential run-in with Hunter as I left the forest and headed into town in search of food.

I'd ignored my hunger as long as I could, but apparently housing a wolf meant I couldn't skip meals without my stomach feeling like it was devouring itself. After our exertions this morning, my wolf was downright hangry, and that didn't bode well for bringing our A-game tonight. The run was going to be difficult enough without adding starvation to the list. So, I followed my nose and stepped onto the path that crossed the common area, leading to the recreational building from where all the mouth-watering smells seemed to originate.

The cafeteria grew quiet when I walked through the double doors, and I drew to a stop, glancing around awkwardly.

Dammit. I'd hoped coming late to breakfast would mean there were fewer pack members around, but that didn't seem to be the case. Apparently, the Ember Wolves loved brunch. The tables were teeming with hungry wolves, all in various states of consuming their food. Forks hung suspended in midair, and all eyes were on me.

A tension I didn't fully comprehend wove through the air.

I was tempted to give them a little wave, take a bow, or something equally sarcastic, but Kenna wouldn't do that. So, I sucked it up and tried to figure out how she would react in such a situation.

She'd probably eat up the attention. Her voice whispered through my mind like a ghost, saying, "Let them look." She'd strut to the buffet tables and get herself whatever it was she was craving without paying the wolves any mind. Or, on second thought, she'd probably have someone fetch her food like the important alpha she was. My father's house was overflowing with servants, but that didn't seem to be the case here among the Ember Wolves—something I appreciated.

Squaring my shoulders, I tried to ignore everyone as I headed for food. Behind me, Tristan followed at what I'm sure he thought was a discreet distance, but it hadn't escaped my notice that he'd been tailing me since we crossed paths in town. His presence made my freedom a mere illusion, but I'd take it for now. If Hunter's and my roles were reversed, I would have put a tail on me, too, so I tolerated Tristan's surveillance the same way I'd always tolerated the enforcers my father had ordered to keep me in line. Nothing had changed, really, but that was the most disheartening part.

At least I'd gotten the drop on him earlier and had some alone time or I'd never have gotten in that practice session with my wolf.

The delicious scents wafting through the air pulled me

from my melancholy, and my stomach growled when I sidled up to the buffet table.

Surveying the breakfast offerings, I decided I may just hug my grumpy mate when I saw him again. There were so many choices, and they all put whatever eggs I would have made to shame.

My stomach felt concave, as though it were eating itself, so I piled my plate high with food and balanced it carefully when I spun to look for a table.

Crap. I hadn't thought about where to sit. Who did my sister know? Who was she friends with? The only ones she'd ever spoken about were close friends from other packs that she'd met at the Summit, an annual gathering of wolves from every pack.

She also hadn't said much about Hunter. Everything I'd gleaned about their relationship spoke of duty and responsibility to their packs, their mating nothing more than a contractual agreement bound with moon witch magic. Nonetheless, since I'd met him, Hunter had seemed intense and committed when it came to their mating.

I felt like I didn't have the full picture when it came to their complicated relationship, and that bothered me.

I hated flying in the dark. It made knowing how to interact with him difficult.

My wolf huffed an amused sound in my head, pushing the memory of his scent and how close he'd stood to me this morning to the forefront of my mind as if to say 'is that the only reason you want to know?'

Promptly ignoring her, I studied the room, noting the table of alphas, betas, and deltas at the head of the room. If this had been our pack, there would be no question that's where Kenna would sit, but their hushed tones couldn't mask their quiet conversations with my new wolfy hearing. Some poked fun while others openly criticized my origin pack. Others were content to snicker or make snide comments about how Hunter could have done so much better. Fuck *that* shit.

Narrowing my eyes, I strode through the room, uncaring about Tristan's scrutinizing attention, and chose a table at random. Plunking down my tray, I held my chin high as I sat, daring anyone to question my decision.

This whole fiasco reminded me of grade school all over again. At least, the years I'd been allowed to attend before having to homeschool myself. I rolled my eyes. Luckily, this meal was worth bearing a little gossip, and I dug in, determined not to let petty chatter bother me.

I was chewing fiercely, inhaling my food, and completely in my own little world when I glanced back up and met the gazes of my table mates. Slowing to a more normal, polite pace, I blushed, swallowed, and took a massive sip of my drink so I could speak.

"Uh, hi." A large part of me hoped they would go back to eating. Receiving more attention, especially from the people whose table I had momentarily hijacked, only made me feel more awkward and out of place. I just wanted to eat in peace and fill the churning hole in my stomach that was part hunger and part dread, warning me that all of this was a bad idea—taking Kenna's place, living here, being under my father's thumb, rising to Hunter's challenge.

I should take my chances and run. I should.

"Rough day?" A girl with dark hair that faded into a purple piped up with a small smile, flicking her gaze over my shoulder toward the table of high-born wolves still having a field day with my reputation.

My throat clogged with emotion when I went to agree. Being thrust into this new life had stilted my grieving process, and it all came rushing back, but I couldn't let myself fall apart here. Last night, I'd been so engrossed in unpacking Kenna's things, it had felt like she was still with me, but in the light of day I was left with the stark reality all over again. This situation only compounded it.

Rough day—more like rough *few* days—was an understatement.

Swallowing harder, I cleared my throat and nodded. "You could say that." I returned my interest to my plate, stabbing a forkful of eggs harder than necessary.

Suddenly, I wasn't as hungry as I had been.

"Moving to a new pack can't be easy," the guy next to her said, misreading what I was upset about. His red hair was a mess of waves that had been pushed away from his forehead, and his smile seemed friendly and approachable. He had an easy way about him that made me want to relax marginally.

"I've always known I wouldn't stay with the Stormborn pack, but I didn't expect it to be this… difficult," I finished, letting them assume I was addressing the disrespect happening behind me when I was talking about so much more.

"They're just jealous," the girl said. "Every one of those girls wants to be Hunter's arm candy."

The brunette from when we got here flashed into my mind, and I had to stuff down my jealousy all over again, along with a retort about how Hunter already seemed to have that position filled.

"And what are the guys' excuses?" I questioned in between bites, my appetite returning enough to allow me to down a few mouthfuls of sausage wrapped in pancakes. I lived for that sweet and salty combination.

"Dominance," the ginger guy answered with a shrug.

"You're going to outrank them, and that rubs their wolves the wrong way."

"Though it shouldn't. Talk about some sexist bullshit. It's not like she hasn't already proven herself as an alpha in the Trials," the girl spat, indignant on my behalf. I decided I liked her, and I smiled at her quick defense.

The guy held up his hands, waving his fork through the air. "Hey, don't snap at me. I didn't say it was right. I was just answering the lady's question."

I hid my smile with another forkful, trying to contain the twitch of my lips but failing.

"Don't tell me it doesn't bother you." The girl scooped a spoonful of her yogurt parfait, waving it around haphazardly while she spoke. I kept waiting for the glob to slip from her spoon and splat on something—or someone. I was prepared to duck, just in case.

Luckily, she popped the bite into her mouth while I responded, "The wolf packs have favored men for as long as I can remember."

"Maybe now that you're here, that'll change for the Ember Wolves. It wasn't always this bad in our pack." The girl shot a glare over my shoulder. "Our Luna demanded their respect, and they gave it willingly."

"Sounds like she was a great woman."

"You didn't know her?" the girl tipped her head, studying me.

Should I? I didn't know when Hunter's mother passed away, but it stood to reason I would have had a chance to meet her at some point in my life. He'd said it had been years, but I didn't know exactly how long that meant.

"It's been a long time." I waved my hand to try and dismiss the question. "And the feud between our packs doesn't exactly foster close relationships," I mumbled, trying to downplay any blunder.

Goddess, this is hard.

"Except for you and Hunter." She waggled her eyebrows, and I wondered how much she knew about our farce of a relationship.

"Right." I stuffed another bite into my mouth, chewing slowly to prolong having to talk. It seemed like a bulletproof strategy.

"I'm Nova, by the way, since we haven't had a chance to properly meet before." She held out her hand and I brushed mine off before taking hers and giving it a quick shake.

"Ma—" I nearly gave her my actual name, pivoting at the last second before I outed myself accidentally—"kenna. Makenna," I repeated, rolling it all together more naturally the second time.

And the Oscar goes to…

I mentally banged my head on the table.

"Or you know… just Kenna." I kept babbling, trying to cover the near mistake.

"Dean." The redhead nodded casually, and I nodded in return.

"Nice to meet you both," I said before shoving another bite into my mouth.

The conversation carried easier after that, and I was grateful for some neutral ground. Making friends Kenna didn't know was like finding a liferaft in the middle of a stormy ocean, and for the first time in days, I actually relaxed.

"It's been a while since you've been here. Do you need any help finding anything before the pack gathering tonight?" Nova offered when we were finished, tossing the remnants of breakfast in the trash can.

I tapped my fingers against my plate as I waited behind her and Dean for my turn to place it in the bin of dirty dishes.

"Actually, could you remind me where I could find the library?" This was my chance to dig for information about the Aether element and anything I could find on Spirit Wolves, particularly, if they could shift.

With the Ember Alpha also being High Alpha, it stood to reason he'd have access to books and resources other packs wouldn't have.

I crossed my fingers and prayed to the Moon Goddess that Nova would agree to help me. It was almost noon, and having her point me in the right direction would save me from wandering around town aimlessly while I searched for the library on my own.

Nova studied me for a long moment, quirking her brow.

"W-what?" I stuttered, wondering if I had something on my face or if she was starting to suspect. I swiped the back of my hand across my mouth anyway, just to be sure.

"I was expecting you to ask to go to the shops in town or something. Everyone knows how much you love to shop and to party. I just figured with the pack run tonight and the gathering afterward, you'd want to buy something new to wear." She shrugged.

"Now who's being sexist," Dean fake whispered.

"It's not sexist if I'm stating something she actually likes to do. It'd only be sexist if I made assumptions. But everyone knows Kenna's fashion forward and enjoys a jaunt around a clothing store."

Both Dean and Nova turned to me, scanning my

current outfit. I looked down at myself, and their appraisal made my simple jeans and tunic top feel lacking.

Dammit. I was not equipped to add 'fashion conscious' to my list of things to pretend I knew anything about.

Before I could defend my choice of clothing, a melodic, feminine voice chimed in from behind me. "I can take you."

Turning, I took in the newcomer, shocked to see the pretty brunette Hunter had run off with the other day. Unfortunately, the soft smile on her face did nothing to stop my stomach from plummeting straight to my feet.

Madison

This close, I could make out the warm chocolate color of the brunette's eyes down to the golden amber flecks interspersed throughout, but behind the warm hues was a quiet intensity. Was this chick really this brazen? Didn't she know I'd seen her with Hunter? She hadn't exactly been discreet about giving him a hug in front of me or disappearing into the woods together minutes after I'd arrived. *What is she up to?*

"Are you sure, Olivia? I can take her," Nova offered, a little put off she was essentially being dismissed. We may have just met, but I appreciated her more than I could say. I could have hugged her for name-dropping. That little tidbit of information was going to prove helpful.

"Of course. Kenna and I have some catching up to do," Olivia said, waving off my new friends who reluctantly left us behind with a wave and a promise to meet up tonight at the run.

A promise I'd need to break if I had any chance of not being found out.

"Did you really want to go to the library?" Olivia asked, moving toward the double doors that led outside.

"Actually, yes. I wanted to find a new book to read for those nights when Hunter and I curl up on the couch together." I didn't know why I said it. It was so far from the truth, but a little part of me wanted to remind her that I was the girl he was living with. I was supposed to be his mate. For now, anyway.

"I can't really imagine Hunter as a cuddler," she mused with a pondering expression that told me she didn't quite believe me.

"Big ol' teddy bear," I exaggerated, and she gave me a confused, yet amused, sort of giggle.

"I'll take your word for it, I guess."

Damn right, you will. I wanted her to keep her paws to herself.

It was annoying just how possessive I felt over a mate who wasn't even mine, especially because he wanted nothing to do with me unless it served his own purposes.

Speaking of which, I glanced behind me before leaving and saw Tristan flirting with some girls, completely distracted from guarding me.

"Tristan will flirt with anything in a skirt." Olivia smirked, and it was then I knew she was behind helping me shake the beta. *Why, though?* "Those are some of my friends.

They were happy to distract him so we could ditch your *bodyguard*."

"You did that for me?" More confusion.

"Us girls have to stick together." She regarded me as if she knew something I didn't, and there was a sad, distant pain buried in her gentle gaze.

"Huh." The little noise was all I could muster. I didn't know what to make of this girl who was supposed to be my enemy. I couldn't get the image of her running into the woods after Hunter out of my head.

"Come on." She motioned for me to join her.

Following Olivia out into the sunlight, we fell into an awkward silence as she led me through town until we reached a path that branched into the forest.

Before I knew what was happening, she glanced around and tugged me down the trail until we were far enough into the trees that we weren't seen, then threw her arms around me and hugged me tight.

"Uh, what's going on?" I stood there stiffly, trying to figure out what was happening as she squeezed me.

"Oh, Kenna. I'm just… I'm so sorry," Olivia said, voice full of regret.

"You're sorry?" I repeated like a confused parrot. Was she seriously apologizing for running off with the guy who was supposed to be my mate? The bond between Hunter and me was a steady thrum in my chest, despite our distance. Even though the bond had transferred to me with Kenna's wolf, I had no claim to Hunter, not really, but my sister had. Moving in on someone else's man like that broke some serious girl code.

"Of course, I am," she said, pulling back with a sniffle. "If I'd known…"

Her words died off, and I cocked my head, studying her.

"You knew, Olivia. Hunter and I have been practically engaged since we were children."

"I… what?" Olivia reared back, studying me wildly.

"You heard me." I propped my hands on my hips, seriously stunned that this chick had the nerve to play so innocent. She may have done me a solid when she distracted Tristan, but that didn't make us even. "I saw you with him the other day. It was pretty blatant."

My wolf pawed in my mind, and I felt her hesitation, her desire for me to re-evaluate. I ignored her, making sure this girl knew that I wouldn't tolerate that kind of behavior. Besides my natural jealousy, my father expected me to carry on with the mating with Hunter, and while I didn't plan to trap him in some shame of a mate bond, it was reason enough to warn this girl away from him.

For now, he was supposed to be mine. So this jealousy I felt… that was natural, expected even. Right?

My wolf huffed, completely put out with me.

"I don't understand what you're talking about. I was just spending some time with him. Is that suddenly not allowed?" Defensive and confused, Olivia crossed her arms and stood her ground.

The alpha in me wanted to stake her claim, to show all the other women in the pack that Hunter was off limits for their flirtations and attempts to secure a mating with him, or worse, the role as his mistress. The wolf inside me was far too possessive to tolerate any of it. I blamed the mate bond, but I'd never felt this way about a guy before. And he was an ass at the best of times. *What's wrong with me?*

As if it answered all my questions, my wolf's growl resonated through my mind, *Mate.*

Yeah, yeah. We get it. You're a thirsty bitch.

She didn't even dispute it.

Blowing out a breath, I faced off against Olivia and decided I needed to handle this once and for all.

"Hunter's the future Alpha, so I'm sure there will be interactions between you two in the future, but I'd appreciate it if you kept your hands off my mate," I declared, and went to brush past her.

"Oh my goddess," she gasped, and pressed a hand to her mouth. Her eyes grew wide with shock, and I knew I'd just made a grave mistake. "You're… you're not Kenna."

My steps faltered at the same time as my heart. *Had she really just said that?*

Turning back to face her, I stared speechless at Olivia and tried to figure out how to respond.

"You're *Madison*," she said on an airy breath.

Shit. Shit. Shit. I was completely frozen, other than the wild fluttering of my pulse. The sound of my actual name completely threw me. She knew. And not in the vague way Hunter accused me of lying to him about something. There was a surety behind her statement. I wouldn't be able to talk my way out of this confrontation.

Had she been friends with my sister? Was that how she so easily told us apart? And if she was a friend, why the hell was she throwing herself at Hunter the other day? He was Kenna's mate. No. Something didn't add up. I didn't have all the puzzle pieces to create a clear picture.

I stood there silently while she began to pace among the towering trees. "I can't believe this," she whispered, then her bright gaze snapped to mine. "Kenna…. she's dead, isn't she?"

I gaped at her like a fish, trying to figure out who this girl was and how the hell she knew everything she did. Just hearing someone else say 'Kenna' and 'dead' in the same sentence made my lungs feel like they were being squeezed. Repeatedly.

"I don't know what you think you know, but you need to keep your voice down," I threatened, peering over my shoulder back toward town, making sure we weren't followed and that no one was listening into this private conversation.

My wolf's power gathered forcefully, ready to be released when I called upon it. The stormy magic churned through me like a powerful gale, and the light breeze around us increased in intensity.

"Oh fuck a duck," she swore, and if it had been any other situation, her ridiculous curse would have made me laugh.

She blinked, then studied me closer. Her gaze flicked over me from head to toe in a way that tried to pick apart any differences from the many similarities I shared with my sister. Anything that would collaborate her theory.

"Everyone knows that the Stormborn Alpha fathered a set of twin girls. We all questioned what happened to the one he said had died. Kenna was always surprisingly silent about it. It wasn't a hard leap to make. None of us trust your father," she said coolly, weighing my reaction to the disparagement. She wouldn't get an argument from me. I held no loyalty to my father. The reminder he had tried to erase me from existence only reaffirmed that.

But talking to Olivia had brought up another concern. If people remembered the old history he'd tried to bury, pretending to be Kenna just got a lot more perilous.

How many others would see through my act and come to the correct conclusion just like this woman had?

Reading my concern, Olivia sighed. "Don't worry. I doubt others will draw the same conclusion. Kenna and I were nearly sisters. I did my research on her and the Storm-born pack. That's why it's fresh in my mind."

"Sisters?" I propped my hands on my hips, feeling protective over anyone else sharing a similar bond with her. *I* was her sister. This girl was…

It dawned on me.

OhmiGoddess. "You're not interested in Hunter, are you?" I winced at the look of disgust that wrinkled Olivia's face and realized I'd just hammered in the final nail in my coffin.

If Olivia had any doubt about who I was, I'd just obliterated it completely.

She knew. I'd practically handed her the truth on a silver platter, and there was nothing I could say or do to take it back.

Madison

Olivia's look of revulsion melted into a burst of inappropriate giggles. "Oh my Goddess. *Ew.* That's so gross. If I needed any proof of which twin you were, that was it." Sobering, she continued, "You honestly don't know who I am, do you?"

I dropped my arms in defeat. "I'm beginning to suspect."

Olivia chuckled. "I'm Hunter's little sister."

I replayed the hug between them the other day through a new lens, and the entire encounter became far more innocent than it had originally appeared.

"Goddess, you were jealous, weren't you?" Olivia

sounded surprised, reading me far too easily. "You like him." She looked flummoxed.

"I… uh… no." I tried to deflect. He might be incredibly hot and the tense chemistry between us might be new and fun, but I definitely didn't like him.

Yet, just like her brother, she saw far too much, and she wasn't having it.

"Oh, you definitely like him," she teased. Then, shaking her head, she sighed. "That's more than I can say for your sister. They never seemed to form a connection despite the years they were promised to each other. They were never a match."

Hearing that from Hunter's sister made my heart a little lighter, easing some of the guilt I had about feeling attracted to the broody alpha.

"No wonder Hunter is so out of sorts with you," she rambled on. "I've never seen someone get so under his skin."

I scoffed. "The only reason I'm under his skin is because he wants to figure out what's different about me."

"Maybe." Olivia had a secretive little smile tipping her lips that made me think she didn't agree, but I chose not to press matters. Let her think whatever she wanted, but we could barely be in the same room together without ripping each other apart. Or bursting into flames.

Olivia sobered some. "This is all too much to digest."

"Trust me, I know." Twisting my fingers together, I asked the question burning on my tongue. "Did Kenna tell you about me?" If she had, I needed to worry about who else she might have told.

"No. When I said we were nearly sisters, it was because she was going to mate my brother and literally make us family. Truthfully, we weren't that close." Olivia flushed with guilt over that little admission. "It wasn't just me, either. She never let anyone get too close. I don't think any of us truly knew her. I'm sure our packs being rivals didn't help. I only know about you because I *see* things." She shrugged like she hadn't just told me she was some sort of psychic.

"See things?" I couldn't help but press.

"It's my elemental gift." She smiled. "I see visions in smoke." Coming closer, she cupped her hands together and let fire erupt from her palms.

I squealed and reared back, worried my eyebrows were about to burn off. The heat was stifling in the warm air, but Olivia controlled the flames easily, burning them down to embers in her hands, letting the smoke build.

When it was thick enough, the smoke gathered and coalesced into a moving picture.

Gasping, I moved closer once more, transfixed by the figures the smoke created. A movie danced among the tendrils. Unlike the black wisps of the Shadow Beast, these were shades of grey, but they reminded me of him all the same. Especially when a miniature of his form emerged in the vision playing out before me.

Olivia's eyes had bled to the palest grey, nearly white, as she watched the scene unfold. The eyes of a seer.

"If I had known, I would have warned her." Regret exuded from Olivia's face, and I turned away before I had to watch the beast kill my sister for a second time. My heart couldn't take it. "I'm so sorry about her death, Madison. I don't always see things before they happen. I had this vision the day you arrived. It was too late by then to warn anyone. I thought…" She bit her lip as her eyes slowly bled back to their normal warm brown.

"You thought it was me—Madison—who died," I filled in.

"When I saw you get out of the car with Hunter, I thought you were Kenna. Goddess, you're identical. You even smell the same." She leaned in, taking another whiff.

"A bewitched perfume covers any of the subtle differences," I replied, waving off the insignificant details of my deception.

"You had me fooled until we started talking. Then it added up quickly." Olivia tucked her hair behind her ear and glanced at me with a gaze full of questions. "I just have to ask, Madison…" she placed her hand on my shoulder, and I stiffened. I still wasn't used to a lot of physical contact, and I didn't know how to handle this situation. She knew. I was completely at her mercy, and I hated that vulnerability. "What are you doing here, pretending to be Kenna?"

I shook my head and began to pace. Reaching for a branch, I snapped off a twig and began breaking it into smaller pieces. I had to give her something, but I couldn't tell her the truth. Not the whole truth, anyway.

Drawing to a halt, I faced Olivia and closed my fist around the twig, letting the wood bite into my palm, and decided to trust her with the parts of my story I could share without painting myself as a traitor and a threat to her pack. She didn't need to know just how dire my situation was. That was my cross to bear.

Instead, I focused on never coming into my elemental powers and how I'd been an embarrassment to my father. That I'd been shunned by the pack, forced to live in the shadows. Since she already knew what happened to Kenna, I glazed over that part, unable to relive the horror of that night again. So, I jumped to how my father sent me to the

Ember Wolves undercover to find her killer, which was only partly true, but she didn't need to know the rest.

The whole time, Olivia listened silently, stunned by my confessions. When I was done, she simply nodded and turned to face the trees for a long beat.

Turning back once she'd digested my story, she appeared calm and resolute. "I'll keep your secret," she murmured, and she could have knocked me down with a feather.

"You will?" I didn't know why I was questioning her when it was exactly the answer I'd wanted, but she'd shocked me. I wanted to understand this girl I hoped to call a friend.

"There are few things stronger than the love between siblings. I don't know if you know this, but I lost one brother already, a few years after my mother passed."

"Goddess," I murmured, my heart panging with sympathy. I understood her pain all too well. "I'm sorry."

Olivia nodded and sniffed. "He was only eighteen. His whole life was ahead of him. Hunter is all I have left, and I'd do anything for him. I understand your desire to avenge your sister's death. If I were in your shoes, I'd do the same."

"I don't know what to say. Thank you for helping me." Just saying those words, however, didn't feel like enough, and I vowed someday I'd repay her kindness.

"Honestly, it's the least I can do. I feel partly responsible." An exhaustion I couldn't explain came over Olivia, as though she'd worried herself sick over her vision to the point she didn't sleep.

"Hey." I reached out and gave her forearm a squeeze, hoping it was a reassuring gesture. "You don't control your visions."

"I know, but that doesn't change the guilt. Every power

comes with a price, and that's mine. I'm just really sorry, Madison. For all you've been through."

"Thank you." I swallowed back the emotion that perpetually attempted to choke me. Compartmentalizing was the only way I'd survive, so I shoved my grief down, locking it in a box I'd open later, when I was alone.

Blowing out a stress-relieving sigh, Olivia hooked her arm through mine and pulled me back along the path we'd taken into the woods like we were fast friends now. Maybe we were. I didn't have any other friendships to compare this to. After a few quiet moments, she broke the silence.

"I understand wanting to keep up appearances. Being Kenna probably gives you a better chance at catching the bastard who did this." Moving a low-hanging branch out of our path, we ducked by. "But it also makes you bait and places you in danger. That means my brother's in more danger too. Do you really think you can pull this off?"

"I'm going to try." *Goddess help me, but I'm going to try.*

"Well, I can help by showing you around so you don't feel so lost here among our pack. But there's one thing I don't understand. Why would your father tell everyone you were dead if you weren't? I understand you didn't come into your elemental powers, but that can't be the whole story."

I tensed, wondering how much more I should share with her. Olivia might claim to be on my side, but I couldn't trust her until she'd proven her loyalty. Her relationship with Hunter still made her a risk, but I also recognized how good it would be to have someone in my corner. Someone I could go to for help, or even just coffee and conversation. A true friend.

I took the leap and spit out my truth. "It wasn't just the powers. I was born without a wolf."

She shook her head, perplexed. "I don't get it. I can sense your wolf."

Fidgeting with the hem of my shirt, I detached myself from Olivia and took a step back. She paused, peering at me with a look of pure confusion.

Triple checking to make sure we still had our privacy, I called on my wolf, hoping she'd respond and emerge as she had this morning. Answering instantly, she pressed against my skin, then passed through me, her iridescent body slipping free. Her black fur glowed that same spectacular teal around the edges, even in the sunlight filtering down through the trees.

"That's… that's Kenna's wolf," she stammered, backing up a step. "How are you doing that?"

I rushed through an explanation, sharing everything I knew while my wolf stayed faithfully by my side. Other than Endora, the witch, calling me an Aether wolf, there wasn't much more to reveal. Still, it felt incredible to finally tell someone, to have a confidant. I just hoped she was worthy of this giant leap of faith.

She seemed to understand the gravity of my situation, and when I was done, I recalled my wolf just as easily, letting her sink back into my body as we became one soul again. Everytime I called upon her, the instinctual flex became more familiar.

Olivia stared at me with wide, stunned eyes, completely speechless. "That was…"—she shook her head rapidly—"fucking insane. I've never heard of the Aether element."

"Me either." I shrugged. "That's why I wanted to use your library."

"Well, if there's information to be found, it would definitely be here among the Ember Wolves. You know my dad's the High Alpha, and with that title comes certain privileges, one of which is having a library leagues beyond what the other packs have." Olivia's excitement over the challenge I presented quickly overtook her shock. Latching on to having a mystery to solve, she focused on what she could do to help.

Grabbing my hand, she tugged me back down the path, but the moment we stepped from the treeline, we came face to face with an angry enforcer.

"First this morning and then again after brunch. Do you have any idea how long I've been looking for you?" Tristan barked.

Olivia pasted on a cheeky smile. "Huh. I didn't expect you to strike out so soon. That's got to be a new record for you. We've been out here for a while but it wasn't *that* long."

"Or maybe he's already finished." My retort was rife with innuendo, and Olivia giggled.

"Oh, damn! I didn't consider that."

"Ha ha." Tristan looked less than amused and ran a hand through his dark hair. "I'm serious. You're not allowed to run off like that. And siccing those she-wolves on me was devious! Normally, I'd approve of such a tactic, but not when it's my ass on the line if anything happens to her...."

His focus slipped to me momentarily, and I saw all the things he'd left unsaid. Sure, he was tasked with my wellbeing, but he was also watching me because his alpha didn't trust me.

Olivia propped her hands on her hips. "First of all, she didn't run off. And secondly, she was with me. Nothing was going to happen to her."

"That's not the same thing as being—"

"Stalked?"

"I was going to say guarded."

Olivia rolled her eyes. "Seriously, Tristan, I know you've

sworn to follow orders from my brother, but as the High Alpha's daughter, I'm telling you that we don't need an escort." Olivia lifted her chin, staring up at the enforcer unwaveringly. I had a feeling she didn't throw her weight around often, which made me feel all kinds of warm inside. Olivia had just promised to keep my secrets, and here she was, already proving herself a friend. "We're within pack territory and we're only going to the library."

"It'll be boring watching us read books," I added for good measure.

Tristan paused for a long beat, studying us both. "Fine," he finally relented. "I'll tell Hunter she's with you this afternoon, but I expect to see you *both* at the pack run." He eyed me like I was a flight risk.

I wasn't, but the mention of the pack run sent a shiver of dread straight through me.

What I wouldn't give for a set of wings so I could fly away right about now.

Olivia smiled sweetly and agreed to Tristan's terms, and ten minutes later the two of us were in the library, surrounded by the scent of aged vanilla, earth, wood, and dust. Long tables for studying lined each side of the main walkway, and comfortable chairs, cushions, and bean bags lined the walls, tucked into every nook to make quiet reading havens. Shelves filled with all sorts of books spanned from floor to ceiling.

The tension of the day eased instantly, and together Olivia and I dove into our searching, using her credentials in the computerized systems to discreetly look for any information that could help.

Surprisingly, Olivia seemed as at home in the library as I did, and before long, we had a stack of books piled between us, skimming the texts for any mention of the missing tenth element.

We spent the afternoon researching, and before I knew it, my stomach was rumbling, demanding dinner. I ran my hand over my abdomen as I closed a thick history book that had been less than helpful.

"Anything?" I asked after reshelving what must have been my thirtieth book, just as empty handed as when we'd started.

Dust flew into the air as Olivia tossed hers back onto the stack on the table. She coughed and waved a hand in front of her face to ward off the particles threatening to make us sneeze.

"I'm starting to think the witch gave you false information. If I hadn't seen your gift with my own eyes, I'd be calling off this search. How is it that there's not one mention of a tenth element?" she whispered, keeping her voice low enough only I could hear her. Thankfully, we were pretty much alone in the library other than the old librarian who gave us squinty eyed looks from time to time.

Depositing the books on their respective shelves, I glanced around and noticed the changing light that bled through the windows as the sun dipped toward the horizon.

We were running out of time. The pack run was in a couple of hours, and I was no closer to answers than I'd been this morning.

"I don't know, but this was my last card to play." I sighed and ran my hands through my hair, closing my eyes and trying to relieve some of the stress from my shoulders by rolling them.

"There are some historical books my dad keeps locked up in his house. They're pretty old, and the paper's getting delicate. It's his way of trying to protect them." I perked up until I caught Olivia's sheepish expression. "I, uh, don't have the clearance to access them. I can get it," she said cryptically, like she could hack into her father's security systems and magically give herself the proper access. "Just… not tonight. If there's one rule to follow here in the Ember pack, it's that you don't bother the High Alpha on the night of a full moon." Olivia looked truly shaken, and I knew I couldn't pry or press her further.

I tried not to let disappointment swamp me "Thanks for trying," I offered, needing to switch tactics anyway and figure out how I was supposed to get through the run tonight. I only had hours left to come up with a plan.

"Tomorrow, okay?" she promised, and I nodded. "Why don't you come to my room to get ready for the run?" she questioned as we left the library and headed for the lodge. Lit up at dusk, it looked inviting and warm, but I couldn't sink into the comfort. Apprehension was a thick feeling that settled at the top of my stomach.

"There's just one more problem," I told her sheepishly.

"What?" Olivia's steps faltered as she focused on me.

"That back there"—I motioned to the woods behind us—"was my only party trick." My hopes sank as I admitted just how screwed I truly was. "I can't shift."

Madison

The magic of the moonlight overhead tingled against my skin as I tugged at the revealing hot-pink bandage top I was wearing, feeling like a fish among wolves as the pack gathered for the run.

"Are you sure this is going to work?" I asked Olivia for the hundredth time, unsure she'd be able to distract Hunter long enough for me to scurry into the woods and find a place to hide during the run.

"The plan is brilliant in its simplicity," she promised with surety. "Besides, Hunter adores me. He's very protective about those in his inner circle. He won't ignore me if I come to him with a problem."

"A made-up problem. Won't he be able to sniff out the lie?" From my experience, Hunter was observant and damn good at sussing out the truth.

"You'll be long gone by then. Just remember my instructions." Olivia waved off my concern, then sighed heavily. "You know, you could just tell him," she suggested, angling herself toward me and lowering her voice to a mere whisper. "It would be a shock, but he'd help you. I'm sure of it. Right now, he suspects the worst of you," she warned.

Smoothing my hands over the sides of my shorts, I shook my head. "No. I can't. He won't be nearly as gracious as you've been." Outing my secret to Hunter was a bad idea for so many reasons. Mainly because he'd never accept the watered-down version of the truth I'd given his sister.

"He's not a bad guy," Olivia pressed, and I nodded my understanding to appease her.

"I know." And honestly, I meant it. "I just need more time to figure everything out."

Olivia sighed but agreed. "Alright. I won't say anything. Just promise me you'll think about it."

"I will."

I didn't get to say another word before the bond between Hunter and I flared so strongly it demanded all my attention. Whatever Hunter and I had was magnetic, despite our mutual distrust, and I couldn't stop myself from scanning the crowd.

He moved sinuously through the gathering wolves, and I held my breath as I drank in the sight of him, hypnotized by the shifting muscles and the tattoos that seemed to come to life on his chest and arms. Wearing nothing more than a pair of sweats, he strode forward like a god among men, and I knew the moment he locked eyes on me.

A warm shiver raced through my body, and I gasped from the near physical sensation of his gaze raking over my bare skin. And there was a lot of it in this outfit. My shorts barely covered my ass and the bandage top I'd found in my closet crossed to cover my breasts before wrapping around the top of my torso, leaving the rest of my abdomen exposed.

Parting naturally, his pack allowed him and his entourage to pass, but he surprised me by moving toward me instead of taking his rightful place before them.

"I want my mate by my side when I start the run," he purred, holding his hand out and waiting for me to take it.

The haze of attraction I'd been floating in eased as I stared at his open palm like it was a snake ready to bite. Hunter's actions may have seemed like a romantic gesture to anyone listening, but underneath the sweet facade of his invitation was a challenge. Another move played in our political chess match.

Still, a thrill electrified me when I placed my fingers in his. Slightly rough and much larger than my own, his hand closed around mine and he brought it to his lips to whisper a possessive, branding kiss along the back.

Tugging me along with him, he settled me at his side and addressed his pack as their future Alpha. Wrapping his arm around my back while he spoke, he trailed his fingers lightly up and down the naked curve of my waist, thoroughly distracting me.

Glowering their displeasure, some of the nearby females sniffed their distaste in his choice of mate, clearly displeased I was the one who held his affections. If only they knew the truth. Each grazing touch on my skin was a promise that he wouldn't let me get away so easily this time.

Hunter had promised he'd unearth my secrets, and he

seemed to be a man of his word. I doubted he'd let me leave his side tonight, determined to see me shift, to scent my wolf once and for all—the one thing neither a shifter nor magic could fake.

The howls that rent the air at the end of his speech chilled me to the bone, and the pack began to strip. Magic filled the air as human forms gave way to wolven ones, and one by one his pack took off into the forest, chasing the call of the moon to run and hunt.

My wolf wanted to join them, yearning to be free to race among the trees, but even she understood the danger we were in collectively tonight and stayed in the background.

Guiding me into the shadows where we had a modicum of privacy, Hunter turned to me with a smirk and toyed with the edge of my top. "Should I help you strip so you can shift, *mate*?"

"I think I can manage," I sassed, and pushed against his chest to gain some extra space. He didn't budge.

Warm fingers delved under the band of my top and trailed slowly upward, pulling the fabric with it until it pooled under my breasts. Grazing his nose against my throat, Hunter inhaled deeply and growled.

"You're brave, I'll give you that." His voice had turned guttural from the nearness of his wolf. The moon pulled at the primal spirit inside of him, commanding him to shift beneath her pale rays. Close to giving in to her seduction, he visibly held himself back, though his tone was pure gravel as he staved off his shift. "If I didn't think you were here to wreak destruction, I might even admire your dedi-cation. But you're also naive if you think I don't see the changes in you. You're nothing like Kenna. You don't act like her, you don't talk like her, and there's something different in your scent, though you're trying your hardest to hide all of it from me. Why?" Nails shifted to claws that pressed into my back. "How far are you willing to go in your subterfuge?"

Another inch and my top was barely clinging to the bottom curve of my breasts.

"Just how much of yourself are you willing to surrender to me in this game of charades?" he pressed as he guided my top upward until it slid over the swell of breasts, exposing my bare flesh to his greedy gaze. His thumbs moved to strum over my taut nipples, and the spark of attraction I'd always felt for him flared into something so much more.

No one had ever touched me like this, and I was *burning*. A sharp spike of arousal had me squirming against Hunter, and he pushed me backward to pin me against a nearby tree. The rough bark against my spine only increased the sensation he had created in me. Inhaling deeply as the heady scent of my arousal perfumed the air, Hunter groaned, grabbed my ass, and lifted me off the ground in one swift motion. As if it were the most natural thing I'd ever done, I wrapped my legs around his waist and pressed deliciously closer. Warm and wet, he closed his mouth around one nipple and *sucked*.

"Oh, *Goddess*," I hissed and dug my hands into his dark hair. My pussy throbbed from the feel of the hard length beneath his sweats. The cotton did nothing to stop me from feeling every steely inch.

Instinctively, I rocked against him, needing more. Needing *him*.

The reasons I had for fleeing from him vanished with the next agonizing pull on my sensitive flesh, and my plan was forgotten when Hunter released a tormented groan.

A tremor vibrated through him as the moon reached its zenith, and I opened my eyes in time to catch his look of confusion as he pulled away.

"How are you denying your shift?" he grunted out, still fighting off the instinctive pull that called his wolf to the forefront. "Is this what you're hiding from me?"

Trepidation washed through me like a cold winter wave. But I couldn't deny it, so I said nothing. Truth was, the moon didn't make me feel anything, even with a wolf spirit. What did that mean?

"You're willing to bare yourself to me, but not your secrets?" Hunter sounded pissed by my silence, which only fueled my anger.

"You're the one who touched me, remember?" I shoved him, and this time he let me down. Feet back on solid ground, I rushed to readjust my top. Tucking my breasts away, I made sure the girls were out of sight from the looming shifter, the mood effectively killed

"Shift," he ordered, his shoulders bulking with the presence of his wolf. His amber eyes were flickering with angry fire. "Shift, *now*."

The order settled over me like a weighted blanket, stirring my wolf into action. She wanted to obey, and I felt the static of her magic under my skin as she rose to greet him. I gritted my teeth and leashed her, holding her back. I opened my mouth, ready to tell him where he could stick it when Olivia's cry of pain pierced through the trees.

"Hunter!" Tristan called loudly. "It's Liv."

For a second, panic filled me for my friend, until I realized this was most likely the plan we'd hatched, and common sense came rushing back with the force of a lightning bolt.

Goddess, what am I doing?

"Stay here," Hunter ordered. He looked torn on leaving me behind, but at Tristan's second shout, he let his shift overtake him and bounded away with one last warning growl, leaving me to sag against the tree sucking in a breath to clear my head.

Pressing a hand over my heart, I felt the rapid beat of my pulse.

I was never going to survive Hunter. But that wouldn't stop me from trying.

Pushing off the tree, I headed for the woods and took off at a dead sprint, using the opportunity Olivia gave me to put as much distance between the surly alpha and myself as I could get before he came looking for me, expecting me to be a wolf. Or before I decided to go after him and finish what we'd started.

✦) ❭ ❱ ❭ ● ❰ ❮ ❰ ❰ ✦

S plashing through a creek, I waded into the water and used it to cover my scent for at least a mile before emerging on the other side. Shivering in the light breeze that rustled the leaves overhead, I looked for a place to hide for a while, hoping I'd done enough to evade being tracked by Hunter for another hour or two.

I just needed to get past the strongest pull of the moon to make my story plausible. Once the moon started to descend, the need to be in our wolf forms lessened enough to allow us to shift back. If I could avoid detection until then, I could pretend I'd been happily running through the woods without his furry ass.

But if he caught me before then, there'd be no way to explain how I was still human.

I'd set up as many false leads as I could, rubbing my scent on trees and weaving a complex path before using the water to cover my trail. But Hunter was smart, and it wouldn't take him long to untangle my web.

Finding a small cave close to the edge of the woods, I reached for the magic I'd felt inside of me since I'd gained a wolf spirit. It tingled in my fingers and grew until I tightened my fist, calling it forth as I slowly opened my hand. A squeal of delight nearly burst from me at the teal electricity that danced in my palm like a zap of lightning.

Using it to illuminate the cave, I deduced it was empty and crawled inside. Playing with my new magic, I let it jump between my fingers for a few minutes before snuffing it out and plunging myself back into the darkness.

Satisfied that I'd done my best, I tried to relax.

Staying close to the lodge meant Hunter would find me faster, but I couldn't bring myself to stray too far with the threat of the Shadow Beast keeping me on edge.

I doubted the Shadow Beast would make an appearance with so many wolves in the forest tonight, but he'd been brazen once, and I was already taking too many chances.

My thoughts drifted as I thought back to the wolves I'd seen shift before Hunter had dragged me off. I'd done my best to catalog their features, but none of them were dark as pitch without markings.

Honestly, I needed a plan to find my sister's killer before my father started pressing me for information on the Ember Wolves. I'd only been here a few days—nearly all of which I'd spent in my room—and already time was closing in on me.

Lost in my thoughts, I didn't notice the silence that had descended on the forest until the hair on the back of my neck pricked.

That keen sense of being watched crept along my skin, and my wolf growled menacingly in my head. The blur of a dark figure in the shadows drew me to the edge of the cave. Suddenly, a shadowy wisp dove for me from between the trees, circling me.

Crying out, my magic rose in a rush. My wolf yipped urgently, and I sent an instinctual blast of lightning into the smokey tendril, satisfied when I heard the eerie hiss it released as it retreated.

"Holy Goddess," I gasped after a few minutes, realizing I was alone again and the shadowy *thing* wasn't coming back. My heart galloped in my chest as I scurried from my hiding place, deciding Hunter was the lesser of two evils.

Hurrying out of the woods, I tried to stop my jittery hands by brushing them nervously along my shorts, but I was thoroughly shaken.

My muscles were already trembling when a brown wolf with red markings and equally red, glowing eyes intercepted my path with a low growl, making my steps falter. A deep warning rumbled from her, and the she-wolf bared her teeth at me.

"Really? You too?" I threw my hands out at my side, truly over the obstacles of this evening. I wanted to go climb into my bed, curl up under the comforter, and forget all the bad things that were stacked against me. Maybe with a pint of ice cream and a chick flick that would give me a reason to cry out my stress, fear, and frustration into my pillow. What I didn't need was a fight.

The wolf just lifted her head and scented me. Brown fur

raised on her haunches, and she released a long, low howl. It was one I'd heard before. A battle cry. A challenge.

"Kenna!" a female voice called, and I dared a glance to see Nova running toward me, pulling her shirt back on. Just behind her was Dean in a pair of sweats, sprinting past Nova to try and reach me.

The brown wolf took my distraction as an opportunity and snapped at me. Instinctively, I used the elemental magic my wolf pressed toward me to retaliate, blasting my attacker with an electric zap that knocked her back.

I glanced down at my hands in shock. *Hot damn!*

Some of the female wolf's coat was singed, the scent of burnt fur making my nose crinkle. Fangs gnashing together, she snarled and bared her teeth in an open threat.

Out of the shadows bled more wolves, circling me slowly.

Dean skidded to a stop before me and growled in warning, blocking me with his broad body. The man was tall and muscled, and seeing him in action easily reinforced the inkling I'd gotten when I first met him—he was one of Hunter's enforcers.

Grabbing onto his arm, I used him as a shield, recognizing that the females wouldn't attack him. He was a trusted member of the pack whereas I was the outsider.

"What's happening?" I asked, needing to know what the hell was going on. Whatever it was, wasn't good.

"You don't know?" Nova cut her way through the wolves and came to a stop on my other side. "They're challenging you for your position as Hunter's Luna." Nova growled, warning the others to stay away.

Dean plastered himself to my other side, and together they squished me between them, leading me toward the lodge.

"We need to get you back to Hunter's apartment," Dean warned.

"I don't understand," I said, a note of hysteria in my voice. "I thought Hunter said they wouldn't challenge me."

"They shouldn't." Nova snarled at the wolf who'd started this shit show. Now every bitch in the pack seemed ready to take a bite out of me. "You've already competed in the Trials, proven yourself as an alpha female, and earned your rank in the pack."

Except I hadn't.… Kenna had.

"The High Alpha chose *you* to be Hunter's mate," Nova emphasized. "The moon must be making the alpha females extra ornery tonight to go against his wishes and take on such a high-ranking female like you. All around, it's not a smart move."

I swallowed. *How the hell are you going to get out of this?*

"Get back, Emery," Nova commanded the brown female wolf, stepping up to block our path. "You don't want to do this."

Emery partially shifted in a tangle of fur, hair, and skin, just enough to allow her gravelly voice to shine through.

"I challenge you for Luna. Submit or die," she bit out, and reverted back to her animalistic form.

My wolf rose, ready to fight, and I felt the electric tingle of a storm brewing in the air as a wave of her power burst from me.

I saw the faintest teal hue around my fingers, an early warning that my wolf was about to do her little magic trick, slip from my body, and reveal our abnormal bond.

"Dammit." Dean winced. "If she'd challenged you for anything else… Kenna, as an enforcer, I can't interfere with a formal challenge."

I nodded, even though I didn't want to. I understood

the repercussions. While a wolf couldn't challenge another wolf simply to improve their rank or settle a dispute, anyone could challenge an Alpha, Beta, Luna, or Alpha-heir for their position and title. I may not be Luna yet, but if I couldn't defend myself and the role I was primed to step into, then in the packs' eyes, I didn't deserve it.

"I'll call Hunter," Nova promised. "He'll want to be here for this." They both gave me a sympathetic look before disengaging.

"No! Wait," I begged.

"Don't worry. I know you can kick her ass," Nova reassured.

Ha. Yeah… Right.

"You got this." Nova sent me an encouraging yet heavy glance before leaving me alone in a pack of bloodthirsty wolves.

The image of my wolf was clear in my mind, her beautiful black fur, her lethal teeth, the gorgeous sky-blue markings on her fur. She wanted to shift, to be let free, but I didn't know how to embody her, and releasing her spirit for the world to see was a last resort.

Magic filled me as I readied for the attack.

Staring down death, I thought my life would flash before my eyes, but I saw nothing but the snapping of jaws as the brown she-wolf lunged straight for me.

EIGHTEEN

Madison

The bite of lethal canines tearing into my shoulder made me cry out, and my wolf snapped viciously from her cage in my mind.

Shoving my hands into the female trying to take me to the ground, I let my power out on instinct. Lightning zapped from my fingers, shocking her until her jaws unlocked from my flesh and she fell back with a high-pitched whine.

I barely had a moment to revel in my small won victory before another wolf, this one stark white, bounded into the makeshift ring and bared her teeth at me.

My eyes widened. "What are you doing? Challenges are

supposed to be one on one." I hissed in pain as I pressed a hand to my wounded shoulder. My arm didn't want to work, the bite having shredded part of the muscle, causing nerve damage.

Blood slicked from the injuries, staining the shreds of my pretty pink top. The wolves around me inhaled, and I cursed. No wonder they were ganging up on me. Besides the moon heightening their aggression, their instincts must be telling them something was off about my scent. Given my magicked perfume, they probably wouldn't make the leap and figure out who I truly was, but it wouldn't matter if I didn't survive.

This is going to be a bloodbath.

I stood a decent chance of surviving against one wolf, maybe, but two? It was a death sentence.

Submit or die.

If I submitted and lost my place as Hunter's Luna, I'd be dead anyway. My father would see to it. He'd hunt me ruthlessly to the ends of the earth for ruining this alliance for him.

Another, and then another joined the fight, circling me, sizing me up. I was the prey to their predator, the bunny to their wolf. I was only human… at least, mostly. I didn't stand a chance.

"Hey!" Nova yelled from the sidelines. "You can't ambush her like that."

I hadn't had many friends, but I decided I liked having someone in my corner.

Another female shifted partially and answered, her voice straight out of a horror movie. "Enemy."

Every wolf had a place within the pack, and their ranking helped keep peace and order. Without it, challenges would be a daily struggle, and the bloodshed and lives lost would be tremendous.

And these wolves? They didn't recognize me as Hunter's mate, because I technically wasn't. I was a lone wolf, a rogue, a trespasser, and I was pretty much free game until I earned a place among them myself.

Goddess, why hadn't I thought of this? I'd just assumed Kenna's rank would have transferred with her wolf, but I knew nothing about our bond, knew nothing about what being an Aether wolf meant.

Without understanding how my powers worked, the odds were stacked against me.

Submit or die.

I held onto those words, letting the seriousness of my situation fuel me as the wolves leapt.

Claws tore into my flesh, slicing it to ribbons. The thick scent of copper immediately stung my nose and I screamed from the searing pain, my mind blinded by agony. I couldn't think. Couldn't do anything but react on impulse. My wolf took over, guiding my actions. She was a lethal ball of energy inside me, helping me any way she could. My hands shook, and she lent me her strength. I felt my senses heighten with her nearness, and she shared her energy. Harnessing her power, I sent one wolf flying across the clearing to land with a crash.

Fire licked from the bite of another who had latched on to my ankle. Literal fire.

I hissed and sent a bolt of lightning into her snout, wounding her badly enough that she released her hold.

Storm clouds gathered in the midnight sky, blocking out the full moon, my element responding to my pain. Fat raindrops fell from the sky to splash onto my cheeks and mix with the tears I couldn't hold back.

Everything hurt. My thoughts were a blur of excruciating pain and the overwhelming need to survive. Every gash, bite, and raw, open wound stung with my movements, but I didn't slow. I wouldn't stop fighting back while there was still breath left in my body. The vast array of injuries I'd sustained all burned like they'd been set on fire. I forced air in and out of my lungs as I dodged attacks, defended myself with magic I was still growing used to, and fought off the wolves persistent enough to reach me. My wolf led me every step of the way, her reflexes making me faster, her intuition guiding me through every step.

Claws raked down my back, cutting through my clothing like butter. And still, I fought, refusing to give up, my stubbornness finally paying off for once.

Calling on the Storm element that belonged to my wolf, I harnessed the wind like I'd grown up seeing others in my pack do, and sent a gust barreling into my attackers. They fell back, fighting against the gale to reach me again.

Emery growled, her eyes glowing red as she stalked toward me. Then she barked, loud and strong. A ball of fire erupted from her mouth and flew straight at me.

I barely had time to gasp before my skin was sizzling.

On a sob, I fell to my knees and tried to pat out the flames, the rain falling in harder torrents to aid me.

Nova leapt to my side, and with her hands outstretched, she recalled the flames. Shifting, she jumped in to defend me.

It wasn't enough.

Blood slicked down my legs and across my arms, and soon the wolves piled on, taking me to the ground with snapping teeth and lethal muscle. Making myself as small as possible was my last hope, and I covered my head as best I could, blocking my neck from their powerful jaws.

Submit or die.

Don't submit, I pleaded with myself, but the cry was on my tongue as the world faded at the edges from too much blood loss.

An image of Hunter flitted through my mind, wavering too much to hold onto, slipping through my grasp like fine sand. Then, I pictured Kenna.

Would she be waiting for me on the other side?

I hoped I'd see her again as dizziness swamped me and my stomach rolled from the pain.

A mighty roar pressed down on the wolves, and the snarls and angry growls of the females fell away.

Rain plinked against my skin as they retreated, and I rolled onto my back, staring up at the grey storm clouds. Droplets of water fell toward the earth in a beautiful dance, washing my blood away in tiny rivulets where they dripped down my body.

Another loud growl filled with rage and possession silenced the world around me.

Vision swimming, I couldn't see anything beyond me until Hunter's stricken face appeared in my line of sight.

"Holy, fuck. Kenna!" He dropped to his knees, his hands flitting over me, not sure where he could touch me without causing me more pain.

"Hunter," I coughed, blood filling my mouth.

Something about choking on my own blood registered just how badly I was hurt. I was dying. I was sure of it.

"Hunter," I tried again, deciding I didn't want to die holding on to my secret. "Not," I slurred, needing to tell him he was right. I wasn't who he thought I was. *Not Kenna.* "Not, K—" was as far as I made it.

"Shhh," he shushed, stopping my confession. "Don't fucking talk. Save your energy."

Strong arms scooped me off the ground, and he cradled me against his chest.

"Anyone who dares to rebel against my mate dares to rebel against me," Hunter boomed, sounding like an angry god among mortals. "What happened here wasn't a challenge, it was a massacre. Touch my woman again, and you'll be exiled."

For a wolf, banishment—a life without a pack—was the worst kind of punishment.

It didn't escape me that he hadn't used Kenna's name, which meant the command actually applied to me—Madison. He didn't trust me, yet, he defended me all the same. His protection settled over me like a warm blanket, and only then did I relax into his arms and let him support me fully.

Exhausted and dizzy, I faded in and out of consciousness as Hunter summoned help and carried me away from the pack.

Everything remained black until I was set down on a soft surface. Working to pry my eyes open, I saw Hunter, Tristan, and Olivia all hurrying to attend to my wounds.

"She's injured pretty badly," Tristan said, eyes flicking to mine briefly. "I don't know, man."

Dainty fingers pressed into my neck. "Her pulse is thready. Hunter, I don't think Kenna's going to make it."

"Mads," I tried to correct her, my voice a raspy, incomplete whisper. Her wide eyes flew to mine, and I knew she was trying to keep my secret.

"The fuck she isn't," Hunter swore. "Out," he barked.

Tentatively, Olivia and Tristan pulled back. They both moved to the door, but Olivia paused, her gaze locked on mine until Tristan pulled her away and shut the door, leaving me alone with the alpha who'd occupied my life these past few days.

"I need you to shift," Hunter pressed urgently. "Shift now, Kenna."

I shook my head, the movement much smaller than I wanted it to be. My energy was gone, leached away from my run in the woods, the fight, pain, loss of blood, and the power I'd exerted. The spirit of my wolf was quiet in my chest now, a phantom compared to the presence she usually was.

In this weakened state, I didn't think I could reach her, or that I'd figure out how to manage a shift before my life faded. Death was so close, its cold grasp already reaching for me.

"Don't do that." Hunter shook my shoulders gently, jarring me out of my morbid thoughts. "Don't give up so goddamn easily. Where's the girl who's been driving me crazy? Huh? Where's my fiery mate? Goddess. *Fuck*. You drive me so insane I can't even fucking think straight."

Climbing onto the bed, he surprised the hell out of me when he gently straddled my waist. His weight dipped the mattress, but he was careful to keep it off of me when he settled over my body. This close I could see the wolf tattoo inked front and center on his chest. Angry, teeth bared, it was a fearsome sight to behold, beautiful in its rage, frozen in time.

I wanted to reach for it, trace my fingers over the outline just once, but I couldn't make my arms lift on command.

Hunter placed his hand just above my left breast. If I'd been stronger, I would have made some snarky comment about how he owed me dinner for how many times he'd made it to second base with me tonight. Somehow, I was less mad about everything that had happened between us earlier. Reaching for my hand, he brought it up and settled it over his heart, holding it against a firm pec.

Goddess, he's ripped.

The connection between us flared to life stronger than ever, and Hunter's amber eyes glowed with russet fire.

His voice was deep and guttural with his next command. "Shift."

Something inside me stirred.

"Shift," he ordered again, infusing it with the power of an alpha.

My wolf responded, drawing toward his voice.

"That's it. Good girl," he purred. "Shift, Kenna."

The command was lost with the wrongness of the name.

I felt my wolf retreat a little, and with her went the hope I'd somehow survive this. If I couldn't shift, even in my own abnormal way, the possibility that Hunter could mend me dissipated. I remembered what he'd said the other day about being able to command my wolf and channel our combined powers into healing. I didn't know how any of it worked. I'd never had powers or a wolf before.

Hunter was my only chance of living through this nightmare, but first I had to trust him with my biggest secret and hope he didn't end me himself.

"Mads," I whispered hoarsely, struggling to get each word out. "My name… is Mads," I told him.

He stared at me incredulously for a long moment, and I shared in his turmoil through our mate bond before he shut it down. Then something hardened in his fiery gaze.

"Shift, Mads," he ordered harshly.

My wolf ripped from my chest in blinding, brilliant teal only to curl up on top of me and stare directly at her mate.

"Fucking hell," Hunter exclaimed, glaring at me in shock. The condemnation spelled out across his face left little doubt that he recognized my sister's onyx wolf.

And yet, I wasn't her.

The muscle jumped in his jaw from the grit of his teeth. Unspoken questions hung between us.

Shaking his head, he came to a decision and moved my hand from his chest, placing it overtop of his, sandwiching my hand between his own.

"Thank you," I said on a shaky breath.

Thank you for trusting me enough to heal me instead of letting me die.

"Don't thank me yet," he told me darkly. "This is going to hurt."

A heat so intense I could barely breathe slowly moved over my body as he twined our powers together, only soothed by the chilled feeling of a cold spring rain washing away the agony in its wake. Slowly, my body knit itself back together with excruciating pain—muscle meeting muscle, flesh meeting flesh.

The last thing I saw before darkness claimed me was the hard press of Hunter's mouth and the disapproval radiating off of him in waves.

Madison

The first thing I noticed upon waking up was the rich scent of Hunter. It permeated everything. The pillows. The sheets. The incredibly soft mattress. Either I was dead and this was my version of the afterlife, or I'd somehow been brought to Hunter's room.

The second thing I noticed was how sore I was when I pushed myself up in bed to investigate. Blearily, I ran a hand over my eyes, trying to shake off the sleep clinging to me and find my bearings, but even that small movement hurt. I felt like I'd run a million miles and then been steamrolled. I stretched and groaned from how tight my muscles were. The bedding pooled around my waist, revealing an unfamiliar t-shirt that also smelled intoxicatingly of Hunter, though my signature now mixed with his.

What the hell?

Confusion warred with my rising nervousness. I wasn't wearing any pants. Or underwear. The sheets were silky smooth on my skin.

What happened last night? Did I sleep with Hunter? And if I did, why couldn't I remember any of it?

Smudges of dried blood stained my skin, and the moment I caught sight of them, everything came flooding back to me. The attack. Telling Hunter the truth. Him healing me.

Oh, shit. This was so much worse than a drunken night and an accidental fuck, even for a virgin. The power that lived inside of me thrummed to the surface. Lightning zapped over my skin with my jolt of anxiety, and the air seemed to charge with electricity.

I jumped from the bed, taking note of the gleaming red numbers on Hunter's alarm clock. It sat on the bedside table along with an open book, face down. I was surprised to note it was a fantasy novel full of adventure and magic. Beside it was an empty coffee mug. A chair was positioned next to the bed, and I noted the bloodied towels that spilled out of the hamper.

Had Hunter… taken care of me?

The scents of Olivia and Tristan hung lightly in the air, but they were several hours old. It had to have been Hunter. His signature was the only one still fresh, still strong, and it was more than just being in his room. He'd been in here as recently as an hour ago. I was sure of it.

Taking a deep breath, I got my magic under control, and found myself rubbing absently at my chest, directly over the spot I could feel the mate bond. I couldn't explain it, but it felt stronger. Visceral. Through it, I could read Hunter's anger, skepticism, and radiating disillusionment.

My feet barely made a sound as I padded to the door and tentatively cracked it open.

Heart in my throat, I slipped through and spotted Hunter at the stove. Muscles tensing, he sensed me behind him. I stood awkwardly, toying with the hem of the t-shirt that brushed against my naked thighs. A shirt I hadn't put on myself.

Shuffling on my feet, I questioned my sanity. I must have hit my head during the attack to be standing in the living room ready to have this confrontation with Hunter when I wasn't wearing any panties.

Goddess help me. *Say something,* I prompted myself, pepping myself up for what I needed to do. Hunter knew the truth about me, and I didn't know what his reaction was going to be. He hadn't killed me yet, and he'd had the chance to let me die. So that was positive. Right?

Open your mouth and fucking apologize.

Instead, I said, "Thank you." It came out as a rasp, and I realized how dry my throat was after several hours of being unconscious. According to the clock, it was after four in the afternoon. "How long was I out?" I asked anyway, wanting to make sure it was only hours and not days.

Without answering, Hunter shifted the pan on the stove, forked a steak, and slapped it on a plate. Topping it with herb butter, he turned and set it in front of me, placing a fork on the plate and pushing it across the island. Filling a tall glass with ice and water, he set that beside it, then leaned back against the counter, eyeing me with a blank expression.

No, not blank. Hidden. Shuttered.

Crossing his arms, he arched a brow and gave one deep

nod toward the food.

A peace offering? Unlikely.

I shuffled closer and pulled a bar stool away from the counter, planting my ass on it. The shirt rode up, barely covering the essentials.

The steak smelled mouthwatering, and my wolf perked up for the first time since I had opened my eyes. She was ravenous. Healing took a lot out of us, so I gave in. Grabbing the cup, I guzzled the contents. The coolness soothed my throat and I followed it up with food. A blush stained my cheeks as my stomach growled loudly when I forked the steak, lifted the whole thing, and took a bite.

Hunter looked amused; the kind of amused when someone looked down their nose at you.

I shouldn't care, but I bristled. How else was I supposed to eat the steak without proper utensils? "Can I have a knife?" I asked and smiled saccharinely.

"Are you going to stab me with it?" Hunter questioned with an angry, yet sarcastic, tilt on his stupidly sexy lips.

I arched my own brow. "Shouldn't I be asking *you* that?"

"I do have plenty of motivation," he growled darkly but reached for the knife block beside the stove and handed one to me. "You turned out to be exactly what I thought. A fucking traitor."

"And yet, you saved me." Fingers tightening on the knife, I sawed away at my steak. "Why go through the trouble if you hate me so much?" I used the fork to shove a bite into my mouth like a fucking lady. My wolf whined, seeing the utensils as a hindrance that slowed down how fast I could fill my stomach.

You really are hangry when you're not fed regularly. I directed that sassy thought straight toward my wolf, who chuffed, not denying it in the least.

Chewing, I glared at Hunter.

He tilted his head, studying me with those perceptive amber eyes. They were dark today, almost honey brown. "Maybe I want to keep my enemies close. Maybe I'm intrigued by you and what the fuck you're doing here."

I shrugged cavalierly. "Curiosity killed the cat."

A growl rumbled viciously in his chest. Prowling around the island, Hunter brushed against me on his way past, leaning in as he warned me. "In case you haven't heard, Goldilocks"—he tugged a lock of my wavy hair—"I'm not some fucking cat. I'm the big bad wolf."

I swiveled my stool around as Hunter moved to the windows. "Is that a threat?"

"It's a reminder."

He braced his forearm against the glass and peered out. Framed by the glow of the late afternoon sun streaming in through the pane, he cut a stunning figure. He was shadowed against the scattered, golden rays spread out over the forest as he surveyed his territory. The master of all.

I studied the tattoos I could see on his arms and the back of his neck, trying to make out the images among the tapestry of inked art. All the while, I wondered what was running through his mind.

The silence stretched until I felt compelled to break it. "My name's not Goldilocks. It's—"

"Mads. Madison," he murmured, his voice a low, intimate rumble. Or at least, that's how it felt to hear him say my name for the first time. My idiotic heart nearly flipped in my chest from hearing it in his deep timbre. The way he said it…. A shiver raced down my spine.

Why did I react to him like this? He hated me, and that was supposed to be mutual. We were enemies for fuck's sake. But for some reason, I was inexplicably drawn to

Hunter Weston. It defied logic, and I gritted my teeth, hating myself for my attraction. I wasn't some weak-minded heroine in a story who swooned on every page.

I was just a girl trying to survive, and despite Hunter healing me and saving my life, he was bad for my health. The emotional whiplash alone every time we had a conversation was enough to make my head hurt.

"Did Olivia tell you?" I finally rasped, clearing my throat and taking another sip of water.

"You told me first, but yes. Olivia may be your friend, but she's my sister first and foremost. Her loyalty lies with me. She filled me in on everything once your secret was out."

"So you know that Kenna is… is…" Why couldn't I say it? I fidgeted with the hem of my shirt, picking at it mindlessly.

"If you're trying to tell me my mate is dead"—Hunter turned, shoving his hands into the pockets of his slacks, appearing far too casual for the harshness of his words—"then, yes. Olivia showed me her vision and told me who, and what, you are. Though I doubt she has the whole story." The look he leveled on me was accusatory and searching.

My heart squeezed hearing him call my sister his 'mate,' which was ridiculous since that's what she was. What she'd been. I opened my mouth, then closed it again. What could I say? The truth—the full truth—wasn't an option. How could I explain what I was doing here? What my father wanted me to do? Keeping secrets was already growing tiring.

"Olivia is far more innocent than I am, Madison. I saw the wolf in her vision. I can only guess you suspect the Ember Wolves killed your sister. I wager your father wrongfully believes it was *me* or, at least, someone in my pack."

My gaze flew to his, my blue eyes wide for a split second before I schooled my features. But that blink, that moment in time, was all Hunter needed to see the truth.

He cursed, and his eyes blazed with fury at the unspoken implications, but anything he was about to say was cut off with a sharp knock on the door.

"Not now," Hunter called, but Olivia didn't heed his demand and hesitantly peeked her head around the door. Catching sight of me, a smile blossomed across her lips.

"Mads!" She rushed toward me, kicking the door closed behind her as she balanced a large box in her hands. "You're awake. Thank fuck. You were out forever. I know it takes time to heal and regain our strength after being injured like that, but holy shit, girl. You scared me!"

"I'm sorry?" I laughed weakly as she discarded the box on the counter and launched herself at me.

Apparently, we really were friends, and while I wasn't used to exuberant hugs from… well, anyone except Kenna… her friendship was welcomed. Especially because of the conversation she'd barged in and interrupted. I hugged her back and then she straightened and faced her brother, who watched on with an exasperated expression.

"Do I really need to tell you not to hug the enemy?" Hunter warned and ran a hand through his hair. His words were condescending, but behind them was only love and worry for his little sister, something I could respect and understand. His boots shifted on the hardwood, and he eyed the two of us.

"Really?" Olivia snarked back. "Do *I* need to remind *you* that everything isn't always black or white? People come in all shades of grey, Hunter. Live a little."

"We were in the middle of an important conversation, Liv," Hunter stated, and it was clear he expected his sister to leave.

Olivia sobered. "It's going to have to wait." Swallowing hard, her voice was stark. "Dad summoned us. And, um, this is for you," she told me. Her fingers drummed on top of the box she had deposited on the counter.

"Me?" I was surprised, wondering what it was and who it was from.

"I'd like to take credit, but it's from the High Alpha." Olivia and Hunter exchanged a weighted look and she reached into her back pocket, retrieving a fancy invitation and handing it to Hunter, who crossed to us.

"What is it?" I questioned, my gaze bouncing between the two of them. There was something they weren't telling me.

"Thank you, Olivia." Hunter dismissed her, and with a weak smile, she took the hint and left, throwing an encouraging "see you soon" before the door clicked shut, closing me in with my enemy once more.

Moving closer, Hunter braced one hand on the counter and leaned in, bending slightly at the waist until we were nearly eye level. His amber eyes burned with serious intent. "This is your last chance to leave before you're in too deep. Whatever it is you think you have on my pack, you're wrong. I may be a dangerous asshole, but I'd never lay a hand on your sister, or any woman, for that matter."

"I know," I whispered, giving him that much of my truth. "I don't think you killed her."

A quiet tension worked through him, as if he hadn't expected me to say that. "But you still think someone in my pack did."

My encounters with those dark shadows played through my memories.

I glanced away, but Hunter captured my chin, bringing my face back to meet his, holding me steady under his scrutiny. I narrowed my eyes.

"You're not as good a liar as you think you are. I see through you. And my father will, as well, if he spends any significant time with you. Whatever your father sent you here to do, you're treading in dangerous waters. Go home," he commanded, tone full of warning.

Anyone else would have missed the note of pleading. The small glitter of worry in his eyes. The care behind the domineering order. As much as he wanted me to believe otherwise, Hunter wasn't as big a dick as he made himself out to be.

"I can't," I whispered.

"Can't? Or won't?" Hunter's grip tightened a fraction, his eyes burning into me as he studied my reaction. My response.

"Both."

My father would hunt me down and kill me if I left, and he'd make my death painful for spiting him. I also couldn't leave Kenna's killer to roam free, with no repercussions for what he'd done. The Shadow Beast was here, among the Ember Wolves, whether he was one of them or not. It may be dangerous, but I wouldn't give up my only lead.

The problem was, I had no idea how I was going to expose the killer once I found him, or how I'd make him pay. I didn't have the strength or skill to fight back against a wolf shifter, which had become painfully obvious when I'd been attacked by Emery and the other she-wolves. The elemental Storm powers I'd inherited from my sister were untrained. I used them on a hope and prayer, trusting my instincts and the guidance of my wolf. And I didn't know the first thing about my Aether element. I was wholly underqualified on every level except for my determination and the need that burned in my heart for revenge. For retribution.

Besides, it was possible the Shadow Beast would follow me wherever I went, stalking me like a wraith in the darkness.

I needed a plan. That was clear. And for now, it didn't involve walking away.

Seeing the truth in my eyes, Hunter released me and stepped back. His disappointment in my decision descended between us, covering me like a blanket.

"This conversation isn't finished, but we're out of time. If you insist on being bullheaded, if you're going to play games, then it's time you realize what you're up against."

Hunter shifted his hold on the invite between two of his fingers and flicked it onto the countertop before storming off. "Be ready to go at seven."

Releasing a pent-up breath when he disappeared into his room, I slid the invitation closer. As I read the first line, dread built in the pit of my stomach, making me nauseous.

You are cordially invited to dine with High Alpha Weston.

Inside the gift was a beautiful red dress. The material was low cut and the bodice was fitted while the skirt flared delicately with slits up each side that were sure to show off a lot of skin. And I scolded myself.

Hunter was right. This was probably a mistake. But I'd made my bed, and now I had to lie in it. In satin, apparently.

TWENTY

Madison

The dress was precariously low and my legs flashed with every step I took, but how uncomfortable I felt in my revealing—albeit gorgeous—gown for the evening was nothing compared to the tension that crept through the foyer as we entered the High Alpha's private residence.

The mountain home was rustic but opulent, everything from the tall ceilings to the expensive art a clear show of High Alpha Weston's wealth, power, and prestige. I expected nothing less, and I slowed to take it in. Feeling like a fish out of water, I sucked in a deep breath, then released it slowly. The High Alpha's power lingered in the air like a bad smell, oppressive even when he wasn't in the room.

My wolf growled. She didn't like being here either. I didn't blame her. I was literally in the den of my pack's most formidable rival.

You've got this. Just play it cool and don't let your nerves show. You don't want them to smell your fear.

Feeling more centered, I moved to follow after Olivia and Tristan, who'd also been invited to this impromptu dinner party. It made sense Olivia was here. She was a Weston, the High Alpha's daughter. And I had a feeling Tristan was never far from Hunter, as a friend, but more importantly, as his beta. Still, I had no idea what this dinner was about, why we had been summoned, or what to expect.

My dress swished around my legs when I moved toward the hallway they'd disappeared down, but Hunter gripped my arm to stop me.

I didn't turn around. Everything about him unnerved me, and this far across enemy lines, I needed to keep my head—and my heart—in the game. I couldn't focus on how complicated everything was between us when I worried I'd blow my cover and fuck everything up.

Invading my space, his nose skimmed into my hair and his hard chest brushed against my back. The loosely gathered strands of my casual updo ruffled as he murmured into my ear. Words quiet and tone low, he made sure only I could hear him. "Be careful tonight. My father isn't known for his leniency." A shiver raced down my spine from the deep rumble of his voice but, also, from his warning.

As if I needed that extra shot of fear to chase the nerves and anxiety I was already swallowing. And yet....

"There you go, surprising me again," I whispered back, turning my face into him as he loomed over my shoulder.

Our lips were only inches apart. I could have brushed the corner of his mouth all too easily. "I thought you'd want me exposed. Locked up or sent home."

As tempting as it was being this close to him, I went to move out of his grip, but I only made it one step before Hunter pulled me around to face him.

A wry expression twisted his lips and his finger twirled a lock of my hair that hung loosely to frame my face. He chose to ignore my accusation. "If you think that's all he'd do to you if he found out your secrets, you're naive, *Sweetheart*," Hunter stressed the pet name.

This close to danger, he couldn't use my actual name, but it seemed he didn't want to call me 'Kenna' any longer, for which I was grateful. Every time I heard her name, it lashed at my heart. It didn't help that it also made me feel like the imposter I was. This wasn't my life, and I wouldn't forget that.

The problem was, I didn't exactly have a life to go back to either.

If I survived, that was. Because Hunter wasn't wrong. His father was dangerous and posed a threat. He absolutely couldn't learn my secrets.

But I wouldn't cave to Hunter's intimidation tactics. I narrowed my gaze.

"Another threat? I'm beginning to think you're all bark and no bite."

It irritated me that he only raised a brow in return, challenging. Almost imperious.

He caressed the silken strands of my hair between two of his fingers. "There you go with that naivety again. You know what I'm saying is true. You're treading in dangerous waters. Shockingly, despite some of your questionable decisions, I hadn't pegged you as dimwitted." Tugging the lock of hair for effect, he released me, straightened, and stepped away. "For your sake, I hope you don't prove me wrong tonight."

He left me gaping after him as he left the room. I'd never been so insultingly complimented in all my life.

"The fucking nerve…" I muttered. Composing myself, I hurried after Hunter and the others, my heels—also known as torture devices—clicking gracelessly against the polished hardwood floors.

I only slowed when a strange, muffled tone sounded through the hallway. It took me a moment to open the small clutch attached to my wrist, realizing it had come from the sleek phone nestled inside. Using it hadn't been part of my plan, regardless of my father's desire for regular updates, but after the ambush last night, it suddenly felt less like a shackle and more like a lifeline if things with the Embers went sour again.

While I had realized I could only trust Jasper so much, I couldn't deny the way he'd looked after me for years. He'd been a friend—sort of—a confidant and a protector. I wouldn't forget his betrayal or how he bent like a reed in the wind to my father's will, but when push came to shove, if I needed someone here, he'd find a way to get to me.

Thumbs fumbling to unlock the cell, I stared at the message.

Speak of the devil….

When I had flipped the phone on earlier this evening, a flood of messages came pouring in from Jasper, and I'd ignored all of them. I wasn't ready to see his apologies and excuses, but the preview of this message was different. More serious.

Biting my lip, I stepped into an alcove and quickly checked over my shoulder to make sure I wasn't being watched. Opening the text, I read Jasper's warning about my father growing impatient to hear from me and skimmed over the plea at the end to be careful.

If only he knew….

I wasn't able, or willing, to deal with him or my father right now. Shoving the cell away at the sound of someone approaching, I feigned a problem with my heel and looked up to see Olivia.

"There you are," she said, pulling me to her side and hooking her arm through my own. I leaned into her, capitalizing on the much needed stability she'd unknowingly provided, and let her guide me into the dining room. The tension between me and Hunter collided like tectonic plates as we moved past. Olivia's warm brown gaze was piercing, and she glanced between me and her brother as she led me away from the others. Her voice lowered. "Are you okay?"

That was a damn good question. I didn't have a good answer for her, though, so I forced a smile. "Fake it 'til you make it, right?" I made light of the crushing weight that sat on my shoulders and waved off her concern.

Olivia smirked. "That's the spirit! I'd say you could sit by me and we'd get through this together, but…" She stopped before the table next to the High Alpha's chair and picked up a place card with her name on it. "It looks like our seats have been chosen for us."

I circled the round table, spotting my name scrawled in elegant cursive placed between the High Alpha's and Hunter's seats.

Goddess help me.

Like a perfect gentleman, my 'mate' waited for me, then proceeded to pull out my chair.

"Oh, uh… you don't have to do that," I murmured, thrown off by the whiplash of going from arguing to civility.

That seemed to be our relationship. Tense. Always trying to figure the other person out. To stay one step ahead. But I didn't have much of an option, so I took the seat he seemed intent on helping me into.

"We might not know each other well *yet*," he said quietly as I situated myself at the table, thanks to his help, "but I am a gentleman, and any man who doesn't look after his date for the evening isn't worth the fucking air he breathes."

My mind fixated on that one little word. *Yet*. We didn't know each other *yet*. What the hell did that mean? And was it a good thing or a bad one? My heart and mind were at odds.

Instead, I asked, "Even when they're enemies?" Turning my chin to face him, I got caught in those golden amber eyes that seemed to strip me bare. Hunter looked at me as if he saw past my skin, as if he could see straight to the heart beating too rapidly inside my chest.

"Especially then," he rumbled into my ear. "Keep your enemies close, remember?" he asked and moved to the seat beside me.

His fingers made quick work of the button on his tuxedo before he sat. The jacket had been tailored to fit his strong physique, showing off his best features, despite the fact all that gorgeous muscle was covered. The sharp lines of his tux only accentuated the hard cut of his square jaw. Power and control radiated from him, but the tattoos peaking above the crisp white button-down hinted at the bad boy beneath the civilized facade. Hunter was pure, refined savagery. A wolf in sheep's clothing.

The arrival of more guests saved me from having to reply, but my jaw unhinged a little when the butler escorted Nova and Dean into the room.

Nova gave me a little wave, appearing uneasy about having been invited to the High Alpha's house. Dean took a seat beside Olivia and Nova sat next to him. That left only two spots remaining, neither with a place card.

"Who else is coming?" I mouthed to Olivia who shrugged just as the door opened, admitting the High Alpha.

I followed the other's lead and stood when he entered, dipping my head to show my respect, but nearly froze when I spotted who was with him. On the arm of the High Alpha hung Emery, the she-wolf who'd attacked me on the night of the full moon.

TWENTY-ONE

Madison

I took comfort in the dark glower that settled over Hunter's handsome features. He was just as unhappy to see Emery, which might be one of the only things we agreed upon.

"What is she doing here?" I growled quietly.

"I don't know. But I'm sure we're about to find out."

"Ah, thank you all for coming," High Alpha Weston cooed graciously with a sweep of his hand, as if we'd had a choice in the matter. Waiting for one of the omegas who was serving us this evening to pull out his seat, he sat like a king before his court, leaving his surprise guest to fend for herself. Only when he was situated did the rest of us settle back into our chairs.

Emery's slinky black dress clung to her curves as she moved to take the empty seat at the far end of the table, facing the High Alpha, but the moment her hand touched the carved wood, he snarled viciously.

"Not that one," he barked.

"That seat belongs to the late Luna, my mother," Hunter admonished. "We leave the table set and the chair empty as a homage to her memory."

Emery threw a hand over her chest apologetically, the move calculated to draw more attention to her cleavage which was on display. Hers was more ample than my own, and she trailed her fingers lightly across the swells, trying to garner Hunter's attention.

When she'd first walked in, I'd thought she'd switched her sights to the High Alpha, but now she was shamelessly flirting with his son. I nearly rolled my eyes.

"Of course," she said. "How silly of me. That's so sweet. I'm just so honored you asked me to join you tonight."

"I didn't," Hunter chastised bluntly. "That was my father's doing."

She waved off his comment, unable or unwilling to take a hint. "Perhaps he knew you'd enjoy my company." Emery was the picture of grace as she took the last remaining place setting, the vacant seat between Hunter and Tristan.

An ugly, twisted sneer curled her lips when she caught my eye. Touching Hunter's shoulder, she settled beside him and dove into an endless round of meaningless chatter while the first course was served. I prided myself on not giving her a reaction, but I had to hold myself back when she laid her hand on his arm like she had every right to touch him so personally.

I hated the casual contact, the ownership in every graze. The blatant disrespect.

My wolf growled possessively in my mind and the bond between Hunter and I tugged.

Muscle jumping in his jaw, Hunter reached for his drink to shake Emery off. Glancing my way, his russet eyes met mine over the top of his glass, and there were so many unsaid things in that shared glance. Could he feel the bond as clearly as I could?

The weight of our unfinished conversation hung between us, thick in the already tense air. Did the others feel that? The way it was harder to breathe? I couldn't fill my lungs fully under his steadfast stare.

It was impossible to look away until the omegas reached between us to serve appetizers that smelled incredible, uncovering one silver platter after another while Emery still chittered on as if she were the reason we were all gathered here.

Truthfully, I had no idea why the High Alpha had thrown this dinner party, but he was lounging back in his throne-like chair, brown eyes glittering in the candlelight. The rustic chandelier overhead was dimmed, setting an intimate mood.

Stomach rumbling, I concentrated on my plate and the numerous utensils sitting beside it. I glanced at Olivia for help, but she was engaged in a conversation with her father.

Now or never.

Swallowing my pride, I leaned over to whisper discretely to Hunter, my voice a mere breath of sound.

"Why are there so many forks?"

He looked at me with incredulous amusement. "Seriously? Were you raised in a barn?"

I glared. "Pretty damn close."

Sobering, his brows drew down as his amusement vanished and he contemplated what I said. There was so much we didn't know about each other....

Yet.

Graciously, he whispered the answer I was after. "Just work your way in from the outside." Lifting a smaller fork, he used it on his salad, and I followed suit.

I focused on stabbing lettuce while the chatter ebbed and flowed around me.

Nova and Dean were mostly silent, but I saw the mischievous sparkle in Nova's eyes as she prodded Emery, contradicting her here and there, making her flustered, as the two of them carried the conversation, talking about some problem in the pack I should probably pay attention to.

Part of my role would be to take on the responsibilities of Luna, but between the overwhelming presence of the High Alpha and the intense, searching glances Hunter continued to give me, I was having a hard time remembering to breathe normally, let alone weigh in on pack discussions about one of their packmates going missing.

Not having finished the steak Hunter had made me earlier, I was ravenous. I dove into my plate when the main course appeared, trying to ignore the heated attentiveness from the man next to me, as well as the annoying blathering from the chick who had nearly killed me twenty-four hours ago.

"Don't you find it odd that it's been three days since anyone's seen him?"

"Honestly? No. He was always a lost soul." Tristan

shrugged, not the least bit concerned. "He'll turn up, drunk off his ass, one of these days."

"He's gone on a bender before," Hunter agreed. It was clear he didn't particularly want to make conversation with Emery, but he seemed to take his role as Alpha-heir seriously. Painful as it might have been, he wouldn't let a concern brought to him by one of the wolves in his pack go unaddressed.

"Well, Mariah is an absolute mess."

"Who's Mariah?" I inquired, trying to follow the conversation as best I could. It was a near thing. I was barely grasping the threads of the conversation and weaving them together to form a picture.

Exasperated, Emery rolled her eyes. "After all these years, shouldn't you know the pack? She's his chosen mate." Going right back to pretending I didn't exist, she set her sights back on Hunter. "He left her and the pups practically penniless."

"I can run out there tomorrow with a basket of provisions, if you'd like," Olivia offered, and Hunter nodded his ascent.

Emery wrinkled her nose in disgust. "A basket? That's just a Band-Aid. They need Blaze home. He was Lyle's best friend."

"Emery," Hunter barked in warning.

She either didn't hear him or didn't care. Cutting her focus to me, Emery smugly filled me in. "Lyle was Hunter's older brother, in case you conveniently forgot that as well."

"And mine, but sure, just ignore me." Olivia muttered into her vegetarian dish.

Imploring Hunter, she laid on the guilt. "I just thought you'd be more concerned. Lyle would—"

A menacing growl cut through the conversation.

Throughout the discussion, the High Alpha had simply watched like we were an entertaining sport, but the mention of his firstborn son had severely soured his mood.

"That's enough. We don't talk about dead traitors in this house, just like we don't talk about my dead mate." The High Alpha's words dripped with pure resentment, his eyes flashing madly.

Whatever bitter history the High Alpha had with his oldest son, Lyle, was steeped in animosity. Removed as I'd been my whole life, I didn't know the story, but I didn't dare ask. Not now, but I filed away the intent to prod Olivia about it the next time we were alone.

Nostrils flared with the High Alpha's sharp inhale and then his rough voice switched to something far more honeyed and conniving. "You know what I'd like to hear about instead?" he mused. "How was the pack run last night to celebrate our guest of honor?" His attention fell on me like a fifty-pound anvil while he took a proffered glass of wine from the omega designated to serve him. "You do look lovely tonight, Kenna," he said while he raked his gaze over me.

Ants crawled over my skin as his leer dropped to the curves of my breasts that were fully on display in this dress. Thin straps held up the cups of a bodice that left little to the imagination. The neckline dipped into a deep, wide *V* that exposed the majority of my chest, stopping at the base of my sternum. The dress hugged my curves before flowing to the ground. In my seated position, the hip-high slits allowed the fabric to fall open to reveal my thighs.

The foreign feeling of wearing a dress aside, I felt sexy in it. But the way the High Alpha looked at me, as if he owned me, tainted my empowerment. I wanted to squirm, but I held steady, refusing to let him see me sweat.

Smiling tightly, I took the glass of wine that was offered by the omega who appeared at my side, murmuring a thank you before I replied to the High Alpha's question as bland and politically correct as I could. "Your land is lovely. The forest is always so beautiful, washed in moonlight. The reception afterward, however, was a bit… hostile."

Emery glared at me, but then, like flipping a switch, she dropped the expression and addressed the High Alpha. "Perhaps I was wrong to challenge Kenna, but my wolf insisted her rank was undetermined. The injuries she sustained wouldn't have been so grave had she shifted and protected herself. She was ripe for the killing." Her shoulder lifted like she was discussing something mundane and unimportant instead of my life, though her tone was caustic, which only increased as she continued. "What kind of Luna will she make if others can destroy her so easily? Hunter deserves better, and the pack deserves a strong Luna who can lead at his side." Her red lips tipped up in the corners victoriously, the color brighter and deeper than the red wine she accepted from the omega. She swirled the alcohol like a pro, arching an eyebrow challengingly.

Nearly growling, I defended myself. "I'm not here to start a war between our packs. I'm here to finalize my mating with Hunter and usher in an era of peace. How would it look if the first thing I did was decimate a member of the High Alpha's pack?" I bluffed, hoping I sounded confident when I was secretly shaking on the inside. Not only at the gall Emery had to ridicule me without provocation—it wasn't all that surprising given how she'd attacked me the other night—but because she wasn't painting an accurate picture. My wolf's snarl filled my mind. She was indignant on our behalf.

"As if you could kill me," Emery scoffed.

Pissed, my wolf released a wave of alpha power that wiped that cocky, arrogant grin right off her lips, and I smirked.

You've been holding back on me, I told her, enjoying her chuff of happiness at my praise.

Hunter stared at me with a look I couldn't decipher. "My mate did fight back," he said before I had a chance to say it for myself.

Completely stunned he was sticking up for me—and that he'd called me his mate, knowing what he did—I held his gaze until it slid to his father. "She used her elemental powers to defend herself. Enough to warn rather than kill, the way a true leader would. If she had shifted, her wolf would have demanded bloodshed, as any alpha would. It was quite diplomatic in my opinion." He lifted his shoulder in a shrug. "She would have held her own, but unfortunately, Emery's challenge quickly escalated into an ambush. Kenna didn't stand a chance in any form," he said, tone darker as he recalled the memory of how I'd nearly died.

"And where were you if not by your mate's side when this all started?" High Alpha Weston berated, growing unhappy.

"I had a vision," Olivia piped in before Hunter could. I caught his narrowed gaze and the quick shake of his head when all eyes turned her direction. "I-I had a vision that Kenna was attacked." Fidgeting with her napkin, she gulped. "I'm sorry Kenna. Hunter was with me when he should have been with you."

I knew Olivia was fibbing on my behalf. She'd distracted Hunter for me last night so I could run, hide, and keep my secret. Now she was taking the heat of her father's wrath to keep her brother from being interrogated.

I'd never had a best friend before. Not really. But in the

past few days, Olivia had proven her loyalty to me over and over again. I just hoped someday I'd be able to repay the favor.

High Alpha Weston steepled his fingers. "Nova. Dean. Tristan. Do you corroborate this story?"

"Of course," Nova jumped to my defense. "Emery started the challenge, but it soon turned into a coordinated attack against Kenna."

"It's no wonder she was gravely injured. She was outnumbered twenty to one," Dean added darkly. "Nova and I jumped in when we realized the challenge had gotten out of hand. Hunter and Tristan broke it up minutes later."

"And before the run? Where was the Alpha-heir then?"

Tristan, who'd been silently observing everything and everyone, spoke up smoothly. "I called him to help me with Olivia after the run had started. He was taking care of her, but when we heard the attack, we rushed in and put a stop to the fighting. Kenna's alive because of him. It all checks out," Tristan promised, though his focus flicked to mine momentarily, telling me he knew far more than he was saying about what happened afterward.

Emery huffed and rolled her eyes, leaning forward to block Tristan from view. The wine in her glass sloshed as she motioned it toward me. "Are we honestly not going to take Kenna's incompetence seriously? For years, she's never wanted to be part of this pack. She wasn't even meant for him," she spat, tightening her fingers around the stem of her glass.

Not meant for him? What the hell does that mean? I didn't get the chance to ask as she continued her tirade.

"Hunter is an incredible alpha. He's going to be a great leader. He needs a woman to stand beside him and support him in all things, just as your Luna did for you." She eyed the seat reserved for a memory and appealed to her High Alpha. "We are the strongest of the nine elemental packs. We don't need some arrangement with inferior elementals. Hunter should be mating someone from his own pack. He should be mating an Ember wolf." Her eyes sparked fire.

Nova rolled her eyes. "Someone like you?" she muttered quietly, her tone dripping with sarcasm.

"Why *not* me?" Emery straightened, looking regal and supercilious. A little grin formed on her lips as she took a sip of her wine, looking for all the world like she'd just solved world hunger instead of nominating herself to sleep her way to the top.

I watched the argument like a ping-pong match, gaze switching from one person to the other while I debated standing up for myself.

But what could I say? Emery wasn't wrong about my sister's lack of interest, and this entire charade of a dinner was all about showboating and the flex of the High Alpha's power. There were times for wining and dining, but in my opinion, solving pack altercations wasn't one of them. Situations like this should be handled privately. Airing punishment as entertainment was a cheap show of power.

The tense set of Hunter's shoulders and his silence spoke volumes.

Dinners like this weren't his style either. I'd wager with everything I owned—well… everything Kenna owned— that the man I shared a mate bond with would be a just and fair leader, ruling without all the pomp and circumstance. It wasn't hard to notice that Hunter and his father were like night and day despite the similar features they shared.

"Are you questioning my authority? My decision-making?" High Alpha Weston asked darkly. Dangerously.

Emery's eyes widened, and she nearly choked on her

wine. Spluttering, she gulped down what was in her mouth and reached for a napkin to dab at her lips, leaving a smudge of red lipstick on the cloth.

Vehemently, she shook her head. "No, sir. You're a wise Alpha and a strong leader." As if she had no self control to swallow her opinion, however, she dove right back into her argument. "It's just that I, and the other single women in the pack—"

"Don't include all the single women in whatever you're about to say," Nova muttered under her breath. "I've got nothing to do with this."

A small growl rumbled from Emery. "As I was saying, we feel as though Hunter's affections would be best directed inside the pack rather than outside it. We don't need the Stormborn's land. You hold all the power. If you want it, you could just take it without signing away Hunter's life to *her*." She wrinkled her nose in distaste as she side-eyed me.

Hunter raised a brow and leaned back in his seat, placing a possessive hand on my thigh, claiming me right in front of the bitch intent on tearing me down. Butterflies fluttered wildly in my stomach while I smiled sweetly in the face of Emery's dislike.

Inside, however, I was still wrapping my mind around the bomb she'd dropped about my pack's land. I'd had my suspicions, but realizing that the High Alpha wanted our mating to take place just to get his hands on our territory was startling nonetheless. His territory was huge, spanning a large section of northwestern Montana and the Idaho panhandle. The main pack was situated in the mountains, well away from the humans. Stormborn pack territory, however, stretched from Packwood, Washington—just below Mt. Rainier—down toward Gifford Pinchot National Forest.

We were smaller and didn't have the numbers of the Ember Wolves, but we had one thing they didn't. Easier access to the Caulder Wolves—the Water elemental pack who resided along the California coastline.

Just because the Ember Wolves were our pack's greatest rival didn't mean *we* were *theirs*. Fire and Water notoriously disliked each other.

Water and Storm, however, had always been allies, joined in their mutual dislike of the High Alpha and the Ember pack. Kenna's mating with Hunter would turn the tide of that alliance, lessening the strength and force the Caulders could leverage against the Embers.

It suddenly felt like my pack was in a wicked game of tug of war. I had to admit, it made sense now why the High Alpha had agreed to the mating and tentative treaty with the Stormborn. We were an insurance policy, and having access to our land, warriors, and resources was a helpful perk.

The High Alpha stared at Emery until the silence weighed uncomfortably.

"O-of course, if you feel differently, I—and the other women—fully support your word as High Alpha," Emery stammered, the glisten of sweat beading along her brow.

"Damn right we do." Nova tucked her colorful hair behind her ear and ducked her head to the High Alpha. "Respectfully."

A wicked glint shone in the High Alpha's eyes as he raised a glass just as the omegas finished serving wine to the table. "To respect."

Hunter's hand tightened on my thigh, and when I met his gaze, it was worried and intense as it tracked the glass to my lips. Dry with fruity notes, the flavor burst over my tongue and slid easily down my throat. I didn't drink much, but I knew this was an expensive wine.

"What's wrong?" I asked quietly, wondering if I'd made some mistake. Dinner party etiquette was clearly not my strength, but didn't you drink after a toast? "Was I supposed to clink glasses or something?"

Riveted in some staring contest I didn't understand, Hunter tipped his own glass to his lips and took a sip in lieu of an answer.

A strangled gasp suddenly broke the spell between us as glass shattered against glass. And the blood-curdling scream that followed rattled the chandelier as wine seeped across the white tablecloth.

TWENTY-TWO

Madison

My mind whirled as I tried to make sense of what was going on. Checking on Nova first, whose scream had nearly stopped my heart, I made sure she was alright before following her wide-eyed, panicked look toward Emery.

She'd dropped and shattered her wine glass, and the broken pieces swam in a puddle on her plate alongside her half-eaten meal. Merlot dripped from the table onto her dress, pooling in her lap. Raking her fingernails across her throat and down to her chest, she left gashes in her skin as she struggled to breathe.

I went to surge to my feet, but Hunter anchored me to my seat with his steadfast, strong grip on my thigh.

"Don't," he whispered harshly. Cupping my cheek, he made sure I was looking at him and not the dying woman beside him. "Don't watch." He studied me for any signs of whatever poison had been in Emery's glass.

Oh Goddess. Am I next?

My heart beat erratically, and my lungs squeezed as I focused on breathing, listening all the while to Emery rasp for the same oxygen I took for granted.

It was as though death followed me like a cloud. First Kenna, and now this? When I closed my eyes, I was right back in the forest, listening to Kenna choke on her own blood.

"Hunter." His name was airy on my lips, barely a sound at all. Something only he could hear.

He must have seen the panic written across my face. The light caress of his thumb smoothing over the arch of my cheek grounded me. "Stay with me," he murmured.

The scrape of the High Alpha's chair against the hardwood floor almost made me jump.

Watchful of his prey, he slowly strode around the table. "You see, Emery, this is why Kenna will make a far better Luna than you ever could. Not only does she have my son's affection, but she knows when to restrain herself or when to make a move. She holds all the cards and knows how to play the ones she's dealt."

His hand grazed me, pausing on the back of my neck as he passed, making me shiver from the wrongness of his touch.

"Such innocence," he purred, eyes flashing animalistically. Like he wanted to see me corrupted. Thankfully, he released me a moment later. "This is a woman who was raised and groomed to serve my son." He clamped his hand supportively on Hunter's shoulder. "You, on the other hand, reek like a bitch in heat."

"A-A-Alpha," Emery wheezed as he moved behind her chair.

"So willing to connive, scheme, and spread your legs to get what you want." Reaching around her, he trailed his fingers over her failing pulse. "Usually, I like that in a woman. It's a shame I couldn't have given your mouth a better occupation tonight, though nothing would have unsealed your fate." Swiftly, he fisted her hair and yanked her head back until she was staring up into eyes glinting with manic brutality. "You dared to question my authority, to second-guess matters that do not, and never will, concern you. You signed your death warrant when you went against my direct wishes for Kenna to mate with my son and attacked the Stormborn heir in *my fucking territory*." Growing increasingly agitated, the High Alpha's voice rose with every word until he was raging, face blistering.

White foam bubbled from her lips, and her gurgling gasp had my nails biting into Hunter's arm as I held on for dear life.

"Father," Hunter growled, turning his body in a way that helped block Emery from view, shielding me from the worst of it. But I still caught the black that bled up her fingertips, and the dark veins around her eyes. The vision would stay with me and haunt my nightmares the way the Shadow Beast did.

"Don't concern yourself." His father grinned cruelly. A small, barely-there expression far more unsettling than a wide smile would have been. "It'll be over soon. It's almost finished working."

Did he think Hunter approved of his murderous

tendencies? It was almost unfathomable. Hunter was nothing like his father. There was a leashed anger, a deep need to react, to help Emery. Her sins didn't warrant this violent death. Even now, she gagged and wheezed as life drained from her body.

I was coming to realize that my father's madness had nothing on the manic viciousness of High Alpha Weston.

Hunter was right; these were dangerous waters, and no matter which way I turned, the sharks circled.

Everyone was frozen around the table when Emery stopped breathing. Something inside me shifted, and suddenly the world burst into colors no one else seemed to be able to see.

Around each person at the table was an aura, a bright, colorful, glowing light burning with vitality. That same light dimmed and flickered around Emery as a wolven form ascended from her chest, leaving her body. She looked straight at me. I'd never forget the haunted despair in her animalistic eyes. Tipping her head back, her wolf howled. Inside me, my wolf joined with her own melody, the mournful cry echoing through my mind as the light of Emery's wolf faded into nothingness.

Satisfied, the High Alpha released her, and she slumped to the table, her face planting into her dish.

"I want you all to spread the word about what happened here this evening. Let it stand as a warning that any who contradict or disobey me will be punished accordingly. By attacking Kenna, Emery single-handedly put my alliance with the Stormborn pack in jeopardy. Such defiance will not be tolerated." Brushing his hands together, he cracked his neck and rolled his shoulders, and all the while, I stared at his strange aura.

I could tell the red color had once been a bright crimson, but now, it was mostly dark and dull, reminiscent of old, dried blood. The vibrance was gone, and it writhed around him, pulsing as the two colors clashed and swirled together like mixing paint.

"And while you're all here, I have some news." Crossing the two steps it took to stand between Hunter's and my chairs, he braced his hands against the backs, one on each. "I've spoken to the Stormborn Alpha and we have agreed, for once, that it's time to finally unite our packs."

"Why the rush?" Hunter questioned darkly, but he must have caught some flicker of emotion emanating through our bond. "We should speak in private."

"There's no need. The decision has been made," the High Alpha said authoritatively, brokering no room for argument. "The packs are growing impatient to see the first simulated 'true' mating since we were cursed over a century ago, and in six days, we will host your mating ceremony at the Summit lands to see you bound by the magic of the moon. It will be a new dawn for all of us."

And you'll get access to our lands…

What the hell was he up to? More and more, I saw the intricate political undercurrents to this world I'd been thrust into.

Hunter's jaw tightened, the muscle seizing as he clenched his teeth and held back any further argument, but I saw the dark look he exchanged with Tristan.

My stomach dropped. He wouldn't share my secret with his father, right? He'd seemed keen on helping me stay off his dad's radar, but maybe his intentions had changed now that he knew we were a hairsbreadth from being bound together for fucking eternity.

"That concludes our business tonight. Please, help yourselves to the wine, and dessert will be out shortly. I'm going to say goodnight, but Kenna…"

Completely overwhelmed, I didn't immediately flinch when the High Alpha reached for my hand, pulling it to his mouth against my will. Hunter bristled as his father brushed the back with a cursory kiss.

"It was a pleasure dining with you. And I want to apologize for the attack last night. I don't expect your safety to be a concern now that I've made an example out of this bitch, but considering your father is adamant about your safety, knowing Hunter cannot be with you at all times, I've agreed to allow one Stormborn enforcer into my territory solely for your protection. As long as he's cleared, I'll have him sent to you."

I nodded, shell-shocked, and cleared my throat to speak past the tightness. "T-thank you."

With that, he swept from the room, and I didn't breathe again until his power lessened. But once it did, a strangled cry slipped from my lips.

Nova was nearly expressionless with her shock, and Olivia had tears dripping down her face, her hands gripping the edge of the table so tightly her knuckles were white. The guys were tense and quiet, but Tristan leapt to action along with Hunter, pulling Emery from her chair and laying her on the floor. Together, they worked to revive her, dumping a vial of liquid Tristan pulled from his pocket down her throat.

"What are you doing?" I asked Hunter, dropping to my knees beside Emery's prone form. But I knew. I knew what none of them did.

"It's the antidote for the poison he typically likes to use," he grunted as he rubbed her throat, helping to guide it into her system before he started compressions.

"Typically? He's done this before?" I asked, incredulous.

"We've heard horrendous stories," Olivia said faintly. "He's got a temper that's only getting worse. But it's never… it's never been like this."

I let Hunter and Tristan work on her for another few minutes, just to be sure there wasn't a chance to revive her body and coax her spirit to come back, but then I reached for my mate, my hand passing through his red aura.

"She's gone."

"She might—"

"No," I told him. Lowering my voice, I murmured, "I saw her spirit leave her, Hunter."

Brows drawn low, he drew to a halt and studied me, then shook his head at Tristan.

Nova leaned into Dean, her hand on his chest, his arm tight around her waist as he held her close. For the first time, I noticed an iridescent shimmer that spanned between them. It glittered in and out of focus like mist.

Suddenly, my power slammed back into me just as quickly as it had flared. Colorful auras leached away until the world was once again normal, and I was left with a wicked headache.

Helping me stand, Hunter shoved a hand through his slicked-back hair. "Listen to me. I need you to go home."

My heart stuttered. Did he mean…

His expression twisted into something dark and possessive. "Back to the apartment," he clarified. "Have Olivia stay with you. I don't want either of you alone."

"Where are you going?"

Something unspoken passed between Hunter and Tristan. Infuriatingly, he didn't answer me.

"Now, who's full of secrets?" A bitter note slipped into

my voice. Unsure why I thought anything had changed between us, I was disappointed the veil had descended between us once more. Whatever tentative truce we'd shared during the horrid events of the evening had evaporated into thin air.

Just like…

My gaze fell on Emery as Tristan hoisted her into his arms. Her head lolled lifelessly against his bicep.

"I'll be back when I can." Hunter shrugged out of his jacket and placed it around my shoulders.

The warmth of it seeped into my chilled skin, and I hugged it around my body as he left me behind in the dining room of death.

TWENTY-THREE

Moonlight streamed through the window as I sat on the couch, waiting for Hunter to walk through the door of our apartment and back into my life. It had been over twenty-four since he'd left me and the others, striding off to Goddess knew where with Tristan at his side.

As ordered, we'd all hurried home last night. Olivia and I had ensconced ourselves in Hunter's apartment, though neither one of us had been able to sleep. We'd spent the early morning hours watching mindless rom coms and eating ice cream. When that didn't work to lift our spirits, we'd moved on to what Olivia called 'retail therapy,' which basically meant we spent the day online, perusing the local shops' inventory and ordering far too many outfits that were delivered right to our door.

Apparently, Kenna had an account, paid for by Hunter, and though it made me uncomfortable to use his money, I was in desperate need of a few essentials along with some new shoes. My feet were so damn tired of wearing heels.

Still, no matter how much we tried to distract ourselves, our worry over Hunter and Tristan stayed with us as the hours passed and day yielded to yet another night. I had to admit I was jealous of Olivia. She'd finally grown tired and had gone to crash in Hunter's bedroom, blessedly escaping the endless circle of anxiety and stress, if only temporarily. I, on the other hand, was still wide awake.

Curling up, I hugged my knees, wrapping the blanket I'd draped over my shoulders more tightly around myself. Hunter's jacket lay over the back of the couch beside me. In the privacy of the apartment we shared, I traced my fingers over the fine material, and against my better judgment, I inhaled his intoxicating scent.

Bourbon, musk, leather, and campfires in the Fall.

It wrapped around me, cocooning me in as much comfort as the blanket. The aroma was rich and addicting, and though his signature shouldn't have an effect on me, I couldn't suppress the fluttering feeling in my stomach.

It was a ridiculous reaction to someone's scent, but more and more, I'd come to appreciate the importance of smell to shifters. All my senses had become heightened—a new depth to what I could smell and taste, more vibrancy in what I could see, greater complexity to the sounds I could hear. And it was all thanks to the wolf pacing restlessly inside of me.

Earlier, between movies and shopping, Olivia promised

me the apartment was safe and wasn't being surveilled, so I took a chance and reached for my wolf. With a stabilizing breath, I let her presence gather under my skin. The beautiful teal glow that always surrounded her lit the dark apartment. Once she was free, she jumped onto the couch beside me and laid her head on my lap. Instead of taking the opportunity to stretch, run, or explore, she comforted me when I needed it most.

I sniffed, grateful I wasn't alone. Somehow, when she was near, my sister didn't feel so unreachable. The pain that lived in my chest lessened.

I blinked the tears away as I reached out and stroked my hand over her dark fur. Her eyes were blue, just like mine, except they glowed brilliantly. Her gaze flicked up to look at me.

"That dinner was pretty horrendous, wasn't it?" Nightmares flitted through my mind every time I closed my eyes, visions of Emery choking to death, memories of Kenna laying in a pool of her own blood. I couldn't sleep, so instead, I was waiting.

For Hunter. For clarity. For answers.

It shocked me that the idea of him coming home was comforting. Our relationship—if you could call it that—was tenuous at best, but somewhere along the way, I decided I trusted him, even if that trust wasn't returned. Enemies though we may be, he wasn't mindlessly vindictive the way my father or his father were. He protected me in his own surly way.

Clearly, I needed an ally.

Telling him what my father was up to wouldn't be easy. It was a risk, but I'd decided it was one worth taking. I was in over my head here.

Especially with the finality of the mating ceremony looming before us.

The look on Hunter's face when he'd learned he was days away from being stuck with me had hurt. It was illogical. I knew that. Of course he didn't want me. I wasn't actually his mate. He didn't know me… not really, and even if he did, I was a broken wolf. No mate for a powerful future Alpha. But it didn't stop the nonsensical ache.

Goddess, everything is so messed up.

However, it was the very reason I knew he would help me. The sooner I found my sister's killer and ended this farce of a relationship we were bound to, the sooner I'd be out of his hair and on my way… somewhere.

Where will I go? I hadn't the faintest clue. But I'd figure it out, just like I always did.

Head hurting, too exhausted to keep my eyes open a moment longer, I dozed into a restless, broken sleep with my wolf protecting me through the night. When I finally woke up, sunlight peeked past the curtains and the front door thudded shut.

"Come on, sleepyhead. The last few days have been a cluster fuck, and we need to do something palate-cleansing and fun today," Olivia chirped happily, if somewhat forced, and I groaned from the raised volume.

Pushing myself up to peek over the back of the couch, I saw her in perfect form, hair done, makeup on, coffee in hand, tossing her car keys onto the counter. She strode into the living room holding two cups sporting the logo of the cafe in town.

"One of those better be for me if you want me even half as alive as you seem to be," I muttered grumpily.

When my powers eased off the other night, I'd been left

with a wicked headache, one that was still clinging to the edges of my brain over a day later. The bright sun wasn't helping either, blinding me as my eyes worked to adjust to wakefulness.

"What kind of friend would I be if I didn't bring you a double shot of mocha espresso loaded with sugar?"

Wrapping my hand around the cup she held toward me, I took a sip, sighing contentedly at the creamy, chocolatey coffee.

"You might be my favorite person," I practically moaned.

"Then prove it by getting your cute ass off that couch." Olivia reached for my wolf and tried to stroke her head, but her fingers waggled right through her incorporeal form. Regardless, my wolf lapped at her hand. Liv smiled and shook her head at the anomaly.

My friend took a sip of her coffee, her eyes going distant as she stared out the bank of windows. "This whole thing is terrible." She visibly shivered and swallowed hard. "I never liked Emery, but she didn't deserve that. And with Hunter still MIA… I can't sit around this apartment worried and stressed for one more minute."

I felt the same way, so I recalled my wolf, stood from the couch, and hurried to get dressed. Washing my face, I blotted it dry with a towel and stared at my reflection in the mirror.

Tired blue eyes stared back at me. The same nose, same mouth, same hair as my sister. I hated that it hurt to look at myself.

I can't keep doing this.

"Hey, Liv?" I called, adopting Olivia's nickname. I hurried to step into some leggings and threw on a slouchy t-shirt that nearly hung off one shoulder, listening as my friend hummed back a response, probably around a mouthful of coffee. "Did you have plans in mind?"

I bypassed the wide array of heels lining the closet and went straight for the pair of cute, slip-on tennis shoes I'd ordered yesterday. Trouble had a way of finding me lately, and I needed sensible footwear in case I needed to run.

Taking a beat, I appraised myself in the full-length mirror. For the first time in days, I felt more like myself, and that was… steadying.

Quickly grabbing the purse I'd adopted as my own, I met Olivia in the kitchen.

"Only getting out of this apartment and finding something to distract us. I hadn't gotten much further than that. Why?"

Hope and a dash of excitement filled me. Given that my life had gone topsy turvy, I was pretty resistant to change, but maybe a little more would be a good thing.

Pulling Olivia from the apartment, I chugged my coffee, nearly bouncing on my toes while we waited for the elevator.

"Are you going to tell me where we're going?" Curiosity burned in her brown eyes, but I could tell she was down for whatever I had planned. Olivia was quickly becoming my 'ride or die.'

Hooking my arm through hers like she always did to me, I grinned.

"I've got an idea. How adventurous are you?"

Four hours later, we were in Nova's apartment on the second floor of the lodge, surrounded by an array of snacks spread out on the coffee table in her living room.

"This is not what I thought you meant when you said you had an adventurous idea," Olivia gasped, turning her face this way and that while staring into her handheld mirror. Bold red highlights newly adorned her hair, making her look like the badass Ember wolf she was on the inside.

Setting the hair dryer aside, Nova fluffed and styled Olivia's hair. "There's nothing like a fresh color to make you feel like a new person."

I desperately hoped she was right.

"You're next. Your color should be set in a few minutes," she told me, seeming totally in her element.

A short while later, rinsed, damp hair tumbled down my back, and I grinned into the mirror. The pink color was vibrant, cheerful. Sexy.

"Not many people can pull off this shade of pink, but girl, you look incredible," Nova cooed as she blow-dried my hair, then styled it into soft waves that framed my face and hung past my shoulders.

I touched my cheek and ran my fingers through my tresses, hardly believing the reflection was mine. "This is exactly what I needed."

It was liberating to look into the mirror and not see my sister staring back at me. To not feel quite so guilty I was living her life. Yipping supportively, my wolf sent a burst of warmth through my chest.

"I wonder what Hunter will think." Nova grinned and waggled her eyebrows.

"Who says his opinion matters?" I teased.

Olivia's sharp laugh had her grinning ear to ear by the

time she controlled herself. "My brother has certainly met his match in you."

I shrugged, not the least bit sorry to be a pain in his ass.

"Have you heard from him?" Nova broached the subject we'd been steadfastly ignoring all day.

Events of the other night were like an elephant in the room, enormous and hard to ignore, but we'd each done our best to cling to a semblance of normality. It was fragile, though, and the moment Hunter's name was brought up, it shattered into a million splintered little pieces.

"No." I looked away, tucking my hair behind my ear, taking a moment to also tuck away the hundreds of things I was feeling. "He wasn't home before we left to come here," I said, truly worried about him.

We may be experts at getting under each other's skin, but I didn't want to see him hurt, or worse.

The High Alpha was as unpredictable as the Shadow Beast and just as lethal. Had Hunter confronted him about that night? Why hadn't we heard from him, and where could he be?

"I'm sure he and Tristan are just dealing with the aftermath of… well, everything." Olivia winced. "They have to deal with her family and the pack as word spreads about what happened."

"Someone has to stop him," I murmured quietly, keeping the treasonous words just between the three of us. Thankfully, Nova and Olivia knew the 'him' I spoke of referred to the High Alpha. Bringing myself to say it, to dance that close to the fire, even if Nova's apartment was supposedly safe, felt uncomfortably risky.

"There's nothing any of us can do. We learned that lesson a long time ago." Olivia sighed, her shoulders deflating as she hunched over. "Hunter's walking a delicate line. He doesn't agree with my father on much, and he hates the way he runs the pack."

"He should…" I paused, looking around like the walls had ears before leaning in to whisper. "Can't he *take care* of the problem?" I murmured, deciding that if Olivia was comfortable enough to speak openly in Nova's apartment, it must really be safe enough. Though that didn't mean I'd raise my voice above a whisper. "I'm sure he'd have support. Hunter will be an incredible Alpha."

Olivia glanced away and wrapped her arms around herself, appearing as though she was trying to keep her secrets inside. "Listen…. I want to tell you everything, but you're new here, and honestly? I don't know how long you intend to stay. I mean, are you really going to go through with mating my brother?"

She looked at me, holding my gaze, searching for the truth while I sat, frozen.

"Wait, why wouldn't she mate with Hunter?" Nova looked to me, then Olivia, searching for answers.

Shit. My attention flew to Nova, whose eyes had narrowed. Olivia was way too close to accidentally letting the cat out of the bag.

"Haven't they been engaged since they were children?" Nova probed. "What am I missing?"

I had a choice to make. As badly as I wanted to bring Nova in on my secret, I didn't want to endanger anyone else. The High Alpha was too volatile to chance putting any more people I cared about in harm's way. The image of Nova in Emery's place solidified my choice.

"Nothing." I shook my head, briefly catching the hint of disappointment that bloomed and subsequently faded on Olivia's face. "I just—"

A sharp knock sounded on the door, making us all jump

and gasp. Blessedly it saved me from having to respond with some half-assed answer.

"Good Goddess," Nova swore, slipping from the room to answer the door.

My wolf barked, trying to tell me something as Nova pulled the door open to reveal Dean on the other side.

"You scared us half to death, you big lug. Did you need to knock like an enforcer?" Nova scolded without heat.

He gave her a winning smile. "I am an enforcer, babe."

"Ugh, that pet name is the worst."

A strange buzz tingled under my skin. I squirmed in place, suddenly uncomfortable, and my wolf barked again.

What? What's wrong, girl?

Dean braced himself against the doorframe, playfully arrogant as he looked down at Nova. "Maybe that's why I use it. You look cute when you're mad."

"Everything out of your mouth is like one big insult," she growled.

"They argue like an old married couple," Olivia mused, popping a chip into her mouth. "Like someone else I know." She sent me a pointed look, and though things had been strained a little while ago, a small smirk tugged at the corner of her lips.

But I couldn't focus.

The ache in my head grew with the unbearable itch under my skin.

"Wait here," Dean addressed someone else, a mere shadow none of us could make out past his larger frame. The door swung shut with a click as he followed Nova into the apartment. "You ladies okay after the other night?" he asked Nova quietly, the two of them heading back toward us, their eyes locked on each other's.

I scratched at my arm absentmindedly, willing the

prickling sensation to go away as they moved closer. I felt like I was coming out of my skin.

"Doing the best we can to distract ourselves. We were just coloring our hair. What do you think?" Nova dug her fingers into my tresses to fluff the strands, her fingertips bumping against my neck as she did.

Between one heartbeat and the next, everything intensified. The world burst into an array of colorful auras before I went sightless.

Against the blinding white light, I saw the image of Dean before it morphed into him and Nova. Together. *Mated*. Their souls matched, their auras reaching for each other, intertwining until I didn't know where one ended and the other began.

Voices filtered to me down a long tunnel, and something crashed. On a gasp, I blinked out of the weird trance and came back to the present. A splitting headache made me sway in my chair, and I nearly toppled to the floor.

Strong hands caught me.

Hunter?

My vision came back like a telescope being focused until the image was clear. But instead of the tall, dark, handsome man I'd been expecting, someone else knelt in front of me, holding me steady with concern swimming in his tempestuous grey eyes.

"Jasper?" I rasped.

TWENTY-FOUR

Madison

Before I knew what was happening, Jasper scooped me into his arms and stalked toward the door, which was splintered into pieces. It looked like a bear—*or an angry wolf*—had demolished it. The muscles in Jasper's jaw jumped from how upset he seemed to be.

My head pounded in time with my heart, each agonizing throb making it hard for me to focus as my friends rushed after us.

"Hey," Dean barked. His typically jovial expression melted into something downright lethal, reminding me that he, too, was a dangerous enforcer. Striding forward in two long steps, he grabbed Jasper's arm and stopped him.

"Get your hands off of me," Jasper warned as he faced off against Dean, the two wolves posturing with me squished between them.

Seriously? I shoved at Jasper's chest, hoping he'd take the hint and set me down, though I wasn't sure I'd be able to stand on my own. I was still coming down from the power that had erupted out of nowhere, and though it had quickly subsided this time, the effect left me shaky and confused. But it didn't matter; his grip didn't budge.

"Who the hell do you think you are, handling the future Luna like that?" Dean's eyes shifted from their normal hazel to the deep crimson of his wolf's with the warning.

That color had me catching my breath. It reminded me so much of the Shadow Beast that my heart stuttered. Between that and breathing in Jasper's musky, rain-soaked forest scent, the evening my sister was murdered came rushing back like a bad dream.

Slamming my eyes shut, I forced the horrific images away and focused on breathing. This wasn't the time for PTSD to rear its ugly head. The Ember Wolves' reddish eyes were incriminating, and I couldn't forget that the enemy was close, but everyone in this room was my friend. Now I just needed to convince *them* of the same.

My lashes fluttered open as Jasper's arms tightened around me. "I'm her enforcer, or did you forget why you're showing me around today?" he spat, voice dripping with sarcasm.

"That doesn't give you the right to manhandle her. Loosen your grip before I make you. You're hurting her," Dean ordered with an animalistic rasp, his wolf close to the surface.

"The Stormborn Alpha personally appointed *me* to serve and protect his daughter," Jasper growled, shucking off Dean's hold. "I'd never hurt her." His grip tightened marginally, possessively, before it relaxed. "I'm taking her back to her room."

"Are you okay with this, Kenna?" Nova asked, peering past the hulking men to catch my eye.

My friend was a feminist through and through. This display of testosterone had hardened her features, and she'd crossed her arms. The glare shining in her brown eyes had softened, however, when she'd zeroed in on me, making sure I was cool with what was happening.

I'd never had girlfriends before. The kind of women you could laugh with but who'd watch your back when things got real. The kind of women who cared.

But it all teetered on the edge. I couldn't stop myself from worrying whether Nova's friendship would shrivel and die when she learned the truth about me.

It wouldn't matter to her that I was Madison, but she'd be hurt and angry I'd lied to her.

Emotion rose up my throat, and I blinked back the pressure growing behind my eyes.

Nova caught my misty look and misinterpreted it. She appeared seconds away from removing her earrings to take on Jasper herself. Funny enough, I'd bet my money on Nova, but we didn't need any more bloodshed.

"I'm fine," I promised. "Jasper is a… friend," I finished lamely, and Nova looked skeptical.

Truthfully, I didn't know what Jasper and I were any longer, and I didn't want to have the talk I knew was coming. But putting it off wasn't an option. He was here now, and it was better to confront our rocky friendship head-on since he was going to act as my guardian.

Plus, I needed time to digest what just happened—those iridescent strings, the vision…

My gaze shifted from Nova to Dean and back again, and I swallowed.

They were *mates*. *Fated* mates. *True* mates.

I was absolutely positive.

It was crazy to think, let alone say out loud. No one would believe me, and I wouldn't be able to assuage their doubt. The wolves had been cursed for decades, making such pairings impossible.

And yet, it was also impossible to ignore what I'd seen. What I'd *felt*.

Explaining how I knew Nova and Dean were mates, however, would undoubtedly put my secret, and thus my safety, in jeopardy.

As if life hasn't thrown enough at me, now I have to choose between selfishly protecting myself and my friends' ultimate happiness?

The lies and secrecy were taking their toll. This was all too much. So, I nodded. Jasper was suddenly a convenient escape. I needed time to process. To breathe.

"Yeah. I'll catch up with you guys later, okay?" I placated.

"You're sure?" Olivia pressed, knowing more of my story than Nova did. "You weren't feeling well a minute ago. Why don't I come with you?"

Jasper's jaw ticked. He wanted to talk in private, and though Olivia was in on my secret, he didn't know that. I didn't want to air our dirty laundry in front of anyone anyway.

"Really, I'm okay. Don't worry about me. Thanks for a fun afternoon. This color is killer." I forced a smile, but it was shaky.

Olivia and Nova looked as though they had twenty questions they wanted to ask, starting with what the hell had happened to me a few minutes ago. Olivia shared a weighted look, and I subtly shook my head.

Please don't press. Not yet.

Luckily, she seemed to understand, but there was a fire in her subtle nod that told me we *would* be talking about this. For now, I'd take the reprieve.

Without further protest, Jasper carried me from the room, squeezing us past a few girls who passed us in the hallway. I heard their whispers and saw the juicy gossip light up their faces as I peered over Jasper's shoulder.

I could practically hear them mocking me as the poor little future Luna who couldn't hold her own. Who needed a babysitter. It set my teeth on edge as we rounded the corner.

"I can walk," I said, and pushed against his chest again. "Let me down." There was more vitriol behind the command than I'd expected. Away from the others and feeling more myself, reality dawned.

I almost couldn't believe Jasper was here, despite the High Alpha telling me last night a Stormborn enforcer was coming, but the relief of having an ally was quickly smothered as I remembered why I was still upset with him.

My emotions roiled through me tumultuously, revving my headache until I felt hungover.

Fuck. Can my life get any more complicated?

I didn't really want to find out.

Jasper's fingers flexed tighter before he acquiesced and set me down. My feet met the hardwood, and I stomped off, knowing he'd follow.

"Mad—" he started before I shot him a look that silenced the accidental slip of my name in public.

My finger jabbed into the elevator button, and I waited for it to descend and the doors to pop open. Once inside, sheltered from the ever-curious eyes of the pack milling through the lodge, Jasper tried again.

"Hey, I'm—"

He was going to apologize, but I cut him a sharp, angry look and shook my head once. It was a warning to shut up, and I threw a glance at the camera in the corner. There was too much technology here within the lodge, and I punched the button for the main floor.

The small elevator vibrated with tension as we waited for it to descend and ding open. Despite my fear of the Shadow Beast, I led Jasper out of the lodge and deep into the woods. The canopy of the trees created a haven, and I made damn sure we were alone before I whirled.

"You can't make mistakes like that here, otherwise you're a liability rather than an asset," I growled. "This is my life, Jasper. A simple slip will get me killed."

"I'm sorry." He had the decency to wince. "Fuck!" Whipping around, his fist thudded into the trunk of the nearest tree. Tempered, but still strong. He'd held back just short of breaking his knuckles. A chunk of bark flew off, the tree vibrating from the force of the hit. "Everything is so fucked up."

"You're telling me," I whispered.

His bloodied hand shoved into the strands of his sandy blond hair. Shorter on the sides, the longer locks on top laid in a messy array, pushed off to one side, sweeping to the left. Jasper looked mussed. Wild eyes stared back at me, full of apology and manic, glittering intensity.

"I've been going out of my mind worrying about you." Suddenly, he was closer, his elemental signature overtaking the calming scent of the forest. His nearness somehow made the great outdoors feel smaller. "You've been all I could think about. Wondering if you were okay. If you were in trouble."

I backed up a step to place a little space between us, but rough bark met my back. Jasper grabbed a low-hanging branch above us and leaned in, motioning to his chest with the other hand. "You haven't answered a single text, and I've been dying inside. If anything happened to you…" Throat bobbing, he reached for me, his fingers flexing as they hovered just off my cheek, unsure.

A stomach-dropping sensation crested inside me at the thought of his fingers grazing my skin, and I dodged away, slipping from the box of his arms.

My insides felt like Jell-O—wobbly and unsteady. I didn't want to acknowledge just how uncomfortable Jasper's touch made me feel, but my wolf's low rumble of unhappiness mirrored my own emotions.

Everything had changed in a matter of days. Once upon a time, I would have welcomed Jasper's affection. But now?

The idea of him touching me intimately was suddenly repellent. It was a *knowing*, a pit in my stomach, the raised hackles of my wolf, the way my body recoiled almost instantly.

There was only one person I couldn't get out of my mind. One infuriatingly sexy jerk.

I wasn't anywhere near ready to analyze why Hunter dominated my thoughts, so I marched farther into the woods.

My gaze scanned the shadows for any sign of danger, my senses on full alert, making sure we were still alone. The peace I'd once found in the woods was a dream—a vestige from a previous life. Between the Shadow Beast and the Ember Wolves, I wasn't sure I'd ever feel like I didn't have to have my guard up. I kicked at the various leaves and sticks that made a bed on the forest floor.

"Mads," Jasper spoke softly from behind me, only chancing to use my true name since we were utterly alone.

I could almost feel his gaze lingering between my shoulders, and I dropped my head. Closing my eyes, I focused on breathing, taking one calm moment for myself before I turned slowly and eyed the man who used to be my one and only friend. Or as much of one as he could be while also serving at the right hand of my father.

And that was the whole problem.

The warmth I used to feel when he was on guard duty, that tingle of excitement when I saw his face and knew for the next twelve hours I wouldn't be so incredibly alone, was muted and distant.

"I don't know what you want from me," I admitted softly.

"How about being fucking honest with me?"

I huffed dryly. "The way you're always so honest with me?"

Jasper reared back and his face became pinched, that pewter gaze narrowing, searching. "What do you think I've lied to you about?"

I shook my head and threw my hands out by my sides half-heartedly. "Nothing. Nevermind."

"No," Jasper demanded. "Don't do that. Just tell me what you're thinking."

I searched his face, but he'd become unreadable. Guarded. "I've just had a hard dose of reality, Jasper. You're my friend, but that friendship has limits."

Jasper blew out a breath, some of the tension in his shoulders easing. "That's what you're talking about?" he asked exasperatedly.

My brow arched. Did he seriously not understand the enormity of that betrayal? "Yes, Jasper. That's what I'm talking about. Your loyalty."

The relief I'd glimpsed was fleeting, and a glower pulled down his brows. "It's yours. It's always been yours."

"Right." Sarcasm dripped from the word. It might be unfair to blame Jasper for something he had no control over, but sometimes what we knew in our heads wasn't what we felt in our hearts.

"You have no idea the things I've done to protect you, Mads." Jasper jabbed his finger in my direction, pointing square at my chest. "The sins I've committed."

"Sins? What *sins*?"

He shook his head, refusing to answer, then stalked away only to pivot and come right back. "Simply befriending you was an act of treason in the eyes of the Alpha."

"I-I know," I relented, blowing out a breath and running my own fingers through my fresh pink locks. A light mountain breeze blew through the trees to further ruffle the tresses.

"I don't think you do," Jasper accused. "Everything I've ever done has been to protect you, especially the things you'll never forgive me for. You might not approve of some of the decisions I've had to make or some of the things I've had to do, but you're alive, in part, because of me. If I weren't the one who was here under orders from your father, it would be another enforcer. Do you really think someone else would be as forgiving of your lack of communication while you've been here? Do you think someone like Reynolds or Crenshaw would have covered for you with the Alpha?"

"Shit." I winced, and some of the wind went out of my

argument. It was hard to hold on to my feelings when Jasper chipped away at the foundation of my anger. I was still upset. Things weren't just magically healed between us, but deep down, I understood his side and knew he was in a precarious situation, stuck between friend and obedient enforcer. So, I relented. "Thank you. For covering for me."

The fight slowly bled out of Jasper, and his taut shoulders relaxed. "You're welcome."

I rubbed one hand over my other bicep, my mind in a whirl. "You weren't wrong earlier when you said everything was so fucked up. I don't even know how we got here, Jasper."

His eyes flashed with something unreadable, and he moved to lean a shoulder against the tree beside me, running a hand through his hair again. "None of this was supposed to happen."

I let silence hang between us for a beat in solidarity, because he was right. It wasn't.

"How pissed is my father?" I dared to ask. Being in Kenna's life had offered me a reprieve from his cruelty, and while there was plenty of merciless savagery in the Ember pack, I had far more freedom than I'd ever experienced before. I had a life here I wasn't eager to relinquish, but with Jasper's arrival and my old life pressing down on my shoulders, it was hard to ignore how short-lived the happiness I'd been able to eke out for myself was.

"I think the true question would be is the Alpha ever not pissed?" A teasing note worked its way into Jasper's tone.

I cracked a smile. "I can attest that I've never seen him in a good mood, but then again, I'm one of his sore spots, so who knows."

"He'll be happier now that I'm behind enemy lines keeping an eye on you."

The small uptick of my lips faltered.

"I just mean, now that I'm here to help. Keep you safe," Jasper amended awkwardly. "But I do need something to appease him. Please tell me you have information for me to relay."

How the hell was I supposed to answer that?

"I haven't found the killer."

Dropping his voice low, Jasper tilted his head and tried to catch my eye. "You know that's not what he wants to know."

"It should be," I growled.

"It should, but I think we all know what he truly wants. What about Hunter?"

"Hunter's not guilty," I snapped, oddly protective.

My hand flew to my chest, and I rubbed the spot where I could still feel our bond. Hunter and I had a love-hate relationship, with more emphasis on the hate, but I couldn't get the way he'd protected me at dinner last night out of my head. The phantom press of his fingers still branded my thigh, and the steadfast way he'd looked at me, trying to shield me from the horror happening a few chairs away, still sent warmth spiraling through me. We had a lot to figure out, but there was something between the two of us that was undeniable. A natural chemistry. A physical draw. The idea of throwing him under the bus made my stomach want to upend.

"Doesn't matter. He was there the night of the attack, which makes him the perfect scapegoat, even if he is inno-cent. Besides, you're living with him." A deep, unhappy edge filtered into his voice, and he threw a disgusted glance into the trees, angled in the direction of the lodge, before returning his attention to me. "Just find something we can use to implicate him, or we'll plant evidence if the guy is somehow clean."

I gaped. "You'd condemn an innocent man?"

"Don't look at me like *I'm* suddenly the enemy," he griped when shock colored my expression. "Your father is growing impatient. We're running out of time, Mads. You're supposed to *mate* this guy in five fucking days."

I wanted to open my mouth and defend Hunter, to tell Jasper he wasn't a bad guy. But in Jasper's eyes, he would always be our rival. Nothing I said would sway his opinion of the Ember heir. And even if it did, I got the distinct impression Hunter did *not* want to mate with me, much to the chagrin of my wolf. His hesitation over our mating ceremony had been clear when his father made the announcement.

On the other hand, I was selfishly torn. My wolf was insistent that Hunter was *ours*, but I didn't want to shackle myself to someone who didn't want me.

Nevertheless, I wouldn't deny I was drawn to Hunter in ways that defied description. The man irritated me and intrigued me in equal measure. Even a day spent arguing with him was worlds better than a 'good' day under my father's rule.

Despite all odds, I'd found a semblance of friendship and freedom I'd never experienced before, and I was hard-pressed to give that up. The High Alpha was a wild card, and a dangerous one at that, but even that didn't scare me as much as being alone and on the run. Because even if my father let me leave, he'd never let me go. I'd simply be on a longer leash.

Loneliness was a hell all its own, but I didn't see a way to rectify the lie and preserve the life I'd started to build here. It would all come crumbling down around me, and I'd be left standing in the ruins.

The thought was depressing, yet determination built within me. I might not be able to save myself, but there were people I cared about now, and I wouldn't let others' lives be destroyed along with my own.

Framing Hunter would destroy more than the High Alpha, it would condemn the Ember pack. Olivia, Nova, Dean… in a handful of days they'd become as good as family to me.

"Listen, I'll figure it out," I said, refusing to give Jasper the validation he wanted to hear. I wasn't going to let him pressure me into a decision that would change the course of my life and that of those I cared about.

Unimpressed with my answer, Jasper pushed off the tree, his gaze intently narrowing on mine as I stared up into his face. Those familiar stormy eyes seemed different somehow. Changed. Hardened. And they matched the threat he left me with before he strode back through the forest and abandoned me to my thoughts. "Find me something I can use, Mads, or so help me, I'll do it myself."

TWENTY-FIVE

Madison

I made it all the way back to my apartment before realizing I couldn't get in. I stared at the fingerprint scanner in exasperation. Thus far, I'd always been with someone who could scan me in. Digging into my pocket, I checked my phone and bit my lip as I sent a text off to Olivia. There was a security camera in the hallway, so I pretended to get a message on my phone and hit the button for the elevator again as though I had somewhere I suddenly needed to be. I went to step into it when it dinged open only to be surprised that Olivia was already here, hopping off.

"You okay?" She peered past me, glancing toward the

door that led to Hunter's apartment, finding us alone in the hallway.

"No," I answered honestly. "But also yes." Physically, I was fine. Emotionally? I was a dumpster fire.

"Come on," she grabbed my wrist and pulled me gently toward the door, scanning us into the quiet solitude of Hunter's place.

I inhaled immediately, and the lingering scent of Hunter calmed my frayed nerves. Strange how this apartment had become a haven of sorts. I felt safe here. Protected. It was the only place I could go to shelter from the world, and something in me relaxed as soon as I passed the threshold.

Olivia badgered me for information wanting to know what had happened when I'd gotten 'sick' and how things went with Jasper. I told her as much as I safely could, but it didn't take long before she realized I wasn't in the right headspace for a chat. I didn't want to be a jerk after all she'd done for me, and I was so damn grateful when she quickly picked up on the fact that I needed a little space to process everything that happened.

"I'm here if you need anything." She reached out and squeezed my arm. "You've got my number. Don't be afraid to use it, okay? I'm only a phone call away."

"I don't deserve such a good friend."

"Pffft." Olivia waved me off with a scoff. "Please. That's the most ridiculous thing I've ever heard. Everyone deserves at least one good friend. After the life you've had, you deserve a whole pod. A gaggle. A, dare I say, pack." She grinned. "Whether you want us or not, you've got me and Nova now. Dean and Tristan too. And Hunter…."

I nodded, a little misty eyed. "Thanks, girl. You've got me too. For as long as you want me."

Olivia shocked me with a hug. "Good. Then it looks like you're stuck with me. No matter what happens between you and Hunter, that won't change. You know what they say… chicks before dicks!"

A startled laugh burst from me as she pulled back with a wicked smirk and a twinkle in her eyes.

I watched her leave and then turned toward the quiet apartment, alone, save for my thoughts. Though it'd been what I wanted, I was almost *too* alone.

My mind whirled as everything caught up to me at once. I warped my arms around myself just before I fell apart and the first tears slipped free.

• ⟩ ⟩ • ⟩ ⟩ • ● • ⟨ ⟨ • ⟨ ⟨ •

Once again, I couldn't sleep. Nightmares haunted my dreams anytime I drifted off, and I didn't fare much better lying in my bed staring at the ceiling either. My eyes were still puffy from crying earlier, and the darkness only preyed upon my churning emotions.

Jasper's threat reverberated through my mind until it drove me from between the sheets out of pure frustration.

Did Jasper really think I'd implicate Hunter if he were innocent? And if I didn't, how would I stop the enforcer from taking matters into his own hands? The silence ticked away like a clock, reminding me just how out of time I was.

I padded to the kitchen worried about Hunter and Tristan, stressed about how to navigate Jasper's threats, and grieving for the sister I wished I could talk to about all of this. I grabbed a glass from the cabinet and moved to the sink. Moonlight glittered through the bank of windows making the water sparkle when I kicked on the faucet, filling my cup.

I tipped it to my lips and took a sip, letting the cold sluice down my throat.

Finding that stalkery, murderous bastard and unmasking his identity needed to be my biggest focus, but doing so meant risking my life. But how was I supposed to protect Hunter if I didn't do something drastic?

I sighed into the dark apartment. At this rate, I was going to have permanent circles ringing my eyes from lack of sleep. I might as well have a raccoon as my spirit animal.

My wolf huffed, and I swore it felt like she was arching a brow at me in her own wolfy way.

The corner of my lips tipped upward. It was equal parts disconcerting, yet comforting, to realize that even when I was alone, I wasn't really *alone*. Using my free hand, I rubbed it over my chest where my wolf now resided. With each passing day, it had become easier to accept she was a permanent part of me.

I was moments away from letting her out, hoping she could offer comfort and ease some of the roiling emotions I was dealing with, when the door swung open, spilling warm light into the apartment and startling me. The water in my glass splashed over the rim as I jumped. Only upon recognizing the man striding through the door did I settle.

Hunter.

His name was practically a girly sigh in my mind, but I leaned into it instead of contemplating my response to seeing his defined, if slightly disheveled, figure.

His white shirt was wrinkled, the buttons open down to his torso, revealing his golden, tattooed abs. The sleeves were rolled up to his elbows to show off his veined, inked forearms. And he was barefoot. Shoes, now slightly scuffed, hung gripped in one hand, as though he'd recently shifted and hastily dressed. Dark scruff covered his strong jaw, and his hair, which was usually styled, lay tousled and untamed.

Even mussed, he was sexy as hell. Seeing him undone cast him in a wild, feral light, and I found myself squirming in place to press my thighs together.

I may have tried to keep busy since I last saw him, but I couldn't lie to myself. I'd missed him. He was a sight for sore eyes, and I drank in every inch of him.

I wasn't the only one.

Hunter inhaled deeply, and his amber eyes flickered with red. The heat of his gaze was visceral as it journeyed down my throat, over the curves of my breasts nestled in the soft tank I'd worn to bed, traveling south to the sliver of my stomach that was visible above the waistband of my cotton shorts. It was like a caress, and open hunger glittered in the flames as he took in the length of my legs. The click of the door closing jolted us both back to reality, and his eyes smoldered to embers that fizzled back to amber.

"You're home," I whispered, almost not believing he stood before me.

"And you're still awake," he replied matter-of-factly. "I expected you to be in bed by now." The scent of the outdoors clung to him, telling me he'd been outside just minutes ago. He'd have noticed that the moon danced well above the tree-tops, fully risen, but he checked his watch anyway to note the time.

"I couldn't sleep," I explained, reaching for a towel to dry the water from my skin.

Hunter hummed his understanding, a low rumble in the back of his throat, and moved to set his shoes near the door.

Despite the heat that passed between us mere moments

ago, things with us seemed stilted. Our relationship yo-yoed between hot and cold, love and hate, trust and scrutiny. I never knew what to expect from him when we interacted.

We hadn't really had a chance to talk since he found out who I was, then we'd gotten sucked into that dinner from hell. It'd felt like something had changed between us that night when he'd protected me with his hand on my thigh, but now, it was as though a football field of space sat between us rather than fifteen feet.

A desperate desire to fix the awkwardness and find a way to move forward drove me to the fridge. I opened it, grabbed a beer, popped the top, and crossed to where Hunter was straightening, shoving a hand through his hair when he saw me. I forced myself to stop before I was standing too close, and my wolf pouted. She wanted me to take that extra step, to feel the heat of his body. The draw to him felt stronger than it had previously, and I could have sworn he swayed closer.

We breathed each other in. One heartbeat, then two.

"Your hair is different," he murmured, breaking the silence. Surprisingly, his fingers captured a loose wave of my hair that lay over one shoulder, caressing the strands as he took in the transformation.

"I needed a change."

He nodded, seeming to understand the weight behind that simple statement. "I like it."

That purred confession washed over me, warming me from head to toe. I didn't need his approval, but I did revel in it. What did it say that I craved his praise? That a nice word from him heated my cheeks and made my heart feel like it had wings?

Resisting the magnetic urge intent on drawing us together, I cleared my throat and leaned back before I did something stupid, like close the remaining distance between us. I made sure I stayed safely in my own bubble of space and held out the glass bottle. "Are you—" I swallowed, peering up at him, trying again to find my voice. "Are you okay?"

Hunter took the beer, and I noted he was careful not to touch me during the exchange. A dry semblance of a laugh crossed his lips, and he took a swig. I watched his Adam's apple bob before he leveled me with a heavy look and moved past me into the apartment.

The air stirred from his movement, whispering over my skin until a light shiver coursed through my body.

"You want me to answer that honestly, Maddie?" He'd shortened my name to something more familiar—and I liked it—except for the slight sarcastic note that soured it.

Yeah, I could do without that surly edge.

"Look," I said, exhausted and not in a place where I wanted to argue, "I was just checking on you. Trying to be a good…"—I almost said 'mate,' but I scrambled for another word—"friend," I finished lamely, knowing it was the safer choice.

"Is that what we are? Friends?" He cut a sharp look at me across the room, then sat on the couch, legs spread, elbows braced on his knees, hands clenching the bottle between them. Focusing on the beer, he studied it like it had all the answers in the universe.

If it did, I hoped he'd share a few of them with me. Everything was so upended, so utterly confusing, so fucking complicated.

"I don't know," I whispered honestly.

The only thing I knew beyond a shadow of a doubt was that there was something between Hunter and me.

We were bonded, but it was more than that.

I *wanted* him.

The yearning I felt for him lived in my chest and made it hard to breathe when he was near. Crossing to him would be so easy, giving in to the pleasure I knew I'd find if I stopped resisting, because on the edge of all the angst between us was blazing-hot lust. Evocative visions of pressing him back into the couch and straddling his waist were so vivid they made my breath catch.

I could still remember the feel of him between my thighs from that night in the forest, and I was desperate to feel him again. Together, we were fire and lightning, and if we let that passion spark between us, it would be all-consuming. It would burn hot and destructive, and I had no idea what would be left of me in its wake.

It was risky and dangerous to feel this way. There were so many reasons to stay away from him, no matter how hard it was to resist the temptation he posed. So, I clenched my hands into fists and withstood the magnetic pull that felt so natural, so unavoidable. Nails bit into my flesh, leaving perfect crescents behind.

Damn, how I wanted him, yet, I couldn't have him.

See? Complicated.

My wolf started to complain, but I blocked her out. I followed after Hunter and went to stand by the window, staring out at the woods and the few twinkling lights nestled in the trees that signaled a house, cabin, or store. The town was dark, the forest even darker. The only other light was the waning, silvery moon.

"I'm sorry," Hunter said quietly. "I shouldn't have been a dick. It's been a challenging last few days."

"If anyone understands that, it's me." My voice carried softly into the dark room, but I didn't turn around. Finally, I built up the courage to ask, "Emery?"

Hunter sighed, and I heard him swallow a pull of beer before he answered. "We did our best to take care of the situation. She's been given an appropriate send-off into the next life. Her family got to say their goodbyes."

I nodded, sure there were more intricacies to the story he hadn't delved into. I knew how much it meant to get a chance to have closure. I hadn't had that with Kenna, and it was like rubbing salt in an already painful wound. The burial, the goodbye—they helped, but it still wasn't enough to make up for the tragedy of a life cut short. If I were Emery's family, I would have been heartbroken and angry. Despite the fact she'd attacked me, no one deserved to die in such a gruesome, vile way. Her death was uncalled for, and I couldn't stop the feeling of guilt that I was responsible.

"I should have realized I wouldn't have a place in the pack. If I had, I would have taken more precautions. Emery wouldn't have attacked, and none of this would have happened. It just never occurred to me…" I trailed off.

"No, Maddie," Hunter interjected, my name softer on his lips, more sincere this time. "This wasn't your fault. You couldn't have known my father was going to…" This time, it was his voice that faded.

For a few minutes, the room was silent except for the light sound of our breathing. There was something cleansing about our quiet confessions, and I soaked in simply being in his presence as I watched the moonlight playing off the leaves on the trees.

Having Hunter close again was like having a weight lifted off my chest. I hadn't even realized it'd been harder to breathe until he walked through the door, but the pressure had lessened, and peace stole over my wolf now that we were talking.

I felt the moment his gaze settled between my shoulder blades before he spoke. It was nearly palpable, like a physical touch.

"How are you doing it?" Hunter broke the silence, his voice low and laid bare.

Curiosity piqued, I turned my chin slightly toward my shoulder, catching sight of him in my periphery. "Doing what?"

A rumble emanated from his chest. "Making me want you." His timbre was raw, flayed open, vulnerable, and sexy as fuck.

I turned, facing him with wide eyes, lips parting on a breath. My mind was a complete whirl even as my nipples pebbled from the intense way he was watching me.

Had he really, truly asked me that? He… wanted me?

I was still processing when I stuttered, "I-I'm not."

He let out a deep, wry laugh. "Oh, but you are, Madison. You're doing something to me. I can feel it." Standing from the couch, he prowled toward me like a wolf stalking a quivering doe.

Beats pounded harder in my chest, and something fluttered deep in my stomach. Adrenaline was a living beast inside my veins, and for some reason, my breath caught. Just for a moment, but it was enough.

Hunter noticed it all, observant, his glance flicking from the fluttering pulse in my neck to my parted lips as I desperately sucked in air.

"Tell me you feel it too," he demanded as he drew closer.

My fingers danced just under my collar bone, above my

heart, where I could feel the buzz of connection, that magical *something* spanning between us. "The bond."

"Mmm," he hummed, a victorious flash blazing to life in his eyes before it fizzled.

I was completely hypnotized as the heat of his body washed over me with his approach, so I nearly missed his next question.

"Why did you do it?" he murmured.

I blinked, the spell he'd woven over me dissipating slightly. "Huh?" I asked, trying to keep up with the shift in conversation.

"Why did you transfer the bond I had with your sister onto yourself?"

I gaped up at him, literally tipping my head back so I could look directly into his amber eyes. He actually thought I'd stolen my sister's bond with him on *purpose*? I couldn't contain the question. It spilled freely from my lips. "Are you serious?"

"Deadly serious."

I bristled, offended. "I never meant…"

"Whatever you say next, don't lie," he chided. That normal intensity he carried dared me to do it. Or maybe it dared me to tell the truth.

"Whether you believe me or not, I'm being honest. I never meant to take on Kenna's wolf… or the bond. I was trying to save her, but it was too late." A rasp worked into my voice until I was swallowing past the lump that had formed in my throat. "Her wolf appeared and I begged her to save Kenna, then the next thing I knew, she dove into me instead and changed everything. The bond?" I motioned between our chests. "That came with her. I never wanted any of this. I never meant for any of it to happen."

Hunter strode closer, leaving mere inches between us.

Large fingers clasped my chin and tilted my face higher for his inspection. He searched every inch, and my lungs stuttered, refusing to work.

Satisfied with whatever he saw, he nodded once. Some of the tension seeped out of me, but still, Hunter didn't release me. Lightly, so damn lightly, his thumb caressed my chin, the tip tracing along the line of my bottom lip. My heart went wild and heat rose up my neck as the bond between us tugged, wanting us to close those last few inches.

It would be so easy to lean in. So simple to rise onto my toes so I was closer to his lips. What would it feel like if I grazed my mouth over his jawline? How would the texture of his stubble feel against the softness of my lips? What would he do if I placed my hands against the hard planes of his chest? Would he close the distance and press his expressive mouth against my own, giving me my first kiss? Or would he reject me, wishing I were someone else?

The thought he might wish I were my sister was enough to cool the heat in my cheeks.

I shouldn't want to kiss him. He'd just been an ass. Like a Sour Patch Kid, one minute he was tart and the next, sweet. I couldn't figure him out. Yet, the enigma of him only served to heighten my interest. My desire.

He's not mine to have.

As if he could hear my internal dialogue, his hand dropped away. The heat he'd brought faded almost instantly, leaving my skin chilled without his touch. I instantly missed it, my heart falling and my wolf letting out a sharp, high-pitched whine of longing.

I stared up at him, noting how he didn't move away. He swallowed, and I traced the bob of his throat.

Breaking the silence, he whispered, "I believe you."

Nodding slightly, I murmured, "Thank you."

"I needed to know you didn't set out to manipulate me using the bond."

My brows drew together. "You think very little of me…."

Hunter tilted his head slightly. "What do you expect, Madison? I don't know you."

His words lanced through me like a spear aimed straight for my heart.

"Right." I took a step backward. What he said wasn't necessarily wrong, so, why was I so bothered by the reality of it?

Maybe because I felt like *I* knew *him*. Not the ins and outs and minutiae of his life, of course. I didn't know what his favorite color was, or his favorite food. I didn't know the defining moments that had shaped and molded him into the person he was today. But in other ways, I *did* know him.

I knew the kind of person he was, the kind of leader he was destined to become. I knew how he looked after and protected his sister, how he stood up for the underdog—like how he'd saved me from the females in his pack, how he didn't shy away from the difficult or unsavory responsibilities that fell on his shoulders. In the short time we'd known each other, I'd witnessed his bravery, his honor, his honesty. Hunter was loyal to those who were loyal to him. He had the respect of his pack, and that spoke volumes about the kind of person he was.

That alone was enough to earn my trust, and—as confusing as it felt, and as loath as I was to admit it to myself—my affection.

I'd lived a solitary life that hindered me in ways I hadn't even begun to realize, but it'd also made me an excellent judge of character. I'd lived my life surrounded by vile people. My father, a pack who'd shunned me, the enforcers who derived joy by keeping me suppressed and doling out punishments whenever I dared to step out of the lines they drew. Surviving their cruelty had served to give me one very important thing—a unique sense of knowing the good in people. And Hunter? Past the dangerous edge he showed to the world, deep down, he had a good heart.

All of this, I knew about him. Part of me had just expected him to understand the same about me. To understand who I was on a soul level. But that wasn't the case. He didn't *see* me.

I wondered if the bond let him feel the ache that suddenly took up residence in my chest.

Goddess, get it together, Mads.

His rejection shouldn't bother me, but it did. It stung far more than I thought it would.

I took another step away, needing the distance between us. Cool air rushed over me, and I wrapped my arms around myself. The walls that had started to drop from around my heart were already rebuilding themselves, brick by brick, and I saw the moment Hunter noticed my shuttered expression.

"Maddie," my name slipped out. His muscles bunched like he intended to follow after me, but he stopped himself, hands clenching into fists.

I envied his self-control. That was the only outward sign that he felt anything but indifferent.

I, on the other hand, was crumbling inside. Growing up basically alone meant I had very few people in my life whom I cared about in any significant way. Somehow, Hunter had landed at the top of that list. I don't even think I'd realized it until he took an eraser to his name. Now, the only people left were Olivia and Nova, and as much as I hoped they were true 'ride or dies', even those relationships hinged on lies I'd told or truths I'd omitted. On things I'd chosen to keep to myself, for better or worse.

I'd never felt more alone.

"Don't worry, Hunter. I know this isn't what you want. The intention was never to mate you," I fibbed. That was exactly what my father had wanted, but I was my own person, and I made my own decisions. I'd figure out how to survive the Stormborn Alpha's wrath. Shoring up my heart until it grew numb, I continued, "I'm only here to find out who killed my sister." Taking a chance that I could use his desire to see me gone to my advantage, I pressed on with what I knew I needed to do. "You're going to help me. Then, I promise I'll be out of your life once and for all."

Hunter tipped his head, studying me. It almost seemed like he was trying to figure out if I was bluffing. "How do I know you're telling the truth?"

My shoulders pulled upward in an exhausted shrug. I'd never been more tired than right now. "You're just going to have to trust me."

Hunter hummed, consideringly, then added, "We're supposed to mate each other in three more days. How will we handle the mating ceremony, our fathers, our packs?"

My gaze flicked between his amber eyes, and it occurred to me what I needed to do.

Growling a low warning as she caught on, my wolf fought me, trying to keep me from making a rash, life-altering decision, but my mind was made up. Electricity zapped over my skin as her presence rose beneath my skin. She tried to force a shift in an effort to silence me. But she and I? We were broken, and she only ended up making my skin glow a soft, pretty teal.

I sucked in a breath for courage and spoke past the

desperate whine that rang through my mind. "I reject you as my mate, Hunter Weston."

As soon as the words left my mouth, my heart shattered more than it already had. Pain splintered down our bond, and my wolf's mournful howl echoed achingly in my ears, a sound only I could hear. Surprisingly, I felt Hunter's pain as well, the fresh agony that sliced through him with precision. Stiffness worked through his shoulders and his eyes widened, revealing his shock, before they narrowed and his jaw clenched.

My throat was rough, my sentiment raw as I left him with a final promise. "And I'll say that again at our mating ceremony. I'll reject you in front of everyone and take the blame for our failed mating onto myself, freeing you to choose another. If you can't trust me now, well, that's on you."

Nearly unable to breathe through the pain, I turned and walked away, leaving pieces of my heart like a trail of breadcrumbs behind me.

TWENTY-SIX

Hunter

Maddie wasn't in her room. In fact, she wasn't in the whole goddamn apartment. Her scent clung to the air like exquisite perfume, making my wolf edgy. He'd paced relentlessly in my mind since last night, refusing to give me a moment's peace.

I splashed cold water across my face before splaying my hands shoulder-width apart on the marble counter, staring in the bathroom mirror as droplets trailed down my skin. The eyes reflected back at me were crackling with flames, the typical amber overtaken by power and the searing frustration of my wolf.

The conversation I had with Madison the night before

replayed in my mind for the millionth time since she'd turned and walked away, the pretty melody of her voice haunting me.

I reject you as my mate, Hunter Weston.

Why had I pushed her, intent on hitting buttons I knew would trigger her? I'd known just what to say to drive her away, and I hadn't held back.

Her rejection radiated down the bond even now, and it left my mind, and more importantly my wolf, roiling.

The agony of it had been unlike anything I'd ever felt before, but it was the hurt in her eyes, the way her expression had fallen as she'd made the decision to release me from promises I'd made before I'd even known she existed that continued to carve away at me.

I didn't want to take a hard look into why I'd decided to keep Madison at arm's length. That she wasn't the woman I was supposed to be bonded with should have been enough. But it was a lie. One I tried to hold on to and convince myself was true; that every time I tried to maintain my distance, I was doing the honorable thing.

But honor had nothing to do with it.

Every moment I spent with the blue-eyed vixen chipped away at the wall I'd erected between us, breaking me down one small piece at a time until I faced the truth.

What the hell did it mean that I was more interested in Maddie than I'd ever been in her identical twin sister?

Over the years, I'd done all I could to ignore that I'd have to settle down with Kenna someday. To be fair, she hadn't seemed eager to mate with me either, which always helped when the occasional guilt reared.

But I didn't experience even an inkling of disinterest with Madison. Just the fucking opposite. She intrigued me far more than I wanted to admit, and that was dangerous.

My muscles were antsy with the need to move. I wanted to run. A jaunt through the forest would surely help settle the unease that continued to build. If only my thoughts would stop betraying me, constantly wandering back to the woman I was supposed to be happy to be rid of.

Hadn't that been what I'd wanted? I mean, how was I supposed to mate a woman under false pretenses? With Makenna, at least we both knew what we were getting into —a loveless pairing born out of duty and responsibility as future leaders.

But that wasn't the case with Madison.

I huffed mirthlessly, trying to contain the thoughts that threatened to roam, that wanted to define exactly what Maddie and I were to each other, that craved to explore what a mating between us would look like, feel like.

I shut it down quickly, slamming the door on the possibilities.

I wasn't wrong when I'd said Maddie and I didn't know each other. I reminded myself of how she'd gained access to my life by lying to me and my pack, that she was here to condemn me for a crime I hadn't committed. I didn't trust her father or any of his followers, especially knowing they were out for revenge.

Truthfully, I hadn't trusted Kenna either. I'd always found the idea of arranged matings archaic. Since the wolves lost the ability to find true mates, matings among the heirs and elite had often become political matches. Love and loyalty had little to do with it.

Nonetheless, I had the distinct feeling that if we followed through with the bonding ceremony and became a mated pair, life with Maddie would never be dull or bland. There were sparks between us that promised to keep me enthralled. The way she challenged me excited me instead of dissuading me from wanting to claim her as my own in three short days.

My fingers dug mercilessly into the marble, bleeding white, in an attempt to hold back what I was feeling.

It's not an option.

I needed to reaffirm my stance, to convince myself, but I had trouble gathering enough conviction.

Despite it all, despite every conceivable reason I dredged up to stay away from her, I found myself wanting to trust Maddie. To help her.

I rolled my head, trying to ease the tension that refused to work itself out of my shoulders. It didn't work.

No matter how I felt, it didn't matter. I had to face reality. Madison wasn't the woman I was supposed to mate. More importantly, she wasn't safe here.

The madness she'd witnessed in my father was only the tip of the iceberg. I hadn't been kidding when I'd warned her of his cruelty. If he found out she was sent here by her father to deceive, he'd take pleasure in making her suffer a slow, torturous death.

There was nothing for her here. I'd done the right thing pushing her away, hurting her enough that she'd walked away from me.

My wolf snarled viciously at the thought. The pure, unadulterated anger vibrated through me, making my head ache with the sheer force he exerted behind his growl of unhappiness.

Mine, my wolf pressed. The word rumbled through the recesses of my mind. Steely. Unwavering.

Fuck.

I scrubbed a hand down my face before pushing away from the sink, refusing to look at myself any longer. Dressing in a pair of sweatpants, I forwent the shirt, grabbed my sling bag, and strode out of the apartment. Stalking past the elevator, I ripped open the door to the stairwell, the energy swirling inside too impatient to wait for machinery. My wolf was right under the surface, demanding to be set free, and I needed an outlet before I burst out of my skin.

I hadn't lost control of a shift since my teens. Doing so now would be seen as a weakness, and that was unacceptable.

Outside, my stride ate up the distance to the forest. I quickly stripped, tucked my sweats into my bag, slung it on, and broke into a run. Magic tingled down my spine as I let my shift overtake me. Sinews stretched and transformed while my bones rearranged themselves. Fur sprouted in place of flesh and, as easy as breathing, between one painless moment and the next, I was sprinting on four legs instead of two.

My hearing sharpened and my vision honed. All my senses came alive in ways that were difficult to describe as the spirit of my wolf pushed to the forefront, eager to race through the trees until we were a blur. The ground yielded beneath our paws, and before I consciously knew his intent, I picked up on the sweetest scent.

Now that I knew what I was sensing beneath the perfume Madison used to change the subtleties of her scent, I easily picked up the notes that were purely hers. The air was charged with the unmistakable smell of thunderstorms and the rich, fruity, sensual fragrance of jasmine. Maddie's feminine musk hung in the air like a beacon.

My willpower was steadfast. Going after her was a bad idea, but my wolf was relentless, exerting his need to see the woman he considered his.

The wind changed as we dueled for control until a second scent invaded my senses. A Stormborn male.

Jasper.

The name was an annoyed growl in my mind. I hadn't approved the enforcer's admittance into pack territory, but there was nothing I could do or say against one of my father's edicts. Until I challenged him, intent on taking away his position as Ember Alpha—and his coveted title of High Alpha—his word was law.

Soon.

It was a promise to myself and to my wolf, who anxiously awaited the day we took over the pack and claimed our rightful place as Alpha.

He was ready. It was me who held back, who understood the long-reaching implications.

I'd been biding my time, waiting until I was beyond certain I could defeat him. My father hadn't earned his high position of power by stroke of luck. He was strong and had years of experience to aid him in a formal challenge. I may have power and strength unmatched by other wolves, but it didn't matter how hard I trained or how many shifters I dragged into the ring and won against. Dear ol' dad, the Ember Alpha, the fucking *High Alpha*, would be a worthy opponent.

Losing wasn't an option.

Leaving Olivia without protection, leaving the pack without a buffer, wasn't an option. But covering for my father's blatant mismanagement of the pack—and not just our pack, but *all* the packs—became harder to maintain with each passing day. His descent into cruelty, into madness, was growing worse, and I was running out of time.

Pushing it all down to deal with later, I ceded control to

my wolf and let him steer us through the woods at a fast clip. He followed the trail through the rocky forest terrain to a break in the trees.

A grassy clearing opened, allowing the sunlight to spill into the small meadow surrounded by towering conifers. At the sound of her voice, I pulled my wolf back, much to his chagrin.

Trust me. When he didn't immediately respond, I urged him again until he ruefully relented. Still in wolf form, I crouched in the grass and crept closer, using the tall brush and unkempt forest to my advantage to stay out of sight as I spotted Maddie.

She was practicing, her wolf prancing around her with that strange yet beautiful glow before she sighed a sound of pure frustration and recalled the creature. Where there were two, now stood one as they merged back into a single being.

"Come on," she grumbled to the sky. "Work with me."

Closing her eyes, she released her wolf once more, but instead of shifting, which I assumed was her goal, her wolf simply bounded out of her once more, manifesting as the same ethereal, luminous presence.

"How much longer are you going to try before you accept that you can't shift, Mads?" Jasper's voice called across the clearing as he pushed off the trunk of the tree he was lounging against. "We've been at this for hours, and you haven't made any progress. I think it's time to admit defeat."

Something about the way he spoke to her brought out every protective instinct I had. The fucking nerve of this *pup*.

If that weren't enough of a reason to be pissed, he was letting her shift out in the open. It might be a secluded section of the forest, but it was still possible for anyone to wander by while out for a run. Case in point: me.

Why the hell was he risking Maddie's life for an impromptu training session if he planned to just stand there and criticize her?

Shifting, I untied my sweats and stepped into them. I didn't even have them fully situated around my waist before I emerged from my obscure vantage point and entered the clearing with the wrath of an impending storm.

"Don't listen to this welp." I waved a hand in Jasper's direction as Maddie spun to face me with wide eyes, her pretty lips parting on a gasp. She recalled her wolf, quickly hiding her from sight while I watched her enforcer partially shift from the threat he perceived me to be.

His instincts were slow. Too slow to be the one gifted with protecting a treasure like Maddie. Was the Stormborn Alpha for real with this asshole? If this was the best they had to protect the woman who should be the most important person in the pack, aside from the Alpha himself, then the Stormborn pack was weaker than I gave them credit for.

If enforcers like this were what we had to contend with, Emery had been right. Their land could be ours with minimal casualties or bloodshed, without arranged matings and political treaties. Not that I condoned territory wars or the need to expand our own. That was beside the point.

I wouldn't trust Jasper to guard my breakfast, let alone a person, especially when that person was Maddie.

The vein in my temple pulsed with the clenching of teeth as Jasper stomped forward.

"What are you, a stalker? Why the fuck are you here?"

"Last time I checked, this was my land. And Maddie," I

nodded toward Madison, and the next words tumbled from my mouth unbidden, "is my mate."

The connection spanning between Maddie and me thrummed, unbroken but injured. The ache of it radiated through my chest like a physical wound, and I saw Maddie flinch, her hand flying to soothe the same spot on herself that festered inside of me.

What would happen when she rejected me publicly? Would the bond break? Fade away like it'd never been there? Or would this ache live with me for the rest of my life always reminding me that something was missing? That something was… wrong.

We were in uncharted territory. None of us were sure how the moon witches' magic worked, especially when it came to forced bonds. It was too new and completely untested.

Neither option, however, appealed to me.

What the fuck is wrong with you?

Apparently, everything. The moment my gaze flicked to Maddie, soaking in her reaction, looking for her thoughts in the deep blue ocean of her eyes, I'd allowed myself to become distracted.

Lost in Maddie as I'd been, I barely noticed the fist flying directly at my face until it was too late.

Rule number one: never take your eyes off your enemy.

Fucking hell. I knew better. It was just one more mistake to add to the growing tally.

TWENTY-SEVEN

Madison

The crack of bone and the splitting of skin echoed through the clearing along with my gasp of utter surprise. The follow through of Jasper's fist sent Hunter's head whipping sideways from the force behind the punch. I raced forward, stopping after only a few steps, unsure if it was smart to intervene.

A low, intimidating growl reverberated through the grassy clearing, vibrating from Hunter's chest as he straightened with arrant malice gleaming in his flickering, russet gaze.

"Jasper!" His name slipped past my lips in airy shock.

What the hell had he done? Attacking a wolf above

your station could be a death sentence. There was a strict hierarchy among the shifters, and Jasper had just stepped *way* outside the bounds of what he was allowed.

Hunter had every right to retaliate, and if he did, Jasper wouldn't stand a chance. What had he been thinking?

The only explanation was that he *hadn't* been.

I wanted to scream at my friend—if I was still calling him that—partly in frustration for his stupidity and partly in fear for his life. There was no question that Hunter would come out on top in a battle of strength and power. Jasper may be an enforcer, but he was a delta wolf, two whole rungs down the ladder than Hunter.

"You told him? *Him?!*" Jasper demanded more than asked. Disbelief warred with anger before his features became guarded.

"Jasp," I pleaded, hoping he'd understand, but it was wishful thinking. He still saw Hunter as the enemy. Some-where along the way, that had changed for me.

"You know what? We'll deal with this later. You need to get out of here, Mads," Jasper ordered, his wolf making each word more of a growl as he spoke.

I reached a hand out as though I was trying to calm a wild animal. "I think *you're* the one who needs to go." Hunter's wrath was nearly palpable, and I swallowed thickly. If I didn't get my enforcer out of here… honestly, I didn't want to replay the possible consequences. Urging him, I added, "Like, right now."

My gaze became glued to Hunter as his fists clenched and unclenched, his nails shifting to wicked claws with every flex of his fingers. A gnarly red color bloomed over his cheek and blood flowed freely from the gash. It dripped off the defined planes of his jaw to trail down his neck.

Lifting a hand, he ran a thumb just under the split and eyed the crimson blood staining his skin.

"That was a risky move, *pup*," he stated dryly, anger tinging what could only be considered a warning. One that said Jasper was lucky his ass wasn't already on the ground.

"Call me 'pup' one more time, and I'll do it again. We're nearly the same age, fucker," Jasper challenged unwisely.

Hunter chuckled, the sound deep and menacing. His muscles coiled tightly with barely maintained control. I could tell he wanted to lash out, but he kept himself reined in, civilized in the face of Jasper's call to violence.

Flicking his attention my way, Hunter's focus bore into me as though he could see straight to my heart. There was something in his eyes. An understanding. A knowing I couldn't put into words.

It was as though he understood how much each of them meant to me, and even though he didn't like it, or even approve of the complicated relationship I had with Jasper, he respected it. I didn't want either of them to fight, to tear into each other and spill more blood.

As brief as his discerning look had been, it held weight.

I couldn't help the pitter patter of my heart. It only normalized when he returned his focus to Jasper. Instead of retaliating physically, he simply bit out, "I think Maddie's right. This is over. It's time for you to scamper off. Your services are no longer required today."

Huffing a single laughing breath, Jasper shook his head and stepped aggressively toward Hunter, chest out in a clear display of opposition. "I don't think you understand how this works. I'm not leaving her alone with the likes of you." He dismissively gestured toward Hunter, giving him none of the respect he deserved as an alpha, an heir, and the fact that this was his pack land we graced.

The level of testosterone was ridiculous. Piping up, I tried to tell Jasper I was safe with Hunter, but he refused to hear a word I said.

"If that were true, would you care to explain to me how you were near death a few days ago? His pack attacked you while you were under his care!"

"It's more complicated than that and you know it," I hedged but he was done listening.

"Mads," he implored. "You're delusional if you think your secret's safe with him. Or that *you're* safe with him."

I opened my mouth to argue, to make him understand, but he slashed his arm through the air in a parental 'we're done talking about this' kind of way, and silenced me before a single noise passed my lips.

"Nothing you say is going to change my mind."

I propped my hands on my hips and narrowed my eyes.

It stunned me that Hunter didn't reciprocate the belligerent hostility Jasper showed him. Instead, some of the tension released from his shoulders and he smirked with that cocky confidence he possessed.

"You're here at your Alpha's request, are you not?"

Jasper didn't answer, glaring where he stood, hands in fists, ready to loose another punch. There was no reason to voice an answer. Everyone here knew the truth.

"You're here only because my father, the High Alpha, approved your presence on Ember lands, around our pack," Hunter continued. "And if I'm not mistaken, the terms of your arrangement specify that you have a mandate to guard and protect our girl over there"—he gestured toward me, and my cheeks heated nonsensically from his phrasing— "when I'm expressly unavailable or request extra backup.

Rest easy that neither of those apply here." Hunter cocked his head, crossed his arms, and jutted his bloody chin toward the woods. "Like I said, your services today are no longer required."

Bristling, Jasper bunched to move toward Hunter again, the desire to pummel the Ember heir written in the tension that pulled across his shoulders. He only made it a step at most. A wave of alpha power detonated through the clearing, staying him.

Hunter's power tingled against my skin, but since it wasn't directed at me personally, I easily ignored the sudden desire to tip my head and bare my neck to the stronger wolf.

Jasper, on the other hand, couldn't defy the berating lash of it. The muscles in his neck became delineated as he fought against the unwelcome effect.

Unable to watch any more male posturing, I went to the man who used to be my only friend and tugged on his bicep. "Jasper, please." I wasn't above begging. "Stop this now, or it won't end well. For any of us."

Reluctantly sliding his attention off his rival and onto me, he searched my expression. "You're really serious." It was a statement, not a question, so I didn't answer him. Jasper shook off my touch and glowered. "Where's your loyalty?"

Hunter growled in the background, but I threw up a hand I hoped conveyed I could handle myself.

The accusatory tone Jasper used made me want to scream.

"Where should my loyalty *be*? With the pack who abandoned me? With the enforcers who made my life a living hell? With my father who undoubtedly hates me and wants to use me for his own political gain? Where do you think it is, Jasper? It's where it's *always* been. With *Kenna*. But, more importantly?" I snapped, "With myself."

For a split second, Jasper looked guilty. I thought he was on the verge of an apology, but whatever had manifested in his expression shuttered just as quickly as it appeared.

His whole demeanor changed. He stood a little taller and squared his shoulders, enacting the enforcer rather than the friend. "We're not going to argue about this anymore. What's done is done, and right now, I need to get you back to the lodge where I have more control over your safety."

I shook my head, flat-out refusing to let this slide. "Things have changed. Don't you see that I'm not the same girl you used to guard?"

It hurt that Jasper didn't *see* me either. When was anyone going to really look at me for who I was? I was tired of being a victim of circumstance, but if I was ever going to overcome the stigma of life as an outcast—or of living a dual life, forced to lie—I needed people to stop returning to their preconceived notions and look beyond the facades that had been forced upon me. If they'd just look under the surface, they'd see I was so much more than the words they, even unconsciously, branded me with: derelict, deceiver, enemy.

Jasper softened infinitesimally and held out his hand. I blinked, just staring at it like it might bite if I reached out to take it.

"I don't know what's running through your head right now, but I've known you forever, Mads, and I've always had your best interests at heart. If you don't believe anything else, believe that." When I didn't move to place my hand in his, his brows pulled down. "I'm not going without you."

"Jasp—"

He cut me off, that light scowl deepening to a full-on glower. I figured he must have taken my lack of response as defiance, but it wasn't. I was just done. "Look, we can discuss this more when we get back to your apartment. Can we just go?" He glanced at Hunter, who was watching this whole interaction from the sidelines. "I don't like the company."

"No." One step backward placed some much needed distance between us.

I was tired of people dictating my life, and right now, whether it was fair or not, Jasper was the embodiment of everything I was trying to escape.

Jasper scoffed and shook his head before running a hand through his hair. A manic sort of energy burned through him, making him fidgety and mean.

It hurt to see him so agitated, but sometimes a girl's got to put herself first and look out for her own wellbeing. Catering to the men in my life was growing tiresome. I wanted to take my power back, and that started with saying 'no.' 'No' to Jasper. 'No' to my father. 'No' to my pack.

Then, once I'd done what I'd come here to accomplish, I'd find my own way in the world. I had to.

"Do you know what you're doing?" Jasper leaned toward me and whisper-yelled.

"Yeah. I'm choosing myself."

Jasper laughed dryly, disbelievingly. "You're picking sides."

"That's not true."

"I'm just trying to protect you. To keep you alive long enough to live the life you deserve."

A resonant, unhappy growl echoed from Hunter, and I wondered briefly if it was in reaction to the idea that I wasn't safe—not here or in my own pack—but mostly, I ignored it, my focus trained on Jasper. "And I appreciate that."

"You have an odd way of showing it." He eyed the space I'd placed between us.

"Don't do this right now. Don't make me choose between my friend and my..." My mouth snapped shut, syllables unfinished. I was unsure how to put into words whatever it was that Hunter and I were, refusing to accept that we were nothing.

"Your what?" Jasper pressed, hurt seeming to flash like lightning in his stormy grey gaze.

Braving a peek at Hunter, I noted the curious tilt of his head from where he stood, easily eavesdropping.

"I don't know. I'm still figuring that out," I admitted honestly, voice no louder than a murmur.

Jasper stumbled back, alternating his incredulous, betrayed gaze between the two of us. His body vibrated, and his muscles bulked. "I see."

Letting go of his tenuous control, his magic erupted in a stormy haze. The air filled with the static charge of a thunderstorm, and after a beat, Jasper shifted effortlessly. The rip of his clothing felt loud in the otherwise silent clearing, and bits of fabric fluttered to the ground around the grey and tan wolf. With one last searing look, he turned and bounded for the forest. The blue markings interspersed throughout his coat were the last things I saw as he disappeared into the shadows.

Footsteps sounded as Hunter moved, and while I was unsure what I'd see written on his face in response to, well, everything, I gathered the same bravery I'd just exuded and faced him as he prowled forward.

"I'm proud of you, Maddie."

It was the last thing I expected him to say. Shock must

have widened my eyes and parted my lips, because I'd fully expected him to call me out on saying I was still figuring out our relationship when I'd clearly promised to seal our fate last night. Instead, he gave me a crooked grin.

"I have a sister, remember? I'm an advocate of females standing up for themselves."

Melting a little at his words, I released a breath and smirked, feeling lighter after the heaviness of the last few minutes. "Let's see if you sing the same tune when *you're* the one I'm disagreeing with."

"I'm an Ember wolf." The amber of his eyes brightened under the sunlight, sparkling like the purest gold. "I think I can handle your fire."

I laughed lightly, and he smiled. Actually smiled, complete with a flash of white teeth and something quite a bit like satisfaction brightening his features in a way I had yet to experience with him. It was the most captivating, breath-stealing, heart-stopping thing I'd ever seen in my life.

For a moment, we just stared at each other, that bond urging us to fix things between us. Begging us to draw closer.

Lifting my hand, I reached for him, my fingers hovering hesitantly near the injury he'd sustained. The nasty cut below his eye and his possibly fractured cheekbone didn't detract at all from how handsome he was. It did, however, make something itch uncomfortably inside of me to see him hurt.

Reaching for my hand, he cupped it gently in his and brought it ever so tenderly to his face, resting just the tips of my fingers beside the wound.

So damn lightly, I stroked them against his skin in a soothing caress. The air around us had heated to something electric, and I swallowed, hoping I wouldn't do something stupid. Like kiss him the way my body yearned to.

"Let's go home so I can take care of this for you," I offered, wondering if I could heal him the way he'd healed me. If nothing else, I was sure I could find a first-aid kit.

"Home," Hunter rumbled. The rich timbre of his wolf deepened the word and made it sound possessive. There was something delicious about the ownership behind it, as if the apartment belonged to me too.

My wolf, who'd been utterly depressed since last night, responded with a happy yip.

Just last night I'd rejected Hunter, but every atom of my being rebelled against the fracture I'd placed in our bond. The idea of not being with him made it hard to breathe. It placed my heart in a vice and squeezed. It made the world colorless.

At first, I blamed the severe reaction on the strength of the moon witch's magic. But the depth of the despair that overcame me every time I thought about what I'd done had me second-guessing myself.

Because, what if… what if the reason I was so distraught over not being with Hunter was because of something else entirely?

TWENTY-EIGHT

Hunter

A frustrated growl rumbled from the back of my throat as I turned my face this way and that, using the steamy bathroom mirror to inspect the injury on the arch of my cheek.

Throbbing pain lanced through my head, and the wound pulled with every expression, which only made the stinging worse.

That cocky little fucker has quite the punch.

It hadn't surprised me that Jasper's fist caused some damage—shifters were naturally strong, far stronger than humans could ever hope to become—but what caught me off guard was that he'd taken the swing in the first place.

He had some balls on him to risk his life assaulting me. An alpha. A rival.

Especially after he'd all but insulted Madison.

If I'd been anyone else, he wouldn't still be breathing, but it was obvious he meant something to Maddie. The 'what' and the 'why' were still to be determined, but just knowing she cared had been enough to stop me from striking back.

She'd gone through enough, and though I hadn't been helping matters up until now, I didn't want to be the cause of any more pain. She didn't deserve more heartache or grief.

There'd been enough bloodshed between our packs, and I had a feeling neither of us wanted to see the animosity continue. I wasn't about to let Jasper rile me into a response that would undoubtedly seal my reputation as the future Alpha of the Ember Pack. I wouldn't rule with violence and fear. I'd worked too long and too hard to differentiate myself from my father to throw it away on a petty challenge with a wolf who felt he had something to prove.

More importantly, Alpha Hale of the Stormborn was known to hold a grudge, and retaliating would've pit me against their pack for life. If I stood any chance of reversing some of the damage done by my father, not just with Maddie's pack, but with all the packs, I couldn't go around killing sanctioned visitors on our land.

Even if said visitor deserved it—or at least a decent pummel that would knock the sense back into him.

Though my quick shower had taken care of most of the mess, blood-tinged water swirled down the drain as I carefully cleaned the tender area around the gash, grateful the bleeding had slowed. My wolf was already fast at work healing cracked bone, knitting flesh, and fixing the bruising that colored my golden skin a lovely shade of fucking purple.

Draping a towel around my hips, I stepped into my room to find something to throw on. In the past, I wouldn't have hesitated to walk around my apartment naked, but with Maddie here…

Yeah, I didn't need to add nudity to the insane amount of chemistry we seemed to share. Sexual tension already charged the apartment. It hung thick between the two of us. So thick I could slice it with a blade if it became any more tangible.

But that didn't mean the idea of seeing her tight little body bared before me hadn't crossed my mind more than I cared to admit. The thought of what she'd look like spread across my bed had my cock growing hard.

The one little taste I'd had of her wasn't enough. I hungered for her, and the longer I denied myself, the hotter I burned.

I wanted to know the exact shade of her pert little nipples. I wanted to revel in the way her breasts filled my palms. I wanted to learn just how responsive she'd be if I closed my mouth around her—

The sound of a soft, feminine gasp filled the room and stole me from my musings. It was difficult to differentiate fantasy from reality when I glanced up and spotted Maddie standing in my bedroom doorway.

Soft golden light spilled around her making her look ethereal. She'd changed into a pair of denim shorts that accentuated her shapely legs and a black tank top that clung to her body like a second skin. I loved the way her waist dipped in and her hips flared. She was so small in comparison, and I found myself wanting to pick her up and carry her around just because I damn well could.

The rosy pink hue staining her cheeks only deepened when her gaze dropped down the naked planes of my chest to where my towel was slung over my hips. I swore my cock hardened to steel at the way her lips parted and her sky-blue eyes darkened with want.

Predatorily, I had the desire to lunge for her. The wolf pressed me to claim. And me? I cursed myself to hell and back.

Madison Hale of the Stormborn Wolves was the one woman I shouldn't want.

So, why do I crave her so goddamn badly?

Madison

My fingers tightened around the smooth metal box in my hand while I reminded myself how to breathe. I hadn't expected Hunter to be practically naked when I lightly knocked on his door.

He'd been hurt and bleeding. The only thing on my mind had been trying to help fix him. It'd taken me twenty minutes of searching to finally turn up the first-aid kit that'd been buried in the back of a closet, and in my rush, I hadn't waited for his answer before entering.

Holy Goddess.

And yet, I couldn't bring myself to be too regretful.

Seeing Hunter with nothing but a towel hugging his hips was orgasm-worthy. The man put chiseled Greek statues to shame. Every visible inch of him rippled in muscle from his biceps to his abdomen.

Out in the clearing he'd been shirtless, but given the fight and the tension, I hadn't had the opportunity to really appreciate the view. Now, however, there was nothing stopping me from taking my fill.

Though I knew I shouldn't, I threw caution to the wind and surveyed the dips and defined planes of his chest and stomach, mesmerized by his vast array of tattoos, down to where the covering dipped low on his hips. I wanted to count the abs that were on full display, but it was the tented fabric that drew my full attention.

Beneath the towel, Hunter's cock stood long and hard. My lips parted in shock and my cheeks heated—partly from embarrassment, but mostly from the desire that slammed into me.

I sucked in a deep breath to steady myself. Steam from the shower he'd taken billowed in from the bathroom, trapping his signature and making it thicker. His arousal only sharpened the scent, increasing the effect it had on me. It was strong, potent, and utterly delicious.

Completely inundated, I had to suppress the needy moan that tried to slip free.

Between the sight of him and that unfairly intoxicating scent, my body was burning. Mouth watering, my clit pulsed, and I had to grasp my last shred of self-control to keep from pressing my thighs together. My body begged for pressure where it needed it most, and my ovaries practically rolled over and pleaded with me to make a move.

I'd never been this turned on before, and it made my head spin in the best way. Desire unleashed, the scent of my own arousal rose into the air to mix with his before I could contain my reaction.

"I, um," I stammered, scrambling to distract him but it was no use. His amber eyes darkened, his pupils blown wide from the smell of my desire. The heat in my face was stifling, and I was sure it showed on the apples of my cheeks. "I found a first-aid kit," I stated the obvious, holding it up and waggling it a little so he understood why I was standing in his bedroom.

He didn't even give it a cursory glance before he crossed the room, tossing the shirt he'd picked up and was about to throw on onto his unmade bed.

Seeing those twisted sheets sent butterflies fluttering through my stomach. Imagining him lounging across the mattress, the sheets tangled around his lower half, his fist gripping that hard length as he lost himself to pleasure. It did things to me. It didn't help that he prowled closer, still just as naked as he'd been, save for that towel.

I wasn't sure if I loved or hated that piece of fabric.

Both. Definitely both, for entirely different reasons.

Needing to get out of his room, needing fresh air—or at least fresher air since the entire apartment was inundated with his scent—I turned and walked back into the living room, knowing he'd follow.

I placed the first-aid kit on the table and began rummaging through the supplies. The chair he pulled out scraped against the hardwood, and turning the seat sideways, he sat facing me. Studying me expectantly.

His legs were spread, the towel pulled taut, the outline

of his hard cock still on full display. He didn't even try to hide it. Almost like he wanted me to look. To see.

Swallowing, I fumbled the small bottle of alcohol I held. It went clattering to the table, then rolled away from me.

I clambered for it, then set it down gently where I wanted it, determined not to lose it a second time.

For the love of the moon. I needed to get it together.

Did I dare tell him that I'd never been alone with a naked man before?

Shifting was one thing. That was tactical. Purposeful. Reasonable. This— having him sit before me, nearly bare, with all of his muscles and tattooed skin on display—was something else entirely.

As he sat, that towel, the bane of my existence, dropped lower, exposing the sexy swath of skin just above his pelvic bone. Seeing him like this was intimate, private.

Deciding to risk it, I raised my face to his only to be snared in that drugging intensity.

Just last night I rejected him, and now I was tempted to call his bluff and jump him, showing him exactly what kind of effect he had on my body.

My thighs were slick, my panties totally ruined. Every breath made me overly aware of my breasts. Behind my bra, my nipples were taut and aching.

If I weren't so inexperienced, I may have tried it, but I couldn't face the very real possibility that he might turn me away. Other than the obvious, Hunter appeared unaffected.

You don't have to like someone to have sex with them. It was a stark reminder that I had a lot to lose. Like my heart.

While I didn't think there was anything wrong with unattached sex, I didn't think I was the type of person who could give her body to someone and not become emotionally invested.

Who are you kidding? You're already emotionally invested.

The ache in my chest panged, reminding me no matter what happened, I wouldn't walk away from this unscathed.

Throwing myself into my task was a last-ditch effort to keep myself under control. Grabbing a cotton ball, I doused it in alcohol and stretched to reach Hunter. Arm fully extended to keep as much space between us as I could, I dabbed lightly at his cut. He hissed, and as sadistic as it might have seemed, I smirked.

"I thought you were the 'big bad wolf,'" I teased, my grin turning into a full blown smile when he arched a brow at me. A light laugh slipped out. "Now, who likes my fire?"

Large fingers hooked into the empty belt loops on my shorts and tugged. I sucked in a sharp breath and my hand stilled, hovering over his skin as he pulled me closer. Too shocked to resist, I let him steer me until I was straddling his leg. Standing, of course, but it didn't stop the rapid uptick of my breathing.

"This may surprise you, but not many people stand up to me."

"Liv does," I countered, but it came out breathier than I meant it to.

He shook his head slowly. "Doesn't count. She's my sister."

I hummed, giving him that. "What about Tristan?"

"Beta. He only questions me when he feels it's warranted, which is in the job description."

"There's always Jasper," I said quietly, then winced. Probably not the best example.

I went back to disinfecting his cut, gentler this time. It was already looking better, the bleeding staunched, but it gave me something to focus on that wasn't how close we were or the fact that Hunter's hands were still at my waist.

Hunter growled at the reminder of the reason he was hurt in the first place. "Jasper's just an asshole."

I couldn't deny that he had been, so I stayed silent.

"My point is, I'm always going to like your fire, Maddie. You push back. You challenge me, and it intrigues my wolf. Just when I think I've got you pegged, you surprise me again. I can never quite figure you out."

His wolf… But what about him?

I spared a quick glance at Hunter before returning my attention to the cut.

"We haven't exactly had time to get to know each other. Not conversationally, anyway," I added, still feeling the sting of his words last night. It was stupid to hope that he could —would—regard me the same way I did him. As much as I wanted differently, I couldn't force him to see me. To understand my soul. My character. But I could have this one moment to actually get to know him.

It'd be fleeting, and when I lost him permanently, it would hurt like hell, but the temptation was as irresistible as chocolate, and I couldn't pass up this rare moment of transparency.

"What do you want to know?" I offered, thoroughly distracted when his thumbs strummed over my hips from where he still had a hold of me.

Hunter cocked his head consideringly. "What's your favorite color?

"Straight to the hard questions, then." I laughed, trying to ignore the rhythmic sweep of his thumbs. "Can't you tell?" I shook my head lightly to make my pink hair dance, then smiled coyly. "Yours?"

"Should have guessed." His lips tugged up in a crooked grin. "Mine's red… but I'm starting to develop an appreciation for the color pink."

Butterflies fluttered wildly in my stomach at the flirta-tious remark, but I tried to quell them, not wanting to get my hopes up. I went to grab the steri-strips to help hold the wound closed, but Hunter's large hand closed over my wrist to halt me.

"Thanks for taking care of me, but I don't need those." He gently stole them from between my fingers and haphaz-ardly discarded them back on the table. "You know my wolf will have this healed in a matter of hours, right? It's minor."

I let my hands drop, a little deflated. "Of course." Truth was, I'd almost forgotten he'd heal on his own.

"You want to get to know each other?" Hunter pressed. Baited, really. "Then, tell me what you're thinking about, because your entire expression just fell." He dipped his head to catch my attention from where it had drifted to the wolf tattoo on his chest. I hadn't even realized I was visually tracing the intricate lines, avoiding eye contact, until his finger hooked my chin and forced me gently back.

"It's nothing."

"If it's bothering you, it's obviously not nothing."

I sighed, resigned to reveal my ineptitude. "I'd almost forgotten you could heal. It's just… I spent so many years having to patch myself up, and it's muscle memory at this point to reach for the first-aid kit. You probably think…"

I trailed off, unsure how to finish that. What did he think? What if he thought I was just trying to come on to him? Clean him up as an excuse to get close? Was that why he'd been so bold? Why he'd pulled me close? Had I given him some signal I hadn't even realized?

Or what if he thought I was naive? He knew some of my story, and it was embarrassing to admit how unfamiliar I was with life as a wolf. Hell, without being able to shift, I might never understand the basics, let alone the more complicated aspects of being a shifter. Having been removed and sequestered at such a young age worried me. I didn't know if I'd ever fully catch up and integrate back into pack life.

Would that even be an option someday? Or would my rare elemental magic make me just as much of an outcast?

Disengaging, I turned around and threw myself into repacking the kit.

"Patch yourself up?" Hunter's voice was guttural, and I instinctively went still at the threat.

I didn't even hear him move, but suddenly the heat of his body licked along my spine and he was right behind me.

"Explain," he demanded.

Madison

A resonant, murderous sound rumbled from Hunter's chest.

"Who hurt you, Maddie?" His voice was full of possessive command, the kind that told me he'd make those who harmed me pay for their sins.

It was almost sweet he wanted to know, but it also brought up old, repressed emotions that made me feel inferior. Delving into my past reminded me just how far beneath Hunter I was—or had been. I didn't really know anymore. Feelings of being unworthy to be here with him, having this conversation, taking up his time, rose to crash over me.

I hadn't been allowed on the Stormborn Alpha's estate since I was six, let alone lived in such luxury. How was I supposed to admit that I'd been lower than the omegas? Considered worthless? Other than my tiny shack in the woods, I had meager belongings, second-hand clothes, and zero money. I lived at the mercy of a father who hated me and would have killed me years ago if he could have.

That kind of long-term oppression was enough to mess anyone up, and those wounds, that trauma, didn't just go away overnight.

I was a strong woman, but everyone had vulnerabilities, and mine were exposed like a raw nerve.

I shifted on my feet, unsure how to answer.

One of Hunter's hands went to my hip, the other clasping my shoulder. His intention to spin me around was clear, but I couldn't reveal what needed to be said to his face.

I didn't want to see pity… or worse.

I tensed, and he seemed to understand.

Finally, after an excruciatingly long time, I gave him the answer he was determined to have.

"Who didn't?"

My soft admission triggered Hunter's hand to tighten on my hip with almost bruising intensity. "Maddie," he rasped, anger brewing in him like a storm. "I'm going to need more than that. Tell me." It was a question more than a command, and that surprised me.

Hesitantly, I slowly turned, but I didn't look at him. I'd never get through this confession otherwise.

Eyes glued to his torso, I tucked my hair behind my ear and shrugged. "I'm not even sure where to start."

Hunter caressed my shoulders, his large palms sliding

up and down my outer arms. "How about at the beginning?"

I peeked at him. "You probably already know some of it."

"Doesn't matter." He promised, "I want to hear it from you." His sincerity covered me like a warm blanket.

The way he looked at me and talked to me, like I was someone who mattered to him, was how I imagined he'd act toward his sister or a friend. Something had changed, and in this moment, in this bubble that seemed to have wrapped around us, we weren't enemies or rivals. Our fate wasn't torn apart. The problems that faced us outside of these walls were tomorrow's concern.

Hunter's eyes glittered with nothing but a genuine desire to understand me, and it gave me the courage to forge forward.

Taking a deep breath, I released it gradually to gather my composure. "My father's hatred of me started the day my mother died. Apparently it was a difficult birth and I was the last to be born. I was just a few minutes behind Kenna, but my mother struggled. I was told she died just minutes after she delivered me."

"That must have been difficult. I know what it's like to lose your mother," Hunter said softly.

"In some ways, it was. But in other ways"—I shrugged—"I think it must have been ten times harder on you. You knew your mother. You spent time with her. You loved her. All I have are stories I remember being told as a child and faded pictures. I never really *knew* her."

"I don't know." Hunter's hands squeeze lightly. "I think that just makes it more tragic. From what I've been told, your mother was a wonderful Luna. Kind, fair, gentle. Had she lived, I'm sure she would have exemplified the same traits as a mom. Knowing you almost had that?" He shook his head. "That can't be easy."

I sniffed and nodded. "She would have been a wonderful mother. But fate is a cruel mistress, and tragic is a pretty good way to describe my life," I stated humorlessly.

"Tell me," he urged, and it was unfeigned. He wanted to know, and it almost bowled me over that he was interested in my past. In the hard life that made me who I was.

"What I remember of my early childhood was happy. Kenna and I used to share a room."

"Let me guess. All pink?" Hunter smirked, so self-assured like he knew he was right.

And dammit, he was.

"Why, yes. Yes it was." I smiled, and it helped ease some of the tension that had built in my shoulders. "We had the run of the woods near the house. We couldn't shift yet, but we used to run through the trees and pretend. We'd draw pictures of what our wolves would look like. Identical, of course, just like us. But when we turned six, Kenna shifted and I-I didn't. She came into her elemental power while I remained barely more than human."

Hunter's gaze darkened once more, but this time it was steeped in wrath. "That's why your father hid you away and spun that story about your death."

I simply nodded, glad he'd connected the dots. "I was an embarrassment to his line. A stain on his hard fought reputation. He believed my lack of power made me a vulnerability he and the pack couldn't afford."

Hunter paced a few steps away, the agitation of his wolf radiating down our connection. "Where did he send you?"

I wrapped my arms around myself like I could hold

myself together. Like I could shield myself from the harsh reality I'd lived and make it hurt less. "Oh, he didn't send me away. I was shunned and cast out of the pack, but he wanted to keep an eye on me. So, he gave me a small cottage, a shack really, on the edge of where the main pack lived and that's where I stayed."

"For twenty-one fucking years?"

"Well, fifteen, since I lived in the main house until I was six, but yes."

"That's inexcusable," Hunter growled, shoving a hand through his hair. His wolf obviously disliked this information. His beast was agitated, his anger on my behalf clear through the bond.

I rubbed my chest. No one had cared that much about my fate, and it hit a chord.

Hunter froze. "Did he—" He closed his eyes and swallowed. "Did he hurt you?"

If he was angry now, he was about to be furious, because I wouldn't lie. Not anymore. "Sometimes," I confessed. "I'll never forget the first time I snuck out to try and see Kenna. He wanted to keep us apart, and I'd broken a direct edict. When he found me, he beat me so badly it took me a month to heal. I don't think I'll ever forget his fist flying toward my face or the explosion of pain when my ribs broke."

"I'm going to fucking kill him," he vowed menacingly.

As terrible a person as it made me, I relished the idea of a world without the constant threat of my father. Someday a stronger male would challenge him for Alpha and win, and when the life bled out of him, I wouldn't grieve. While I tried not to harbor hate, because I truly believe it darkened your soul, I held no love for my father. When he was gone, I'd breathe a sigh of relief and revel in my freedom.

Freedom. What would that even look like? I almost couldn't picture it. I hadn't been free since my failed awakening.

I looked at Hunter, letting him see the lifetime of pain that lived inside of me. "I wouldn't stop you," I murmured. It was sinful to say it, but it was also honest. "He had enforcers stationed with me around the clock. I was always watched, guarded, except instead of keeping me safe, they were there to ensure I stayed in line and didn't do anything to draw attention to myself. I couldn't leave. I was basically a prisoner.

"There were set rules, and if I stepped outside the bounds of what I was allowed, I was punished, either by one of my father's enforcers or by the Alpha himself."

"Jasper?"

He'd be able to tell if I lied, so I swallowed and nodded.

Fur blurred in and out along his arms in a partial shift. The low snarl that slid from his throat promised blood and death as he stalked toward the door.

The pure vehemence of his visceral reaction shocked me. I didn't know where I stood with my rejected mate, but no one had ever had such a strong reaction to the abuse I'd suffered. My father reveled in it. My sister never knew how bad things were. And Jasper? He turned a blind eye—he had no other choice.

Growing up suffering punishments at the whim of others had desensitized me, I realized. Threats, violence, and loneliness were normal, and that was disconcerting.

Hunter's primal instinct to protect me was disarming. So much so, he'd already crossed the room while I stood staring after him as my heart squeezed. It was a combination of astonished bewilderment, blooming devotion, and utter heart-breaking affection.

I had to force myself out of my stupor, to breathe, to react before he killed someone on my behalf.

"Wait!" I ran after him, my short legs working double time to keep up with his long, furious strides. My hands closed around one of his arms just as he touched the doorknob, and I tugged. "Hunter, he didn't have a choice. Whenever Jasper was ordered to conduct my punishment, he went easy on me. Honestly, it was a blessing."

He whirled, and a dry laugh broke past his lips. "A *blessing?*"

"He was the only enforcer who was nice to me, and over the years, we became friends," I explained, needing him to understand. "It wasn't perfect, but in his own way he protected me. He snuck me books and magazines, brought me desserts I was never allowed to have, but mostly, he talked to me. My existence was lonely. Other than my all-too-brief secretive visits with Kenna, Jasper was the only bright spot in my miserable life for so long."

Calming enough to contain his wolf, his arms returned to normal, and while he remained tense, he'd stopped trying to rip the door off its hinges to track down Jasper.

Hunter shook his head and paced into the living room, like he needed to put space between himself and the temptation the front door posed. Understanding his primal side, I figured his wolf was still fighting him, pressing him to leave and seek vengeance for me.

It was sweet, really. No one had ever truly stuck up for me before. As much as I wanted to read into things, I had to remind myself it was most likely just a reaction from his wolf. We were still bonded, and until I fully rejected him in front of the pack—and hopefully reversed the moon witch's bonding spell—his wolf still considered me his future mate. His responsibility to protect.

"Alright," he said and blew out a breath. "So, what happened with you two? The entire time I've known you, things between you both have seemed tense."

I bit my lip. "I realized his friendship would always take a backseat to the orders he's sworn to follow." Content he wasn't going to go murder my enforcer, I followed after him and curled up on one side of the couch before I continued. "As much as he tries to protect me, he's a pawn for my father first and foremost." I fidgeted with the hem of my tank, averting my eyes. "It was honestly silly of me to hope for anything different. It's not his fault. He's as trapped as the rest of us."

Hunter sauntered to the coffee table and sat directly across from me. Leaning forward, he braced his elbows on his knees. "*Fuck.* I think I hate him a little less now."

The sheer distaste splashed across his features made me crack a smile, and it brought a small measure of levity to the heavy mood.

"Speaking of Jasper," I started, hoping to turn the conversation to Hunter for once. So far, I'd been doing all the talking, but I wanted to learn something about Hunter. "What happened today?"

Brows drawn down, he shrugged like it was obvious. "He disrespected you, Maddie."

"By telling me I should stop trying to shift?"

Hunter bristled, the reminder of the earlier fight riling him all over again. "No one should ever tell you what you can and cannot do. Not Jasper. Not your father or mine. Not even me."

He paused and let that settle over me. His words held weight. Power. And I whole-heartedly wanted to believe that. To have that power for myself.

"I can feel your power, Maddie. Your magic is strong.

Stronger than you realize. Jasper belittled you by suggesting you couldn't shift."

I blushed, unused to compliments from him. "I think in his own way, he was trying to tell me I'm fine the way I am and I don't need to try to meet some societal expectation of what a wolf shifter should be."

Hunter frowned, clearly not having interpreted the comment the same way. "Of course you are. You don't need to change yourself for anyone. But why should he be the one who decides what your limits are? Just because you didn't master shifting in one training session, does that mean you should give up ever trying to connect with your wolf in that way?"

He was right. I knew he was, but niggling doubt crept in unbidden.

"You want me to be able to shift." I dug a little further, wondering if the restless, troubled thoughts that rushed in to cloud my mind were right. The ones that screamed Hunter wanted me to master shifting so I was a more acceptable mate. One he'd want instead of one he was relieved to be rid of.

Hunter's eyes narrowed with intensity. "You're misunderstanding me...." He shook his head and leaned forward, capturing my hand in his. Large fingers squeezed mine lightly as he made sure he won my full attention. "From everything you've told me, you've never been normal, Maddie, and I don't mean that in some fucked up way. You're special, and so is your wolf.

"Shift. Don't shift. It doesn't matter to me. But you need the freedom and the fucking time to explore everything you are and could be. Powers take time to develop, and while shifting may seem basic to most of us, you've lived your entire life without a wolf. I feel like it's natural that it might take you two a while to acclimate to each other, especially because she's not used to you either. There's going to be an adjustment period."

What he said made sense, and I nodded slowly, letting it sink into my mind and my heart.

"I didn't think of it like that. You're right." I slowly released a breath, but it didn't do anything to steady my troubled heart. "I don't know what I'm doing, Hunter."

It wasn't easy to admit. Control was the one thing I'd struggled to hold onto. Growing up, I'd had almost no control over my own life, but what little I could garner, I guarded like a dragon hoarding a precious treasure.

To tell the man I was supposed to frame for murder that I was struggling? To give up that small piece of myself to him? A lifelong rival. A supposed enemy. To show more vulnerability? It was stupid and risky and confusing. My heart was exposed, the walls down, the defenses I'd worked so long and so hard to build dismantled and laid at his feet.

This was all of me, bared before him. The real, true Madison.

Hunter's thumb strummed over the back of my hand. "Tell me how I can help."

I'd half-expected him to bring up our deal from last night—his help for my rejection of our bond—but his offer seemed authentic and without condition.

It hung heavy in the air between us, and I thought about how best to answer.

What do *I need?*

My goal hadn't changed. One way or another, I planned to take down the Shadow Beast and expose him for the monster he was.

But I had a notion that I didn't need to hunt for him. *He* was hunting *me*. Stalking me from the shadows, toying with me, thriving off of my fear, and when he deemed the time was right, he would make himself known.

Unless I made *myself* known first. Used myself as bait to lure him out.

Unfortunately, I was nothing against the vile, beastly wolf without whatever powers I now possessed. Besides the Storm element I had inherited from Kenna, I was also an Aether wolf—a Spirit wolf—and I still had no idea what that meant or what magic apparently now resided within me. I needed to learn and master what I could in the short time I had left, because the mating ceremony was on the horizon and with it came the end of my life here among the Ember Wolves. Rejecting Hunter would see to that.

Three days, come nightfall. That was all I had until everything changed. Again.

"I need to learn more about my element," I said. "I couldn't find anything in the library the other day, but Olivia mentioned the High Alpha has an extensive collection of old books. She thought he might have something on the tenth element, on Aether Wolves. On what I am."

Hunter tensed, and that light, comforting caress on the back of my hand paused. "You want to see my father's private collection?"

"Unless you'd rather take a trip to see a witch who seems to have at least some of the answers, yes."

Hunter's lip twitched in a feral way, the outward reaction of a wolf who wanted to bare its teeth. "I don't particularly trust witches, especially ones so easily bribed by money. Particularly the one who works with your father."

"I don't trust her either, but I'm at a loss for choices. I'm getting desperate, Hunter." I paused hesitantly before continuing. "The creature that killed Kenna is here," I confided softly.

"On Ember land?" He was incredulous, and his hand tensed around my own. "When?"

"I haven't seen the same wolf again, but I've seen those same wispy shadows that chased us that night, and I feel him. I can't explain it, but I know he's close."

A million things clashed behind Hunter's amber-turned-russet gaze. He had the look of an alpha, always planning, plotting, staying one step ahead.

"I'll alert the enforcers about a possible intrusion on our lands, and I'll inform the most loyal of the bunch that we may have a traitor in our midst." He squeezed my hand in a reaffirming vow. "I can't promise the offender isn't one of my pack, but I do have my doubts. I would have known if one of my wolves wielded the kind of strength and power I witnessed in Olivia's vision.

"It's not impossible, but it's a slim chance the Ember Wolves are actually at fault for this. But if it turns out one of my own wolves is to blame for Kenna's death, I swear they will face the full extent of my wrath."

It was the most he could promise, and I'd take what I could get. I had an ally, and that's what mattered most.

My hand tightened around his in return. "Thank you."

"As for the High Alpha's private library collection"—there was something hesitant in Hunter's features, but it was there and gone faster than a lightning strike—"my father keeps it locked away from the pack for fear they'll accidentally mishandle the older tomes. He's the only one with access. I can get the clearance," he said cryptically, "but it will take time. As soon as I have it, however, we can search for answers together."

The information I needed was so close, and I was antsy

about the delay, but there was nothing to be done except to thank him for his help and survive what promised to be an agonizing wait.

Burying that edge of disappointment, I lifted Hunter's hand and used my other hand to lightly stroke my middle finger over the ridges of his knuckles. There was a small scar on the back of one, and just below where his fingers ended, his tattoos started.

I wanted to trace the lines, but refrained. Barely.

Today had undoubtedly brought us closer, and just like I thought, that only made all of this harder.

If I didn't know before, I definitely knew now. I was already in too deep.

Lifting his hand to my mouth, I pressed a small kiss to his knuckles, then lowered it to my lap.

"Thank you, Hunter. For everything." I didn't know what to say, but 'thank you' felt inadequate. It wasn't strong enough to express how I felt. He'd listened, truly engaged in everything I said, and from my lowest point, he'd built me back up, encouraged me, validated my strength, and volunteered to help.

My heart was absolute toast. Because that fracture in our bond? Yeah, that was still there, and it was only bound to get worse.

"You don't have to thank me, Maddie. You're my…" His voice halted and his jaw jumped with the clench of his teeth.

"Mate?" I said, barely above a whisper.

His silence was a cavernous ache that yawned through the center of my chest.

And I just knew I was right.

Taking him up on his offer fulfilled our agreement, and

I couldn't help the intrusive, heart-dropping thought that grew heavy in my mind like a darkening rain cloud.

His help for my rejection.

I was pretty sure I'd just sealed our fate.

I was falling for Hunter Weston, and in a matter of days, I was going to have to let him go. For good.

THIRTY

Hunter

The makeshift graveyard was eerily quiet. Under the light of the waning moon, the low headstones cast harsh, long shadows across the grassy meadow. The small clearing was located on the very edge of our territory, an obscure spot surrounded by briars that made it undesirable for most of the wolves in my pack to roam. Only those who knew what lay beyond the brambles ever visited.

Squatting down, I brushed the forest debris off the headstone in front of me, then ran my fingers over the engraved name.

"I'm almost out of time, Lyle." I sighed heavily, unsure why I was talking to the spirit of my dead brother. I never had before, but the burden that sat on my shoulders since he passed weighed heavier today. "His madness grows by the day, and if I don't stop him—" I trailed off.

If I didn't stop him, I worried about the repercussions of his dissent into cruelty and violence. But the headstone in front of me was a perfect example of what I had to worry about if I issued a formal challenge against my father. It felt like no matter which choice I made, death was imminent.

Our pack wouldn't take much more. Neither would the others under our rule. It was only a matter of time before one of the Alphas grew ballsy enough to attack in hopes of attaining the power of my father's position for themself.

I needed to secure my place as the Ember Alpha soon, and thus, the title of High Alpha, and start mending relations with the other packs. If I didn't, I'd have far more challenges to contend with than the one I had to fight against my own flesh and blood.

Starting with Madison's father, Thaddeus Hale.

Given that I outranked most of the Alphas—my strength and power making me a formidable force—there were many who'd be happy to see me take over my father's positions, especially if it benefited their packs. But there were a number of Alphas who'd relish the chance to usurp the line of succession in a bid for power.

It didn't help that relationship between the packs and the High Alpha had devolved to a place of hate and grudging obedience.

More and more whispers were reaching my ears about shifting alliances and the possibility of a war between packs, so much so that I worried the gossip was based in truth more than rumor.

It wasn't surprising, but it was also the last damn thing I needed.

I already had my father to deal with, and now I had to worry about Maddie's safety from some murderous lunatic.

The sound of snapping twigs infiltrated the night, and I whirled, bracing one hand on the ground in front of me while the other partially shifted into claws. I surveyed the forest through narrowed eyes with my wolf at the ready right below the surface, coiled tightly, shift imminent, prepared to spring the moment the perceived threat advanced.

I relaxed at the sight of Tristan and Kip as they appeared from between the towering trees. I'd asked them to meet me here. I could have assumed it was them, but I hadn't become a powerful alpha by taking foolish risks. As remote as I was, with my territory's borders only a few short miles away, anyone could have ambushed me.

With the possibility of the intruder Maddie had told me about, there wasn't room for errors or lapses in judgment. The life of a shifter could be dangerous, but the life of a future Alpha was downright deadly. One slip would get me killed and change the perceived line of succession, and I didn't plan on dying. Not today, anyway.

"Alpha," Tristan greeted as he crossed into the makeshift graveyard.

This was the place we buried the wolves who would never see a proper send off into the next life. Ember Wolves usually had a ceremonial pyre where we'd burn the body to set the soul free. Burying an Ember wolf almost felt cruel, but we did the best we could by wolves who'd been branded traitors or killed for one nonsensical reason or another.

Most of the headstones in this place were victims of my father's tyrannical rule. Like the freshly turned earth two rows beyond, where we'd laid Emery to rest, her life reduced to a small plot and a simple grave marker. Much like my brother's.

"Alpha," Kip, my most trusted enforcer, repeated the greeting and dipped his head respectfully. "What can we do for you?"

I straightened to my full height as the two men drew to a stop in front of me.

"We've got a problem," I stated, then filled them in on the information I had regarding the potential trespasser. I left out the part about Kenna being killed, stating only that my mate had acquired a dangerous stalker. Tristan knew the truth, and I trusted Kip, but the fewer people who knew about Maddie, the better.

The more Kip listened, the tenser he grew. "The borders are secure. I haven't heard any inklings about an outsider crossing into our territory, but I'll send out teams to investigate and do a sweep through the pack lands to be sure we didn't somehow miss something."

"I'm not suggesting you did, but thank you for your vigilance."

"Do you think the threat could be coming from inside the pack?" Tristan asked, scrubbing a hand along the back of his neck, a clear sign he was uncomfortable even suggesting the notion we had a traitor in our midst.

"It's a possibility. I'm not ruling anything out. My mate's safety is of the utmost importance to me." It surprised me how much I meant those words too. The thought of Maddie hurt or worse… It angered me enough that a deep vibration started in my chest. My wolf would consider it a personal failing if she were injured on our watch. Again.

But soon, she wouldn't be my concern, and I was… Fuck. I was conflicted.

On one hand, it was clear she wasn't safe here. On the other, was she safe anywhere? Would I be able to let her go knowing the risks? It'd be simpler if I knew she had a life to go back to, but learning what I had about her past earlier tonight, that wasn't the case. That woman was a survivor. She was strong, and it wasn't just the power I felt radiating from her. It was *her*. Her tenacity. Her loyalty. Her ability to keep going in the face of such adversity. She'd lived a depressing, oppressive life, and I found myself wanting to give her fucking everything.

How much of that was *me* and how much was my wolf projecting his feelings for the woman he considered his, was hard to differentiate. I pushed it all to the background for now, focusing on the plan Tristan and Kip were hatching to comb through the pack.

Approving their ideas, I thanked Kip and watched him leave before turning to Tristan. He studied me with a knowing look. Trying to avoid the question I knew was coming, I motioned him to follow me down the path and into the truck I used when navigating rough terrain. We barely made it a mile down the dirt road when he gave up on holding his tongue.

"Your mate?" he asked, voice rising on the last word, the question hanging, demanding an answer.

I adjusted my grip on the steering wheel. "That's what she is."

For now.

I shrugged the unwelcome thought off and focused on the road, unsure I wanted to have this conversation, even with the guy I trusted the most. Tristan was exceedingly loyal and would naturally take his place as my second—my official Beta—when the time came for me to ascend to a position of power. I didn't keep much from him, but this wasn't something I was ready to open up about when I didn't even know where I stood in my own mind.

The fuck you don't. But I wasn't ready to open that door and step through it.

I could feel my friend's intent gaze on my profile, and when I peered his way, he had his head cocked, one brow tipped upward. "You fucking like her."

What I felt went beyond like. 'Like' was too casual a word for the turmoil going on inside of me when it came to Maddie.

I didn't need to respond for Tristan to see the truth. Every heir-apparent had a beta, and he had been mine since we were children, fresh out of our awakenings. Over the years, he'd become my best friend. It was hard to hide things from someone who knew you so well.

"Holy shit. I'm right, aren't I? You *like* her." Tristan shoved a hand through his hair, shocked. "Fuck, man. I thought you didn't trust her."

I sighed and tried to roll some of the tension from my shoulders. "I didn't, at first. But I've come to know her." I didn't know how to explain it. "The bond may connect us, but it has nothing to do with the chemistry I feel every goddamn time I'm around her."

It was addicting, and not entirely unwelcome, now that things had changed with Maddie.

"Damn." Tristan was silent for a long time, stealing glances at me occasionally as we drew closer to the heart of our territory.

"I've seen that look on your face before," Tristan said cryptically, and it was my turn to raise a brow.

"What the fuck are you talking about? What look?"

"That self-sacrificing, for-the-good-of-the-pack, of-others, of-the-world, stubborn-ass glint in your eyes. The one I've come to recognize means you're burying what you want for the good of who-knows-what," Tristan smirked, the smart ass.

I straightened in my seat, assuming my full alpha countenance complete with an arched brow and a mock sardonic expression.

Tristan sobered, but he knew I'd never truly exert my alpha will over him. I wasn't angry. In fact, I appreciated his honesty and candor, even if his delivery could use some work.

"Look man, I know we don't talk about feelings and shit very often, but I've known you your entire life, and I've never seen you look so torn up over a woman. You put the pack first. Always have, even to the detriment of your own happiness. That's part of what makes you such a damn good alpha, and what will make you a great leader one day, but let's get one thing straight," he paused and looked me straight in the eye, holding my gaze though it made the beta in him squirm to do so. I reined in some of my alpha command, not wanting to bowl him over with it. "You deserve to be happy."

Those words struck a chord, and I purposely checked the road, taking a minute. After a beat, I gave him a sharp nod, not knowing how else to respond but appreciative of his support. I scanned the passing forest blindly, not really seeing it. "It's not as easy as that."

"The fuck it isn't," Tristan stated matter-of-factly.

I huffed and shoved a hand through my hair, realizing I

was inadvertently staring toward where the bond in my chest pulled—toward the lodge and the woman nestled inside my apartment.

"She rejected me," I informed him, and hearing it out loud brought a new sense of reality to it. My hand tightened on the steering wheel. "She thinks it's what I want, and she plans to reject me in front of the pack at the mating ceremony and break our bond, essentially setting me free."

Tristan whistled, a deprecating, high-pitched sound. "You really are in some shit, aren't you?"

I growled, and he chuckled.

"Is rejecting you what *she* wants?"

"I don't know," I admitted. "I don't think so. I've seen the way she looks at me. Her wolf is just as drawn to me as mine is to hers, but I don't know if that's just the effect of the bond or a reflection of what she actually wants."

"Did you want Kenna in the same way?"

Another low growl broke from my throat. The thought of mating anyone else was massively unappealing, going as far as to turn my stomach. *Goddamn.*

"I'm going to take that as a 'no,' which I already knew. But I think that answers your question, doesn't it?" Ensconced in my truck, we could talk freely, but Tristan kept his voice low anyway. "You didn't desire Kenna the way you do Madison, but her wolf is the same, isn't it?"

"In a sense, it is, yeah. But her wolf feels like her own, not a vestige of her sister."

Though the bond had transferred with the spirit of the wolf that once belonged to Kenna, it was hard to remember that the she-wolf hadn't always been solely Maddie's. It could've been because they were twins, but I had the suspicion it was more. My gut told me there was something greater at play here, and I intended to dig deeper and find out.

"What are you thinking?" I asked, needing to hear whatever was running through Tristan's mind. He'd sent me spiraling down avenues I hadn't considered, and I needed validation that I wasn't grasping at impossibilities.

"You're blaming the connection you feel on the mate bond between you and Madison, but you just openly admitted you never felt drawn to Kenna, even though you were bonded to her. Your wolf may have accepted your fate when that witch bound you together, but you never, not once, actually wanted her.

"Those of us closest to you, who know you best, saw how unhappy you were. Once again, you were sacrificing your own happiness to duty and responsibility. Sound familiar?" Tristan adjusted in his seat, crossing his own arms and staring me down, challenging me to lie and disagree. "It's the same thing you're doing now, except this time, it's worse."

I squeezed my eyes closed for a moment and swallowed. Everything he said hit the mark. And he was right. I knew things with Maddie were different. I'd acknowledged as much to myself. But traveling down this path was dangerous. Hope was dangerous. Allowing myself to actually want something was dangerous.

"Haven't you wondered why you're drawn to Madison when you weren't with Makenna?" Tristan questioned, and I snapped my gaze to his. "They were identical twins, so it wasn't based on outward beauty. They shared the same wolf, the same bond to you. The only difference is the person the wolf resides in now. What if that *means* something?"

I understood what he was getting at.

True mates.

"Our kind has been cursed, Tristan. It's not possible," I said gruffly, trying not to entertain the thought.

Wolves were meant to mate for life. Not having that connection was unnatural, and when shifters came of age, that loss became an unsettled ache that never eased. Bringing up everything we wanted but couldn't have was like rubbing goddamned salt in the wound.

Had I wished that Maddie was my true mate? Fuck, I was man enough to admit I had. Briefly. But it wasn't worth wasting time hoping for the impossible. For some reason, it hurt worse when I pictured her as mine.

My wolf rumbled at the image that branded itself in my thoughts. Maddie with my mark on her neck, right at the crux of her shoulder, for all the world to see, mated by the power and blessing of the Moon Goddess instead of some witch being paid a hefty sum to betray her own kind—the very kind that cursed us to begin with.

Tristan shrugged. "I think there are those of us who know when we meet our mate regardless."

I caught the way Tristan's eyes strayed toward the lodge neither of us could see through the forest. Was I an ass and hadn't realized he had met someone? Or were his musings the emergence of a hidden romantic? Seeing the longing that sparked in his gaze—there and then gone in a blink of an eye—I leaned toward the former.

And I knew I appeared just as pining as he seemed in that brief moment, maybe more.

I was fucked.

There was no way I was going to be able to get Maddie out of my mind. She was like a drug—potent and addicting, keeping me coming back for more.

And if what Tristan was insinuating was right?

I couldn't let her go.

Tristan tore his gaze from the woods and slanted his solemn stare to me, and I could almost feel the gravity of his next words before he'd even spoken. My beta had never been more serious. "We may be cursed, unable to form our fated bonds, but that doesn't mean our spirit doesn't recognize the other half of our soul. If that's Madison for you, the real question is, what are you going to do about it?"

THIRTY-ONE

Madison

A sharp knock on the door startled me as I tossed another top into my suitcase.

My mating ceremony to Hunter was tomorrow night, and I was woefully unprepared for the transition from Ember packlands to the Summit—a central meeting ground where all the packs could gather in neutral territory without killing each other. The Ember pack's private plane was scheduled to depart in the morning, but as pertinent as it was for me to get ready, I was thoroughly distracted.

When I woke up this morning, Hunter was gone again. I knew pack business kept him occupied, but I also felt like he was distancing himself. I'd barely seen him since our talk the night before last, and I was more confused than ever. Though I hated to admit it, I missed him, and I was mostly packing to keep busy while I waited for him to come home.

I wanted to think my desire to see him had a logical reason, like his promise to help me gain access to his father's private collection of old books, but deep down, it was more. The need to be close to him buzzed under my skin, almost like my wolf knew the remaining time we had together was ticking away rapidly. There was only one day left until I rejected him for the final time and, hopefully, severed our bond. Afterwards, all of this would be gone.

I gazed longingly around the apartment as I crossed to the door. I wasn't naive enough, however, to think it was the apartment I'd miss, though I'd felt more at home inside these four walls than I had anywhere else. It was Hunter. It was always Hunter. The thought of not seeing him everyday was a physical ache I didn't know how to soothe.

The banging knock sounded again as I reached the door, closing my hand around the handle.

"I'm here, I'm here," I grumbled at the impatient person on the other side of the mahogany. Yanking it open, half-expecting to find Jasper or Tristan waiting for me, I almost swallowed my tongue when I saw High Alpha Weston on the other side.

"High Alpha." I dipped my head respectfully as I stood back, door wide, allowing him in. "I apologize. I wasn't expecting you, or I would have cleaned up."

I'd heard through the grapevine that the High Alpha liked order and cleanliness, and having visited his home, I knew those rumors to be true. The apartment was in relatively good condition, but I eyed the pile of clothes haphazardly strewn across my room, visible through my wide-open bedroom door. I hoped he wouldn't mind. The last thing I wanted to do was anger him in some way or give him a reason to find me lacking. Visions of the last time I'd seen him swam through my mind, constricting my airway, as a heavy dose of fear pumped through my veins like adrenaline.

"Kenna," he all but cooed and pivoted to face me as I hesitantly released my white-knuckled grip on the edge of the door.

I had no excuse to hold it open without looking suspicious as hell. This was supposed to be my future father-in-law. My future pack Alpha. And as always, my High Alpha. My fealty wasn't just expected, it was required. What kind of message would I send if I held the door open like I expected him to leave as quickly as he'd arrived? But my blood ran cold at the snick of the latch all the same.

"I can smell your fear, my girl," he tsked, and yet, I swore I saw a gleam in his eyes that revealed his glee at my apprehension. He desired his subjects' fear. He all but feasted on the sense of import it gave him to see those he considered lesser wolves squirm beneath his power.

I knew the type. My father was the exact same way.

Two peas in a misogynistic, power-hungry pod.

I schooled my reaction, tamping down the trepidation and nervousness that swirled inside me like an F5 tornado.

I laughed nervously, not having half of my sister's poise and grace. I'd have to fake it, downplay my reaction so he wouldn't be suspicious. There was only one surefire way to do that. Stroke the hell out of his ego.

I pasted on a smile as sweet as sin. "I was simply thrown off by having the most important man in the territory stop in for a surprise visit. What can I do for you, High Alpha?"

I dipped my head once more, showing him my obedience and respect.

As anticipated, the High Alpha puffed up from my ass-kissing praise.

My wolf released a jumble of unhappy snarling noises at having to appease this asshole, but I shushed her quickly. The name of the game was survival. I'd already witnessed this man kill once. I didn't want to be his next target.

"I'm here for you, my dear." He reached out a calloused, rough hand, waiting for me to take it.

Everything in me screamed against touching him. My eyes flicked from his outstretched hand to his face, noting the tight lines at the corners of his eyes.

This is a test.

High Alpha Weston liked to challenge people. Find their limits. Test their power, wit, and loyalty. But mostly, it was a game. He wanted to prove his strength and cunning. Knowing he threw me wildly off balance while simultaneously making me uncomfortable was all the better for his entertainment and enjoyment. Being Alpha, especially High Alpha, was a sport to him. One he intended to win.

Straightening my spine like a puppet suddenly pulled up by its strings, I placed my palm in his.

I don't know what I expected. The world to implode? His power to slam into me and make me submit? Anger to darken his features as he told me he knew all my secrets? Death? None of those things happened.

Instead, he lifted my hand to his mouth and pressed a chaste kiss on the back like a gentleman. I had to keep the cringe off my face from the contact, but otherwise, there was nothing untoward about the gesture.

"Tomorrow, you will mate my son and become the

future Luna of my pack in front of my allies, as well as my enemies."

It was a statement, not a question, so I stayed silent, which appeared to be the correct move when his lips tipped up in the corners like a man with a secret.

"More so, you'll be stepping into a position of power I doubt your father has adequately prepared you for." He sneered, and disdain dripped from his features. Reaching for the door, he opened it and barked, "Caroline!"

A crew of omega wolves filtered in, spreading out in all directions.

"W-what's happening?" I asked, tracing their movement with my eyes. A light breeze stirred through the apartment as they flurried about, setting to tasks I hadn't asked them to do. The demand for them to leave bubbled up my throat, but I swallowed it back. I had no say in the matter, and the High Alpha didn't give one iota about what I wanted.

The wolf in me hated other shifters in Hunter's private quarters, touching our things, but I bit my tongue.

"I don't know what kind of pack your father is running, but you're days away from being a member of mine. There is no reason for our future Luna to pack her own belongings. This is why there is a pack hierarchy, my dear. Let the low-level wolves do the menial labor."

He brushed them off as if their lives were of little importance to him, and he turned toward the living room, pulling me after him by the hand that was still captured in his. Luckily, he didn't see the flash of indignation I was sure darted through my eyes or the way I gritted my teeth at his dismissal of the omegas he considered no more than servants.

"Now," he said, finally releasing me so he could clap at a handful of omegas nearby.

They scurried into motion and moved the furniture until the couches were against the windows and the floor was wide and clear. A round pedestal was placed in the center of the rug and two more omegas hustled in with a heavy, ornate mirror that they set down on the edge of the carpet. Others unfolded a makeshift screen like a vintage changing station. I almost couldn't keep up with the whirl of activity. The omegas worked like bees in a hive, each with a purpose, buzzing to and fro without questioning the orders coming from above. Two more funneled in fresh from the elevator wheeling a portable clothing rack that held more dresses than I could count. They hung in elegant, colorful cascades.

"It's time for you to choose the outfit you'll wear when you mate my son. As future Luna, you will be the envy of all who lay eyes on you. You will be the unattainable center of the men's desire, and the women will covet not only your newfound position of power, but the man you'll claim as your own before the packs. They'll hate you while wishing they could *be* you." He gestured with his hands while he spoke. "You're mating into the strongest pack in the country, taking the most eligible bachelor as your own, and with that comes a responsibility to portray an air of wealth and superiority." The High Alpha waved me toward the dresses, and I turned hesitantly to scan the options. "You must dress the part."

His hand landed on my lower back and nudged me toward the offerings, and I moved simply because I disliked his touch anywhere on my body.

The luxury fabrics were soft and silken under my fingers, and the hangers scraped along the metal bar as I shuffled them to study the options.

Surprise, surprise.

I shouldn't have been shocked all the choices were revealing in one way or another.

As if he could sense my hesitation, the High Alpha began pulling dresses from the rack and thrusting them at a waiting omega. Caught unaware, she gasped before adjusting her hold on the gowns, careful not to crush the silk, satin, or crepe fabrics.

"Shoo. Go on," he ushered me after the girl and behind the curtain. Alone, except for the two attendants, I sighed and stopped resisting.

If the High Alpha wanted to see me in dresses, then I'd truss myself up and parade around the room.

Selecting an emerald-green gown with sturdy fabric, I made the omegas turn their backs while I stripped and shimmied into the dress before requesting their help with the fastenings. Without the mirror, there was no gauge for how I looked, but the bodice dipped far too low in the front and the satin hugged my curves, constricting me in ways that made me want to take the gown right back off.

That wasn't an option. I walked myself out in front of the High Alpha who'd taken a seat in the sole accent chair left in the room, lounging as though it were a golden throne. A blush immediately heated my cheeks at the way he studied my figure. Hunter was the only man who should be looking at me that way, but I held my tongue and spun when the High Alpha twirled his finger through the air.

Catching sight of my reflection in the longline mirror, I almost gasped. Far too much of my chest was on display and the satin I'd hoped would feel covering, shielding, did the exact opposite. Despite the yards of fabric, I felt naked and exposed.

"Gorgeous. Just as I knew you'd be."

Hands fluttering lightly over the neckline to keep my

breasts hidden from sight, I laughed nervously. "I'm not sure the color is right. Pink hair, green dress. I almost feel like a watermelon."

"Delicious and dripping with juice," the High Alpha replied silkenly.

The innuendo did not evade me. Now uncomfortable in my own skin, I excused myself to try another dress and quickly shucked the green one off like it burned, uncaring how many zero's there were on the price tag.

Fuck this.

Angry, emotional tears pricked my eyes. I didn't want to go back out there to be objectified. If it had been anyone else, I would have said screw the consequences and refused to play a part in this charade.

But it wasn't anyone else, and I didn't have a choice.

High Alpha Weston ruled our world, and that included me.

I blew out a steadying breath and blinked rapidly, knowing if I didn't compose myself soon, the High Alpha would read my moment of weakness in my red, watery eyes. Sniffling, resigned to my fate, I reached for another dress.

THIRTY-TWO

Madison

Trembling fingers made it difficult to unhook the next gown from the hanger. The younger of the two omegas with me stepped up and took pity. With a soft, sympathetic smile, she brushed my hands away and readied the dress, helping me step into it. Grateful for her help, I almost didn't mind being mostly naked in front of a perfect stranger. Abandoning my human ideals of modesty was difficult but necessary if I wanted to survive in this world of wolf shifters.

Dress after dress I tried on, and time after time, the High Alpha appraised me like a meal he longed to savor.

Exhausted and not a fan of any of the options, I let the

omega, whose name I'd learned was Bex, pick the next dress while I slumped against the wall and drove my palms into my eyes.

"You'll mess up your makeup, and that will anger the High Alpha," Bex chastised softly. "Come on," she prodded, and I straightened with a sigh. "You have a few more options, but none of them will be any better than what you've already tried on. There is one, though, that's truly stunning, and while it shows off some skin, it's not as revealing as some of the others."

"That one. Whatever it is, I'll take it." I was tired and done playing dress up for the amusement and titillation of the High Alpha.

Smiling more genuinely, Bex pulled a sparkly number I hadn't seen before from where it'd been wedged between two other gowns. The off-white fabric looked as delicate as finely spun gossamer and sparkled as if it had been created using stardust. I gasped and dared to reach out to touch it.

The corset bodice cupped my breasts perfectly when I stepped into the dress, and the fit was sublime when Bex finished fastening each hook. While everything below the supportive cups of the corset was sheer, showing off my stomach and back beneath the sparkling material, the skirt was opaque at the top, fading to transparency toward the bottom in an ombre effect. A lot of skin showed, but all the important bits were concealed from view and fabric covered me from chest to toes.

"This is the one." I smiled without needing to see more. It was just a feeling. I could nearly picture Hunter's face when he saw me in this, but that thought was quickly followed by what I'd have to do while wearing something so stunning. Reject him.

My excitement lessened. Shaking the thought from my

mind, I almost stepped right back out of the garment, wanting Hunter to be the first person besides Bex to see me in it, regardless. But the High Alpha had come for a show, and he wouldn't be happily deprived of the grand finale. Steeling myself for another leering reaction, I moved around the screen and stepped on to the pedestal, letting him get a good, long look at me.

I spun for him when he indicated I should but stopped when I spotted the mirror. My breath caught.

That wasn't me. No. The girl staring back at me was a pink-haired, captivating goddess.

I swished this way and that, enjoying the way the light played off the diamond-like sparkles and the unbelievable softness of the skirt that danced around my legs.

All High Alpha Weston had to do was growl in dismissal and the omegas dropped whatever they were doing and headed toward the door. I watched wide-eyed as Bex winced an apology, dipped her head, and fled with the rest of the shifters until the door closed, leaving me to fend for myself.

My eyes met the High Alpha's as he pushed from his chair and strode in purposeful strides to stand behind me. The pedestal beneath my feet didn't do enough to close our height discrepancy, boosting me a mere five inches. Stepping to my back, the High Alpha towered over me.

It was harder to breathe when the weight of his power pressed along my spine. My wolf hated him, but she recognized when she was outmatched. If he wanted us to submit, there wouldn't be a choice.

We were, well and truly, at his mercy.

"A fitting choice," he purred. "You sparkle like the stars on the darkest of nights. A fitting juxtaposition for how you will be the light our pack turns to on dark days." Nausea churned in my belly as he lifted a hand and rearranged my hair, pushing some of the pink locks off my shoulder. "Yes. This will do nicely. You will be the envy of every woman. They will all want what you have, from your mate to your beauty."

Some of my hair was suddenly captured in his fingers, and he caught my eye in the reflection. "You look absolutely captivating, though the hair is an interesting choice. Bold." Unwelcomed heat flashed in his eyes as he wrapped the strands around his finger, then let them unwind slowly. "I hope it's a testament to how you will be at my son's side, both in the public eye and in… private." His gaze lowered suggestively.

The sensation of a million ants crawled over my skin and made it hard to hold still, but I didn't move a single muscle. The air stalled in my lungs. I didn't dare breathe.

"Soon you'll be mated to my son." One hand snuck to wrap around my waist and he jerked me until my back was plastered against his chest. I almost fell off the pedestal, which caused me to lean heavily into the High Alpha's body for support. His grip turned possessive, fingers digging into my belly like he owned me. "And once he's had you, I'll no longer deny the temptation you inspire. I don't care which of us impregnates you," his fingers splayed over my stomach, "as long as you're carrying a Weston and the future heir to my empire."

My stomach revolted and acid burned as it crawled up the back of my throat. I was going to be sick. Head spinning, I tried to wrap my mind around the vile things that spewed from his mouth. He planned to *rape* me, because there was no way I'd ever willingly let him touch me.

Had he made inappropriate moves on my sister before? Sexual harassment was completely unacceptable. If this had been the treatment Kenna was subjected to when visiting the Ember Wolves, I didn't fault her for wanting to turn it all down and take a lover.

Everyone deserved happiness, and my heart ached that Kenna hadn't gotten to have hers.

The combination of grief and revulsion choked me. I wouldn't stand being treated this way, to be touched by someone without consent. But, who was I to stand up to an Alpha? And not just any Alpha, *the* Alpha. How did I get myself out of this situation?

"My father won't stand for my abuse," I declared, putting far too much faith in another man I didn't trust. There was no love lost between my father and me. But High Alpha Weston thought I was Kenna, and my father had favored her our whole lives. That had to mean something. Hold some kind of weight.

"Your father sold his soul to me when we arranged your mating, darling. Why do you think the treaty remained intact when I *killed* my eldest son?"

I held back the gasp of surprise that wanted to break past my lips, but the High Alpha must have seen the shock in my expression, because his lips curled. He loved an audience, and I was his unwilling captive.

It wasn't shocking that High Alpha Weston was a murderer. That was an easy leap. I'd witnessed as much myself. But having killed his own son? What kind of ruthless monster murdered their own flesh and blood?

Apparently the High Alpha was capable of untold evils. Underestimating him would be a grave mistake, a lesson I wouldn't forget.

"You were never meant to be Hunter's, Kenna. Or had you forgotten?" he mused.

Shit. Was this common knowledge? Something Kenna

knew about? I felt my carefully guarded secrets beginning to unravel.

"You were always supposed to mate with Lyle, but the moment that smug little bastard turned eighteen, he thought he could challenge me and win." High Alpha Weston snarled, and my stomach bore the brunt of his revived anger. I'd have bruises on my skin from where he gripped too tightly while holding me prisoner against him while he raged. "I bled that dream right out of him. Watched the dawning realization that he wasn't prepared to beat me as life drained from his cowardly eyes. He was a traitor. And with his death should have come the annulment of the treaty that united the Ember and Stormborn packs. But your father, the sniveling little kiss-ass, wants the position at my right hand so badly he was willing to re-sign you over to my second son, the new heir-apparent to all I've built."

Hunter. He was talking about Hunter.

"You were young, just nine when I ended Lyle," the hand in my hair toyed with the locks as he reminisced. "I don't blame you for not remembering. But you see, girl, there is nothing your father would do to jeopardize our little arrangement. Your life means nothing to the whims of powerful men. You belong to me. Your life will be whatever I make it. Whatever I deem it to be."

"I won't live like that," I rasped hoarsely. I couldn't. I'd rather die.

Wrapping my hair around his hand, he tugged my head backward painfully. "You don't have a choice." Before I could come up with a retort, High Alpha Weston buried his nose in my hair and inhaled. Deeply.

"There's something about your scent," he murmured, his breath tickling my neck and bringing about another wave of nausea. Dots swam in front of my vision as I scarcely breathed.

I struggled to right myself, to loosen his hold, to put some space between us, but the bar of his arm tightened painfully and his grip on my hair refused to ease.

Shit, shit, shit.

He couldn't know. He couldn't find out who I was.

"Ah, ah, ah," he scolded, sounding far too jovial. "I see you're still struggling in the face of your reality. We can't have you misbehaving."

He adjusted his hold, and my wolf's angry, warning growl reverberated off the corners of my mind just as I caught a glint of silver flash in the mirror. A sharp prick pierced my flesh before I could react.

"No!" I wrenched myself in his arms, trying to break free, trying to fight back, but it was too late.

Sweet lethargy worked through my muscles, rendering them useless. A tear leaked from my eye to trail down my cheek as my body unwillingly sagged against him, feeling heavy and limp. My tongue was thick in my mouth and my head grew fuzzy until I couldn't make sense of the jumble of thoughts and animalistic snarls. Stripped of my power and my dignity, the darkness reached for me and pulled me under as I collapsed against my enemy.

THIRTY-THREE

Hunter

The door crashed into the wall with a resounding bang.

"Where is she?" I stormed into my father's chambers at Ember House, our pack's private residence whenever we visited the Summit lands. Voice no more than a growl, shift impending, I was ready to issue a formal challenge right then and there if he didn't answer me quickly enough.

Everything was fucking wrong. I wanted to claw at the unsettled feeling in the center of my chest, right where the mate bond resided. The unease spread like cancer, growing slowly, poisoning my body until all I wanted to do was cut it out.

I'd been feeling this way for hours. To say my wolf was on edge would be the biggest fucking understatement.

"Calm down," my father chided, barely glancing up from the book he read at his ornate wooden desk.

A snarl sounded from Aiden, his Beta, who stood at his side with his own book in hand. A book that looked oddly familiar.

One fucking thing at a time.

"Tell me where she is, and as long as your answer warrants the response, I'd be happy to 'calm down.' Until my wolf knows what happened to my mate, I'll do no such thing."

Maddie had been missing since sometime yesterday. The note she'd left on her bed said she was coming here early, but I didn't trust it. Aside from the crippling sense of unease, the bond we shared was somehow muted, like a picture that'd been leached of color; you could still see it, yet it wasn't as vibrant. The connection was still there, but the magnetism wasn't that same overwhelming pull. It was soft and quiet in the background.

It wasn't enough to locate her. Fueled by the feeling of wrongness that only seemed to grow, I'd searched my entire territory only to confirm what I already knew—she was gone. Hell, I'd even called Jasper out of sheer desperation, but the fucker's number kept going to voicemail. Pissed and worried, I'd set off to the airstrip to fly out immediately. Except when I arrived, I found my father had already commandeered our private plane that afternoon, and it wouldn't be back until morning to refuel and pick me up.

It was all too convenient, and there was no fucking way I was going to wait that long, so I opted for option B.

I'd spent the last twelve hours trapped in a car driving from our territory in Montana to the Summit lands near Manti-La Sal National Park in Utah. All the while, my wolf slowly lost it.

As soon as I'd arrived, I'd nearly ripped the door to the Ember House off its hinges in my haste to find her. I'd just finished tearing every damn room apart and still hadn't found her, not so much as a fucking whiff of her scent. So here I was, confronting the man my instincts screamed was responsible.

My father stood swiftly, snapping the book closed with a loud thunk. Dust from the unused pages flew into the air, the musty scent tickling my nose. All my senses were heightened with the nearness of my wolf, the overstimulation dizzying.

My father's face twisted in disgruntlement.

Rage simmered through me, and I growled another warning, daring him to start spewing lies. "I know you were there. I smelled you in our apartment when I returned home yesterday," I accused, cutting through whatever bullshit he'd been ready to feed me.

I'd been in the middle of scouring my father's old tomes yesterday when the sinking feeling hit my chest. I knew immediately something wasn't right.

Regret at staying away from her for so long was instant and biting. I'd always planned to take her with me to search for answers to her elemental power, but after my talk with Tristan, I'd needed time alone to think. To fucking process. So I'd kept my distance, staying busy with meetings and my various pack responsibilities. All the while, my promise to Maddie had stayed with me, and when my schedule cleared for a few hours, I decided to go scope out the security on my father's library collection rather than going home.

When I found his office empty with a block of time marked off his calendar, I took the opportunity. I'd called Olivia, who hacked into this system and gave me the clearance I needed, all so I could search his old books and get the hell out before he came home.

I'd convinced myself it was safer that way.

My father was suspicious by nature. Since I'd never cared about his old books before, he'd no doubt take an interest in sussing out what the hell I was up to if he learned I'd been nosing through his collection. As the heir-apparent, I had enough attention bearing down on me. I didn't need additional scrutiny when I was trying to keep Maddie out of danger.

Lot of fucking good it'd done me.

My mate was missing, and I hadn't found one useful piece of information in the hours I'd spent exploring those old texts. It was like the Aether element and Spirit Wolves had been erased from our history. All I'd turned up were hand-written journals filled with useless information, old territory maps, lists of Alpha successions, and histories of various supernatural creatures from vampires and fae, to the moon witches who'd cursed us over a century ago.

When that uneasy feeling settled into the bond, I cut my losses. Though I hated to disappoint Maddie, the over-whelming need to see her forced me to return everything to its natural state and hurry home.

Except when I got there, the apartment was fucking empty.

"I know you have her. Tell me where," I demanded.

"Kenna is just fine," my father barked at my insinuation. "I brought the omegas over to help her pack her things. She met with our seamstress and picked a dress for your mating ceremony tonight. You have to remember, she's a woman. They like to make grand entrances. She didn't want you to see the dress, so she asked to come to the Summit lands early to get settled and have some privacy before the event." He waved me away like I was a pesky fly who irritated him. "Her father requested she spend her last day as a member of his pack at the Stormborn House. You'll see her in a matter of hours."

I inhaled and released it slowly while my mind turned over that information, measuring it for the truth.

All I knew was that Maddie was gone.

Stray belongings had been strewn across her room back home, but most of her things were missing. The note she'd left stated she'd see me at the mating ceremony, but I hadn't trusted it. I didn't know if she'd actually left it, or if someone had left it for her. Fuck, I couldn't even recognize her handwriting. The paper smelled like her, but that didn't mean much. Anyone could have transferred her signature to it. A million scents had filled the apartment, commingling with our own—including my father's.

I trusted Jasper over the man who'd fathered me, and that said a fuckton.

Olivia and Nova were just as surprised and concerned when I asked them. It didn't seem like Maddie to up and leave without a word to any of us. Deep down, I knew she wouldn't go without saying goodbye, unless there wasn't a choice.

But in the back of my mind, niggling doubt ate away at me like acid. Maybe she was distancing herself before she officially rejected me, forcing us apart.

Fuck. I didn't know what to think.

Was she really alright? The need to see her—to *talk* to her—rode me. I wanted to rush over to the Stormborn House and tear it down until I found her. However, if her father didn't want her to see me tonight, there wasn't a damn thing I'd be able to do to persuade him.

While the Summit lands were neutral territory among the packs, the different houses were exclusively for pack members. They were as heavily guarded as our territories back home. I doubted I'd make it to the front door of the Stormborn House without starting a fight with an overzealous enforcer. With tensions already frayed, it would be reckless to piss off Thaddeus hours before our treaty was solidified.

"If I find out you're lying…" A dark promise dripped from the unveiled threat.

"You'll do what?" my father boasted. His eyes turned to slits and his chin tilted up so he could stare down his nose at me. The effect may have worked when I was younger, but I was nearly his equal now. Strong enough to challenge him. Wise enough to lead.

A muscle in my jaw ticked. Hands balling into tight fists, I held my wolf back from ripping into a man he no longer viewed as his superior.

Sensing the threat I'd become, Aiden released a warning growl. The book he held hit the ground with a thump as his nails shifted to claws. I caught a glimpse of the cover, noting the title had something to do with elemental history. As did the one my father had been studying.

What the fuck?. The unease in my chest erupted. Even if Maddie was okay now, that didn't mean she was safe. I wanted to eradicate the threats against her, starting in this very room.

My wolf was ready to issue the formal challenge.

Maddie first. Once I knew she was safe, then I'd deal with my father.

His taunt hung heavy in the air, mixing with his Alpha

authority. It pressed down on me but barely elicited a reaction. What used to feel like an elephant sitting on my chest now felt no heavier than a feather.

I pushed my own alpha command into the room, letting it suffocate Aiden to the point his eyes widened. Served the fucker right. My father's Beta and I had a mutual dislike for each other. Me, because I always knew Aiden was an asshole, and him, because everytime he looked at me, he saw his inevitable demotion. Someday, I'd replace my father, and when that day came, Aiden would be out on his ass faster than he could blink.

Leveling my gaze on my father, I let my glower bore into him, hoping he felt every ounce of truth behind my threat. "Test me and find out."

Leaving them with that warning, I turned and stalked from the room. There wasn't anything else to say. I'd exhausted any answers I'd hoped to find when I stormed into my father's chambers, and I was done wasting time.

I strode purposefully down the hallway, already digging into my pocket for my cell. Tristan answered on the first ring.

"What did you learn?" he said in lieu of a greeting.

"He says she's at the Stormborn House."

"Do you believe him?"

"Never, but I also can't prove him wrong." My anger flared in the background like a wildfire, ready to unleash its wrath on the world. "I can't get a strong enough sense from the bond to locate her, but I've searched the entire Ember House, and she's not fucking here."

"I hear the determination in your voice, Hunter," Tristan warned with a sigh. "You know you can't go over there and demand to see her. Treaty or not, Thaddeus will have your head for challenging his authority in front of his own pack. There's a reason the pack houses are off limits to outsiders."

"And if it was your"—I swallowed—"your mate?"

Tristan was silent. Tension radiated across the line. "So you *do* think she's your true mate...."

I shoved a hand through my hair, tugging on the strands until it was painful. "I haven't been able to get the possibility out of my fucking mind. I haven't been able to get *her* out of my mind."

"Then you do what you need to do. But Hunter?" Tristan said seriously. "Don't get yourself killed, alright? The pack needs you. So does Mads."

Ending the call, I shoved my phone into a side table for safekeeping and stalked from the Ember House. Breaking into a run, I shifted in mid-air, letting the beast inside take over. My clothing fluttered to the ground in tatters and I headed for the woods.

I only had hours left until the mating ceremony started, but I'd spend every last second I could trying to protect the woman I was starting to consider mine.

Running the distance to the Stormborn House, I stalked right up to their border. Enforcers moved in the shadows.

Good. They saw me.

We met with a gnash of teeth and growls. Sunlight glinted off their fangs, and the hair on their grey backs stood on end. Vicious snarls echoed on both sides of the invisible line that separated us. They dared me to set a paw on their property, practically taunting me to kick their sorry asses.

I let my wolf bulk to his full height. As an alpha, I towered above them. My nails flexed, digging into the dirt, and the warmth of my Fire element flooded through me. The flames that lived within blazed to life and heated my deadly gaze, making me look like a demon wolf as I bared my teeth.

Tristan was right. I couldn't do much without starting a war between our packs, but I could do this. I wanted them to know I was here. That I was watching.

I stared them down, exuding alpha authority until they were forced to break eye contact. With one last warning growl, I prowled on, staying recklessly close to Stormborn land. Smoke curled from my paws as I stalked the edges of their territory like a nightmare with a vendetta and a vow. One that threatened if they dared touch one hair on Madison's head, there'd be hell to pay.

I reached for the bond, trying to pour reassurance down the connection. There was nothing. No tug. No warmth or consuming magnetism.

Yeah. Something was very fucking wrong.

I'm here, my Little Wolf. Where are you?

THIRTY-FOUR

Consciousness was a bitch. My lashes fluttered open as I slowly awoke, and everything came rushing back. The soft mattress below me barely registered before my body began swinging. Or at least, trying to.

In reality, I barely moved. My limbs felt weighted and heavy, and while my groggy mind screamed at my muscles to move, to fight, they were sluggish and disobedient. I struggled to breathe through the rising panic as the High Alpha's threats, and his tight hold on my body, came flooding back. My ribs ached like they were bruised and my mind was fuzzy and unfocused, making me slow to connect the dots.

Forcing my elbow to bend and my arm to lift, I sloppily reached for my neck, willing my fingertips to skim over the area I'd felt that sharp prick.

That son of a bitch drugged me.

Gaze wild, my eyes flew from one corner to the next, looking for threats. From where the bed sat against the wall, I had an unobstructed view of the unfamiliar room I'd been left in. I was alone.

At least one thing is going your way.

Vulnerable as I was, I couldn't protect myself, and that had me feeling caged and panicked. I steeled myself with a deep breath, gathered my slowly returning strength, and tried to get up. I made it as far as the headboard, propping myself up against it. It was progress. I shifted the covers off my body. My limbs already felt too heavy, and I didn't want anything else obscuring my ability to move.

It was then I noticed the soft t-shirt and cotton shorts I wore, and my teeth gnashed together as anger surged through me. I'd been wearing a dress before. And that's when the nausea hit.

Listing sideways, I almost took myself out on the corner of an old nightstand when I leaned over the side of the bed. I dry heaved, my body convulsing on each purging wretch. There wasn't anything in my stomach to upend, but I swiped the back of my hand across my mouth when I was done anyway. Shakily, I slipped my legs off the mattress, then swayed to my feet. Pain sliced into my hip as I tilted too far sideways, banging into that godforsaken nightstand. I braced myself against it, using it to my advantage until the room stopped spinning and the floor ceased its rolling.

Slowly, steadily, I stood upright. My hands slid down my

body as I checked myself, patting down my clothing, and assessing my physical state. Tears pricked at my eyes when I realized I was okay. Unharmed.

Untouched.

Other than the expected soreness from being manhandled, nothing else hurt. There was no pain or unwelcome slickness between my thighs. I was even wearing underwear, though my breasts were free-range behind the oversized cotton tee.

He didn't rape me.

Wet streaks trailed down my cheeks freely. Being a girl was so goddamn vulnerable sometimes, and I hated feeling victimized or weak. I was so tired of my fate being decided by the whims of authoritarian, entitled Alphas who paraded around as though they were superior.

The sound of the door handle rattling had me fumbling for something to protect myself with, but the room was barren except for a few sparse furnishings, and I highly doubted I could beat someone to death with a pillow. I could strangle them with the sheet, however, and I fisted the fabric in my hand as the door swung open.

The person I saw was vaguely familiar to my drug-addled brain. It took a second to place her as the maid who'd served me breakfast back at the Stormborn estate that fateful morning after Kenna's death. I didn't know her name, but her eyes lit at the sight of me on my feet.

"You're finally awake," she chirped cheerfully, like I'd simply overslept instead of woken from a drug-induced coma. I guess I couldn't judge her too harshly. It seemed she was always kept in the dark, only fed whatever lies my father wanted to perpetrate.

Two important questions swam to mind, and I asked

the one that seemed most pertinent. "How long have I been out?"

"Long enough." The male voice dripped with disdain, and the click of dress shoes preceded my father into the room. He had to duck past the door frame, which was oddly small.

Seeing him was a trip, and I wanted to pinch myself to make sure I wasn't still stuck in some weird dream state. How did I get here? What happened? And where the hell was I?

"Dismissed," he barked at the maid, who dipped her head and quickly scurried away.

He swung his attention back to me, and I quickly swiped at my wet cheeks, not wanting him to see my moment of weakness, but it was too little too late.

"Alpha Weston tells me you've been… difficult," my father growled. His stormy eyes flashed like lightning, the same disapproval he'd always felt toward me gleaming in the forefront.

"That man is a predator," I spat back with fury and vitriol.

"Aren't we all?" he drolled. "I think you've forgotten, Madison"—my name fell from his lips like he had an aversion to forming the syllables—"you are dirt on the bottom of my shoe, good for nothing unless I give you a purpose."

Stalking forward, he invaded my space and gripped my face. I wanted to fight back, but I was barely remaining upright. Locking my knees and making my spine rigid, I glared back at him as he sneered. "You're only breathing because I allow it. You had one job. *One.* Keep Hunter and High Alpha Weston happy while finding a way to frame them for your sister's gruesome murder. Yet, here you are, hand-delivered to me like a disobedient child by the very man I despise almost as much as you," he raged.

My wolf roused, but her growl of unhappiness was low and quiet. It was the first time I realized she wasn't fully awake yet either. The bond in my chest was just as hushed, like it, too, was fighting the effects of being tranquilized.

"Be careful, Thaddeus." A feminine voice floated into the room. "You don't want to bruise the girl before you've presented her as a gift to the High Alpha and his son."

Endora, the moon witch, swept into the room dressed in a beautiful gown that flowed like shimmering, silver moonlight.

My father was just as well-dressed, in a crisp navy tuxedo with black lapels. Paired with a grey shirt beneath and a black tie, he looked like dark rain clouds, a physical manifestation of his element.

Static electricity infiltrated the room, brewing from the Alpha. My father didn't like being dictated to, especially by the witch he paid to do his bidding.

"I'll bruise her if I damn well please. That's what all the makeup you cover yourselves in is for, is it not?" His tone was biting, his grip tightening ever so slightly until my inner cheeks were abraded by my teeth.

"Hunter will notice," I promised, hating the smooshed sound of my voice.

A resonant snarl of unhappiness vibrated through my father, and then he released me with a shove that threw me off balance. I crashed onto the mattress, catching myself before I was flat on my back. Unable to contain my reaction, I bared my teeth at his retreating back but swallowed down the accompanying sound.

My strength was returning, but I was no match against my father in this condition. I still had questions that needed answers, and I'd catch more flies with honey and all that shit.

"Where are we?" I asked, rubbing my face where I was sure fingerprint-sized bruises were already forming.

"We're at the Summit lands, darling," Endora answered saccharinely. Her melodic voice almost put me in a sugar coma.

Digesting that information and eyeing their style of dress, I came to my own conclusion. "The mating ceremony?"

Endora hummed her agreement. "It's almost time."

"You will bathe and dress. Then Jasper will be here to escort you to the ceremony." My father turned on his heel to face me. "You will do nothing to embarrass me. You will follow through with the mating, and once you are claimed by that ill-equipped bastard, you are to stay out of my way. Do I make myself clear?"

My mind whirled. Stay out of his way permanently? Or was he insinuating something far more imminent?

I nodded to appease him, but meekly asked, "What's happening? Do I need to be careful?"

I didn't give a damn about myself, but if I played the self-serving card and acted like my interest was only in keeping myself safe, the way he would, he might just buy it. But if Hunter was in danger, if Olivia, Nova, Tristan, and Dean were in the crosshairs of whatever scheme he had planned, I needed to know what it was so I could warn them.

My father wanted power. I wouldn't put it past him to use this opportunity to seize any and all he could get.

"Since you have been unable to do the one simple thing I have asked of you, I had to improvise. You are lucky you're still useful to me, or I'd end your pathetic life right here, right now."

"Thaddeus, is that any way to talk to your last surviving daughter?" Endora paced toward me, floating more than walking. I flinched as she reached for my head and ran the back of her finger along my pink hair. Her power tingled against my skin, but it was different from anything I'd ever felt before. "She's needed. Play nice," she warned him. There was something there. Something heavy and intentional in the way she'd worded that.

Needed? What is she talking about? An ominous feeling took up residence in the pit of my stomach.

With a glower, he waved his hand through the room and stormy magic swirled to life. The heavy scent of mist and electricity charged the air, a little tempest forming over the small tub shoved in the corner. Lightning flashed and the clouds opened, unleashing a small monsoon. Rain poured into the basin until it was full enough, then the shower evaporated as quickly as it started.

"Jasper will be here in an hour. Be ready," my father ordered and stomped out. His footsteps echoed down the hall, growing faint until there wasn't a trace of sound. And he took my answers with him.

Endora glided across the room and skimmed her fingers over the surface, whispering a chant I didn't recognize. Steam lifted from the heated bath, and she offered me a small smile that didn't reach her eyes.

"You'll feel much better once you're cleaned up. Your dress is in the wardrobe, along with a stunning pair of shoes," she stated. "Come." She held her hand out.

Pushing gingerly to my feet, I clumsily made my way toward her, my body still awakening. She turned and gave me her back, making it apparent she wasn't going to leave and I should strip.

Gritting my teeth, I got naked and slipped cautiously into the tub. The heat was blissful, and I sighed as I sank below the surface to wet my hair. A bar of soap was waiting for me when I reemerged, still tingling with Endora's evident power. I eyed her suspiciously as I picked it up and scrubbed myself clean. By the time I climbed out, I realized there was something about the water that invigorated me until I felt much more myself.

I dried off and wrapped a towel around my body as I eyed the witch's back.

"I don't understand. You hate me, yet you're helping me. Why?"

Endora took my line of inquiry to mean I was modest and spun gracefully to face me. "I don't hate you, Madison," she said with a tilt of her head.

Like my own personal fairy godmother, she twirled her finger through the air, and my hair dried instantly and spun itself into an elaborate updo. I faced the small mirror on the wall to see soft curls framing my face. The rest swept upward in loose twists and cascaded down my back in a fancy ponytail. It was modern, yet ethereal, a look I never could have created myself.

"I don't understand," I shook my head, my pink hair swaying lightly.

"You're smarter than that, Madison. Haven't you been listening? I have use for you." Her eyes gleamed, and it made my stomach sink.

"And what exactly is it I can help you with?"

She smiled genuinely for the first time, and the look was unsettlingly savage. "That's for me to know and you to find out, my dear."

Madison

I'd been trying to find a way out of this room for the past twenty minutes, but there weren't any windows or doors besides the one Endora locked behind her when she'd left.

So the next time the door opened, I cried out in relief.

"Jasper," I gasped. The last time I'd seen him, we'd parted on bad terms, but despite our muddled history, I launched myself at him. His familiar scent wrapped around me with his hug, and I let myself soak in his strength and comfort. "After High Alpha Weston, then my father and Endora, it's nice to see a friendly face," I murmured into his chest.

"Shhh. It's okay. You're safe now," Jasper promised, and his body shuddered against mine. "I'm sorry, Mads. I'm so damn sorry. I was upset and angry, and needed some distance. I was keeping an eye on you from afar, and I didn't know. I should have been there. I should have stopped him," he rumbled, and his hand stroked my back soothingly. "I won't fail you again, Mads. I swear it."

Tears pricked my eyes once more, but I was mindful of the makeup I'd applied and didn't want to get snot all over his dark dress shirt. I couldn't lose it now. If I started crying in earnest, I might never stop. At least not until I'd downed a gallon of ice cream and decompressed from the hell I'd been through. But it could've been worse. So much worse.

Pulling back, he cupped my face and locked those stormy grey eyes on my blue ones. "He didn't..." Jasper trailed off and swallowed, but he didn't look away.

"No." I quickly shook my head.

He released the breath he'd been holding. "Thank fuck." He reeled me back in and gave me yet another squeezing hug.

"I'm so happy to see you." I sniffled, then pulled myself together. There were people counting on me, and I wouldn't let them down. I stepped out of the circle of Jasper's arms and gazed up at him, searching for the truth. "My father's planning something tonight, isn't he?"

My friend's eyes darkened with anger. "He plans to use you as a pawn to secure the rightful succession of the Ember Pack."

"Meaning he wants me to mate with Hunter," I stated, which had been the plan all along.

It was funny how my heart gave a little flip at the mere mention of claiming Hunter as my own. There was a rightness to it. Bitterly, the rejection I was supposed to issue sat heavy on my tongue.

I didn't know if I could do it. Just the thought of it threatened to fracture my heart into a million pieces.

The ghost of his fingers lingering on my skin would haunt me forever, as would the possessiveness that flared in his eyes when he looked at me sometimes. Those were the moments that made me question everything.

Was rejection what Hunter truly wanted? Because I was woman enough to admit it was the furthest thing from the desires of my heart.

Jasper moved toward me and gripped my biceps, practically begging me to really think about this. "You can't do it, Mads. You can't mate with him."

I was on the verge of asking why, but I wasn't sure I was prepared to hear his answer. There was a wildness to Jasper I hadn't seen in him before, and it made me wary.

Besides, the point was moot. I wouldn't go back on my promise to Hunter unless he said otherwise. I wouldn't tie down a man who didn't want me, no matter how much it killed me to let him go, my certain death be damned.

As grateful as I was to see Jasper, I wasn't about to open up about matters so personal. He despised Hunter, and he'd never understand.

Instead, I stated the obvious, unsure what else to say. "He'll kill me if I don't." We both knew who I was talking about.

"I'd stop him," Jasper growled, but it was an empty promise. He didn't stand a chance against my father.

It was a sobering thought. There were so many ways this night could go, and I needed contingency plans for every single one.

If I issued a rejection the way Hunter expected me to,

my father would be out for my blood. I'd need a quick escape so I could make a run for it, which meant I needed to be prepared. I should pack a bag of essentials and find a way to get some cash. Jasper would help if I asked, but none of this was what I wanted to waste my time thinking about.

Somehow, my own life didn't matter as much to me as those of my friends—or Hunter's. I cared for them almost as much as I had for Kenna. They were my people now, a family I'd chosen rather than one I'd been born into, and I'd protect them with my own life if necessary.

"And if I mate with Hunter? What are my father's plans then?" I pressed, and Jasper growled possessively.

He swallowed it back enough to answer, "He's been gathering allies, planting seeds of doubt that the High Alpha orchestrated a treasonous plot that involved his son attacking you in a failed attempt to end their alliance."

"He has no proof of that," I spat angrily, pulling away from Jasper to pace the room. "The other Alphas can't possibly believe him."

"I told you we'd find a way if you didn't do your part, Madison." Jasper's voice grew callous, and a quick glance showed his face shuttering. Gone was the open affection, and in its place was the hardened shell of the enforcer.

"What does that mean?" I stopped where I stood and waved my hands through the air, beyond frustrated with the cryptic messages I'd received recently.

"He has the witch on his side," Jasper said. "He's been promising mate bonds for the Alphas' heirs if they side with him in a rebellion. They're planning a war, Mads."

"*Tonight?*" It came out high-pitched and incredulous.

"Once you officially take your place as the future Luna of the Ember Pack, he'll attack. The plan is to take out

High Alpha Weston, Hunter, and all of their loyal followers." He paused and let that sink in while my face paled and my heart practically stopped beating. "Then, with you under his control as the sole surviving leader of the Ember Pack, your father will rule more territory than any of the other Alphas, giving him a greater bid for the position of High Alpha. With the witch on his side and the promises they've made, he doesn't expect any of the other Alphas to issue a formal challenge."

It was both expected and shocking all at the same time. But there was something that didn't make sense....

"I've rarely heard of a Luna ruling a pack after the death of her mate." I almost choked at the thought of Hunter dead, but I forged on, needing to understand. "Don't get me wrong, I think it's asinine we don't have more single female rulers, but since we base our succession on brute strength over brains, everyone knows another Alpha would challenge her and win on sheer power alone."

Lunas and other female alphas were strong, but we were outmatched when it came to the alpha males of our kind. It was the whole reason separate Trials were held for men and women when they were ready to prove their strength and find their pack ranking.

"My father or one of the others would have to challenge me for the right to the Ember Pack."

"They won't attack you, Mads." He sounded so sure, but there were strained creases at the corners of his eyes telling me he knew more than he planned on sharing. That wasn't about to fly with me.

"Tell me everything. *Now*, Jasper. I'm running out of patience," I demanded, and it was backed with the rousing power of my wolf.

There you are.

Jasper hesitated but finally caved. "Your father expects you to simply hand it over without the need for a fight."

That wasn't surprising. He thought he had me under his thumb.

"And the others?"

He shoved a hand through his hair. "The Alpha and the witch didn't just promise *magicked* mate bonds. They promised *true* mate bonds."

Color drained from my face. "But that's impossible."

"Is it?" Jasper crossed his arms and raised a brow.

"What's that supposed to mean?" I rasped, but the fight had bled out of me, because I knew.

Yet, I couldn't wrap my mind around it.

They couldn't know about the auras and that shimmering connection I'd seen between Nova and Dean, right? That little secret was mine and mine alone. Besides, my powers were brand new, and I wasn't sure I'd even made the correct assumption that those two were true mates. I could be wrong. I didn't understand anything about being a Spirit wolf.

But Endora does.

Chills raced through me as I remembered her honeyed threats.

Is this what she needs me for? It was possible, but the way she'd phrased it had also felt like *more*.

I didn't know what to make of the witch, but she was undeniably an enemy. I had bigger things to worry about right now, however.

"You have untold powers, Madison. They won't touch you. Not when you're the answer we've all been looking for." Jasper sounded so hopeful, but I didn't share his faith in my father, Endora, or the other Alphas.

"All the Alphas know about me? About Kenna?" I

gasped, trying to wrap my mind around all this information. My thoughts were swimming, twisting and coiling around each other so fast I didn't know where to focus.

"Not exactly. He plans to unveil all the details tonight, but he's told everyone that you're the key to breaking our curse."

"I-I don't understand. That doesn't make sense." My eyes had grown wide, and my arms wrapped around myself. I smoothed my hands over the goosebumps on my skin. This was all so unbelievable.

Me? The answer to breaking the curse? Were they out of their minds? I barely knew how to view auras let alone distinguish mate bonds, and even if I did detect a connection like I had between Nova and Dean, I didn't know how to solidify a true mate bond.

My instincts were screaming at me that Endora did, though. She and my father were consorting together, planning to use me as a tool. A means to an end.

I hated feeling so in the dark, and the idea of being used sent an inky feeling creeping down my spine. It simply added to the foreboding that made me physically ill. I was close to dry heaving all over again, but I held myself together.

Hunter and my friends were in danger, and I needed to warn them. I couldn't let anything happen to any of them. My heart couldn't take another loss.

I had to get out of here. I had to find him.

Jasper was standing between me and the doorway. I needed his help, or I needed him out of my way.

I swallowed down my hesitancy. "If you're so sure the other Alpha's won't attack me, why do you want me to reject Hunter?" I pressed, needing to know.

Jasper huffed a dry laugh, incredulity twisting his

features. "If you don't know the answer to that by now, I must be doing something wrong."

He stalked forward so fast I barely had time to take more than one step backward. Large hands closed around my upper arms, and he yanked me against him.

"Jasper," I sputtered in shock and reprimand. My arms were trapped between us like a barrier, and my hands curled into fists. I pushed against his chest, trying to dislodge his grasp, but he either didn't notice or didn't care. His fingers tightened and he buried his nose into my hair, nestling against the curve of my neck and inhaling deeply.

"Mads," he groaned.

I jerked backward. "Jasper, let me—" I didn't get to finish scolding him before he interrupted.

"Don't fight it. There's always been something between us. I know you feel it too. After tonight, we won't have to hide it anymore. As long as you obey the Alpha, he won't care that we're together."

His mouth slammed down onto mine before I could respond and set him straight.

Aghast and dismayed, I gathered my returning strength and pushed against his chest with as much force as I could muster. A low, angry sound thundered from my wolf. She hated the feel of his body against mine as much as I did. I crushed my lips together against the moist swipe of his tongue. The wrongness of it sat like lead in my stomach. I was repulsed by his touch and the feel of his lips moving over mine. The sound of his rapturous groan made me want to vomit.

I wrenched my head backwards, breaking the kiss, but Jasper just stared down at me with a smile on his face, completely blind to the revulsion painted across mine. His eyes glittered with possession and hunger.

He's fucking delusional.

I was seconds from slapping him across the face or kneeing him in the balls for taking liberties, but I wanted out of his grasp more than I wanted to punish him.

With a heave, I finally broke free of his imprisoning hold. I stumbled back on my heels, catching my balance before I fell on my ass. The arches of my cheeks were heated and flushed with anger, and I scrubbed at my lips.

He'd stolen my first kiss.

I was absolutely gutted, while Jasper appeared love-struck. Besotted. He gazed at me like I hung the damn moon. "Your father doesn't need you to mate with that fuckwad. We have enough allies and power to take the High Alpha down. We can take what we want without you, my Maddie."

Still reeling from the feeling of his mouth on mine, the sound of Hunter's name for me on Jasper's lips caused my stomach to cramp nauseatingly.

He took a step toward me and I mirrored the movement with a step back. I didn't want him anywhere near me.

Some of the light dimmed from his eyes, and he shook his head slightly. He backed up until he stood in the doorway. Snatching the crystal perfume bottle that held Kenna's scent from where it sat on a small shelf by the door, he tossed it lightly and caught it with ease. "You won't be needing this anymore. You're getting a brand new life, Mads." He slipped it into his pocket. "I'll be back for you when it's all over." With a final smile, Jasper backed out of the room before I could react and slammed the door.

No! Chasing after him, I yanked on the knob just as I heard the lock latching into place. Enraged, I screamed and banged a fist against the wood that tingled with the presence of magic.

Endora. Her name was a pissed-off curse.

Panting, my hands shaking with anger, I stepped back, Jasper's betrayal a hot fire burning in my chest.

Slowly, gradually, the icy calm of resolve snuffed the flames of my rage.

I was done being a victim. Done being pushed around. Done, done, *done.* This final act of betrayal snapped something inside me. A power, still foreign and new, rose with a vengeance.

With a deep, bracing breath, I called my wolf.

THIRTY-SIX

Madison

My wolf leapt from my chest in a glorious burst of black fur. Intricate blue markings decorated her coat and her brilliant teal aura glowed softly throughout the small, dim room.

She was gorgeous, but it wasn't the femininity of her build or the graceful way she moved. It was the raging fury in her striking blue eyes promising retribution that made her stunningly beautiful.

Her lethal fangs glinted in the warm lamplight as she bared her teeth at the magically reinforced door.

A snarl so menacing it sent shivers racing along my skin reverberated through the musty air. My wolf was just as viscerally repelled by Jasper as I was, and she was supremely pissed he'd dared to lay hands on me. She wanted to draw his blood in vengeance.

I didn't fucking blame her. Deep down, the animalistic, primal side of myself demanded at least that much in retaliation.

Reaching for her, I buried my fingers in her ethereal coat. The soft caress grounded me, and I released a shuddering breath. That slow exhale kept me from the full-on meltdown that threatened to take over, but this wasn't the time or the place.

My wolf seemed to understand how dire our situation was. The only way out of this room was through that door.

"I need to get out of here and warn Hunter," I told her. "Help me. Please," I begged. She craned her neck to nudge my hand with her head. Her wet tongue lapped gently at my wrist, glowing blue eyes staring up at me reassuringly.

They were so much like Kenna's that it stopped my heart for a second. Even though those eyes were also just like mine, I held onto the comfort that blossomed from thinking I still had a part of my sister with me.

Without a second of hesitation, my wolf turned, ran full-tilt for the door, and leapt through it.

Alone, I wrapped my arms around myself and rubbed my hands up and down my biceps. The pounding beat of my heart echoed in my ears, marking time like a clock. Slow and creeping, a headache formed at my temples, a low ache that grew in intensity until I gripped the sides of my head with a groan.

"What's happening?" I gasped and curled my fingertips into my scalp.

I groaned at the sudden, sharp crescendo of power that rose within me like a tidal wave. It filled every part of my being and had the distinct flavor of my wolf's magic. It buzzed through my veins, growing more potent as it mixed with my adrenaline. Air whooshed from my lungs as something tugged at my mind. The throb in my head increased to something sharp and stabbing.

My panic rose, and my wolf sensed it. She pressed a feeling of calm right into the center of my chest. A request that said 'trust me.'

The pain in my head grew until I didn't think I'd survive it. Another agonizing throb, and suddenly my vision fractured. I was both inside my one-room prison and outside of it, padding down a dark hallway to a set of stone stairs.

Holy shit. *My wolf.*

The two sides of myself coexisted simultaneously. It felt like one step closer to being able to shift, and yet, we were still two distinctly different individuals. I was split between two worlds. Hers and mine.

The effect was dizzying, like a weird version of seeing double. I blinked rapidly, and with a steadying breath, I latched onto my wolf's mind and brought it to the forefront.

She sent a proud wave through our connection, happy I'd figured out what she was trying to teach me.

Wandering carefully to the bed, I sat down and clasped the edge of the mattress in a white-knuckled grip so I could focus solely on my wolf. She was climbing the stairs cautiously, stopping at a cellar door.

Where the fuck am I? Underground?

It didn't matter as long as I got the hell out of here.

I braced myself as she leaned back on her haunches and leapt, sailing through the solid wood.

I squealed like a total girl, my hands flying up to cover my face the second her nose collided with the door. I expected pain to lance through me, but there was only a bit of pressure when she flew through it.

My sudden reaction tossed my own consciousness back to the forefront, and I had to scramble to bring her mind back into focus.

This shit is going to give me mental whiplash.

Finding my way back into her mind, a deep breath of relief flew past my lips when I noticed she'd made it outside. Carefully, my wolf crept through the trees, staying to the shadows, watching for enforcers or other wolves. Her soft, glowing aura was like a flashlight in the darkness. If we ran into anyone, our secret would be out. There was no reasonable explanation for why my wolf glowed in the dark, but it was a chance we had to take.

Hunter. His name reverberated through my mind on repeat, an anthem that fueled my determination to break free.

Mate, my wolf echoed, feeling that same desperation that made my pulse beat faster with a mix of worry and adrenaline. It was the first time I'd heard her speak, and it felt right to hear her voice lilting through my mind.

I reached for the mate bond, but it felt like a quiet afterthought rather than the addictive humming pulse it used to be. Still, it was louder than it had been when I woke up, and that was a good sign. Except it felt... distressed.

In the distance, howls of the enforcers rose into the night, followed by ferocious warning growls. Not wasting another second, my wolf took off into the trees at a fast clip. We were still alone, but for how long? We needed to move.

The forest flew by in a blur of greens and browns. Experiencing it all through my wolf's eyes was incredible. All my senses were heightened beyond anything I'd experienced before. I could almost taste the flavor of the woods as she moved through the trees. Colors had shifted into high definition, becoming more vibrant, and everything sharpened to crystalline clarity. The world came alive in other ways too. The scents were layered, deep and rich. The added sensory input was addicting. It made my typical existence seem almost bland in comparison.

I could sense the moment she left Stormborn territory just as keenly. The taste of the magic in the air changed from something stormy and electric to something neutral and nondescript.

I inhaled deeply, taking it all in, and almost stumbled.

Hunter! I could have sworn I caught his scent on the wind. The notes of smoke and leather teased my senses, calling to me and almost making my wolf shift direction, but they were there and gone in the blink of an eye.

I hesitated, but my wolf pushed us onward. We were almost there. The sound of music and the low din of too many people chatting at once filled the air, and the first twinkle of ambient light was now visible through the trees.

I almost cried out when she stopped and made a sharp left, traversing deeper into the forest and away from the hive of activity. I didn't have a game plan for keeping her out of sight, but help was through that treeline. Hunter and Olivia, Nova and Dean… they were all at the damn ceremony she was heading away from.

What are you doing? I pleaded. *We need to warn them!*

My wolf yipped quietly. A clear 'no,' or at least a 'not yet.'

Padding down a steep decline, she drew to a stop in a small rocky grotto, ducking out of sight by a cluster of ferns situated next to a gurgling stream.

We don't have time for this, I grumbled, but she wasn't listening.

Closing her eyes, she blocked out my view until I receded from her mind, back into my own. I blinked, and I was staring at the same four walls and the blasted door I couldn't break through.

Hurrying over to it, I banged my fist against it once, then twice. Hopelessness crept in as it looked less and less likely I'd be getting out of here anytime soon. Frustrated tears flooded my eyes.

"Dammit," I whispered angrily. "Think, Madison."

I had to get out of here. I *had* to.

My wolf yipped, the sound ricocheting off the corners of my mind. Her magic, the same magic that had pressed in on me earlier, flared to life again, making my head ache. But this time, she wasn't pulling at my consciousness. She scratched at my mind, begging for entrance. For control. But it wasn't natural for a wolf's spirit to invade a human's body and mind in such a way. I'd only ever seen the connection go in reverse. The human became the wolf. The wolf *never* became the human.

Still, her spirit filled up every inch of me until my skin felt too small to fit us both.

Goddess. Her presence was a feral thrum in every limb, her consciousness an urgent press against my own. The foreignness of my body gave her pause, and unease shot through our connection. Returning the favor, I sent her a stream of reassurances, and she quickly smothered her hesitation to continue that unrelenting press.

Every part of me resisted the invasion, but a desperate whine from my wolf once again asked for my trust.

Shaking uncontrollably, I sucked in a breath and

released it slowly. Working past the shocking assault, I found a way to let her in.

The pressure in my head hit an all-time high and then, suddenly, we were symbiotic, her mind right alongside my own. And I understood.

The knowledge my wolf was eager to impart was just there as though I'd always had it.

And I *knew* what she wanted me to do.

My eyelids fluttered shut in concentration, and my wolf, now assured, receded, allowing me to focus.

I reached my magic, summoning the Aether element I knew lived inside of me. At first, I didn't think anything would happen, but after a few moments, a spark flared in my chest. I coaxed it slowly, the way my wolf told me to, and let it grow until it became a beautiful, glowing ball of power in my mind's eye. Channeling it the way my wolf instructed, a static sensation bloomed in my fingers and toes, working through my body until all of me felt fuzzy and disconnected.

Peering down at myself, I huffed an incredulous laugh. My body was shimmering, flickering in and out of existence. Not even my dress was visible.

My wolf yipped with jubilation. She tugged at some invisible threads and then I was flying. Not literally, but it sure as hell felt that way. The rush was dizzying, and my body was nothing but pins and needles. The whirl made my stomach drop, and between one heartbeat and the next, I was shimmering back into existence in front of my wolf.

The forest surrounded me on all sides and the moon glowed overhead. I dragged in a deep breath, hoping the extra dose of oxygen would help my head stop spinning.

"That was insane," I told my wolf, who looked immensely happy with herself.

Kneeling down, I dug my hands into the fur on either side of her face and pressed my forehead to hers.

"Thank you," I whispered, blinking through the emotion that clogged my throat and threatened to spill down my cheeks. We had a lot to learn about each other once this terrible night was over and we were all safe.

Mate, my wolf growled into my mind.

Yes. Hunter, I pressed back and stood swiftly.

Now that I was free from the cellar, the mate bond increased, and Hunter's agitation flooded me.

My wolf peered up at me with a frenzied glint in her gaze before it was overtaken by sheer determination. Eyes narrowing, tongue sneaking out to lick her nose, she crouched like she was about to tackle me to the ground.

And then she did. Kind of.

She leapt into my chest, disappearing from sight, but even as she settled into her usual place inside of me, her presence never truly receded. It hovered close, buzzing below my skin like a live wire and rising to wrap around my mind.

For the first time since I'd gained my wolf, I felt truly connected to her. She felt like mine in a way she never had before. What we'd accomplished tonight had deepened our bond on so many levels. Not just as a shifter, but as friends, companions, and allies. I didn't know how to thank her for all she'd done. She'd significantly changed my life, probably saved it, and I hoped I'd make her just as happy and proud as she made me.

Reading my thoughts, a burst of warmth suffused my chest, letting me know the feeling was mutual.

Sensing her familiarity with the grounds, I once again let her take the lead. The need to get to Hunter drove us both, and I'd do anything to get to him faster.

I slid my heels off, hiked my dress to my knees, and we took off into the shadowed trees. Her power fueled me until I was moving faster than I'd ever run before.

Is this a taste of how Hunter and everyone else feels when they shift into their wolf forms? This fast? This fearless?

With my wolf at the forefront, I felt untamed. Wild. Feral. Savage. I was a passenger in my own body, but at the same time, I felt closer to my wolf, more like a shifter than I ever had in my life.

Forcing myself to slow when I broke from the treeline so as not to draw attention, I strode quickly down the pathway that led to a large stone mansion where the mating ceremony would be held. The place looked like a merge between an academy and a medieval castle with its grey stone, lighted turrets, and numerous balconies.

My instincts told me not to go through the main doors, so I wove through an intricate side garden, cutting around to a set of double doors that were thrown wide. People spilled out everywhere. No. Correction. *Wolves* spilled out everywhere.

And here I was, heading directly into their metaphorical den unprotected except for the new facet of magic I'd just learned how to wield.

Without the perfume Jasper had stolen, I smelled like myself instead of Kenna. My only hope was that people would be too busy socializing to notice the differences between our scents.

I straightened my shoulders, pretending I had nothing to hide. People were less likely to question you if you proceeded with confidence.

My only goal was to find Hunter. After that, I didn't care what happened to me. I just needed to know he and the others were safe.

Following the bond, I hurried through the garden. I'd just made it past the rose bushes when a hand snatched me and pulled me deeper into the darkness.

I was spun around and crushed to a very masculine chest, but the hold was protective. Loving.

"Goddess above, Kenna," a masculine voice breathed as a hand cupped the back of my head. The guy couldn't have been much older than myself, but he looked like he'd been through hell. "I've been worried fucking sick."

I barely had time to take in the oceanic eyes or the white hair of the man who held me before his lips crashed to my own.

My wolf gave a surprising whine filled with anguish and longing, and it stunned me enough that I just stood there like a statue.

I didn't understand it, but my wolf felt close to this man, and though this was my second stolen kiss this evening, I didn't fight this one. I also didn't join in, but something told me it would be cruel to push him away.

The man felt my hesitation and pulled back. His gaze flicked between my eyes, searching for something.

Kenna. This was Kenna's boyfriend. The man she'd told me about that fateful night.

No. It was more than that.

Mate, my wolf said, but it was tinged with sadness.

The man skimmed his thumb over my cheekbone, confusion creasing his forehead.

I shook my head, my heart breaking from loss all over again. I had to tell him. Had to explain, but there was no time.

A dark, wolven shadow fell across us, and with a growl, the man was ripped away from me in one brutally swift move.

Hunter

My wolf ripped Silas off Maddie with a growl, tossing him carelessly aside like yesterday's garbage. Stalking over to him, I bared my canines with a rumbling snarl, and he scrambled back in the grass. Pure hot anger turned my vision into a red haze. His hands had been on *my* mate. He'd fucking kissed her. He'd stolen something from me, from Maddie, and my wolf wanted to tear his throat out.

I reined him in at the last second, reminding my wolf the Summit was supposed to be neutral ground.

"Hunter!" Maddie gasped, darting in front of me and

holding her hands out to stop me before I got the chance to draw blood.

Fuck. She was a sight for sore eyes. I left Silas to climb to his feet while I rested my forehead against her chest. I nuzzled her stomach, and her hands dug into my fur, practically petting me. No one had ever dared touch my wolf like that, but from her, I liked it. She could touch me however the hell she wanted to, and I'd be grateful for her attention. Her affection.

My heart thundered in my chest. When I'd felt the bond strengthen, I'd chased the feeling. Hunting it. Tracking it. The need to see her burned in my veins, and then when I finally fucking found her, that asshole had his mouth plastered against her own, holding her like she belonged to him.

"It's okay," Maddie whispered soothingly. "It's okay."

But it wasn't. Nothing would be okay until I had her in my arms, felt her heartbeat, and convinced both myself and my wolf that she was safe.

Silas brushed the dirt off his coat sleeves, glowering at me with a mixture of confusion and contempt. The Caulder wolf was a powerful Alpha-heir in his own right.

I growled again in warning, infusing the sound with alpha power, and gently nudged Maddie to the side, wanting to protect her in case Silas got the idea to start a fight.

"Kenna." Silas said the name like a fucking prayer, holding out his hand for her. "You don't have to go with him. You don't belong to him. You don't belong to fucking anyone."

Did he just call her Kenna?

"No wonder she liked you," Madison murmured quietly, mostly to herself, but I heard her.

Goddammit. The pieces clicked into place. So this was who Kenna had been seeing? Of course she'd fall for my other rival. Fire and water didn't mix, both in nature and among the packs.

I bet they'd bonded over their mutual dislike for me.

Madison looked full of regret. "I promise to explain, but I can't right now." She took a step backward. "I-I have to go." Turning, she gave me a heavy look, hiked her dress, and ran down the path with me at her side.

"Kenna, please," he pleaded, but when she didn't turn around, his voice changed. It lowered with the power and nearness of his wolf. "This isn't over, Weston," he warned, but I ignored the threat that floated away on the evening breeze.

For the first time in my life, I felt bad for the guy. I knew firsthand how devastating it was to lose a mate, and if he considered Kenna as much, I didn't envy him the pain he'd go through when he learned the truth. Tonight could have ended much differently for me, and I swore never to take Maddie for granted. Happiness was fleeting, and I wanted to hold onto it for as long as I could.

Avoiding prying eyes was difficult in this crush, and we kept to the shadows while we ran through the gardens. I guided Maddie away from the crowd, then nudged her toward an enclosed patio that led to a small, empty event room. She easily scaled the stone balcony and opened the door. We spilled inside, and she slammed it shut, encasing us in darkness. I called on my Fire element and let it shoot out to light the sconces on the wall as Maddie leaned against the door, panting.

My shift already sparked over my body, and I rushed her on my next breath.

Her eyes darkened with hunger at the sight of my

naked body, and something primal and proud rose inside of me.

"Fucking hell, Maddie." I heaved her into my arms and crushed her to my chest. Her heels clattered to the floor, and her arms wound around my neck. I cradled her like the precious treasure she was and buried my face into the crux of her shoulder.

"Hunter," she breathed, the sound barely more than an airy sigh.

My name on her lips roused my cock, and it only grew harder as I drew in the scent of her. Until an unhappy rumble vibrated my chest at the stench of another man on her.

No. Not man. *Men.*

Silas and…

"Fucking *Jasper*," I gritted out.

Anger brought my wolf right back to the surface. My muscles bulked, and I had to push back my shift before I burst out of my skin. There would be plenty of time for retribution later. Right now, I had my woman in my arms, and taking care of her was all that mattered.

"Shh," Maddie soothed. "It's okay."

"They touched you," I bit out, but I wasn't upset with her. It was self-loathing. I was pissed I hadn't been there to protect her. I should've started a fucking war by rushing the Stormborn House. I should've been there. I should've—

Maddie pulled back and traced a finger across my forehead, brushing back a stray lock that had fallen forward. She shook her head slightly. "Not in any way that matters."

It made my stomach twist violently, but I needed to fucking know. "My father?" I swallowed. "I know he was involved in whatever the hell went down." I braced myself for the answer.

"He drugged me, but he didn't… he didn't…" She couldn't bring herself to say it.

I growled as every protective bone in my body reacted. "I'm never going to let another man touch you again." It was a promise I fully intended to keep. I pressed my forehead to hers, breathing in the air she exhaled.

"Let me help you forget, Maddie." I needed her closer. Needed to assure myself she was truly okay.

Reaching down, I gripped her ass and, using pure strength, lifted her up until she wrapped her legs around my waist.

"Hunter," she gasped when I settled myself between her sweet thighs. Her dress bunched around her hips, and her fingers tightened in my hair, keeping me close.

I walked her over to the wall and pinned her against it.

"I'll erase it all until the only person you can think about is me." I skimmed my nose along her neck, reveling in the shiver that wracked her. She was so fucking responsive, it made my dick ache.

Maddie gripped my face in her palms, her eyes searching mine. "Too late. You're already the only person I ever think about." Those pretty blue eyes fell to my mouth, and then she pressed her lips against mine.

I groaned, letting her sweet mouth work over mine hesitantly. I could tell she was new at this, and it made me fucking ecstatic.

I wanted to teach her *everything*.

Mine, my wolf rumbled possessively, and I was in total fucking agreement.

I only let her have control for another minute, and then I devoured her.

With every press of my lips, I staked my claim. With every swipe of my tongue, I told her she was mine, showing her how to move, how to explore. Her fingers skimmed back into my hair, and she tugged.

Growing more confident, she guided me right where she wanted me, angling my head to deepen our kiss. The first glide of her tongue against mine was nearly my undoing. I groaned, letting the sound vibrate my chest. Pressed against her as I was, I wanted that sensation against her nipples. She squirmed, and I let out a satisfied hum of approval as she playfully bit my lip.

Fucking hell…

Together, we traded dominance. Giving. Sharing. Taking. Capturing.

She filled my senses. For the first time, the purity of her signature wrapped around me, the mix of summer thunderstorms and midnight jasmine calling to my wolf in a way I'd never experienced. And the little sounds she made? They were like a stroke against my cock, making me burn for her. I couldn't get enough.

"Thought you were dead," I growled between kisses. "Thought you were hurt." I bit her plump bottom lip, then soothed it with my tongue. "Couldn't find you," I rasped and stole another kiss. "Couldn't feel you."

I braced my hand on the wall beside her head, my fingers digging into the damn drywall as I fought for my self-control. Maddie drove me wild with every graze of her tongue, with every little mewl.

"Almost lost my fucking mind without you. Goddess, Maddie," I groaned as she arched against my hard length. "Fucking need you."

"Goddess above," Maddie hissed with the next rock against my arousal. "I need you too."

My hand went to her ribs, and my thumb curved below her breast. Slowly, I slid it over her bodice, teasing her through the layers of fabric. My other hand slid from her ass to gather her dress. I watched her cerulean eyes darken to sapphires as I stroked my fingers up her thigh, letting the sparkling ivory material bunch as I journeyed onward.

I met the thin strap of her underwear, and with a sharp tug, I ripped it apart, baring her. With a smug tilt of my lips, I set the delicate golden panties off to the side.

"What do you plan to do with those?" she breathed quietly.

"Keep them, of course. They're mine now, Little Wolf."

I enjoyed Maddie's wide eyes and parted lips as she glanced at her ruined panties, then back to me. Her mouth was a beautiful rosy color, as were her cheeks. Knowing I'd put that flush on her face nearly had me groaning all over again.

Goddamn, I was lost for this girl. Why had it taken me so long to admit it?

I slid my hand up to grip her hip, my thumb dancing dangerously close to her center.

"Hunter." Maddie's voice was pure sex. My cock jumped and my balls ached. My hands tightened with my need, but I held onto my self-control even tighter.

This was about Maddie.

My thumb moved, dipping to her sex and slowly circling her clit.

"Oh fuck," she whimpered. Her lashes fluttered closed and she dropped her head back, exposing her neck to me.

I ran my nose along the column of her throat, breathing her in. I rubbed my cheek against her neck, letting my stubble abrade her soft skin while I smothered out the others' scents and marked her with my own. I nipped at the curve of her neck, right over the very spot I was supposed to sink my teeth into tonight to complete the mating bite, and I felt her shiver in my arms.

"Don't do it, Maddie," I murmured against her ear as my thumb circled again. "Don't reject me. I changed my mind. Can't fucking let you go," I rambled as I pleasured her, loving the way her hips canted into my hand, seeking *more*. "You're fucking *mine*. You're my *mate*."

Her eyes flew open, and there were a million emotions flying through those blue depths.

"Tell me you won't reject me." It was an order and a plea all rolled into one. "Say it, Maddie." My thumb stilled, and I waited.

"I don't want to reject you. I never did." Her hand moved to the plane of my jaw, her fingers stroking lightly. Possessively. "You're *mine*, Hunter."

"Fucking hell." My arms shook with the effort it took to hold myself back from lifting her up and slamming her down on my cock, wanting to mark her in every way. "Say it again," I demanded.

"You're my *mate*, Hunter. And I belong to you. Only you," she swore with a vehemence I reveled in.

Her declaration sunk into my soul, and I growled. My cock was ruddy and straining.

"Trust me?" My timbre was deeper and huskier, than I'd meant it to be, but that was what Maddie did to me.

"Always," she promised, and her blue eyes sparkled like stars in the low firelight.

I wouldn't take things too far, but I was dying to *feel* her.

I changed my hold, gripping her hips in both hands, moving myself between her thighs. Slowly, carefully, I slicked myself through her folds, letting the head of my cock stroke over her clit.

"Fuck," she cursed. "This is so much better than doing it to myself."

My hips jerked at the vision of her lying on my bed with her fingers buried inside her pussy. If I wasn't steely hard before, I was now.

"Dammit, Maddie. You can't say stuff like that to me when I'm this fucking close to being inside you."

She grinned cheekily until I ground against her. She inhaled sharply, and her mouth dropped open in a pretty little *O*.

"Tell me to stop, and I will," I promised.

"Don't you fucking dare," she ordered. "I want you to…" She trailed off, and the blush staining her cheeks deepened.

"You want me to make you come, Maddie?"

She nodded.

"I need you to say it."

She bit her lip, hesitating, and I stilled, prolonging her beautiful torture until she gave me what I wanted.

"Say it," I commanded.

Her eyes caught mine. "Don't stop, Hunter. Make me come."

I groaned, thrusting against her, careful not to penetrate.

She wasn't ready for that. Not tonight. But it didn't stop me from grinding against her, making sure I hit that sweet spot with every stroke.

"Oh Goddess," she moaned, and I growled.

"So fucking wet for me," I praised. "That's it, my mate. Cream all over my cock."

Madison

I shuddered in Hunter's hold as he rocked up against me. The silken steel of his cock brushed my clit over and over again, making pleasure coil tightly in my belly.

With his dirty words in my ear and his possessive claim that I belonged to him still playing through my mind, I was a goner.

His cock was thick and long, and I was desperate to know what it would feel like buried inside of me, but Hunter seemed content to give me time to adjust to all of this. I didn't want our first time to be some rushed tryst, so I clung to his tattooed shoulders as he lifted and dropped me, creating delicious friction that had me seeing the fucking stars.

"Holy shit," I gasped, practically unable to form words. I was a tangle of feelings. And the things he made me feel were intense and new and so damn delicious I didn't want them to end.

The way he moved his hips in long, powerful, fluid strokes was sexy as hell, and every time he grunted or groaned sent me teetering to the edge of release.

Adjusting his hold, he freed a hand and tugged down one cup of my bodice. Dipping his head, he sucked my nipple into his mouth with a pull that sent tingles shooting to my core. His eyes rolled up to watch me, and I lost it with the next pull of his mouth and swirl of his talented tongue.

"Hunter!" His name flew off my lips on a hushed scream as my orgasm hit me. My pussy pulsed and fluttered. With a pop, Hunter released my breast. The cant of his hips became uncoordinated as he rutted against me.

"That's it, Maddie. Come for me, my Little Wolf," he coaxed.

Hunter chased my release with his cock nudged between my folds, rocking relentlessly against my clit and prolonging my bliss.

With a jerk, he yanked himself back just enough to grip his cock and stroke himself through his own release. "Fuuu-uck," he hissed, spilling across the floor.

Our foreheads came together, our panting breaths mingling between us.

"My mate. My Maddie," he rumbled possessively, and I loved it.

With a strong arm under my ass, Hunter carried me away from the mess we'd made and set me gently on my feet. My dress fell back into place, and though I was probably mussed to hell, I was once again presentable. He left me for a moment, finding some tissues and cleaning up after himself before returning to my side.

Hooking a finger under my chin, he lifted my face to his and silently leaned down to give me a claiming kiss. Everything that'd been wrong about the other kisses I'd received tonight was right about Hunter's.

"Since I haven't had the chance to tell you this yet,"—his gaze dropped down my body appreciatively—"you look fucking beautiful."

I blushed. "Thank you."

"I meant what I said, Maddie. I don't want you to reject me. That wasn't just the sex talking."

My heart swelled in my chest, and a genuinely happy smile curved my lips. "And I meant what I said. Your mine, Hunter Weston. I'm not letting you go."

Hunter purred, and I breathed in his musk, loving the strength of his scent.

Until I realized mine was just as strong.

"Hunter…" I leaned away as a sense of urgency came rushing back. It had never truly left, simply been pushed to the background while I stole this time with my mate.

There was so much hanging in the balance, but deep down I knew my father wouldn't start a war until Hunter was standing at the High Alpha's side. He wouldn't want any loose ends to deal with in the aftermath of his vile plan. As long as Hunter was with me, we had time, but it was dwindling fast. It wouldn't be long until the High Alpha sent enforcers to look for his son, intent on starting the ceremony.

I had to tell him everything before that happened.

"My scent. Jasper stole the perfume I use to make myself smell more like Kenna. People are going to know.

Not that it matters since my father is planning on outing my secret tonight, but I—"

"Wait," Hunter held up a hand to stop my ramble. "Your father is going to do *what?*" He was angry, and I didn't blame him. So was I.

"I have a lot I need to tell you." I quickly filled him in on the essentials, and Hunter shoved a hand through his hair.

"I always knew your father was an asshole, but fuck. He's actually claiming I killed Kenna?"

"Attacked her," I corrected. "He hasn't told anyone about me yet. As far as everyone is still concerned, I'm Kenna. Without the perfume though, everyone will know I'm not who I say I am the second I walk into that ballroom. As much as I'd love to drop the facade, I think your father will kill me the second he finds out the truth."

"I'd like to see him try. He'll have to kill me first," he swore.

"How about we both stay alive?" I couldn't take one more mention of Hunter dying tonight. My heart couldn't take it.

A knock sounded on the door to the patio, and Hunter held a finger to his lips, telling me to stay quiet. He motioned for me to get against the wall, out of sight. I did what he said as my wolf pressed below my skin, ready to help me protect our man.

Holy shit. Hunter was mine.

It was still sinking in as Hunter tore the door open, his shoulders already bulked from the presence of his wolf.

Tristan raised an eyebrow at Hunter.

"Is that anyway to greet your fucking lackey?" He pushed into the room, unfazed by Hunter's nudity. The scent of the room gave him pause, but he barely missed a beat, letting it roll off his back and refusing to say anything about the smell of sex and pheromones in the air.

My respect for Tristan grew in that moment, and I understood why Hunter chose him as his beta. He was loyal and had Hunter's back no matter what, two qualities I appreciated.

"Do you know what it's like carrying a proper garment bag as a wolf? It's not easy, I'll tell you that." He pulled a garment bag off his shoulder and held it out to Hunter after he'd closed the door again. "Here. I already dressed. You get whatever's left."

"Thanks, man." Hunter clapped Tristan on the shoulder and took the bag. He tossed me a wink as he strode away. I caught myself staring at his ass as he passed, and looked away as he hung the bag from some window trim and unzipped it.

"I'm telling you. I don't get paid enough for this," Tristan complained good-naturedly.

Hunter huffed a laugh as he tugged on his formal attire. "You don't get paid at all."

"And therein lies the problem. Is this what it's going to be like when you're High Alpha? Me running around, cleaning up your messes?"

I giggled. "Probably worse."

"See?" Tristan motioned toward me. "She knows. I need a vacation. And a raise."

"I'll get right on that," Hunter mused dryly, but I could tell he loved the banter.

It'd lightened things, and we needed that before we left this room and faced everything that lay beyond.

Dressed in a black tux with a black shirt and tie, Hunter looked like a dark god. I noticed him discreetly stash my ruined panties into his pocket as I moved to him. He threw me a wink, and my face warmed as I straightened his tie, fiddling with it unnecessarily. I wasn't ready to leave yet. Wasn't ready to put him in danger. If we could find Olivia, Nova, and Dean, I had half a mind to make a run for it. But running would only be a temporary solution.

"It's going to be okay, Maddie. I've got you." Hunter held out his hand, and I took it. Large, warm fingers closed around my smaller ones.

"What's going on?" Tristan asked, sobering.

I looked toward the dark-haired beta, meeting his deep brown eyes. "My father plans on attacking the High Alpha and killing him, Hunter, and any of their loyal supporters."

"He's got the backing of the other Alphas," Hunter added, and Tristan's eyes darkened.

"Well, fuck." He shoved a hand through his hair, pushing the strands away from his forehead. "You got a plan?"

"Yeah," Hunter said, and squeezed my hand. He peered down at me, and I didn't like what I saw. A part of me grew cold as the flames flickered to life in his eyes. "As soon as the mate bond is complete, I'm going to challenge my father for the position of Ember Alpha. When I win, I'll inherit the title of High Alpha. With Maddie by my side, we're going to win back the support of the other Alphas and stop the bloodshed between packs."

"Oh good. I thought it would be something difficult," Tristan quipped sarcastically.

"**Y**ou need to be careful," I murmured quietly to Hunter as we stood at the back of the ballroom. I glanced around nervously, keeping our conversation just between the two of us. My tone was low, hidden easily beneath the pleasant music flowing through the room.

"It's going to be okay," he promised and squeezed my hand reassuringly. Again. He'd been continuously trying to soothe me since he revealed his plan, but no matter how much comfort he tried to offer, I couldn't shake the sinking feeling in my stomach.

I gazed up at him, trying desperately to keep the worry off my face so no one would see. "I can't lose you. I just got you."

Hunter swooped down to give me a quick peck, and I captured him, keeping him there for another kiss. Then another. He groaned as I sipped from his lips until I felt we were drawing more attention than we already had as the guests of honor.

He practically purred when I pulled back, a glint of possession in his eyes that said he liked me staking my claim so publicly. He wanted others to know he was mine.

That *I* was *his*.

"You trust me, right?"

I didn't hesitate. "Yes. Completely."

Hunter looked so certain. So steadfast. "Then have faith, my Little Wolf."

He lifted my arm and pressed a sensual kiss against my wrist, right over the place he'd scent marked me before we'd left our private little haven. I didn't think I'd ever forget the way he'd dropped to his knees before me to rub his face against my stomach, thighs, and wrists to help cover my natural signature with his. Spinning me, he'd done the same to my back, then given the curve of my ass a sharp little bite before he'd stood with a satisfied tilt pulling at his sexy mouth.

So far, the scent marking seemed to be working. No one looked at me weirdly, trying to suss out what was different. Well, except for the stares my pink hair and public displays of affection received, but those couldn't be helped.

"I have all the faith in you," I told him ardently, needing him to really believe it. What kind of Luna would I be if I didn't back my Alpha completely? "It's not you I'm worried about. But you and I both know your father won't play fair, and neither will mine."

"I know," Hunter murmured, and it was the first time even a hint of trepidation had worked into his tone. He covered it quickly. "I've been preparing for this day since I became the heir. I've trained for this." His fingers traced a lock of my hair, tucking it gently behind my ear. "It's time. I won't stand for you to be in danger. I'd do anything to keep you safe, my Little Wolf. I'm ready."

I nodded and cupped his face, my thumb stroking over the line of his jaw. "You're going to be a wonderful Alpha," I whispered.

A mixture of heat and determination flared in his amber eyes, turning them into that fiery russet I loved. "And you'll be a strong and kind Luna."

My heart flipped. I lifted his hand in turn and pressed a kiss along his tattooed knuckles.

"What? No good luck kiss for me?" Tristan inserted, butting into our private moment from where he stood behind us. "You know I'm his second, right? What if I get a boo-boo?"

Hunter released a guttural growl. "You better watch it, or *I'll* be the one to injure you."

"And here I thought our bromance meant more to you. I'm wounded."

I laughed while Hunter raised a sardonic brow in Tristan's direction.

"Ooo." Tristan pantomimed being burned. "So touchy." He grinned, knowing exactly which buttons he was pressing. And he hit each one purposefully, playing his role of beta to perfection. Hunter needed to be completely focused, and Tristan seemed to know how to help redirect his alpha to the right headspace. Through his humor, he eased the impending separation between the two of us while also rousing Hunter's protective nature. It was a subtle reminder of what he was about to fight for.

For us.

For our future and that of his pack.

Each of us completed a part of Hunter. Together, we were his *pack*. His counsel. His support.

A good Alpha needed an inner circle he trusted, and Tristan and I were the start of Hunter's.

The mood between us grew more serious as Tristan and Hunter shared a silent, brotherly moment before getting back to business.

"Tristan?" Hunter murmured.

"Hmm?"

"Call Dean and Kip. Once the mating is complete, I want Maddie out of danger. They're the only ones I trust to protect my mate while we're otherwise engaged."

"On it." Tristan pulled out a sleek phone and hit a button. I tuned him out as he coordinated in the background.

I wanted to interject and tell Hunter I could take care of myself, but if he needed to know I had backup, I wouldn't deny him such a simple request. Besides, after everything I'd been through, it wasn't smart to turn down extra muscle. I liked Dean and Kip. Hunter trusted them, and so did I.

Then Hunter turned to me, and with one last searing kiss, he asked, "You ready?"

With a succinct nod, Hunter looped my arm through his and led me toward the dais his father sat upon. The power in the ballroom was almost stifling with so many Alphas in one place, and I breathed through the cacophony of scents, trying not to feel overwhelmed.

The crowd parted easily to allow us passage. Murmurs moved through the wolves, some complimentary, others downright vicious, but I was solely focused on the dais and the wolves who stood as we approached.

I lifted my chin as the High Alpha locked his gaze on the pair of us. I couldn't decipher the look in his eyes, but I refused to be cowed by the man who'd drugged me. Who'd promised he'd rape me as soon as I was mated to his son.

The son of a bitch needed to go down, and I'd revel in his downfall. There was no room for corrupt leaders in the world Hunter and I wanted to forge together, and the High Alpha needed to be the first to fall.

Followed closely by my father.

The rumble my wolf released into my mind was blood-thirsty. She wanted revenge, but more than that, she wanted to show these men just how much they'd underestimated us.

I spotted my father at the front of the crowd and caught the look of approval on his face. I felt sick at having put it there. I didn't want to do anything to please that man, but I was claiming Hunter for me. For my own wants and needs. Not for some scheme my father had drummed up.

What hit me was that he didn't look surprised to see me....

It had been Jasper's plan to call an audible and lock me up. To tell my father they could take what they wanted by force, without the mating. But my father didn't seem shocked or confused at my presence.

Did that mean Jasper hadn't gotten to him yet? I searched quickly through the crowd, looking for the man I used to call a friend. He was nowhere to be seen, but I could've just as easily missed him, blinded by glitzy dresses and crisp tuxedos everywhere I looked. Everyone here was dressed to the nines, and there were more people than I'd expected.

Among the crowd were the other Alphas, their Betas, their heirs, and some of the wolves who were classed as elites—higher-ranking wolves and those whose bloodlines were undiluted enough to be considered purebred. It didn't used to be a designation, but in the years since our kind had been cursed, the wolf packs had begun breeding solely within their own elements.

Before, wolves could have found their soul match in anyone. Pack lines didn't matter. Now, many of those mixed bloodlines had been eradicated, and those with the purest lines were considered elite. Better. Stronger. It was like they were trying to convince themselves they hadn't lost something precious by lying to themselves that being 'pure' was a good thing. It was absolute horse shit if you asked me, but years of inbreeding had obviously taken its toll on higher thinking.

Hunter's bicep flexed beneath my hand as we finally broke through the throng of people to stand before the dais. The cruel twist of his father's lips had my hand tightening infinitesimally on Hunter's arm, and I felt him reach for our bond, letting me know we were in this together.

Always.

"Ah, my son has finally decided to grace us with his presence," the High Alpha crooned, and a chuckle wove through the crowd. Despite the politics, the High Alpha had many loyal followers. Seeing how they pandered to him made me question the validity of my father's plans.

Off to my side, Olivia and Nova broke through the masses with Dean and Kip trailing just a step behind. The looks on their faces were a mixture of relief and curiosity. They didn't need to speak. I knew exactly what they were thinking. Their gazes burned into me, asking where the hell I'd been and if I was alright.

I sent them a reassuring glance, one I hoped conveyed I was okay. Or as okay as I could be given that my mate was about to throw down a challenge that could end in his death.

"Come and greet your High Alpha," Hunter's father demanded.

Hunter radiated pure confidence as he led me past my father and Endora who stood at the base of the dais with members of the Stormborn pack behind them. My father's attention bored into me as I passed, warning me to obey and act according to his plans, but I didn't acknowledge him.

Clinging to my mate, we climbed the steps of the dais, and I dropped into a small curtsy when we reached the top, murmuring, "High Alpha."

"Father." Hunter dipped his head respectfully, though I knew it killed him to do so.

Under the dim lights, the High Alpha's umber eyes glittered like obsidian, and something in my stomach clenched when the weight of his gaze fell upon me. "Kenna. Let me be among the first to tell you how lovely you look tonight." There was a crude undertone to his otherwise benign compliment, and Hunter tensed beside me.

I forced a tight smile to my lips, wanting him to see that he didn't hold any power over me. I wasn't afraid.

Somehow, that only made the spark of inappropriate interest in his gaze burn hotter. He liked the fucking challenge I apparently presented, and it made me want to go home and take a shower to scrub the feeling of his stare off my skin.

A low, vicious rumble sounded from Hunter, drawing his father's attention off of me.

"Curious, is it not?" the High Alpha remarked, only continuing when we weren't baited by his open-ended question. "After all these years, you've finally taken an interest in your mate. Makes a man wonder what's changed."

"Nothing's changed. I simply have duty and honor," Hunter replied with a half-truth.

For a brief moment, my heart seized, worried he viewed me as a commitment he was obligated to fulfill. But I knew better. What Hunter and I had, ran deep. We had real chemistry. Real connection. And while the mate bond drew us together, it wasn't responsible for what we felt for each other. After all, Hunter had been promised to Kenna far longer than he'd been bonded to me, and the two of them hadn't shared one ounce of real affection for each other.

Hunter's hands on my body earlier told the real truth. The desperate way he'd needed me would forever be branded into my memories.

Right now, Hunter was embroiled in a dangerous game. We both were. Anything we had to do or say tonight was in the name of survival.

I threw up the walls around my heart. I was in a den of

wolves, and there was no room for softness or vulnerability here.

"And what of your duty and honor, *Kenna*?" He said the name with a suspicious lilt that made the hair on the back of my neck stand on end.

"I'm sorry?" The question rolled off my tongue while my mind spun, trying to figure out what he implied.

Hunter vibrated with angry energy. "What are you trying to get at?"

His father ignored him, crossing his arms behind his back as he stared me down like he could force the truth out of me with his intensity. "Your loyalty. Does it lie with the Ember Wolves?" His eyes narrowed as he threw a brief glance over my shoulder. I followed it down the dais to where my father stood, waiting for our formal greeting of the High Alpha to conclude so we could get on with the mating ceremony. And thus, his plans.

Little did the High Alpha know just how far my loyalties strayed from my birth pack. And little did he know that my answer had absolutely nothing to do with him and everything to do with Hunter.

"It does, and always will," I vowed, my fingers tightening on Hunter's arm in silent, secretive support.

Heat washed through our bond, chasing away the chill that always crept over me whenever I had interactions with the High Alpha.

"That's my good girl," the High Alpha praised, and I wanted to wrinkle my nose in disgust at the ownership in his voice and the way he made me sound like his pet.

Hunter dropped my arm and stepped toward his father. From below, it probably looked like they were having a bonding moment, but Hunter dropped his tone to something that resonated with warning. "Don't fucking talk to her that way."

A manic sort of glee lit the High Alpha's features, and he clamped his hand around the back of Hunter's neck in a faux embrace. "And if I don't comply, what is it you plan to do, hmm?"

Tristan emerged behind me, clamping his hand on my shoulder. Whether it was in support or to pull me out of the way if the two men started brawling, I didn't know, but I was too focused to care. My hands clenched into fists, nails biting into my palms as the High Alpha bared his teeth in a feral smile.

He leaned into Hunter's space, looking for all the world like he was enjoying himself, and uttered two little words. "Challenge me?"

THIRTY-NINE

Hunter

Sharp, painful pricks pierced my neck as my father's nails shifted to claws.

"You think I can't smell the dissent on you?" His eyes flashed with fire as he inhaled. "I can practically taste your hatred," he purred.

It wasn't exactly news that I disliked my father. Though we kept up a facade of respect for each other, there was very little truth behind it. My father tolerated me because he had to. He needed an heir, and once Lyle was gone, I was all he had left.

And I tolerated my father because I didn't have a choice. There were too many lives sitting upon my shoulders to challenge him prematurely. As badly as I wanted to try and take him down years ago, I had Olivia to think of, as well as Tristan and my pack. Despite being in his fifties, the man was in his prime. Undeniably strong and savagely cunning, he would make a vicious opponent in a challenge.

If that weren't enough, unseating the High Alpha would send a ripple effect through the packs. It wasn't just my father I'd have to face, but any of the other Alphas who thought they stood a chance of besting me and procuring the title and position of High Alpha for themselves.

We were talking about an upset that spanned far and wide. Bloodshed wasn't what I reveled in or desired, but the packs needed a shake-up, and there'd never been a better time than now.

I meant what I'd told Maddie. I'd do anything to keep her safe.

She meant that fucking much to me now.

"I see the challenge in your eyes. It's waiting on your tongue for the perfect opportunity, isn't it?" he taunted. His hold tightened, digging into my flesh enough to draw blood.

I kept my expression blank and my tongue silent, refusing to reveal my plans or allow my father to rattle me, and that irritated him to no end.

My father was a sadistic bastard. He thrived off conflict and discord, got off on making other people's lives miserable. Ruling by fear was his mantra, and with each passing year, he grew more creative in the ways he inspired fealty.

So, my lack of reaction dug right under his skin like an unrelenting itch. He wanted me to squirm, to sweat, and I wouldn't give him the satisfaction.

Whether he realized it or not, I wasn't the same scared kid I'd been when I watched my brother bleed out from a torn throat. I was a man now, with a woman I wanted to ardently protect. I was an alpha who already had the support of his pack behind him. I was a wolf with a thirst to right the imbalance of power that had been skewed for far too long. My pack deserved their freedom from tyranny, and my mate deserved not to live fearfully in the shadows— hunted by a murderer, oppressed by her father, and forced to live a double life.

Fuck all of it.

It ended tonight.

As soon as Maddie wore my crescent-shaped bite mark and our mating was blessed by the moon witch, I'd issue my challenge and fight to the death.

My father sighed and pulled me with him as he began to pace. His arm stayed drooped over my back, hand gripping the scruff of my neck, claws still embedded in my skin. I growled quietly, but went along with the charade, parading with him to keep up appearances for those celebrating and partying down below.

Music still flowed from the string quartet he'd hired for the evening and waiters flitted through the crowd with trays of hors d'oeuvres and glasses of wine and champagne. Endless chatter created a low din in the cavernous ballroom, and we'd mostly lost the attention of our guests who were waiting until my father addressed the room at large and began the ceremony. To anyone who still paid us mind, my father probably appeared as though he was giving me advice on mated life, or simply wishing me luck with my future, rather than issuing threats.

I could have overpowered him or fought back, but I didn't want to make a scene. I needed him and Thaddeus to go through with their treaty, and as much as it vexed me, I needed that damn witch.

Since Maddie and I didn't know if her Aether powers

could truly bind mates together, this was our best chance of solidifying our bond, and that was something I wasn't willing to leave to chance.

There was too much that could go wrong. Being officially mated would deepen our connection and allow us to speak into each other's minds at will without having to be in our shifted forms—something my Little Wolf couldn't do yet. I needed Maddie bound to me in all ways if I stood any chance of keeping her safe from the threats stacked against her.

If my father wanted to try and cow me before the ceremony started, so be it. I'd grit my teeth and take it knowing this was the final time I'd be subjected to his beratement or mad rants.

His claws dug a little deeper as he sighed. "I'd hoped you were smarter than your foolish brother." I tensed at the mention of Lyle, and sensing he'd struck a chord, he forged forward like a dog with a bone. "Yet, I sense your willingness—your sheer desire—to go down the same road that led to his brutal end. You have no idea how foolish you even are." He pulled me forward bodily, and the gouges in my neck tore from the force. My teeth gnashed together, but the pain was a pinprick, nothing compared to what I'd experience when we battled for dominance and the right to rule. I let it roll off my back, even though his words refused to. "You think you can kill me and there won't be repercussions? You have no idea what would happen if you tried to challenge me. And if by some twist of fate you succeeded, which we both know you wouldn't, you still wouldn't win."

What the fuck is he talking about?

"Your brother wore the same look of confusion when he found out just moments before I dealt the final blow that ended his sorry life. You have no idea how long I've waited to play this card. To see your face when you learned the truth."

I hated that he had me right where he wanted me, but whatever secret he held had him practically vibrating with mad energy. If it was something that put Maddie in danger —or my sister, Tristan, and the pack—I had to swallow my pride and figure out what bomb he was prepared to drop.

"What truth?" I questioned.

My father drew to a stop and finally released me so he could face me, wanting to fully witness my reaction, if I had to hazard a guess.

"Let me tell you a story about two Alphas who fell in love with the same woman," he started.

"Not what I expected…." I mumbled. "Continue."

My father bristled at the command in my voice, but he let it slide, too gleefully excited to shock me with whatever he had to unveil.

"It was the one and only time I lost to another Alpha, but the woman I wanted chose to mate with another." His contemptuous gaze fell to Thaddeus.

Well fuck. He had to be talking about Maddie's mother. I hadn't known the vendetta he had against the Stormborn Wolves went deeper than land, power, and easier access to the Caulder Wolves' territory, but it finally made sense why he hated Thaddeus so much. It was fucking personal.

"The High Alpha at the time was growing older and his power was beginning to slip, both Thaddeus and I planned to challenge him for his position. The young Stormborn Alpha was just as hungry for power as I was, but I refused to lose to him a second time."

"I don't see what this has to do with anything," I remarked, trying to figure out where he was going with this and why he thought any of it mattered when it came to me issuing a formal challenge against him.

"You never did have any patience," he spat. "A trait you got from your mother, no doubt. But I'll cut to the chase since we have far more important things to accomplish this evening. Once I made the decision to issue a challenge for the position of High Alpha, I hunted down a witch and made a trade."

My brows drew together, and I crossed my arms, eyeing my father suspiciously. This was the first I'd heard any mention of yet another witch. "What kind of trade?"

"My wolf's soul for more power and strength."

He said it so nonchalantly that it took me a minute to digest it. He'd signed away his wolf's *soul*? To a fucking *witch*? "That's dark magic, against all the supernatural laws," I gritted out quietly, shifting my gaze around to make sure no one was listening in on our conversation.

I caught sight of Maddie standing with Tristan, a concerned crease between her brows as she studied us across the distance my father had put between us. His enforcers stood nearby. Watching. Waiting. Unease crept in.

"Witches will do almost anything for enough money. Besides, it was a mutually beneficial arrangement. She draws on my soul for her magic and spells, and in return, I wield invincibility like a sword, slaying all who dare to stand against me. Don't you see?" he crooned. "I'm practically unbeatable."

"All living things can die," I threatened.

His eyes flashed dangerously. Maniacally. Madly. And I knew then it was the true cost of living without a soul. I'd watched my father descend into cruelty, into madness, for years. It made sense now. He was cursed. Soulless. Separated from the very essence of his wolf. Over time, it had fractured his mind. He was literally going mad.

"There are few who can stand against me," he warned, but a flash of vulnerability crossed his face, there and gone so fast I would have missed it if I'd blinked. "If the Moon Goddess herself came down from the heavens and struck me dead, I suppose. But that's the greatest part of my little story, you see, for even if by some twist of fate I die, the curse will transfer to my heir. And thanks to your brother's selfishness, that honor is now bestowed upon *you*."

Ice ran through my veins and my wolf snarled so menacingly in my mind that my temples throbbed. The idea of my wolf's soul being ripped from me had a sense of forlornness spreading through my chest. Aside from what it would do to me, all I could think about were the consequences that would affect Maddie. Once we were mated, our souls would be connected. Bound together forever.

My parents were chosen mates, not true mates or even bonded mates, and my mind roiled as I thought back to how my mother had been sick for years.

Did my father's curse have something to do with why my mother wasted away?

Why she *died*?

I staggered back a step as the gravity of what I'd learned sunk in.

If my realization were correct, Maddie would suffer far worse, because our bond was stronger than anything my parents had shared.

I peered up, almost unseeing. My vision tunneled until the room faded away and all I could see was Maddie. My little wolf. I wouldn't—*couldn't*—condemn her to such a life.

Sensing my distress, she fought against Tristan to get to

me, but he held her back, trying to subdue my feisty little mate.

"I see you've connected all the dots. You always did have the quickest wit of all my children." His large hand clamped down on my shoulder, but I didn't react. I couldn't tear my gaze away from Madison. Away from the future I'd been so close to having. "Let's hope that serves you well throughout the rest of your evening."

With a shove, he pushed me toward the edge of the dais to stand at his side while I tried to figure out how the hell I could stall the ceremony he was about to commence. And how I was going to tell Madison.

"Ladies and Gentlemen…. I want to thank you for coming out to celebrate this momentous occasion with my son and his future mate. However, before we get to the real reason we're all gathered here this evening, it's been brought to my attention that there is a traitor in our midst. A cockroach willing to scheme. To plot against me in the background." Gasps tore through the wolves gathered throughout the room, and murmurs rose with accusations and questions.

"What the fuck are you doing?" I growled under my breath, trying to figure out what motive he'd have for calling me out so publicly by telling the room at large I'd been about to challenge him. For trying to paint me as a traitor.

My father ignored me and smiled sardonically. "It's entertaining really, that he thinks he can beat me. So, how about a little preceremonial entertainment, hmm?" My father locked his eyes on his victim like a predator ready to take down its prey. "I formally issue a challenge against Thaddeus Hale, Alpha of the Stormborn Pack, who has been spreading lies and planning to stage a coup this evening in an effort to usurp me. Thankfully, most of my Alphas are rather loyal and brought his traitorous actions to my attention."

Thaddeus seethed from where he stood at the bottom of the dais, glaring daggers at my father. "This is absolutely preposterous." His tirade went on, but I was too busy communicating with Tristan to get Maddie out of the room.

She didn't hold any love for her father, but that didn't mean she needed to watch him die at my father's hand.

But all three of us froze when the High Alpha threw one last curveball at us.

"Since this is my favorite suit," my father brushed a hand down the expensive fabric of his jacket, "I'm naming my son, Hunter, as my proxy."

With a vile grin, my father leaned close. "You wanted to fight? Go on and prove yourself, boy. Let's see if you have what it takes to try your hand against me. Win and you can have the girl. Lose, and… well, you'll be dead, so you won't mind if I decide to sample her for myself."

FORTY

Madison

The High Alpha snapped his fingers and suddenly Tristan and I were surrounded by enforcers. My heart hadn't regained a steady beat since Hunter was named as his father's proxy, and being boxed in by strange men only prolonged the stutter. Hunter growled furiously beyond the wall of muscular flesh separating us. Tristan added his own intimidating snarl to the cacophony and shoved me behind him, prepared to defend me in his alpha's stead.

My wolf pressed swiftly to the surface, and I bared my teeth like an animal, daring the enforcers to lay a hand on me.

I could barely hear the High Alpha bark Tristan's name past my wolf's own thundering sounds of unhappiness.

"Tristan." He infused his command with power that demanded obedience. "You will serve as Hunter's second. Leave the girl and attend to your alpha."

Tristan's jaw jumped, but there wasn't a choice. He couldn't defy a direct order, and a public one at that. Wolves had been killed for lesser offenses.

"Go," I urged. "Watch his back. I'll be fine." Hunter held my heart, and I'd much rather Tristan serve at his side than mine.

"Dean," Hunter called brusquely, his wolf turning his smooth timbre to grit and gravel. He nodded in my direction.

My redheaded friend started shoving his way toward me through the crowd, who'd formed a wide circle in the center of the ballroom for the brawl. Hunter and I shared one last heavy look. A million things flashed in his eyes— concern for me, anger at his father, determination to win, lingering heat and passion that told me just how much he cared about me. I put just as much into mine, telling him he better be careful and come back to me in one piece. He gave me a confident nod as he descended the stairs to fight and kill the man who'd fathered me.

"Take the girl," the High Alpha commanded his enforcers. "If the rumors I've been hearing are true, she's too important to risk, and if I have my way, things are about to get violent." He waved me away as though I were an object and not the future Luna of his pack.

His dismissal didn't bode well. There was a smugness to his expression telling me he held more cards than I'd given him credit for, and the dread that had taken up residence in the pit of my stomach turned to lead.

Not willing to go down without a fight, I swung at the first enforcer who reached for me. The punch landed with a thud across his face, and pain lanced through my fist. Unfortunately, it only angered him.

"No!" I cried as two of the enforcers lifted me off my feet and roughly dragged me toward one of the side doors.

I caught glimpses of Dean fighting off enforcers while Olivia and Nova tried to shoulder their way through the crowd to reach me. Hunter turned swiftly at the sound of my distress, his russet eyes searching for mine through the crowd as I fought to free myself. The resonance of his growl reverberated off the walls.

"Take your hands off me!" I spat.

But I was a distraction Hunter couldn't afford.

Dark storm clouds formed overhead, swirling along the high ceiling. Lightning flashed and thunder boomed loud enough to rattle the walls.

True to his nature, my father had shifted before the challenge officially commenced. His clothing rained down in tatters across the marble. The last thing I saw as the enforcers hauled me from the room was my father launching himself at my mate before he even had a chance to loosen his tie.

❖·)·)·)·)·●·(·(·(·(·❖

A boom echoed through the room as the heavy doors of the large, connecting event room swung shut, blocking out the broken glimpses I had of Hunter and the fight. The enforcers cursed as I kicked and scratched, doing all I could to break free against opponents that outweighed me by one hundred pounds each. They had natural strength and training that I didn't.

In the midst of my struggle, my surroundings were a blur until I was tossed haphazardly onto a soft surface. Manhandled like a prisoner, the enforcers slammed a cuff around my wrist, then secured it to a post and moved back to survey their handiwork.

Seething, I memorized their features. They were going to pay for ripping me away from Hunter. Vicious sounds from the challenge filtered through from beyond the door. My heart seized with worry, but I swallowed hard and forced myself to focus.

Get free, then get back to Hunter.

I looked around at the makeshift room, cataloging everything I could about where I was and how to get out of here. I was sprawled across a four-poster, king-size bed. Gauzy fabric hung from the canopy above, tied elegantly at each ornate bedpost. Beyond the edge of the mattress was a throne-like upholstered seat with other chairs flanked off to the sides.

"What the hell is all of this?" I bit out at the enforcer who wore a sneer.

He cocked his head at me, amusement turning his sneer into a leering smile. "You seriously don't know?" He peered over at the other guy and laughed, even though the second enforcer didn't join in his amusement, looking uncomfortable.

I gritted my teeth. Oh yeah, Mr. Sneer was definitely going to pay. My wolf was in full agreement. The fucker.

I tugged at the shackle on my wrist, testing its strength and tightness while I responded. I needed to keep them talking so they didn't notice the way I tried to manipulate my thumb so I could slip free. "Apparently not. Care to explain?"

"Your mating to Hunter is as close to a true mating as we've gotten in fucking *years*. After the ceremony is complete, given the importance of your union and the treaty set to be signed between our packs, The High Alpha intends for your mating to be *witnessed*."

Sex. He meant sex.

Usually when wolves *mated* for the first time—whether they were chosen or true mates—they marked each other with bites that would remain as permanent scars. It was always done in private. But since our mating was such a public affair, I'd thought we would share those bites in innocuous places before Endora completed our mate bond using magic.

My stomach twisted. The skin on my wrist and the base of my palm grew raw as I fought my restraint.

I huffed in shock and shook my head. But I should've known the High Alpha would have tried something like this. "Like a fucking bedding ceremony?"

The practice of having a newlywed couple observed by numerous witnesses as they consummated their marriage was an archaic, degrading spectacle. I'd never heard of the wolves adopting such customs.

Our kind were possessive and private.

"You didn't know?" The second enforcer asked, rubbing at a gouge I'd scratched into his cheek during my struggle.

"No, and the High Alpha's mad if he thinks I'd ever agree to such a thing."

And Hunter? Heads would roll before he allowed anyone to see me so intimately. He was the epitome of a protective and possessive wolf, and I was *his*. I might as well have a sign hanging around my neck that said 'For Hunter's Eyes Only.'

I glanced at the other chairs, counting how many were present beside the throne obviously meant for the High Alpha. There were nine.

"The other Alphas and Endora?" I asked, barely needing the confirmation.

"And their Betas will most likely stand at the back. Alphas never go anywhere without their bodyguards." Mr. Sneer glared and rubbed at the bruise forming along his jaw from where I'd punched him. "If I'd known being Beta would come with such perks, I'd have fought Aiden for the honor. What I wouldn't give to see you stripped bare and put in your place."

I wasn't a bloodthirsty person by nature, but my wolf and I both agreed this asshole deserved to feel our wrath. That simple bruise wasn't enough. I growled just as viciously as the sounds echoing in from the ballroom.

"Come on." Mr. Sneer gestured his arm into the second guy, tapping him on the chest with the back of his hand. "She's not going anywhere, and I'm not going to miss a good fight to babysit." He moved for the door. "Have fun, *sweetheart.*"

"That's Luna to you," I spat.

"Not yet, it isn't."

"You better run, wolf," I warned, "because once I'm part of your pack, I will make you regret the day you were whelped."

Once Hunter was in charge, we'd have to weed out the bad apples from his father's regime, and I planned to start with this guy.

He skimmed his hand over the light bruise. "Yeah, I'm

really scared of a bitch who doesn't even know how to throw a proper punch. I look forward to seeing you try."

I roared as I reached for my wolf, begging for Kenna's Storm element so I could fry his ass with a bolt of lightning. Warmth flared in the center of my chest, then abruptly cut off as heat simmered to life along my wrist instead. My skin burned beneath the manacle, the pain searing, and I screamed.

The enforcer chuckled. "That's silver, sweetheart. Locks down your wolf and any powers you possess. Why do you think we chained you up with only one shackle? It's that fucking effective. Now shut that pretty little mouth and wait until the High Alpha has need of you."

His laughter melded into the roar of the crowd as he ripped open the door and walked through it with the second enforcer trailing after him unsurely. I used the brief few seconds to catch a precious glimpse of my mate amidst the battle, but all I could see as I strained against my binding were flashes of fur between the crowd as the two wolves tore at each other. The noise muted again as the door slammed shut in the enforcers' wake, and the snick of a latch slid into place as they locked me in.

I screamed a loud, long, frustrated sound while my wolf snarled. A headache pounded behind my eyes when I was done. Together, my wolf and I tried to find a way around the silver cuff. My skin blistered and melted, and eventually, I couldn't take any more.

Angry tears leaked from my eyes.

"Dammit," I hissed as I propped myself against the headboard and curled into myself. My fingers shook from the pain, and I balled them into a weak fist.

Hunter's distress bled into my own through the bond until I didn't know where I started and he ended.

I stared out the bank of windows along the back wall, blinking to get my emotions under control. Moonlight spilled across the gardens, outlining the shadowed roses and topiaries. I tried to draw peace from the tranquil scene.

Maybe if I could clear my mind, a plan would come to me. If I could just get out of this shackle….

Lost in my thoughts, I almost didn't notice the shift in the room. Smoky tendrils seeped through the seam where the french casement windows met. They slithered in like ink, circling back to press against the panes until the window flew open. Dark, cloud-like matter poured into the room unbidden, creeping across the ground like low-hanging fog.

I watched with wide, disbelieving eyes. Panic seized me, and my struggle to break free renewed. I yanked, pulled, and wrenched against the silver cuff. The smell of scorched skin assaulted my nose as my wolf rose protectively, and a gasping, airy keen rent the air. It took me a minute to realize it had squeezed from my lungs. The agony of the third-degree burns on my wrists was so painful, I couldn't help but cry.

I nearly broke my thumb trying to escape. It gave me an idea, and I looked at the headboard, gauging whether I could use the hard wood to my advantage. If I angled my palm just right, could I hit it with enough force to crack the bone, and escape? I was useless in this shape, and the tendrils were too damn close.

Try as I might, I couldn't call my wolf. I couldn't teleport out of there or summon any defensive magic. I was pretty much a sitting duck, and my heart beat against my ribs like it was about to escape without me.

The black wisps curled together, coalescing into a solid mass. A shape formed out of the shadowed tendrils until I stared into the face of a beastly wolf—the very one who'd *killed* my sister.

"You," I rasped, anger and terror fighting for dominance in my shaky voice.

Lethal teeth flashed as the wolf's jowls rippled back, and a deep rumble vibrated through his huge body. He stalked closer, teeth bared, eyes on fucking fire. I pressed myself against the headboard as he circled the bed, prowling, watching me like he was sizing up how many bites it would take to devour me.

I'd never felt more like prey in my life.

His tongue snuck out to lick his chops, and I tracked his movements. He was toying with me. Feasting off my fear. The fire in his eyes blazed brighter at the growl that rolled from my own throat.

Surprising the fuck out of me, the tendrils that formed his body shifted, becoming insubstantial until the dark matter molded into the shape of a man. The wisps dove inside him in much the same way I recalled my wolf, disappearing until only the human was left. But he wasn't any less terrifying.

He strode toward me at a slow, methodical clip. Dress shoes clicked against the hardwood, and he tugged on the lapels of a black tuxedo. There was something familiar in the way he moved, and yet I couldn't pinpoint why. From what I could see of him, he didn't look like anyone I knew. He had hair as dark as pitch and pale skin that contrasted lightly against his crisp white shirt.

Straightening his bow tie, he moved to the edge of the mattress and gazed down at me. A masquerade mask made of those smokey tendrils writhed around the upper half of his face. It obscured most of his features from view except for a long, jagged scar that started at his jaw, slashed down his neck, and disappeared into his dress shirt. Hard, black eyes devoid of any natural variation in color stared down at me. They were as dark and flat as coal and yet, when he looked upon me, there was a spark in them. It flared hard and fast, like a knife striking flint, and just as quickly ignited fear into the center of my chest from the look of pure fixation churning in the depths.

I wasn't timid by nature, but I couldn't stop myself from clambering as far away from him as I could get. There was something minacious about the man who stood silently before me, and all my internal alarm bells blared at once. He was dangerous, and there was something distinctly *off* about him. Every part of me rebelled at his nearness, and my wolf had barely stopped growling, filling my head with fervent warnings.

Without saying a word, he lifted a hand into the air, and those same black, shadowed tendrils spiraled from his fingers. They snaked forward, and I reared back as they touched me. Uncomfortable heat warmed my skin at the contact, and my magic instantly responded. It rushed to the surface, recognizing something in him I didn't.

Pain lanced through my wrist while my mind tried to make sense of it.

What the hell?

"Hello, my sweet Madison," the murderer said, his tone a deep bass that resonated through me like the beat of a drum. Those onyx tendrils glided over my face to caress my cheek even as I tried to turn away. "I've been waiting for the pleasure of this moment for longer than you can imagine."

FORTY-ONE

Madison

Tension tightened the muscles in my neck, back, and shoulders. The endearment he'd used sent a mixture of fear and revulsion spiraling through me.

My sweet Madison.

Knots formed in my stomach, and my lungs worked overtime, breathing in fast, shallow pants.

I wasn't his sweet *anything*.

The retort sat ready on my lips, but I swallowed it down.

Don't piss off the murderer, Mads, or you could be his next victim.

The terror of our first encounter came flooding back in

a torrent. Kenna's phantom howls haunted me. Her gurgled 'love you' still played through my mind. The heartbreak I'd learned to live with ached from the fresh wave of agony.

My sister was dead… and this man was responsible.

He'd *killed* her. He'd fucking ripped her throat out and let her die a gruesome, painful death. And for some reason, he'd left me alive to deal with the aftermath. The pain, the hurt, the fear.

Blood pounded in my ears and my breath shuddered out haltingly. I was on the verge of a panic attack, unsure which emotion to settle on. Heartbreak? Guilt? Anger? Terror?

Thick, stifling concern shot through the mate bond, radiating from Hunter. I swallowed and sent a soothing wave of reassurance I didn't actually feel back to him, worried my distress would distract him during his fight with my father. A single moment of inattention could be the difference between life and death.

Stay alive. I pushed the thought—the sheer need—down the bond. Then, I suppressed our connection to the best of my ability.

Locking the enemy in my sights, I growled. My human teeth were blunt and unintimidating, but that didn't stop me from baring them at the man like an animal.

"Who are you?" I demanded harshly. I didn't expect him to respond truthfully, so I infused every ounce of alpha command I possessed into the order, hoping to force out the answer I so desperately needed. I'd been searching for this asshole for nearly two weeks while he stalked me from the shadows, and I was no closer to figuring out his identity than I'd been that very first night.

"Nice try, Sunshine," he purred, not fazed by my show of power, "but that remains my secret for now."

"I'm not your *sunshine*," I spat.

He tilted his head. "Oh, but you are. There's not another name that epitomizes you so perfectly. Sunshine just fits."

He slowly circled the bed, and I shifted on the mattress. Silken, glittery fabric pooled around me as I rose onto my knees and angled myself toward him. My intuition told me not to give him my back.

"You're fiery and passionate. A fighter, a survivor— just like me. No matter what they do to you, your fire can't be extinguished." Those wisps glided down my arm like a finger trailing along my skin. I batted them away, but my hand flew right through the onyx haze. Unfazed by my struggle, he continued, "Like the sun, you're a light in the darkness. People are drawn to your warmth. They'll look to you with hope in their eyes, awaiting a new dawn. And those who thrive in the shadows will either want to possess you or destroy you."

I narrowed my eyes. "And which do you desire? To possess me? Or destroy me?"

"Ah, Sunshine. Why would I ever want to destroy you when I've done all of this simply to *awaken* you?"

I recoiled. Chills skated down my arms, and goosebumps rose like tiny mountain ranges along my flesh.

The corners of my lips drew down.

"I see the confusion written across your face. You're like an open book. So expressive." He tsked, like I should be more careful. "Would you like me to enlighten you?"

My free hand curled into a fist. I wanted to lash out at him so damn badly, but I'd never be able to get close enough. He stood just outside of my reach and knew exactly what he was doing. Thriving off taunting me.

"I don't want anything except to see you burn in hell for what you've done."

His eyes flashed with dark intrigue. "That mouth," he growled.

Great job at not upsetting the psychopath.

He reached for my face like he wanted to cup my chin and press his thumb past my lips, but I snapped my teeth at him like a savage beast, threatening to bite his fingers off if he drew any closer.

A feral smile curled his mouth. "So feisty. So full of *life*."

"Get away from me," I growled.

"That's no way to treat the man who freed you," he lightly scolded, but there was no harsh rebuke behind it. His words were all chosen strategically. They dangled like tempting bait I couldn't resist.

"'*Awaken*' me? '*Freed*' me? Nothing you say makes any sense." I hated giving him exactly what he wanted. My attention. My curiosity.

"Hmmm," he hummed and continued his slow trek around the bed. His fingers trailed over the comforter, then skimmed over the arch of the footboard. "That's because you don't understand your own destiny. You're mad now. It's understandable given the tragic death of your sister, but you'll get past it. Death is fleeting." He sounded flippant, and he waved Kenna's life away like it meant nothing.

I leaned forward, tipping my chin up. The cuff clanged against the post as I strained against my restraint. It held me back as I seethed. Anger covered my grief, muting it until I was a ball of fury. "She's dead because of *you*."

His eyes hardened. "Makenna was always meant to be fodder. If she didn't die at my hand, she would've died another way. Her destiny has always been tied to yours. One to rise. One to fall."

"What does that even mean?!" My rage beat behind my eyes like a pulse, steady and requisite.

He smirked, enjoying his secrets and the way they tortured me. I loathed him.

It was surreal that the killer—the Shadow Beast—now stood before me. So close, yet so fucking far.

I tugged against my shackle again, begging it to break, wishing more than anything I could launch myself at him. My shoulder ached from the way my bound arm strained behind me, and my nails dug into the bedding like claws. The bloodthirsty predilections of my wolf smothered out my human sensibilities, and I craved revenge. I wanted to rip into his face. To tear into him and make him feel even an ounce of the pain I suffered daily. My muscles were primed, ready to leap. But I was a prisoner.

"Perhaps I should bring a friend to help explain it to you." He paused at the end of the bed and with the flick of a wrist, he summoned more of those tendrils. They poured in through the open window to unite at his side.

Slowly, in just the same way, they formed the vague shape of a person, then solidified into a man.

I sat back on my heels as I gaped at the familiar newcomer. "Jasper?"

No. It wasn't possible. I blinked hard, willing my vision to correct.

Shadows flitted over Jasper's features. He clenched his jaw, and anger stormed to life in his eyes. "Mads. I told you to stay put."

"No. You locked me up against my will," I spat, furious about the multitude of wrongdoings. The pulse in my neck fluttered wildly, and my gaze moved between the two men.

"I don't understand." I had questions. A lot of fucking questions. Like how had Jasper just appeared out of the damn shadows like the Shadow Beast? But I only asked the most pressing one. "What are you doing with *him*?"

"It's easy, really," the Shadow Beast explained. "Jasper and I have a partnership of convenience. He wanted to free you from your dismal life, and I wanted to awaken your powers. He pledged his allegiance, and in return, I orchestrated the attack and killed your sister."

Pounding in my temples made my head throb, and I blinked to keep the tears at bay.

"Mads." Jasper took a step forward. "Your sister needed to die so that you could truly live."

A smack across the face would have been less shocking. "W-what?"

Jasper shoved a hand through his already mussed hair. "You're a twin, a shifter born without a wolf. Without power. Your sister got all of it. Didn't you ever wonder why?"

"Of course I did! But the answer doesn't matter."

"It matters, Madison. You weren't born as powerless as you think. You're a Spirit wolf. The pack couldn't see it, but your powers have always been there, waiting dormantly in the background. If your mother had lived, she would've helped you realize your potential all along."

"My mother was a Stormborn wolf," I retorted, trying to follow the path of our conversation and failing.

Jasper shrugged. "But not an *elite*."

That little nugget hung between us. I didn't know if he was to be believed. Truth was, I didn't know much about my mother.

The Shadow Beast clamped a clawed hand on Jasper's shoulder, pulled him back, and stepped past him, closer to me. "You get your Spirit element from her. Generation after generation of diluting the bloodline buried it farther back, making it harder to find, but it's there. And it was passed on to you."

It didn't make sense. Despite any mixed bloodlines from the parents, children always inherited whatever elemental power the bloodlines favored. Even if they were split fifty-fifty, the power that passed down would've come from the stronger parent—usually the father.

My mother and father both had powers from the Storm element. So did Kenna. So what made me different? Did the fact that I was a twin allow room for *both* powers to manifest? One in Kenna, one in me?

It was possible. There wasn't much known about twins since they were exceedingly rare among our kind. When Kenna and I were born, we'd given my father a status boost that had increased his standing among the Alphas and other packs. It was the one and only time my father had been proud of me. Until the fateful day my wolf—and subsequently my powers—didn't awaken, and he tried to forget I ever existed.

If only he'd known that I wasn't as powerless as he'd always assumed....

"How do you know all of this?" I asked them. I didn't care who responded, as long as I kept them talking. All the while, I was still working on contorting my thumb past the silver.

"I started looking into it when I was assigned as one of your enforcers. You weren't anything like I'd expected," Jasper admitted.

"And I sensed it the first time I laid eyes on both you and your sister." The Shadow Beast hooked his hands behind his back, staring down his nose at me. "Kenna was average. Nothing special. Not the way you are."

The chill I'd been fighting turned absolutely glacial.

We met before? No wonder he seemed familiar. But where did I know him from? Unease refused to abate, and I studied him for anything that'd jog my memory of who he was. But there was nothing remarkable about him except for the strange power he wielded.

One corner of his lips pulled up in a smirk. "I'm almost hurt you don't remember me, but we were quite young. Then, when you didn't shift during your awakening, you were ripped away like a dream I couldn't catch. But I always remembered you. It took me years to figure it all out, to realize what I now know to be true."

I hesitated, unsure if I wanted to know more. "And that is?"

He stopped before me, his presence demanding all my attention as I stared up at him. "It's a rarity, even among twins, but you and your sister shared the spirit of one wolf. It resided in her, but it was waiting for you. I just needed to set it free so it could find its way home. And once you were made whole, your powers roared to the surface, the way I always knew they would."

Tears burned behind my eyes and my chin quivered. I sniffed, looking past the enemy to Jasper. "That's why you weren't with Kenna that night. You left her in the woods unprotected. You let *him* kill her."

He moved to grip the footboard in both hands and fervently squeezed the wood. "I'm sorry, Mads. I know it was gruesome to witness, but her death was the only way I could give you the life I knew you desperately wanted. Everything Kenna had should have been yours."

He's not sorry she was murdered. He's just sorry I saw it.

He'd helped the Shadow Beast kill my sister. For *me*.

I couldn't look at either of them without being sick.

"Death is a part of life, Sunshine. You'll learn that soon enough. It surrounds you even now." The Shadow Beast motioned toward the door and the sounds of the vicious battle Hunter was fighting.

I'd do almost anything to get out of here and back into Hunter's arms. The longing to go back in time to those stolen moments we shared together before the ceremony was staggeringly sharp.

Hopelessness seeped in like the slow creep of spilled ink. I didn't know if we'd both make it out of this night alive, or if those fleeting moments would be all we'd ever share.

Acid rose to scald the back of my throat.

The Shadow Beast was a sadistic bastard, a sick and twisted psychopath, and all of this was his fault. Yet, somehow, the guilt I already shouldered grew exponentially. I couldn't stop blaming myself for what he'd done. It was *because* of me that Kenna was gone, and I didn't know how to live with that.

I blinked, trying to keep the tears at bay.

Angry heat flushed into my face, and I clenched my teeth, begging myself not to break down in front of my enemy. Neither he nor Jasper felt any remorse for their actions, and I wouldn't give them the satisfaction of seeing me cry. Showing weakness was a surefire way to get yourself killed, or show your opponent exactly where to hit you to do the most damage.

They'd already taken Kenna from me, but there were other people I cared about now. Olivia. Nova. Dean. Hunter.

"Mads," Jasper cooed, seeing how emotional I was. He rounded the bed and moved to my side. I scrambled back, but he sat on the mattress and reached for the hand that wasn't chained. The Shadow Beast growled, but it didn't deter the fervent way Jasper squeezed my fingers. "I did it for you. I know it hurts now, but eventually, the grief will pass, and you'll have all the things you always deserved. You were miserable, guarded twenty-four seven, with zero freedom. Now the pack will see what I see. They'll know how incredible you are. I want you to have fucking *everything*. I want… fuck. I want us to *be* together, just like I've dreamed."

He swooped down to press his mouth to my hand, and I jerked—hard. "*No*," I stated forcefully, fighting against him, but he didn't react. Using my foot, I leveraged my heel against his chest and used all of my strength to kick him away. I didn't want him laying a hand on me again. "Don't fucking touch me."

"Good girl," the Shadow Beast purred as though I'd put Jasper in his place just to please him. The satisfied notes dropped from his voice as he faced Jasper, and it went steely hard. "You heard the woman." He waved a hand through the air before Jasper could right himself, and suddenly, his body convulsed. A thunk sounded as the enforcer hit the floor in a heap, and I gasped, peering over the edge of the bed to see his eyes going wide. Gurgling and choking, Jasper gasped for air to no avail. Those same smokey tendrils slid past his lips from the inside out until they spewed from his mouth.

I gasped, throwing a hand over my mouth and scrambling against the headboard. I held onto it for dear life.

The Shadow Beast came to a stop beside Jasper's dying form and leaned down.

"We have a deal, remember? Your spirit *belongs* to me. You do what *I* say. And Madison? She was never yours. I let you believe in the delusion that you two could be together, because I needed your inside access to the Stormborn and my Sunshine over here. It's *pathetic* you thought such a powerful woman could ever belong with a low ranking *delta*." A cruel smirk curled his lips. "I'll admit, you were helpful, for a while. But I no longer have any use for you." His tone grew darker with every word.

Jasper tried to scream, but it came out strangled as he suffocated. His grey stare landed on mine, full of regret and panic. Horror, disgust, and sadness flooded me, but so, too, was there a sense of relief and satisfaction as the tendrils poured from his throat. Wisp by wisp, his life drained away until he was an empty husk, no more than a shell once used to house a man I'd once considered my only friend.

How very, *very* wrong I'd been.

My enemies were everywhere.

Slowly, Jasper's body disintegrated into that same smoky matter, which the Shadow Beast absorbed into himself. Pressing back to his feet, he brushed off his hands.

I was thoroughly shaken. "What do you want from me?" I dared to question, my voice tight and quiet.

"For tonight, all I wanted was to see my handiwork." A blast of Alpha power stronger than I imagined he possessed rolled from him in waves. His magic warmed the air and skated along my skin. My wolf responded with a growl from the depths of my soul. Risking the pain it would cause, she released our own torrent of power, pressing his back and away from us. Our magic clashed, our powers fighting for dominance. "Ah, there she is. You're both magnificent. Tell me, does it feel good to finally be whole?"

"I'd rather have lived my whole life in the shadows as an outcast, than have sacrificed my sister's life for power." I forced my voice to remain strong even when it wanted to waver with emotion.

The darkness in his eyes flashed with a brief flicker of flame. "No matter how badly it wants to, the sun cannot live in the shadows."

I shook my head, my hair swaying lightly against my back. I wasn't going to sit here and listen to him spew bull-shit. I needed to get out of here. I needed to get to Hunter. The blood pounded too loudly in my ears to hear much of the fight next door, and I had no idea who was winning or losing.

Still, I couldn't focus past the man slowly approaching the bed like a shark stalking its dinner. It only took two steps until his knees brushed the mattress.

"You never should have been chained, Sunshine, but I admit, I'm appreciative it's given me an opportunity to see you without having you run or fight back." Reaching for the bedpost I was shackled to, he toyed with the metal chain attached to the cuff. "I've been watching you, waiting for a time I could get close. To think I could've missed this opportunity for some quality alone time if I didn't have so many eyes in so many places, informing me of your every move."

Who else can there be?

Clearly, Jasper had been working with him—or *for* him. Now, he was implying there were others involved in what-ever his cold-blooded plans were.

He smirked, reading me easily, and his ruthless eyes captured me. "If you only knew just how close those you'd consider enemies truly are. Right under your pert, little nose."

Fear shot through my veins like a drug. Just how many

others did he have working for him? As if I didn't have enough problems…

I felt like I was drowning in quicksand. No matter which way I moved, I sank deeper. The hope I always tried to hold onto sputtered like a candle in the wind.

The Shadow Beast called forth the smoky tendrils, letting them drift far too close to my body for comfort. With a wave of his hand, he redirected them and sent them spiraling into the keyhole on my cuff. They twisted and swirled, then to my complete disbelief, the manacle snapped open and fell off, swinging into the bedpost with a loud clunk.

There was no time to cradle my wrist into my body to baby my injuries.

I jumped from the bed with a growl, not wasting a second. Warmth bloomed in my chest as I called my wolf, and she surged forward without hesitation. There wasn't much her glowing, incorporeal form could do, but she growled viciously while I clawed at the man with a savage scream. Infuriatingly, he disappeared into a dark cloud to avoid my attack. Smoky tendrils poured from him until he was once again shapeless.

Multiple times now, he'd formed and unformed at will. I'd never seen anything like it.

The wisps wound around me in revolving circles. I whipped this way and that, trying to track them, but it was no use. They were everywhere and nowhere all at once. Strong arms formed from the shadows and grabbed me. Imprisoned again, the bar of his arm pressed against my stomach, caging my back against his half-formed chest. Snapping her lethal but spectral fangs, my wolf tried to help.

"Yes, fight me," he growled hoarsely in my ear. "I like your *spirit*."

"Go *fuck* yourself!" It wasn't my most clever comeback, but I was so far past done it wasn't even funny. Power tingled to life in my fingers, and I sent a bolt of lightning into the writhing matter.

He hissed and released me. I caught myself before I stumbled too far forward. Whirling around, I saw his masked face bleed back into onyx shadow.

"You still like my spirit?" I mocked, ready to release another blast.

A chuckle sounded from the darkness. "You have no idea."

The smoky tendrils flew around me once more, brushing against my arms, my back, my shoulders, my neck. I wanted a shower to wash the feel of him off my body.

"You and I—we're destined for great things," he rumbled into my ear. "I have plans for you, Sunshine. Be good until I see you again."

As fast as he'd appeared, the smoke bled out of the room through the same open window. I ran for it, bracing my palms against the sill. He disappeared into the darkness, and I nearly came out of my skin with the need to go after him.

Furious growls tumbled from my wolf.

He needed to pay for his sins, but with each labored breath I inhaled and blew back out, the vicious snarls and pained howls sounded from the ballroom.

Shaking, I reached for the bond. Pure, unadulterated wrath and fury rained down on me, along with a worry so thick, it choked me. But underneath all of that was *pain*.

Hunter.

I looked toward the door, then back out the window at the dark, retreating mass. It wasn't even a choice.

As badly as I wanted vengeance for Kenna, I had to come to terms with the fact that nothing I did would bring her back. Chasing a phantom I didn't know how to fight was pointless. Hard as it was to accept, Kenna was my past.

Hunter was my future. And right now, he needed my help.

Agony and anguish rolled through the bond, and I just *knew*. Something was wrong with my mate….

Without wasting another breath, I turned and bolted for the door. I threw myself against it and wrenched the handle, trying to open it, but just as I expected, the enforcers had locked me in. It wouldn't budge.

I looked at my wolf. She was our only hope of getting out of there, but using our power was risky. Anyone could see us, and that meant revealing our secret.

My wolf and I shared a look. Her tongue snuck out as she licked her nose, ready for our next challenge. I smirked and closed my eyes. Pressure built in my head until that familiar tugging sensation pulled me into the mind of my wolf.

More determined than ever, she ran for the door and bounded through it, right into the middle of the crowd surrounding the makeshift arena.

Madison

I couldn't see Hunter through the legs of the bystanders. An array of colorful dresses draped to the floor, making it impossible to catch more than glimpses of the fight beyond the crowd, but his roar of pain shook the walls.

I threw myself from my wolf's consciousness back into my own and summoned the magic of my Aether element. It rose instantly to heat my chest. Focusing on what I'd learned earlier, I channeled the magic until that static sensation tingled through my limbs. Flooded with dizziness and a distinct sense of detachment, I reached for my wolf and urged her to do her thing. That same uncomfortable tug pulled at the center of my being where my magic resided. Then, time and space blurred.

I reformed in front of her, finally free from the room I'd been trapped in. Stumbling on my heels, I caught myself before I fell on my ass and drew unwanted attention, then immediately recalled her. My wolf dove into my chest and disappeared while I peered around to see if anyone had noticed us. Her glowing aura wasn't exactly inconspicuous, but all eyes were riveted on the fight.

I started shoving my way through the crowd that had pressed closer to the wall, widening the circle of the battlefield. Through the valley of shoulders, I spotted Hunter, who stood in the middle in wolf form. He cut an imposing figure with his black fur and red tribal markings. They decorated his legs and haunches like tattoos. Smoke curled from his paws and fire burned in his eyes even as blood dripped from the gashes on his sides and legs. Fangs bared in a snarl of warning, he limped in a circle around his opponent—Robert Cassian, the Alpha of the Caulder Wolves.

He was the only other Alpha I recognized, and I only remembered him from my childhood because the Caulder Wolves were the Stormborns neighboring pack and closest allies.

I shook my head. None of this was right. Challenges were supposed to be one on one with the occasional involvement of the wolves' chosen seconds. Where was my father?

Chills skated down my spine at the blood covering the light marble floor, making it slippery. Wolven bodies were scattered here and there across the makeshift arena, the spirits of the dead ascending to shimmer out of existence, but my father wasn't one of them. My mind raced as I noticed Tristan in wolven form fighting nearby, helping Hunter in what had become an *ambush*.

Ember enforcers held Olivia and Nova captive at the edge of the crowd, and the High Alpha still sat on his dais, looking gleefully entertained as his son bled in his stead.

Anger suffused my chest as Tristan and Hunter faced their opponents, and I scanned the various wolves, trying to identify who was fighting.

I recognized a handful of Stormborn enforcers, including Reynolds, Crenshaw, and Juno. They battled two carbon-grey Ember Wolves I didn't recognize but guessed were Dean and Kip.

My father's Beta, Griffon, dodged around Tristan, ripping chunks of his flesh out with each lunging nip he took. Blood slicked Tristan's fur, but he didn't waver. He watched, learned, then struck, catching the overconfident Beta off-guard. It was enough for Tristan to leap and take him down. I couldn't bring myself to watch the carnage as he ripped Griffon's throat out before defending himself against a barrage of Stormborn enforcers who leapt into the fray in anger.

Struggling against the crowd, I caught an elbow to the stomach that knocked the breath from my lungs. I growled, but it was a whisper compared to the roar of the fighting wolves.

Hunter and the Caulder Alpha clashed in a furious tangle of teeth and claws. My heart nearly stopped as they battled with such force, I felt the vibrations of it through the floor. With a sharp bark, Hunter released a burst of fire at Robert, who countered with a swish of his tail, throwing a blast of water that engulfed the flames, extinguishing them before they scalded his fur. Smoke wafted between them as they parried, lunged, attacked, and retreated in a deadly dance. Trading elemental blows amidst their physical fight, they both tried to catch the other unprepared.

The Caulder Alpha looked smug when they finally pulled apart, glancing past Hunter before returning his attention to the Ember heir. I followed his line of sight to the edge of the arena, and my heart fucking stopped.

Canines bared, my father lowered his shoulders and crept along the floor predatorily. His grey coat was covered in splotches of blood that plastered his fur to his body. Grey, elemental clouds grew around his haunches until half of him was amassed in a stormy haze. Electricity charged the air, a warning of things to come. Muscles bunching, my father readied himself to strike. I looked between him and Hunter, whose back was to the threat, still fending off attacks from the Caulder Alpha.

The Alphas are working together.

My blood ran cold. They were going to kill my mate.

I peered up at the High Alpha who leaned forward in his seat, gripping the edges of the armrests as he watched with keen interest, seeming more entertained than concerned for the well-being of his only living son.

Didn't he care about his succession, if not about his own flesh and blood? Even my father, who hated me, cared about his lineage and having an heir.

Or maybe this was all a game to the High Alpha, a test of Hunter's strength. A formal challenge was one thing. There were rules that should've been enforced. It was supposed to be fairly supervised. This, however, was more than an ambush. It was a slaughter. A *war*.

The other Alphas shifted uncomfortably on their feet, eyeing the High Alpha to see if he'd eventually put a stop to the madness. Taking their cues from him, however, they followed his lead and didn't protest when their leader did nothing but watch with fervent interest.

This wasn't their fight, and they weren't about to stick their necks out.

I wanted to laugh mirthlessly at just how corrupt they all were, but it was a testament to their fear. They didn't dare move against the High Alpha, afraid if they did, they'd lose their positions, or worse, their lives. Better to grit their teeth and bear the tyranny than dare to make a move against the man who ruled over our world.

Some of the heirs, however, seemed to feel differently. I spotted a number of men around my age who exuded alpha power. They stood around the edges of the arena with clenched fists and tight jaws, sharing weighted looks with each other as they bided their time, silently deciding when to act.

But Hunter didn't have another second to waste.

I sent a warning through the bond, but Hunter was engaged with the Caulder Alpha. The older man drove him backward with a well-placed assault, herding him closer to where my father crouched in wait to attack.

Magic roared to life in my fingers.

Head low, ears pressed tightly against his head, the Caulder Alpha continued to bombard Hunter. But it was just an elaborate scheme to distract my mate, who met each blow with a stronger one.

My father bounded sideways, lining himself up for the perfect strike.

It all happened in slow motion.

Hunter dropped his shoulders and bared his teeth, coiling to leap at the Caulder Alpha when my father lunged, aiming for Hunter's throat. His muscles flexed, and he was airborne.

"Hunter!" I screamed, fighting to get through the throngs of people in my fucking way.

My power filled me, buzzing under my skin, the warmth of it nearly palpable.

The choice between keeping my secret and trying to save Hunter came as naturally as breathing. Truthfully, it wasn't a choice at all.

I was irrevocably falling for Hunter Weston. A deep knowing inside my soul told me he was my mate. I simply refused to imagine a world without him, and I reacted on pure, innate instinct.

A blast of magic tore through me with the speed of a bullet firing from a gun, and between one breath and the next, I summoned my wolf, seeing through her eyes instantly as she sprang from my body.

She didn't fight as I took control of her mind and bounded through the crowd. Our apparitional form passed through anyone who stood in our way. Every person we traversed had a sense of good or evil to their spirit. The flavors, the senses, overwhelmed me, but I forced myself to focus. I pumped my legs harder, faster.

Gasps and whispers broke through the masses as she blasted past the edge of the crowd, a radiant, glowing powerhouse of sleek, muscular, pissed-off wolf. My wolf's ears pricked backward, and her growl was ominously loud as she covered the remaining distance and threw herself between my mate and my father.

I slammed back into my own consciousness with a sharp inhale, and my magic was reactionary. It read my intent and complied. One second, my human form was trapped amidst the crowd, and the next, I was *Spirit*. Like we'd done so many times tonight, my wolf tugged on those strings that connected us, directing me toward her like a beacon. Time seemed to slow.

The second I rematerialized, my magic was ready. I threw a hand out, loosing a bolt of lightning. The Storm element came so naturally, it was like I'd been born with it all along. Unsure if it were even possible, I willed it to split into four branches, visualizing each target and directing the blasts. To my shock, it worked. Each one struck the enforcers fighting Dean, Kip, and Tristan, as well as the Caulder Alpha trying to distract Hunter. It gave our side the upper hand we so desperately needed.

It'd only taken a single breath to release the power, and I exhaled as I zeroed in on my father. He was death incarnate, and he was heading straight for me. My other hand was already lifted skyward, and I called forth so much power it raised the fine hairs along my entire body. Fingers curling into a fist, I swiftly brought my hand down, pulling the lightning from the roiling storm clouds covering the ceiling. It struck my father full force.

The scent of burnt hair and the agonized whine from his throat told me I'd struck true, but my split attention had cost me.

I was too late.

I barely had time to brace for impact before he was on me.

FORTY-THREE

Madison

Teeth and claws rended my flesh as he drove me to the floor. I used my arms as shields to protect my throat from his attack. Through the bar of my arms, I saw the saliva that dripped from his maw and the blood that stained his lethal fangs.

Each bite was burning hot agony. He ripped into me with the force of a tornado intent on destroying everything in its path.

Tears flooded my eyes, and my mouth flew open on a sharp, crying gasp. Blood welled from the severe gashes on my arms and abdomen. Everything *hurt*. I could barely breathe past the pain. All my mind could focus on was the intensity of each agonizing breath, one after another.

Lurching back, my father gazed wide-eyed at me through the eyes of his wolf as he realized what he'd done. My blood coated his muzzle and stained his paws. What started as a low growl grew stronger as anger replaced his shock, and his gaze turned to veiled slits.

A high-pitched whine pierced the air from somewhere behind us, followed by the gurgle of a torn throat, then Hunter leapt past me with a blood-curdling growl. His fury over my being hurt flooded our connection with a ferocity that stole what little breath I had left. Blood dripped from his mouth, and he only added more as he attacked my father with fiery vengeance.

Incensed beyond reason, he put all his wrath into the fight. His wolf was a lethal beast. Five feet of pure, murderous muscle. All of it aimed at avenging me and ending this fucking challenge.

Hunter circled my father, biting at his legs and tearing at his sides. Waiting, watching, he bided his time for the perfect opportunity to slip past my father's defenses. Pushing up with one hand, I used the other to clutch at my stomach with trembling fingers. A whooshing filled my ears. Vision going hazy from blood loss, focusing was difficult, but I saw the moment things shifted.

"Hunter!" I wheezed, as a bolt of lightning shot from the clouds surrounding my father.

It tore toward my mate, but Hunter was already moving. He dodged it and sailed through the air, slamming into my father's side and knocking him off balance. Both wolves tumbled to the slicked floor, sliding from the sheer force. Electricity jolted through Hunter, but he didn't stop.

He didn't slow. The snapping of jaws and echoing snarls played through the room like a sick melody.

I marked time with the ragged breaths I slowly dragged in and forced back out. *One. Two. Three.*

That was all it took for Hunter to have my father flat on his back. His jaw clamped down on his enemy's neck and snapped shut with crushing ferocity. With a jerk, he ended my father by ripping his throat out. Brutal but quick.

The spirit of my father's wolf rose from its battered body to loom above it. In a fit of fury, it snarled and charged straight for me. Soft fur brushed against my injured arms as my wolf dove in front of me protectively, but it was no use. My father's wolf bolted straight through her and into my body like it could rip me apart from the inside out.

I clawed at my chest and choked out a cry. Every atom of my being rebelled against the vileness of my father's spirit. His darkness chilled me, turning my fingers to icicles. But instead of absorbing his wolf the way I had Kenna's, it passed straight through. I turned despite the agony twisting caused, and watched as the wolf disintegrated into mist and disappeared forever.

Hunter's wolf ran to me, and I buried my hands in its fur. Magic blazed to life and suddenly it was Hunter kneeling before me.

"Maddie!" Hunter rasped urgently as the chaos of the fight continued to rage around us. His arm went around me to keep me from listing sideways while the other hovered over my torn stomach. "What the fuck were you thinking? You could've been killed!"

I gazed into his russet, fiery eyes as I clung to him. "Had to save you," I murmured, but it hurt to talk. To breathe.

Hunter growled a deeply possessive yet unhappy sound. "I'd rather die than see you hurt."

I pulled him closer, enjoying the feel of his bare skin under my palms. He was alive, and that was all that mattered to me. "I feel the same way about you." I had to speak in between heaving lungfuls of air, and deep concern pinched Hunter's brow.

His grip tightened, and he glanced from my glowing wolf back to me with a shake of his head. "You risked everything, Maddie. Everything."

"You're worth it," I ran my hand up the steely column of his throat and into his hair, holding onto him as he rested our foreheads together.

"Fucking hell." He swooped down and captured my lips in a fast, drugging kiss, but I gasped when he pulled me closer. He ripped himself away. "Dammit. I'm sorry," he swore, and bent to survey the damage beneath my ruined glittering gown.

Blood. There was blood everywhere. A river of red ran across the white marble, and my own welled steadily, adding to the mess along with Hunter's. Gashes and vicious bite marks marred his skin, but he was barely fazed by them.

"We need to get you out of here so I can heal you," he stated desperately.

But as if the Moon Goddess herself was against us, suddenly more Stormborn enforcers joined the melee that still raged. They poured in through the side doors from the gardens and stepped from the recesses of the room where they'd been lying in wait, spilling into the arena to box us in. Tristan, Kip, and Dean fought to keep them away from us, acting as our first line of defense, while more and more wolves joined the fight. My mate blocked my body to the best of his ability, thrusting a hand out and releasing blasts of fire to take out our opponents.

"This may be your best chance to go through with your plans," I cautioned quietly, unwilling to risk turning toward the dais to eye the High Alpha. I hurt too much to twist or do anything that'd exacerbate the pain, but Hunter knew what I meant.

"I promise you, Little Wolf," Hunter dropped his voice to no more than a whisper kept just between us, "one day I will destroy that man until there's nothing left of him, but it can't be tonight." A caustic expression flashed across his face at the end of his vow. There was something he wasn't telling me, something that had changed, but it wasn't the time or the place to ask questions.

I nodded. "For the best. You're hurt." If he was going to fight his father, I wanted him in peak condition, physically, mentally, and spiritually. After all that had happened, it was clear that tonight was not a night any of us had anticipated.

Reaching to cup my face, his thumb stroked over the curve of my cheekbone adoringly. I leaned into him, uncaring about the blood that smeared across my skin. "You're the one who's hurt, Little Wolf. Mine are just scratches."

I laughed, because his were far more than 'just scratches', but it ended abruptly as I spluttered on blood that crawled up my throat to choke me. It was then I knew just how grave my injuries were.

Hunter's eyes flew wide with the same kind of terror I'd felt when I'd been ripped away from him, not knowing if he'd live or die, then they narrowed with rekindled determination. His hand pressed over mine on my stomach to staunch the worst of the bleeding.

I swallowed down the blood, and my wolf sent a wave of healing through me, trying to buy me some time by focusing on the areas that needed it most.

Hunter kept his head on a swivel, scanning the crowd for any kind of opening he could use to get me out of here, to someplace safe, but our options were bleak.

Caulder enforcers moved to join the Stormborn ranks, but surprisingly, the man who'd kissed me earlier stepped to the forefront and laid down a growl laden with Alpha power. My vision swam as I regarded him over Hunter's shoulder, and there was a wealth of emotion poured back at me when he met my eyes.

Now that I saw him in the light, it was easy to notice the similarities he shared with the Caulder Alpha. Was it possible he was Robert Cassian's son all grown up? I had fond memories of playing together as children until my world fell apart.

He growled again, his shift bulking his shoulders, and his enforcers wrenched their heads, exposing their necks in submission. "Since my father was not challenged and did not die defending his title, I, Silas Cassian, am the new Alpha of the Caulder Wolves. And I decree that my pack stands down. There has been enough bloodshed for one night," he announced in a booming voice that filtered above the din of the room.

The Stormborn enforcers sent an ominous howl into the air as they prepared to wage another wave of attacks. They wanted the High Alpha dead, which also meant cutting through Hunter. They split into two groups, one prowling to the base of the dais to be met by Ember enforcers who shifted to greet them in battle, while the second circled us like sharks stalking their dinner.

But the proverbial head had been chopped off the

snake. They were disorganized, led by greed, hatred, and a rivalry that had lasted far too long.

With Hunter's help I stood, some of the haze clearing as my wolf focused on trying to knit me back together. I peered up at him, hoping he wouldn't hate me for what I was about to do. My injuries alone were enough to kill me tonight, but the next words to leave my mouth could very well be a death sentence for so many reasons.

I strained upward and pressed my lips to his in a desperately fast kiss. He captured the back of my head and devoured me for one brief moment before pulling away.

Hunter's brows slashed downward, reading me easily. "Little Wolf," he growled in warning, low and quiet.

Guiltily, I tore my eyes away from his—knowing he wouldn't approve of what I was about to do. My being a Spirit wolf was out, but almost no one knew the other half of my secret.

I surveyed the crowd, and my attention landed on the High Alpha who stood from his throne and strode to the edge of the dais. Gone was the amused light that'd sparkled in his eyes, and in its place was voracious avarice.

He was driven by ambition, vindictive greed, and an unending thirst for power. He thrived on the mayhem of battle but wouldn't hesitate to cut someone down the moment their sights shifted off his son and onto him. And despite the chaos raging around him, he didn't seem the least bit concerned. His sole focus was settled on me and the glowing wolf at my side.

I took a hobbling step away from Hunter to face the High Alpha and urged my wolf to move with me. A rapacious sort of hunger simmered in his dark gaze as he took us in.

Hunter moved to my back, his warmth spreading along my spine in unending support.

Help me, I begged my wolf, drawing from her strength and reaching for my power. It flowed through my veins and filled me until I couldn't contain it.

With my wolf's help, we let it build, then released it in a torrent over the crowd. Stormborn Wolves stopped in their tracks, and though many of them fought against the command, they exposed their necks in submission. Shocked awe filled me, giving me a small burst of energy that kept me standing tall. The only time I'd ever felt more powerful was in Hunter's arms as he lost himself in the pleasure of my body.

Taking a shuddering breath to steel myself against whatever might happen, I let that same command flow into my voice. "I, Madison Hale, the last surviving heir of the Stormborn pack, also decree that my pack stands down."

Raucous whispers hissed through the air to reverberate off the gilded walls.

"Enough," the High Alpha boomed, and the whole room silenced as his stifling power blanketed the room. It forced Alphas and enforcers alike to drop to their knees and tilt their heads. Only Hunter and I were left standing, spared from the onslaught.

"From the rumors comes the truth," the High Alpha stated mysteriously. "I wasn't sure I believed you when you first told me of the girl." His attention never left me though he addressed someone else.

The silver sheen of a dress caught my eye first. Endora climbed the stairs of the dais to stand at the High Alpha's side.

"I wouldn't lie to the High Alpha, especially given how much you paid me for reliable intel. She's really quite remarkable," the witch purred with a cunningly cruel tilt to her lips, openly admitting that she'd played my father and my pack for fools. This whole time, she'd been feeding information back to the High Alpha.

How long had he known who—and *what*—I was? It couldn't have been long, but it explained why I'd felt a shift in him this evening—a blatantly obvious suspicion.

I wasn't loyal to my father by any means, but the witch bitch was a two-timing, double-crossing hussy, and nothing would convince me otherwise.

Maybe it was the blow of new information or the injury and blood loss, but I was running out of energy and the backbone that'd made me stand up in the first place. My focus swam in and out, and my legs grew tired and numb. Weakness crept in, zapping my strength. I didn't know how much longer I could remain upright.

"My, my, my," the High Alpha crooned. "A Spirit wolf. It's been so long, I truly believed they were just a myth."

"I assure you she's very real. And extremely powerful," Endora remarked. "Just as I promised."

The High Alpha strode down the steps magnanimously as though he were blessing us with his presence. He kicked a Stormborn enforcer out of his way, clearing a path straight to me. Hunter tensed at my back, and one of his hands came to rest on my hip.

"I knew there was something different about you," the High Alpha purred. "Madison Hale, back from the dead."

"I was never dead," I told him. "It was just another of my father's lies."

"Oh, I know. Just another intricate web he spun thinking us none the wiser. We always questioned what happened to you. To think your father had you squirreled away like a prisoner all these years when untold power lived within you, just waiting to be realized." He tsked. "Thaddeus Hale never was a smart man." He sneered at my father's dead body. "He thought he could send you in here, pretending to be your late sister, and I wouldn't find out about his deception?"

I kept my chin high and my eyes focused on a random spot beyond the High Alpha. My fate was in his hands, and I nearly shook as he scrutinized me. He circled Hunter and me, his slimy gaze sliding over me avidly.

"He should've known he had no true allies, not even the ones he bribed. The packs are exceedingly loyal, and those who question my authority eventually come around"—he spared a glance toward Silas—"when they realize they could never win against me. Isn't that right, Hunter?"

The father and son locked eyes tensely, and Hunter's hand tightened on my hip. Not giving him the satisfaction of an answer, my mate redirected the conversation. "Perhaps we can save the posturing for later," he suggested tersely. I held my breath, and the High Alpha's eyes went to slits. "Seems to me we have some traitors to deal with—the quicker the better."

The High Alpha's expression eased some, and he didn't lash back the way I'd expected. Instead, his cold eyes glittered with the promise of violence. Lifting a hand into the air, he snapped his fingers, and the other Alphas, Betas, and enforcers jumped to do his bidding. Suddenly the Stormborn renegades were surrounded. Still held by the High Alpha's power, they didn't so much as twitch a muscle in protest, though their whines rent the air.

"Thaddeus Hale poisoned the minds of his so-called pack, and now they'll die for his crimes. Let this be a testament to all the packs. Move against me, and I'll take my pound of flesh in retribution."

I leaned back into Hunter. My legs were shaking and my breathing grew shallower, but I refused to faceplant in front of the High Alpha. Hunter became my rock. He held me up and lent me his strength.

"Kill them." The High Alpha stared right at me, daring me to defy the fate he dealt my packmates, but he'd get no protest from me.

My father's enforcers knew what they'd signed up for the moment they decided to wage war against the High Alpha. There was no saving them now.

I nodded once, one small decline of my chin, and the High Alpha's lips curled in the corners. "Good girl."

My teeth gnashed together from his praise, but I held my tongue while the other enforcers shifted in preparation of what would be a swift and brutal ending to an entire line of Stormborn wolves.

"With all due respect, my mate doesn't need to watch this," Hunter insisted. "She's badly hurt, and it's imperative I tend to her injuries. As you yourself said, she's rare. It'd be a shame to lose her simply to make her witness the death of a pack she's not been responsible for until today."

"*With all due respect,*" one of the Alphas spat, stepping forward, mocking Hunter. "She's not really your mate, now is she?"

"Dad," another gentleman stepped forward, placing his hand on his father's arm, but the older man shook him off.

"No," he growled. "This needs to be said and I know I don't speak solely for myself. Thaddues touted that the girl had the power to make true mate matches."

My stomach dropped. They knew. They all knew. Jasper had hinted at as much earlier, but hearing it outloud and facing the stark reality made it so much more real. Worse still was that I didn't even know *how* to make true mate bonds. So far, I'd only sensed a connection between Nova and Dean. I had no clue how to turn that connection into a bond.

The Alpha continued his tirade, "Now, we find out her true identity and that she's a Spirit wolf. My pack and I are unendingly loyal to the High Alpha, but I think we can all agree that this new information changes everything."

Hunter's jaw jumped as he faced the man who opposed him—and our mating, apparently. "I can assure you the bond I share with Madison Hale is stronger than any chosen mate bond."

"And yet that doesn't make her your mate. Your legally binding contract—the entire treaty, for that matter—were all tied to your mating *Makenna* Hale."

"What are you getting at, Vincent?"

Vincent… Judging by his name, dark hair, and the pale grey, nearly white eyes the man had, my best guess was that he was the Alpha of the Lunar Wolves.

"With the new information that's come to light, I believe we need to hold a tribunal to discuss matters, as this is not the time nor the place for such important *negotiations*." He enunciated the last word pointedly as he pivoted to the High Alpha and dipped his head. "Respectfully, of course, High Alpha," he added, actually meaning it this time.

I could see the High Alpha's mind churning behind his veiled expression. The man was always one step ahead, and it showed when the corner of his lips pulled up in a smile, like he'd been expecting this all along.

"I agree there may need to be a change in terms. But if you don't mind, I'd like to get this messy business taken care of. Death really does bring down a perfectly good party."

Vincent gave him a controlled smile and turned to address the enforcers under his own command. "Do as the

High Alpha has decreed. Let's end this pathetic attempt at a war so we can discuss more important matters."

He cast a greed-filled glance my way, but the effect was lost thanks to my darkening vision.

"Hunter," I whispered, my weight now fully against his chest as I teetered on the edge of consciousness. My wolf bounded back into my chest to fortify me, but even her presence wasn't enough to keep the darkness from attempting to pull me under.

"Seeing as I have no choice in the matter, do what you must," Hunter conceded angrily. Carefully, so very gently, he scooped me into his arms, cautious of my injuries, and cradled me against him. His muscles were tense with anger, but he held me like a precious, breakable treasure. "But I'm taking Madison out of here right now. She's lost too much blood and I need to heal her, otherwise you'll have nothing left to *discuss*."

My head lolled against his arm as he turned, strode through the parting crowd, and left the ballroom.

The last thing I heard before darkness claimed me were the dying sounds of my pack, and my mate's fervent promise.

"I've got you Maddie. I've got you."

Madison

Stifling heat surrounded me, and I snuggled deeper into its embrace, not wanting to wake up. A deep, masculine chuckle had me prying my eyes open. The first thing I noticed were the hard muscles and tanned skin that belonged to a very naked chest.

"There you are, Sleeping Beauty," Hunter teased huskily and trailed a finger across my forehead, tucking a lock of hair away.

I hummed as I stretched, then propped myself on his chest in a way that allowed me to gaze into his handsome face. "I like it better when you call me 'Maddie' or your 'Little Wolf,' but how long was I out?"

"Seventeen hours this time," Olivia butted in, startling me. My gaze flew to her worried one. I hadn't realized we had company, but Tristan, Nova, and Dean were also in the room, leaning against the wall with matching concerned expressions.

Tristan brightened considerably, a smirk tugging up one side of his mouth. Hands in his pockets, one foot propped against the wall, he tilted his head. "I mean, I've heard of beauty sleep, but damn, girl. You were comatose."

I blushed and bolted upright in bed, then winced from the uncomfortable sensation in my abdomen.

Hiking up the tank I was now dressed in, I lightly ran my fingers over the newly healed skin. There wasn't so much as a scratch left to tell the tale of our horrible night, but I could tell my wolf was still taking care of any remaining remnants after Hunter healed me.

My arms and wrist were healed too, though the silver cuff had left a lasting mark, the palest silver scar. It looked like I'd gone tanning with a bracelet on. Hopefully it would fade, but it could've been so much worse.

"I don't know if I'll ever get used to this." In my past life, it would have taken me weeks to heal from my injuries, if they didn't kill me first.

"Bonded healing is a handy power to have," Olivia stated, but there was a heaviness to her voice as she crossed the room and perched on my side of the mattress.

Somehow, I'd ended up in a darkly decorated bedroom that smelled entirely too seductive—like smoldering camp-fires, smooth musk, bourbon, and leather. I took another whiff, letting the distinctive scent of my mate soothe my frayed nerves. I was safe now, but it was hard to transition from my last waking memory to the present. Dying howls still haunted me as did the strong odor of copper that made my stomach churn. I understood Olivia's pinched look of concern.

We'd been through hell. Again.

"I thought we might lose you this time," Olivia admitted. She swallowed and looked down, picking endlessly at one of her nails. "Thank you," she finally whispered.

I reached for her arm and gave her a light squeeze. "For what?"

Gaze glassy when she finally lifted her face, she covered my hand with hers. "For saving Hunter. He… he's all I have left." She still had her father, but I knew what she meant. Hunter was the only family she truly cared about, and it was understandable given how sadistic her father was. If anyone understood having a shitty father, it was me.

"You're welcome," I rasped, my throat suddenly tight.

Then I turned to Nova and Dean. Neither of them had known my secrets, and hurt burned like simmering embers in Nova's brown eyes.

"I can't believe you didn't tell me," she murmured.

"I'm so sorry. I thought it would put you in danger."

"The fewer people who knew, the better." Hunter swung his jean-clad legs over the side of the bed and reached for his shirt. I drank in the sight of him as he tugged on the dark graphite-colored fabric, his tattoos rippling with the motion. "That's all it was." He pressed to his feet and implored both Dean and Nova. "You're among some of the only pack members we know we can trust."

Nova nodded, but her attention swung back to me. Her pain was palpable and made me feel like the worst friend. My heart panged with the echo of loss, and I went to my knees on the mattress, crawling toward the edge of the bed and unfolding myself to stand beside Hunter. I wobbled, the blood rushing through my body making me lightheaded while my muscles remembered how to work. Hunter caught me, wrapping his arm around my waist and holding me against his side.

"Please, Nova. Please tell me you understand," I pleaded. Having friends was new to me, but now that I had them, I didn't want to lose them. They were the only people I had in my life who mattered, and the thought of losing Nova because I wasn't honest broke another piece of my heart. Worst of all, it was completely my fault.

She motioned with her hands and she responded, "I do, but that doesn't make it any easier. I need some time." Her palms skated over the outside of her jeans, and she moved toward the door. Throwing Dean a look over her shoulder, she silently asked if he was coming.

He glanced between all of us.

"Go," I urged. I didn't know when or how to tell them I thought they were mates, but after all we'd been through, they needed some time to process and come to terms with the bombs that had already been dropped. Right now, Nova needed his support. The kind of support only a mate could provide.

"I'm glad you're doing better, Mads," Dean said, adopting my old nickname. Coming from him, it was good to hear. He rubbed the back of his neck and nodded at Hunter. "We're cool, man. We're going to give you your privacy, but good luck with your father. Holler if you need anything."

The mention of the High Alpha quickly deflated the rest of my good mood.

"I think we can handle the old bastard." Tristan half-jested, half-crowed.

Hunter shook his head. "You're going to get yourself killed someday if you keep talking like that."

"Gotta keep things interesting." Tristan shrugged.

Olivia sighed, looking downright frazzled. She stood and propped her hands on her hips, turning to face us. "I think we've had enough interesting shit to last us a lifetime, thanks."

Tristan huffed a laugh. "Somehow I think we're only getting started. Come on, Liv. Let's give these two some time to get cleaned up." He paused in the doorway, sobering as he addressed Hunter. "Your father and the others will be expecting you now that Madison is awake. See you there?"

Hunter nodded. "Give us ten minutes."

Turning my head toward my armpit, I gave a cursory sniff and wrinkled my nose. "I don't know what magic he thinks I possess, but give us twenty. If I have to face off against the High Alpha again, I need time to make myself presentable."

Hunter shifted me in his arms and tugged me closer. "I don't know what you're talking about. The girls gave you a sponge bath to scrub the blood off, and you smell fine. You're beautiful just the way you are," he purred, burying his nose in my hair and skimming it along the line of my neck.

Pleasant little tingles raced through me.

"A sponge bath is no replacement for a long, hot shower."

"Want some company?" Hunter offered seductively, and I was on the verge of saying 'yes,' but we didn't have time for the type of shower I wanted to share with him.

"Get a room," Tristan reprimanded playfully.

Hunter growled. "This *is* my room."

"Semantics," Tristan complained good-naturedly on his

way out the door, but neither one of us paid him any attention as it clicked shut.

Finally alone, I gave life to my worries, murmuring into my mates ear. "I don't have a good feeling about this tribunal, Hunter."

My mate placed three little kisses along the column of my throat before pulling back and gazing down at me. His amber eyes were bright and intense. "Neither do I, but I promise, Maddie. I've got you."

They were the same three little words he'd whispered to me last night, and I held them close, hoping they'd be enough.

FORTY-FIVE

Madison

The thud of the heavy door swinging shut behind us reverberated through the private study. The High Alpha stood behind an ostentatious desk, his arms spreading in welcome.

"Ah, there you are. Madison, I trust you are feeling better?" he said in lieu of a greeting, suffusing his words with what I could only surmise was feigned concern.

"Uh, yes. Thank you." I tried to remain respectful, but it was a hard emotion to fake.

The High Alpha didn't give a shit about me unless it pertained to whatever ways he deemed I could serve him.

"My mate was able to use our bond to heal me." It was

an intentional mention, a reminder that Hunter and I were, in fact, bonded. The circumstances surrounding how we'd ended up connected weren't important. And for now, they didn't need to know I suspected he was my true mate. I held that little kernel of truth in my heart, guarding it closely.

The less I said—about anything—the better I'd be.

That became clear when the Alphas in the room bristled at the mention of our bond. Obviously, they'd already discussed my mating with Hunter amongst themselves.

I glanced up at my mate, and he gazed down at me. Intertwining our hands, Hunter gave my fingers a squeeze in support. Together, we moved farther into the room.

Warm afternoon sunlight spilled through the windows behind the High Alpha. He sauntered around the desk as we approached, and I dropped into a courteous dip of respect before righting myself while Hunter bowed his head briefly.

"High Alpha," we both murmured.

I motioned around the room. "I see the Alphas have already convened without me. As the new ruler over whatever is left of the Stormborn pack, I'd like to have a say in whatever decisions are being made here today."

The High Alpha's eyes brightened, glittering maniacally. "After all you've been through, I admire your fortitude, my girl. That fight, that drive, to jump right back into your duty tells us all we need to know. You will make a wonderful Luna someday."

I caught the dismissal easily, and cocked my head, narrowing my eyes slightly. "Someday?"

"The other Alphas and I have been talking." The cruel slash of his lips curled at the corners.

I almost huffed a laugh.

Of course they had.

I might be new to this whole wolf and power thing, but I wasn't born yesterday. "About my mating with Hunter? My claim to the Stormborn pack? Or the fact that I'm the only living Spirit wolf—the sole member of the Spirit pack?"

"All of it, my girl. All of it."

He motioned toward a chair, offering me a seat, but the rest of the Alphas were standing, and I refused to be placed below them. Literally or figuratively. My wolf chuffed her agreement. These men could shove their misogyny right up their asses.

Frustration fueled me—a churning tornado of anger in my chest.

"Let's start with the Stormborn pack," one of the Alphas suggested, and the High Alpha agreed.

"What about it? I am the last surviving heir, am I not?" I looked around the room, daring them to contradict me. Hunter had a little smile tugging at his mouth, standing slightly behind me and off to the side in silent support. His arms were crossed, and he watched me proudly. That he believed I could handle this battle made me fall just a little bit harder. He was there if I needed him but perfectly content to let me show them exactly who they were messing with.

"Technically, that is true," the High Alpha stated. "But how can you claim the Stormborn pack, girl, when you have no rank among them. Or any of the other packs, for that matter? Including the long-lost Spirit pack."

My stomach dropped, and the High Alpha's smile grew wider. More vindictive.

He motioned toward the other egocentric Alphas, who all shared shrewd glances, except for Silas Cassian, who wore a frown.

They're going to pull the rug out from under me.

They were planning something, all too giddy to ruin the small bit of happiness, of power, I'd fought like hell to get. My head swam nauseatingly with all the possibilities. Even Hunter's arms had tensed, and the muscles in his jaw stretched tight.

"Honestly, you don't have a pack at all," he tsked. "We can't have that, now, can we?"

"Madison is the only living Spirit wolf that we know of. She belongs to her own damn pack—the Spirit pack, even if it's a pack of one. Regardless, she's about to become my Luna," Hunter growled. "If nothing else, she'll become part of the Ember Wolves. But her claim stands true. Madison *is* the only remaining heir of the Stormborn Wolves. She deserves a chance to defend the title, at the very least. Those are basic rights given during any succession, whether male *or* female."

I knew just how much Hunter would despise seeing me fight in a formal challenge. He didn't want to see me hurt, or worse. Yet, he jumped to my defense anyway. He fought for me vehemently, regardless of his own personal feelings, and it made me appreciate him even more.

"Not without an official rank," the High Alpha spat at Hunter. Disapproval colored his tone from his son's interruption.

"What are you suggesting?" I asked, playing his game for a moment.

"Maddie," Hunter warned, reaching for me, but I shook my head.

"The High Alpha already has a plan he intends to carry out no matter how hard we argue. Might as well hear him out so we know what we're fighting against."

"A wise choice," the High Alpha praised, and a spark of lust flared in his dark eyes, making my skin crawl.

Ick. Shivers slithered down my spine. *Gross motherfucking asshole.* The fear I'd felt when he drugged me tried to creep in, but I suppressed it, refusing to be cowed by this man. Especially now, when my future hung in the balance.

"Since you are, in fact, currently rankless, the Alphas and I have decided to cancel your mating ceremony to my son."

My heart instantly stuttered, refusing to beat correctly.

"That's bullshit!" Hunter raged, marching forward with a finger pointed at his father's chest.

I lunged for him and wrapped my hands around his straining forearm. Pulling him back, I tried to ease him with soothing words meant only for him.

Hunter's father was delighted by his outburst, and he paced before us, tucking his hands behind his back. "Despite how you feel, boy, the rule has always been that every wolf must compete in the Trials and receive their pack ranks. Only then can they possibly be mated off. Since we use rank as an important part of the decision-making process when determining the most advantageous matings, this is the next natural step for Madison's integration back into polite society and pack dynamics."

"No sense holding back the rest of the plan," Vincent, the Alpha of the Lunar Wolves, prodded the High Alpha, who's power flared from being dictated to. The air in the room thinned, making it harder to breathe.

Pivoting, the High Alpha drew to a stop before me. "It's clear you're a powerful heir, Madison. The only one of your kind, with powers we're all eager to learn more about. Particularly about your ability to find true mates. The other Alphas have convinced me to allow their own heirs the chance to court you for themselves while you prepare and compete in the Trials."

"No." I shook my head. "I'm sorry High Alpha, but I'm *bonded* with Hunter," I stammered, shocked he'd ever allow such a thing.

Politically, having me mate his son was a power move. Bringing me into his pack, having my power under his thumb, only benefited him. So why would he allow the other Alphas to have such pull, such sway, over the decision of who I officially mated? It didn't make any sense.

My wolf growled, begging me to pay attention, and my gaze fell to the High Alpha's desk. Territory maps were strewn across the surface along with stacks of cash and various valuables.

Holy shit. They're bribing him. For me.

Of course. The High Alpha didn't make a move unless it somehow benefited him, and there were plenty of things the other Alphas could barter for a chance to have a Spirit wolf bound to their pack: land, favors, borrowed warriors, money, power, fealty.

All the Alphas may be cordially standing in this room, but tensions between packs were often strained. Each pack had their own alliances and rivals, and though they were forced to comply with the High Alpha, that didn't mean they weren't secretly planning his death just like my father had. These Alphas were driven by territory and power.

To the High Alpha, I was a tool, a powerful bargaining chip. In a world where the packs were at each other's throats, loyalty, even if it was bought and paid for, was an invaluable asset.

All at once, my ability to sense true mates was suddenly my greatest strength and my biggest downfall.

"Bonds can be broken," the High Alpha promised

darkly, and the color drained from my face as Hunter and I locked eyes.

No.

My wolf raged in my chest, completely devastated by the possibility. Not much was known about true matings, and I feared that if Endora ever tried to break the bond she'd magicked, she'd somehow destroy our true mate bond with it.

It had been the moon witches who'd cursed us to begin with, concealing our fated mate bonds from us. With this new threat hanging over our heads, I wanted her as far away from Hunter and me as possible. Losing him, in any way, was now my greatest fear.

The High Alpha took two steps and stopped in front of his son. "Given that you've had pre-emptive time to get to know Madison, I have agreed that you will stand down and stay out of the other heirs' way as they court the Spirit wolf. Do you understand?"

Hunter's jaw jumped, and he fixed his gaze somewhere out the window. He dipped his chin. Once. One sharp movement. If he felt the devastation I was feeling, it was probably all he could manage. But neither of us had a choice or a say over the High Alphas' decree.

I scanned the faces of the other Alphas, searching for anyone who would stand up for us, but I was met with hard, unmoving determination. The only sympathetic face in the whole bunch was Silas's, and I could barely look at him without the pang of loss my wolf felt toward him.

"Excellent. Since the next pack Trials don't take place for six months, I've decided that we'll host a special set of Trials specifically for Madison, set to start immediately. Time is of the essence."

Hunter scoffed. "No. No way. Maddie needs time to

prepare. She just got a wolf. She's still learning her powers. You can't expect her to be Trial ready so soon. Some of them are dangerous, and she's too important to risk."

The High Alpha resumed his pacing and pursed his lips. "What are you suggesting?"

I knew Hunter hated asking for his father for anything, but he swallowed his pride to make a plea on my behalf. "Give me a month to train her. I'll get her ready."

"She's no longer your destined mate and, therefore, none of your concern."

"Bullshit. I may have to let others throw their damn hats in the ring, but that doesn't mean I'm backing down. If they want to win her, then they have to go through me. Give me a month."

"One week."

"Three."

The High Alpha paused and glowered at his son. "You are ranked second only to me—not just in our pack, but across a whole division of wolves. If you're still that same talented wolf, you'll do it in two weeks. That's my final offer."

"Done." Hunter nodded his assent while my head spun. I felt lightheaded and completely caught off-guard. I didn't know what to expect from the Trials, but that was a problem for another day.

"That just leaves one last little problem," the High Alpha proclaimed.

Maybe for him, there was only one problem left, but I had a mountain of them. My sister's psychotic murderer was still on the loose and had powers the likes of which I'd never seen. The traitorous witch had mysterious plans for me. My father was dead, leaving what was left of my pack leaderless. I still knew precious little about my Aether element. And now, I was being ripped away from the one man I was fated to be with. Oh yeah, and I had to compete in my own special brand of the Trials to prove myself worthy of being 'auctioned' off to the highest bidder. I could only hope the Alphas wouldn't come up with some type of Hunger Games shit. With my luck, I needed to be prepared for anything. Literally, anything.

I swallowed and closed my hands into loose fists so my fingers wouldn't tremble from the wealth of adrenaline storming through me.

"What problem?" Hunter asked the question I couldn't force past my lips.

"The problem of your pack, Madison. Right now, the Alpha council and I view you as packless. Without the sponsorship of a pack, you cannot compete in the Trials."

I shook my head. I realized I could no longer claim the Ember pack as my future home, but I still had a birth pack I inherently belonged to. "Even if I'm not considered the Alpha, I belong to the Stormborn pack," I stated ardently.

"As far as we're all concerned, your father disowned you when he cast you from the pack and lied about your death."

"None of that is Madison's fault." Hunter jumped to my defense.

"I was six," I pleaded simultaneously. My heart beat faster as it dawned on me just how hopeless this had become. The High Alpha wanted Stormborn land, and there was no way I'd be able to stop him from claiming my pack as his own.

"Unfortunately, that has no bearing on my decision. It's a catch twenty-two, really. Your father is dead, and since you have yet to compete in the Trails, you're essentially a rogue. A lone wolf."

"If nothing else, I belong to the Spirit pack."

"A pack of one?" The High Alpha chuckled derisively, and the other Alphas joined in. "My girl, I may sense alpha power in you, but without a rank, you once again cannot claim to be Alpha of that pack, and without an Alpha, there ceases to be a pack at all."

My mind spun from the circles he was sending me in. No matter what I did, what pack I claimed, I wouldn't be able to refute his twisted logic. His word was law.

"You are packless, my dear. However, I'm not cold-hearted enough to leave you in such a position."

I wanted to scoff. Of course he was, but I zipped my lips and continued listening.

"If you kneel and swear fealty to me, I'll allow you into *my* pack and the Ember Wolves will sponsor your Trials."

My wolf wanted me to growl and bare my teeth. This was just another way for him to chain me to him. To control me.

The High Alpha circled me and leaned close, lowering his voice, though I was sure the others in the room could still hear his murmured threats. "If not, I'll just have to assume you're a traitor and imprison you. Rogue wolves are afforded no respect, no rights. I could use you in whichever way I deem necessary."

I easily picked up on the double meaning, and a shiver of dread shot down my spine at the thought of him forcing himself on me. My stomach revolted, churning wildly, but I schooled my expression, hoping he didn't notice that his words had an effect.

"Or you can agree to swear fealty and be under the protection of my pack. You'd be afforded rights and protections, you'd live in luxury, and be given the opportunity to compete in the Trials and earn your spot among the packs." To sway me fully, he went in for the knockout, keeping his tone low. "Let me put it this way, it's the only chance you'll get to fight for the mate bond I know you truly want—the one with my son. I'll look more favorably upon your wishes if you work with me, instead of against me. But I'm not afraid of a woman with a little fight in her. It'll just make you all the more fun to break."

Hunter released a low growl that never seemed to end.

But once again, the High Alpha was a step ahead, and he knew it.

If I didn't want to be locked away in whatever creepy dungeon he probably had, to be pulled out and paraded around as the Alpha's shiny new toy, forced to use my powers at his beck and call, I had no choice.

No matter what, he controlled me, but his offer gave me a fighting chance at a better life.

"Choose," the High Alpha commanded, running out of patience. He circled back in front of me, and waited.

I looked at Hunter, whose jaw clenched so tightly it could break at any second. The emotion reflected in his fiery russet eyes seared me to my very soul.

My gaze stayed locked on his as my legs gave out, and my knees hit the floor.

I turned to the High Alpha at the last second, catching the covetous greed contorting his features.

I fought my wolf to tilt my head ever so slightly, exposing my neck in submission. "I swear my fealty to the Ember Pack," I vowed, the words like ash on my tongue.

I hated giving him what he wanted, hated the helpless position he'd forced me into. I hated being on my knees before him and the heated satisfaction burning in his eyes.

I may have just signed myself over to the Ember Wolves, but in that moment I made a vow to myself, too.

I would do whatever it took to find my way through this and claim Hunter as my own…

Even if it meant making a deal with the devil.

To be continued….

Ready for the next chapter in Madison's adventure?

Preorder Book 2, Mate Blessed, now!

Need more Hunter?
Read Hunter's POV from the first time he sees Maddie by signing up to Elena's Newsletter.

Come join Elena's reader group on Facebook to keep up with all the latest news, teasers, and sneak previews of book 2!
Elena's Pack of Readers

AUTHOR'S NOTE

I don't even know where to start! First and foremost, thank you for reading Rejected Fate!

I poured so much of myself into this book and truly fell in love with Hunter and Madison's story. I hope you're enjoying the journey and are ready to devour more of this series!

Book two, Mate Blessed, is already on preorder on Amazon. Are you as excited as I am to see what adventures await these characters next? There is so much more to come!

I would be remiss if I didn't take a moment to say some very important thank yous to the people in my life who helped make this book possible.

To my alpha readers, Beverly, Stacy, and Missy, thank you for the support, encouragement, and insight you provided (and continue to provide) throughout the writing process. For listening to me ramble about plot points and helping me through the messy twists and turns that come with writing a book. I could not have done this without you.

To The Beta Pack, thank you all so much for your feedback, critiques, guidance, and help in polishing this book to such a beautiful shine. This book wouldn't be what it is today without you.

And to my AMAZING editor Heather, thank you for your dedication and tireless effort in making this book the best it could possibly be. You are incredible, and you're stuck with me forever and ever!

Lastly, to my family. Thank you to my husband for being a sounding board, for always listening to my crazy ideas, for letting me read chapters out loud to run story beats by you, and for your endless encouragement and support. I don't know what I did to get so lucky, but I'm thankful for you every single day. I love you more than you know and appreciate you so very much. And to my three busy, energetic children, I hope you know that I work so hard for you. I love you to the moon and back!

BEFORE YOU GO

Please consider leaving an honest review.

Even a few words or a simple star rating are great ways to share your thoughts on a book or series.

ABOUT THE AUTHOR

Elena Forest writes fast-paced new adult paranormal romance reads.

When she's not busy writing about sassy heroines and dreaming up dark vamps or protective wolves that would make addictive book boyfriends, she spends her time watching reruns of The Vampire Diaries, enjoying time with her family, or playing Zelda.

She loves reading almost as much as she loves writing, and is often found curled up with a good book or her laptop and a mug full of hot chocolate.

facebook.com/authorelenaforest

twitter.com/AuthorEForest

instagram.com/elena.forest.author

tiktok.com/@authorelenaforest

amazon.com/stores/Elena-Forest/author/B09HXYKB4T

bookbub.com/profile/elena-forest

ALSO BY ELENA FOREST

Elemental Wolves: Spirit Ascending:

Rejected Fate

Mate Blessed (on pre-order!)

Anthologies:

Rejected Mates: A Limited Edition Collection

www.ingramcontent.com/pod-product-compliance
Lightning Source LLC
Chambersburg PA
CBHW021329310726
48971CB00001B/46